DRAGONS OF ISENTOL

THE COMPLETE SERIES

OTHER BOOKS

Dragon Riders of Osnen

The Price of Honor
Trial by Sorcery
A Bond of Flame
The Warrior's Call
The Coin of Souls
Wing of Terror
Eyes of Stone
Tooth and Claw
The Servant of Souls
Smoke and Shadow
The Dark Rider
The Song of Bones
Sword and Crown
Tides of Darkness

Marked by the Dragon

Scale of the Dragon
Egg of the Dragon
Call of the Dragon
Wrath of the Dragon

The Fallen King Chronicles

Dragonsphere
The Fallen King
The Valiant King
The Restored King

DRAGONS OF ISENTOL

THE COMPLETE SERIES

RICHARD FIERCE
PDMAC

Cover design by Richard Fierce
Cover art by Rosauro Ugang

Dragonfire Press

e-Book ISBN: 978-1-947329-58-4

Print ISBN: 978-1-958354-16-2

First Edition: 2022

THRONE

OF

DECEIT

BOOK 1

CHAPTER 1

GWEN

The Seven Stars inn was busier than normal. That was good for business, but it also meant that Gwen had been rushing around most of the evening, filling tankards and delivering steaming food. It was warm, uncomfortably so, and Gwen was glad the night was almost over. The air was thick with pipe smoke and boisterous laughter, a rarity these days.

Gwen spotted a man waving his arm, tankard upside down on the table. She heaved a weary sigh and hurried to the table, forcing a smile.

"More ale?" she asked.

"Yes, and keep it flowing," the man replied.

Gwen could tell by the way he slurred his words that he'd probably already had too much, but she nodded and refilled his tankard. The inn would be closing soon, so not much more ale would be "flowing" anyway. Gwen's father had been in the kitchen since opening, fulfilling the endless stream of orders and cursing when he burned himself, which was quite often.

A bard began playing a cheerful song, his fingers

passing through and tonight would be his last performance at the inn. She did another loop of the tables, making sure the patrons were taken care of, then sat behind the bar and listened to the music.

Gwen found the bard handsome. He was young and energetic, his face clean shaven, and his brown hair trimmed short and neat. Her father would never allow her to marry someone with a profession that required constant travel, but she didn't see any problem with admiring the man's attractiveness. Besides that, it was common knowledge that Gwen would take over the Seven Stars once her father retired.

As the bard finished his song, a commotion outside the inn caught Gwen's attention. She looked to the windows, but it was too dark to see anything other than vague shadows. The noise drew the attention of the inn's customers as well, and the people quickly congregated in front of the windows. Those who couldn't squeeze in among the others exited the doors to see things up close.

Gwen heard angry shouting and groaned. Drunken men fist fighting one another wasn't uncommon, especially when the place was busy. She removed her apron and hung it on one of the hooks on the wall, then walked to the door and cracked it open, peering out into the night.

A single man was surrounded by a group of the king's soldiers. Their black leather armor made them blend in with the darkness, but Gwen knew the attire. The soldiers had become a common sight around the inn, and around Dawsbury in general. Rumors of war had been circulating for years, but now there were signs of it. Aside from the presence of the king's men, there were also whispers of dark magic and sightings of dragons.

Gwen didn't know what to think about any of it. She lived a simple life working at the inn, and she wanted it to stay that way. The king could make war on the surrounding kingdoms if he wanted to, so long as Gwen's way of life wasn't impacted. Her attention was jerked back to the present when one of the soldiers kicked the back of the man's legs, knocking him to the ground. The man being harassed scowled and tried to get back up.

"Stay down, dog," one of the soldiers said.

"Yeah," chimed in another. "If you know what's good for you."

Someone bumped into Gwen from behind and she looked over her shoulder to see Tobias, the baker's son.

"What's going on out there?" he asked.

"Some of the soldiers have taken an interest in Garre," Gwen replied. "Garre's angry, but I think he'll keep his temper under control."

"I can't stand those soldiers," Tobias muttered. "They think they can come to our town and do whatever they want just because they wear the king's emblem."

"As long as we stay out of their way, we don't have anything to worry about," Gwen said. "They're just following orders."

Tobias snorted but didn't say anything.

Garre was glaring daggers at the soldiers, but he stayed where he was.

"Good dog," one of the soldiers goaded. "Now lick the dirt off my boots."

"Screw off," Garre spat.

The soldier who'd spoke drew his sword and

leveled the tip at Garre's throat. "What was that, dog? Did I tell you to speak?"

Silence fell over everyone in the inn. Gwen watched intently, her heart hammering in her chest with anxiety. "They can't kill someone for no reason," she whispered.

"That's what you'd think, anyway," Tobias said. "When left unchecked, that tyrant's hired hands will do anything, including murdering innocent people."

"Watch your words, boy," one of the patrons said. "You'll bring the king's wrath down on us all."

Gwen watched with bated breath, silently praying that Garre wouldn't be hurt. She wasn't friends with him, but she knew who he was, and they'd never had any issues. Even if they had, Gwen would never wish harm on anyone.

"Get to licking," the soldier demanded, lifting his boot near Garre's face. For a moment, Gwen thought he was going to lick the soldier's boot. Instead, Garre grabbed onto the soldier's leg and pulled, forcing the soldier to fall onto his back.

"Yeah!" Tobias shouted. "Give him what for!"

Gwen had a feeling something terrible was about to happen. The soldier scrambled back onto his feet and kicked Garre in the face. Garre crumbled backward awkwardly, his legs tucked under his body.

"Gods," Gwen said, flinching and looking at Tobias.

"Someone has to do something," Tobias said. "They're going to kill him."

"Don't say that," Gwen replied.

Tobias stared at her, jaw clenched. "No more," he said.

Before Gwen could figure out what he meant, Tobias drew a dagger and pushed past her. He sprinted toward the soldier that had kicked Garre and leaped onto his back, driving the small blade into the soldier's chest.

The world froze.

Gwen's eyes widened in horror and surprise. She screamed, and the world began moving again, but now it was a blur. The other soldiers grabbed Tobias and forced him to the ground, wrenching his dagger away. The soldier he'd attempted to stab was uninjured.

"Some dogs don't understand loyalty," he said, then lifted his sword up threateningly. With a sudden grunt, he staggered forward as Garre pushed him from behind. Another soldier drew his sword and thrust it into Garre's back.

Gwen stepped back from the door, shaken. Garre screamed and fell to the ground, writhing in the dirt. There was confusion among the rest of the soldiers as they glanced at each other with uncertainty. Tobias broke free of the men holding him and sprinted to the left, running down the alley beside the inn.

The apparent leader threw his arms up. "Don't just stand there, get him!"

The others chased after Tobias and Gwen quietly shut the door and returned to the bar. The patrons slowly went back to their tables, but the mood had changed. The bard had stopped playing his music and the conversations became muted.

Gwen wrung her hands together nervously, not knowing what she could do to help Garre. Should she help him? What if he had done something to warrant the interest of the soldiers and she wasn't privy to that knowledge? She started to head around the bar when the kitchen door flung open and Tobias ran in, followed by Boris, Gwen's father.

"What's going on?" Boris demanded.

"I need somewhere to hide," Tobias replied. He looked around the inn, frantic. Gwen thought he looked like a frightened deer, ready to flee at any moment.

Boris looked around the room, noting the patrons, then grabbed onto the edge of the bar. "Help me, will you?"

Tobias grabbed the other end and, together, they heaved the stout wooden structure forward. Gwen was surprised to see a trap door hidden in the floor.

Boris opened the small door and motioned to the darkness within. "Go," he said. "Hurry."

Tobias didn't question the order and hurried down into the hidden space. Boris closed the door and tried to move the bar back into place, but it was too heavy. He looked at Gwen, then changed his mind and turned to the customers.

"Someone give me a hand!"

A few people leaped to their feet to help and, within a few moments, the bar was back in place.

"Father," Gwen said softly, following him into the kitchen. "You never told me about that door."

"Forget that you ever saw it," Boris replied, washing his hands off in a bucket of clean water. He went back to preparing meals as if nothing had happened.

Gwen watched her father work, wondering why his demeanor had changed so suddenly. There was something he wasn't telling her, that much was obvious. There was shouting in the common room and Gwen rushed out of the kitchen. The soldiers had entered the inn and were harassing the customers.

"Gentlemen," Gwen greeted loudly, offering the largest smile she could muster. "Drinks?"

"We're looking for a criminal," one of them said. Gwen turned her attention to him and recognized him as the leader of the group from outside.

"I don't think I've seen anyone shady in here, but I'll help if I can," Gwen said cheerily. She was surprised her voice hadn't cracked.

"This person is an enemy of the king. He's dangerous and we need to remove him from the streets. He's about my height and build, with black hair."

Gwen put a puzzled look on her face and slowly shook her head. "I can't say I've seen anyone like that in here. Would you like a drink while your men ask my customers?"

"I'd love one, but I must refuse. I'm on duty."

"Right. Can't have you out there staggering around on the job." Gwen laughed. The soldier didn't share her mirth. The kitchen door opened as Boris came out, carrying a tray full of food. The soldier jumped, obviously startled, then calmed when he saw there was no threat.

"Evening," Boris greeted as he passed them, delivering the food to a table by the windows.

"If you see anyone matching the description, please report it to the local constabulary. They'll get word to us."

"I will," Gwen replied.

The soldier turned his back to Gwen, and she noticed the uneasiness of the customers. Most were minding their own business, but a few people were staring death at the soldiers. Boris returned to the bar and the lead soldier stopped him.

"Are you the owner?"

"I am," Boris replied, offering a grin. "It's a humble place, but it's served me well."

"It's a dump," the soldier grunted. "I've also heard that it's a den of protection for the king's enemies."

Boris looked pained. "I hope no one questions my devotion to the king," he said. "I've been a staunch supporter all my years."

The soldier stared at Boris intently, then nodded, seeming satisfied.

"Anything?" the soldier asked his men.

"Nothing," someone answered.

"Let's go, then." The lead soldier looked from Boris to Gwen, then headed for the door. His men followed after him and they exited the inn. Gwen sighed in relief and leaned over the bar.

"That was close," she whispered.

There was a pounding noise at the door and Gwen realized that the soldiers were securing it so that no one could leave.

"Father, what's happening? Why did he say we're hiding enemies here?"

Boris suddenly looked older to her. Deep lines spread across his face and there were bags under his eyes.

"There are things I haven't told you because I wanted to keep you safe," Boris replied.

The customers of the inn began to panic and started kicking at the door. A few others picked up chairs and broke some of the windows, but they were greeted with flaming torches that were thrown into the inn. People scattered out of the way, knocking over tables and spilling drinks. Alcohol hit the torches and flames spread across the floor.

"We've got to get out of here!" Gwen shouted.

Boris grabbed her hand and led her through the kitchen to the backdoor, but when he pushed on it, it didn't budge.

"They've blocked us in," Boris said grimly.

CHAPTER 2

CONAL

Shackled to the thick iron rings hammered into the granite walls in a dank prison was not the outcome Conal had in mind when he agreed to lead the latest raid on the market city. Once again, he berated himself for ignoring his gut feeling.

"It'll be easy," Oscon had said. "A walk in the park. Get in, get out and by the time yer back here they won't know what happened."

"Why me?" Conal frowned at the bandit chief, a hulking lummox of a man, beetle browed with a sneer for a smile.

"'cause nobody'd expect you. Ya got that baby-face look like yer a choirboy."

Conal's first instinct was to ask him the real reason for this sudden elevation to lead a raid. Until then, he had been little more than a gopher or a lookout. It wasn't until he overheard Oscon talking about moving on because they had pretty much skimmed all they could from the area towns and cities and the constabulary and soldier patrols were becoming too frequent that caused Conal to wonder why do another raid? When he heard Oscon talk

But vanity overruled his misgivings, and when Oscon poked a thick finger at him and said, "Yer gonna lead this one," Conal had squashed his reservations and stepped forward. His uneasiness was somewhat allayed when Oscon selected a few of the best men and women to go along.

The setup played out to perfection.

Once in the town, Conal had been recognized and immediately surrounded by four guards and four swords pointed much too closely at various parts of his body. When Conal frantically looked for help, there was none. The six men and women who had so assiduously listened to his plan and followed him into town had melted away like morning dew. Had Conal paid more attention to his followers, he might have noticed them disappearing one by one that by the time he was in the market center by the tax boxes, he was quite alone.

The ultimate insult was when he swore the voice calling out, "I know him. He's a bandit," belonged to his second in command, Jestyn.

And now here he sat amidst the overlapping stench of unwashed bodies and the layered decay of the dead, wondering why Oscon had decided he was no longer useful, and vowing that he would hunt him down if it was the last thing he ever did, which by the look of things might be a tad difficult.

His broodings were interrupted when he heard the far cell door grind open and a nobly dressed man, flanked by several guards eased his way through the cell, holding a handkerchief at his nose and mouth. Conal watched as the man occasionally stopped and pointed whereupon two guards would grab the prisoner, unshackle him or her before handcuffing them and leading them away.

When the man stopped in front of him, Conal flashed a loopy smile and received a pointed finger in return whereupon he was yanked up, unshackled and handcuffed, and led through the squalid mass of bodies, out through the door and recesses of the prison keep to finally emerge into the mid-morning outside and fresh air.

Conal inhaled a deep satisfying breath then glanced to his left and right at the other prisoners lined up on both sides of him. There were ten of them, six women and four men, all young and healthy, all handcuffed.

The sergeant of the guard stood imperiously before them. He was a toad of a man, all body and skinny legs wrapped in an ill-fitting uniform of the town's constabulary: crimson jacket with gold buttons, straight tan cotton trousers tucked into calf-high boots, and a leather helmet capped with a bristle that looked like someone had lost a shoe brush.

Behind him the noble man stood, aloof bordering on ennui, the handkerchief still at his mouth. He wore a long-sleeved white silk shirt, covered by a white cream-colored vest of the finest calfskin. His ebony trousers were handcrafted from rabbit skin, and his boots a work of art in reptile skin. He eschewed a hat and his full-bodied blond hair fell about his shoulders, framing a handsome face with square jaw and dark brown eyes. Conal guessed him to be closing in on 40.

"In accordance with Kingdom Statute 43 dash 12," the sergeant bellowed, reading from an unfurled parchment, "and with the honest and whole-hearted concurrence of the Burgomaster of Hemlyn, you have been redeemed by Lord Pharyl. Your death sentences have been commuted to a life of servitude until such time that you die or are provided your freedom according to the wishes of Lord Pharyl, Prince of the realm of Vandyr. You are henceforth to be branded so that all may know the depths to which you have fallen. Should you choose to escape, know that you are subject to the laws of exile and retribution. Anyone finding an escaped slave may kill him or her."

Pharyl. Conal knew the name. The man ruled this part of the kingdom with an iron fist inside a velvet glove. He could be as cruel as he was generous. Conal felt a flash of relief, knowing he would stay alive if he played his cards right. Those poor fettered souls left behind in the prison were as good as dead.

Rolling up the parchment, the sergeant nodded to the guards who force-marched the newly anointed slaves to the center of town so that the entire populace could witness their debasement. Men, women, and curious children stood in a thick circle around the branding pit, the heat from the fire keeping them back while providing enough space for the guards to hold the victim down for the Branding Master who instructed the poor soul to stay as still as possible. Moving while being branded caused a bad brand, requiring a second one. The normal location of a slave brand, concentric circles the size of a large coin, was on the cheek.

Despite the rising fear of having his face forever marred, Conal noticed there were four irons in the fire. He knew the reason. Some slaves had a different brand placed on the outside of the right shoulder – the death's head, a skull with horns. These slaves were bound to protect the master with their lives. Two other branding irons consisted of a viper and a rose.

The viper brand was placed on the upper left arm. Vipers were the master's enforcers, assassins, and muscle. They lived well and it was considered an honor to be a viper, for vipers could marry and the children of the marriage were considered freeborn.

The rose brand was placed on the right thigh. A rose slave was a pleasure slave. Conal prayed to whatever god or gods were out there that he would not be a rose slave, for he knew what happened to rose slaves. Sure, there were the few who had pleased their masters and allowed to live a life of privilege in the harem. But the majority of rose slaves, those whose beauty had faded, were sent to the farms to spend the rest of their lives in back-breaking labor.

The fourth iron? Conal frowned in puzzlement for only a moment until his attention was diverted by Lord Pharyl who causally strolled down the line to stand in front of the first person, an attractive blond woman about Conal's age.

Staring at the woman for only a moment, Pharyl dipped a finger at her. "Rose."

As the woman was dragged off to be branded, Pharyl side-stepped to the next slave, a tall strong teenager. "Death's Head."

Conal was seventh in line and his prayers increased in urgency and pleading as Pharyl continued down the line, announcing, "Rose." "Death's Head." "Rose." "Rose."

Pharyl stopped to appraise Conal as though he were judging a good horse. Folding his arms, he scrutinized the young man, impressed that the slave didn't avert his eyes or appear to grovel. Instead, the young man stood firm, appearing to be unafraid.

"Either you're a sheep who has no clue of what's going to happen, or you've resigned yourself to fate.

Which is it?"

"Fate, m'Lord."

"You answer with a strong voice," Pharyl said with a slow nod, noting the young man didn't call him master as was required. "Men like you tend to be wild, like a stallion that needs to be broken. They're too high-spirited. Are you high-spirited?"

Conal smiled at him. "It all depends upon the rider, m'Lord. A skilled rider knows his mount, knows how to direct and coax with just the right words. A gifted rider and mount are a team to be envied."

A smile flitted across Pharyl's lips. "You talk as one educated. Are you educated?"

"Yes, m'Lord."

"Where was the failure then that you end up like this?" Pharyl looked down his nose at him.

Conal shrugged. "Bad crowd, bad choices. Not everyone who calls you friend is one."

"Well spoken," Pharyl acknowledged. "You're too pretty to have your cheek branded, and you're not big or strong enough to be a Death's Head."

Conal's hopes took a nosedive, especially with the "too pretty" comment. What was it with these people and his looks? There were plenty of men who were better looking. Why couldn't people see that he was smart, that he had a brain? Steeling himself for the inevitable and already dreaming of a way to escape, he was startled when Pharyl gently pushed a finger into his chest.

"Viper."

Without thinking, Conal did a fist pump and exclaimed, "Yes," causing Pharyl to smirk and flash a bemused glance at this curious fellow. He started to sidestep to the next one in line when he stopped at turned back to Conal.

"What is your name?"

"Conal, m'Lord."

Pharyl nodded and continued, the next three all designated a "rose." With the choices decided, Lord Pharyl stepped away to watch the branding, noting the demeanor of each slave. Amidst all the shifting and squirming and fear, only Conal seemed unaffected. In fact, the man seemed more than ready to get branded.

After the woman before Conal had the rose mark burned into her skin and went sniveling to the medicine tent, Conal marched up, sat down and pulled off his shirt, revealing a wiry and strong body, which elicited some whistles and catcalls, causing him to scowl. Bracing himself for the pain, he clenched his jaw, determined not to show weakness.

"Hold," Lord Pharyl commanded as the Brand Master withdrew the glowing red-hot Viper iron. He pointed to another iron next to it. "Use that one."

Suddenly fearing Lord Pharyl had changed his mind, Conal struggled to determine which iron held the rose brand. His anxiety elevated as his gaze narrowed on the Brand Master carefully retrieving the branding iron then approached him. The head was small like a rose, yet the design was wrong, and he frowned, twisting his head to glance up to Lord Pharyl.

"The cobra," Lord Pharyl calmly answered. "Do not disappoint me." He turned and walked away, the guard sergeant hustling up next to him, obsequiously nodding and agreeing with the lord's softly spoken conversation.

The Cobra.

Conal's fear morphed to confident elation as he

watched the not-so-subtle change in the crowd. Some were immediately intimidated, others unsure, and still others scoffed that so inexperienced a man should be chosen as a Cobra. Yet they knew the reputation. The Cobra was a leader among assassins, the silent unseen killers. Still, a sense of relief spread through the crowd for they knew this man would be taken away from here, for he was known.

Conal flinched then strained to remain immobile as the hot iron burned his flesh, the smell of burnt skin and the pain on his arm causing tears to well up in his eyes. Yet he sat rooted like a statue, grimly enduring the suffering.

Finally, the Brand Master pulled the iron away and surveyed his work. "Looks good. A good image." He dipped his head in admiration. "You sat very still. Go to the tent for them to bandage your arm."

Conal was halfway to the tent when he heard the screech of the next victim, a woman given a rose brand. Inside the tent, three healers applied salve and bandages to the branded areas. All too soon, the ten slaves were again in line, no handcuffs this time. The crowds had drifted away, and few remained to witness their departure.

Lord Pharyl sat astride a magnificent dappled stallion at least 17 hands high. He waited as the slaves were loaded into carts, leaning forward when Conal made ready to grab the wagon rail and climb aboard.

"You, young Conal."

Conal lowered his leg and turned to face his new master. "Yes, m'Lord."

"Do you ride?"

"Yes, m' Lord."

Pharyl nodded and flicked two fingers at his travel steward, a tall lean man with close cropped hair and beard. A few moments later, a servant led a sorrel mount almost as tall as Lord Pharyl's steed to stand next to the Lord and Master.

Pharyl narrowed his focus on Conal. "You will ride with me."

"Yes, m'Lord."

With practiced ease, Conal swung up into the saddle, took hold of the reigns and slipped his feet into the stirrups.

"We are ready, m'Lord," the steward announced.

"Then let's get started. I want to be in Denhelm by dinner time."

"Yes, m'Lord."

The steward bustled up to the first wagon and climbed aboard, ticking his head at the driver who flicked the reins causing the wagon to lurch forward. Soon, four wagons containing nine slaves and supplies surrounded by a dozen men at arms, their Lord and Master and the newest Cobra plodded out of the city. Conal rode next to Pharyl who remained silent until they were out of the earshot of the city walls.

"It's a three-day ride to my castle," Pharyl spoke. "We have plenty of time to get acquainted. You will tell me everything there is to know about you, and I will tell you what I expect of you."

"Yes, m'Lord."

"You may perhaps wonder why I chose you to be a Cobra when you have so little experience."

"The thought did occur to me, m'Lord."

"I have an eye for talent, and I believe you have the gifts I require. Do not worry, you will be trained as required for a Cobra. You perform well for me and I will consider giving you your freedom."

Conal reverently tipped his head. "It will be an

honor to serve you, m'Lord."

"Yes, I know," he replied with an indifferent nod. They loped along in silence for a bit. "Tell me, young Conal, what is the first thing you wish to do as a Cobra?"

Conal didn't have to think about the answer. "Find a certain outlaw… and make him rue the day he was born."

Pharyl chuckled. "All in good time, my young friend, all in good time."

CHAPTER 3

GWEN

Gwen digested Boris's words and realized that they were likely going to die.

"What about the trap door? Where does it lead?"

Boris grabbed a long knife from a stack of cutlery and led Gwen back into the common room. The customers had put the fires out, but the soldiers were still outside. He surveyed the damage and shook his head.

"There are a few things you should know, but now is not the time. If we get out of this alive, I promise I'll tell you everything. For now, know that the trap door is one of a few entrances into an underground tunnel that leads to the cemetery."

"That's outside the city," Gwen said.

"Exactly," Boris replied. "It's an escape route."

"An escape from what?"

Boris looked at the soldiers waiting outside, and Gwen followed his gaze.

"Why would we need to flee the king's soldiers? They're supposed to protect us. None of this makes any sense."

"Gents, someone help me. The rest of you, block

the windows so those brutes can't see what we're doing."

The patrons lined up, shoulder to shoulder, and blocked the windows. One large man helped Boris push the bar forward, and Gwen marveled again at the fact that she'd never known the door was there. Boris pulled it open, then took one of the lanterns off the wall and handed it to Gwen.

"At the bottom of the ladder you'll see two tunnels. One is a decoy and leads to a pitfall. Follow the tunnel on the right. It's a bit of a trek, but just keep going until you reach the stone door."

"You aren't coming with me?" Gwen asked.

"I'm afraid not," Boris answered. He wrapped Gwen in his arms and hugged her close, holding her for a long moment in silence. When he released her, he smiled at her and tucked some stray hairs behind her left ear. "Find Tobias when you get out of the tunnel. He'll keep you safe."

"I don't want to leave you," Gwen whispered. Her eyes welled and a tear slid down her cheek.

"Don't worry about me, girl. I've still got plenty of fight in these old bones. Those soldiers won't kill me so easily. Keep your tears for the grief that is sure to come in the future. Now go."

Gwen clenched her jaw against the sadness and nodded. She held onto the lantern and climbed down the ladder. She heard Boris ask if anyone else wanted to leave, and three people joined her in the tunnel. Then the trap door closed, and the world went dark except for the dim light of the lantern.

She lifted it, shining the light in an arcing motion, and saw the two tunnels. "This way," she said, leading the others along the one to the right. Wooden beams were spaced every few feet, lining the walls and the ceiling overhead. Gwen wondered if her father had been involved in digging the tunnels, or if he had discovered them. Considering the events of the night, something told her it was the former.

They walked for what seemed like an eternity before Gwen noticed the ground began to slope upward. After another fifty feet, the lantern illuminated an archway. The stone door Boris had mentioned was partially open. Gwen pushed on it, forcing it fully open and stepped out into the night. The others followed her, then left the cemetery and headed for the road.

Boris had told her to find Tobias, but how did he expect her to do that? She had no idea where he might have gone. Besides that, he was a wanted man now. How could someone considered to be an enemy of the king keep her safe? Tobias would have his hands full evading the authorities. She sighed in frustration, facing more questions than answers.

Gwen glanced around the cemetery. There were tombstones scattered everywhere, but they were lined in an orderly fashion. A crypt towered over the rest of the graves, its white marble walls shining eerily under the light of the moon. Perched atop the roof were several gargoyles, their stone maws open in silent roars. Moss had overtaken their bodies, covering them in a thick green blanket.

The sound of approaching horses filled the air. Gwen killed the lantern, hid behind a tall headstone, and waited. As the horses drew closer, Gwen peeked out and saw it was more of the king's soldiers. They were heading toward Dawsbury. Gwen assumed that word must have reached the outpost and these soldiers were reinforcements. She waited until the horses were gone before stepping back into the open.

"Where do I go?" she whispered. It was hard for her to fathom how quickly her world of comfort had been ripped away.

A stick snapped nearby, and her heart leaped within her chest. Before she could hide, a figure stepped into view wielding a sword. Gwen turned to run and slipped, falling and scraping her right knee on some rocks. She heard the figure running at her and screamed. A warm, sweaty hand clamped over her mouth.

"Quiet!"

Gwen knew the voice. She slapped the hand away and turned to look at Tobias. "You scared me!"

"I didn't mean to. I thought you were one of the king's soldiers. They're crawling all over Dawsbury."

"I wonder why," Gwen snapped. "You tried to stab one of them!"

"Keep your voice down," Tobias said. "What are you doing out here?"

"My father sent me. The soldiers locked everyone in the inn, accusing my father of hiding the king's enemies."

"Word finally got out," Tobias muttered. "I suppose it was only a matter of time."

"What are you talking about?"

"I know everything. You don't have to put on an act now."

"What act?" Gwen asked. "I have no idea what's happening!"

Tobias stared at her for a moment, then started laughing. "Gods! He didn't tell you, did he?"

"Tell me what?"

"It makes sense, though. He was probably trying to protect you, but he should have told you what he was involved with.”

“Stop talking to yourself and answer my question. What didn’t my father tell me?” Gwen demanded.

Tobias sheathed his sword and closed the tomb door Gwen had come out of. “There’s a war brewing.”

“People have been saying that for years,” Gwen said.

“This is different. I’m not sure what rock you’ve been under, but the king is not a good man. He’s the source of most of our problems.”

“What does that have to do with my father?”

“Boris has been helping the rebellion since it started. After his wife died, he put everything he had into the Seven Stars, but the king has raised our taxes so high that Boris lost ownership of the inn last year.”

“He lost ownership of the inn?” Gwen closed her eyes and sighed. “Why didn’t he tell me?”

“Maybe he thought he’d lose you, too? It’s hard to say. The death of his wife was hard on him.”

“Yes, I know. My mother’s death was hard on us both.”

Tobias went quiet, but the look on his face told Gwen he wanted to say something.

“What is it?” Gwen asked.

“It sounds like Boris told you less than I thought. Isabelle …”

“What about her?”

“She wasn’t your mother,” Tobias said. “And Boris isn’t your father.”

“Why would you say something like that? That’s just hurtful.”

“I’m being honest, Gwen. You were an orphan. Boris and Isabelle raised you like their own, but you were never in Isabelle’s womb. Why do you think you're an only child? Isabelle was barren."

Gwen couldn't believe it. Tobias was making up outlandish tales at a time like this? Did he take her for a fool? She turned away from him and started for the road.

"Where are you going?"

"Away from you," Gwen replied.

"Gwen, wait. What *did* Boris tell you? Surely, he said something before sending you out here?"

"He told me to find you and that you would keep me safe. He must have been overwhelmed when he said it, because he was clearly wrong about you."

"So, it's time then? We're not ready, but what choice do we have?"

Gwen paused. "Not ready for what?"

"To overthrow the king," Tobias said. "That's what Boris has been helping with. This tunnel has ferried more than people through it. We've been stockpiling weapons and other goods for months now."

"You're insane," Gwen blurted, tossing her hands into the air.

Another group of men were approaching. The galloping of their horses echoed off the headstones with an odd drum-like sound. Gwen dropped to all fours, and Tobias crawled over to her.

"We need to get moving," he whispered. "Boris wasn't wrong about me. I *can* keep you safe, but you're going to have to trust me."

"Why should I? You tried to kill a soldier."

"For good reason," Tobias replied. "Would you rather have let them kill Garre with no intervention?"

"Does it matter? Garre's dead now anyway."

Tobias groaned. "You're missing the point, Gwen. If we continue to let the king stomp on us, nothing will ever change. But if we stand up for ourselves and fight back, we can force change."

Gwen heard the passion behind his words and considered what he said with more seriousness. If her father had truly been aiding a rebellion, there was a reason for it. Tobias said the king was depraved. Added onto the knowledge that her father had been taxed until he lost the inn he built with his own hands … it made her angry.

"What can we do?" she asked. "Honestly? The king has more men, more money, and more reach than any of us."

"That may be true now, but it won't always be that way. We've been working hard and spreading the word. More people are joining our cause every day."

"You said the rebellion is going to overthrow the king. What does that look like, exactly? Most of the people in Dawsbury aren't warriors. Are you going to march an army of farmers against the castle and demand the king step down?"

"Of course not," Tobias said. "We've been training people to fight, to defend themselves. We can't put a castle under siege. Not yet at least. The plan is to draw Torian out of his fortress, bring him face to face with his victims. If we can cause enough problems for him out here, he'll take the bait."

It was a lot for Gwen to take in, not to mention above her head. She knew nothing of war or battle, and even less about weapons. She considered running away and leaving Dawsbury behind in the proverbial dust, but the thought of her father helping the rebellion gave her pause. If her father, an easy-going inn owner, could help people under duress, so could she.

"Where's this rebellion at? Is there a headquarters

or something?"

"It's everywhere," Tobias answered. "Anywhere that people are tired of the oppression, that is where the tinder of rebellion lies. They just need a flame to ignite them."

"I—" Gwen was interrupted by shouting from the road. Tobias was peering past her, squinting. "What is it?"

"Prisoners, it looks like," Tobias replied. "They're being pulled by rope."

They waited in silence as the procession passed the cemetery. Tobias's eyes widened.

"What do you see?" Gwen asked.

"It's everyone from Boris's inn."

Gwen's heart dropped into her stomach. "Everyone?"

Tobias turned his gaze on her, and Gwen was certain he could see the fear etched on her face.

"My father, too? Is Boris with them?"

Tobias nodded.

Gwen couldn't stomach the thought of her father being held in prison. "We have to do something," she said. "We have to free him."

"We can't. There're too many soldiers. Even if you were trained with a sword, we wouldn't stand a chance."

"What about the rebellion? Won't they help one of their own?" Gwen asked.

"Of course they will, but there's a time and a place for everything we do. It'll need to be well planned. Unfortunately, we'll have to wait until they get the prisoners to the outpost. It's risky, but I think this is what we've been waiting for."

"You've been waiting for the soldiers to take prisoners?" Gwen asked, confused.

"We've been waiting for an opportunity to raze the outpost," Tobias clarified.

"Count me in," Gwen said. "I want to help rescue my father."

"I'm not in charge, but I don't think that'll be a problem with Eradore."

"Who's Air-uh-door?" Gwen asked, trying to sound out the odd name.

"He's a wizard."

CHAPTER 4

CONAL

For the next three hours they lazily wended their way along the wagon trail through the thick forest. Conal responded to Lord Pharyl's questions, surprised that the Lord spent so much time with him, especially when the travel steward attempted to insert himself in the discussions.

"Beg pardon, m'Lord," the Steward interrupted. "Where would you prefer to lodge for the evening?"

Pharyl's face tightened and he raised an eyebrow. "Where do we normally spend the night?"

The man swallowed and stuttered, "I… I, um, thought that with the addition of the slaves, you might want to adjust our arrangements."

Pharyl cocked his head to the left. "What are you rambling about? How many times have I come this way with more slaves than I now have? Why are you bothering me? Is this not why I made you the travel steward, to handle these affairs?"

"Yes, Yes, m'Lord. I just wanted to make sure." He dipped his head several times. "Just making sure."

Pharyl shook his head as the man rode off to the front where the lead soldiers led the wagons on the well-traveled road.

"You see what I have to put up with?" he bemoaned. "I made him travel steward as a favor to a cousin." He turned and narrowed a stare at Conal. "Your first mission as a Cobra will be to rid me of that incompetent fool. Permanently. Understand?"

"Perfectly, m'Lord." Conal wondered what the steward had done to warrant the death sentence.

As though sensing his thoughts, Pharyl asked, "Do you not wish to know why I want him dead?"

"Is it necessary that I know, m'Lord? That you commanded it is explanation enough."

Surprised at the response, Pharyl smiled. "A wise answer. I see a great future for you. What do you know about my demesne?"

"I've traveled the breadth and width of it m'Lord. I am familiar with most towns and cities."

"And the people?"

"The same wherever I go," he gamely shrugged. "The common folk want to be left alone to go about their lives. The burgomasters run the cities and local towns, collect the taxes and skim off what's above owed to you."

"Have you been outside the demesne?" Pharyl asked, ignoring the barb at the tax burden.

"No, m'Lord, but I should like to, especially the kingdoms of the dwarves and elves. I've only ever seen them at the port towns, dwarves mostly, elves rarely."

"Sometime perhaps," Pharyl replied. "For now, it is important that you stay closer to home, learning about the demesne and its part in the kingdom. What do you know about Caldyr?"

"The king?" Conal blinked at the mention of the most powerful man in the realm.

"Yes."

"I know little, m'Lord. He is king. You rule here. That's the extent of it."

"It is time for a simple lesson," Phayrl said, assuming the role of a tutor. "There are many kingdoms in the land, some more powerful than others. Some ruled by men, others by elves and dwarves… and still others by creatures I will not talk about."

Conal pretended to pay attention, the instruction common knowledge.

"Caldyr rules the kingdom of Tir Manach, of which my realm, Vandyr, makes up a quarter if the kingdom. I rule here because Caldyr has only one son, but he has three daughters, one of whom is my wife."

Pharyl might not have been so pleased with Conal's rapt attention had he known the young man was only half listening. The other half was paying attention to the surroundings and the much too relaxed demeanor of the guards.

"Caldyr is my uncle," Pharyl droned on. "My father is, or was, his younger brother."

Conal momentarily looked away so that Pharyl would not see him rolling his eyes. While some folks lived and breathed lineage study, he'd rather watch pigs mate than listen to some dribble about an ancestor 200 years ago. He turned back and nodded, putting on his 'my-God-this-is-just-so-fascinating' face.

Noting the devoted attention, Pharyl started to explain what had happened to his father when his smile abruptly turned to a frown upon seeing the steward take the left at the fork in the road.

"No. This is wrong," he called out. "You're going the wrong way." Spurring his mount forward, he snapped, "What is wrong with that idiot."

Conal likewise spurred his horse to stay just behind Lord Pharyl whose temper increased the farther down the road he traveled. Flicking their whips to above the draft horses, the wagoners increased their speed to catch up with their disappearing Lord.

The road curved sharply to the left and Pharyl and Conal came to a sliding halt, confronted by the travel steward and Pharyl's guards surrounded by what appeared to be highwaymen. The wagons lurched to a halt, bunching up behind them.

"What's the meaning of this," Lord Pharyl demanded.

Conal did a quick assessment and calculated they were outnumbered at least two to one. The highwaymen were armed with bow and arrow, crossbows, and swords. One curious thing he noted was that they were clean and relatively well-dressed, causing him to wonder if they were who they pretended to be. Oddly enough, the steward didn't seem to be all that upset.

A tall well-built man with saucy confidence strode up and over-dramatically bowed. His auburn hair was cut short as was his beard. "Welcome my Lord. I trust your journey has been uneventful so far."

"Who are you and what do you want?"

"I am called many names," he said with a smile. "For now, 'Jock' will do… and I think you already know what we want."

Pharyl's gaze shifted from the man to his steward whose smug grin said enough. "You will pay for this with your life."

"Perhaps," the steward shrugged, "but not because of you." He nodded to an adjacent bowman who pulled back on the bowstring.

"Wait," Conal exclaimed, his hands spread. "Wait. Just hear me out. Please."

Jock ticked his head at the bowman who eased up on the bowstring.

"What are you doing?" the steward fumed at Jock before glaring at Conal. "He's a nobody, a slave." He jerked his head at Pharyl. "Kill him."

Ignoring him, Jock directed his attention to Conal. "Well?"

"I don't know what's going on, but it seems to me to be foolish to kill Lord Pharyl," Conal said, making up an excuse on the fly. "He's royalty. You kill him and you'll bring all hell down on yourselves." He held up a hand to stop Jock's interruption. "Because he's royalty… You just can't have some highwayman take out royalty anytime he wants and not expect a reaction, especially when word gets out."

"We're wasting time," the steward fussed.

Jock flipped hand at the steward telling him to be quiet. "And why would word get out?"

Conal ticked his head at the steward. "He's the one who would talk. And he'd put the entire blame on you."

"He's a liar," the steward exploded. "Why are you listening to him? We've got a job to do. Let's get on with it."

"And another thing," Conal pointed out. "Did you plan on killing all the slaves here too?"

Jock stiffened. "Of course not. You are free. I should think you would be happy about that."

"We would be, except for one little problem. If you kill Lord Pharyl, we have no letters of manumission freeing us. Therefore, we are all considered runaway slaves, and anyone can take vengeance on us."

Jock frowned then half-smiled. "Manumission. That's quite a word for a slave. I see the dressing on your shoulder, and I have to ask myself 'Why is this slave riding beside Lord Pharyl?'"

"He's marked with the Cobra," the steward interjected.

Surprised, Jock regarded Conal with new appreciation. "What is your name?"

"I am called Conal."

"You are educated?"

"Yes."

"How did you end up marked as chattel?" Jock was beginning to like this brash young man.

"Like I told our Lord here, not everyone who calls you friend is one."

"Well Conal, what do you suggest we do? We've been paid for a job, and it would be bad for our reputation as highwaymen if we renege on contracts."

"You are hardly highwaymen," Conal grinned, "though I will accept the appearance for now. You've already been paid to permanently dispose of Lord Pharyl. Why? Not my business. However, like I said, killing him creates all sorts of problems for the slaves here and for the surrounding towns for you know they will bear the brunt of retribution." Conal paused. "Instead of killing him, why not ransom him off?"

"That's crazy," the steward snapped. "You've been paid to do a job. Now do it."

"You shut up," Jock threatened then turned back to Conal. "We've already been paid. Ransoming him creates problems for us."

Conal stared intently at him. "If you were really highwaymen, it wouldn't matter."

Jock snorted a laugh. "Well spoken. I will give

consideration to your suggestion."

"You can't do that," the steward exploded. "Blayne will find out what you've done."

"Blayne?" Pharyl roared. "Brody's bastard son put you up to this?" He twisted his head to focus on Jock. "Whatever he paid you, I will double it."

Jock's smile widened. "A tempting offer."

"See?" Conal said with an impish smile. "Already your prospects are improving."

Jock smirked and curled his fingers at Conal. "Come down and talk with me."

Conal dismounted and followed Jock several paces away from listening ears.

"Do you trust Pharyl to do as he said?"

"Not at all," Conal replied. "Once inside the safety of his castle, he'll state that he doesn't deal with highwaymen. But you've already been paid, so what does it matter? What matters is Blayne and his father Brody. But again, what does it matter? Now that Pharyl knows Blayne meant to kill him, he will want to return the favor. Why not offer your services to Pharyl and be paid twice for the same effort?"

Jock barked a laugh. "That is an excellent idea, with one exception. You will stay with me. I can use a man with your brains."

Conal dipped his head and smiled. "It would be a privilege." *Finally. Finally, someone sees that I'm smart.*

Jock walked back to the group, Conal behind him.

"I have made my decision. Lord Pharyl and his group are free to go with the exception of Conal here."

"But he's mine," Pharyl snapped, bowing up.

Conal briskly closed the gap between him and Pharyl, motioning him to bend down. "It's all I could do, m'Lord," he whispered. "My life for yours."

Pharyl sat back up, astonished and ashamed he had this selfless man branded. "I will not forget this. I am in your debt."

"As a benefit," Jock spoke, gazing directly at Pharyl, "we will offer our services to you to eliminate the man who wished to do you harm."

Pharyl stared back at him then at Conal and immediately understood what Conal had done, impressed that this man had so easily turned the tables on his enemies. "I like your suggestion. Perhaps you can send a man to negotiate terms."

"It would be our pleasure," Jock grinned.

"What about my steward?"

"He is of no use to you," Jock answered, noting the steward's face had assumed an ashen color and he was beginning to sweat.

"I demand justice," Pharyl growled.

"A fair demand," Jock acknowledged. "Let's ask our friend here what he thinks." He turned to Conal. "What are we to do with him?" He flicked his hand at several highwaymen close by the steward who reached up and dragged him off his horse.

Conal gazed at the man held firmly between two burly men, a cockiness flowing inside him that everyone was looking to him for a solution. Everyone wanted to know what he thought should be done. *This is a nice change from Oscon.*

"You know he can't be trusted," Conal sagely stated. "He was more than willing to betray his Lord for who knows how much. Ask him. How much was it?"

Jock shifted a glance at the steward. "Well? Answer the man."

When he didn't answer, one of the men holding

him poked him in the side with a dagger.

"Fifty regals," he sputtered with a hard swallow.

"Fifty regals," Conal repeated in a loud voice. "The man betrayed a Lord for a mere fifty regals. I assume they were gold regals. Apparently, a Lord's life isn't worth much… unless they promised him something more." He folded his arms and stared at the steward.

Realizing his life was on tender hooks, the steward blurted, "And a pub of my own."

"There you have it," Conal announced as though he were a barrister playing to a jury. "The man sold out for a mere fifty regals and a pint of ale. What makes you think he won't betray you when the time is right… and for a lot less than fifty regals?"

"You're right," Jock agreed with a nod.

"Wait," the steward struggled. "You can't do this. We had a deal. Blayne will make you pay for this. Please."

With an extravagant display, Jock slowly looked around the group. "What say you? Death or life?"

The shouts of 'death' reverberated. Jock turned to look up at Pharyl whose pleased demeanor told him his answer. Yet Pharyl nodded and added his own voice to the crescendo.

"O God, please no," the steward begged, sinking to his knees.

Jock walked over to one of his highwaymen. Taking the man's crossbow, he strode back to Conal and thrust it into his hands.

"Here. Kill him."

CHAPTER 5

GWEN

An hour after departing the cemetery outside Dawsbury, Gwen and Tobias were nearing the outpost that the prisoners had been escorted to. Gwen had spent much of the walk deep in thought. Tobias had thrown so much information at her, and she was still working through it all. When she spotted the outpost, she stopped walking.

"I thought we were going to see Eradore?"

"We are," Tobias replied. "His place is past the outpost."

"Aren't you afraid the soldiers will see you?"

"Not really. I don't think the men we encountered will remember my face from the many others they've seen today. Besides, it was dark. If any of them happened to memorize what they saw, I'd be impressed."

Gwen wrung her hands anxiously, but she reminded herself that she agreed to trust Tobias, and this would be the first opportunity to prove her word. She nodded at him and continued walking.

"Besides, we're going to need a horse, maybe two. How much do you weigh?"

"That's none of your business," Gwen snapped.

"And I didn't know the soldiers sold horses at the outpost."

"They don't," Tobias said. "We're going to steal one."

"I'm sorry? I don't think I heard you correctly. You said we're going to steal a horse from the king's soldiers?"

"It sounds to me like you've got great hearing."

Gwen shot a glare at Tobias, but he was grinning from ear to ear. "You must think yourself amusing," she said.

"Absolutely. Life is too short for delusions." Tobias chuckled at his own joke, but Gwen rolled her eyes.

"Don't worry. I've done this several times. We'll be long gone before they even know a horse is missing. Trust me."

There were far too many warning signs for Gwen's comfort, but she was determined to keep her word. Tobias was proving to be brash and overconfident, but he was the only person Gwen had right now.

Tobias took them off the road, keeping a wide berth of the outpost until they passed it, then circled back and hid among the shadows of a copse of trees. Gwen was tempted to ask why he wasted the effort, but then she spotted the stable. It was a squat wood building with a thatched roof outside of the main compound. A lantern hung next to each of the stalls, illuminating the area more than Gwen was comfortable with.

"Stay here and wait for me. Once I'm free of the stable, you need to be prepared for a hasty exit. We're going to fly like the wind."

"What about all that light? Someone is bound to

see you moving around."

"The lanterns are new, but that just makes my job easier," Tobias said. "I don't have to fumble around in the dark."

"What if something goes wrong? What should I do?" Gwen looked around for anything that might be used as a weapon, but aside from a few busted wagon wheels, she didn't spot anything useful.

"If I whistle, that means go."

"Go … where?" Gwen asked.

"Anywhere, just get away from here. Find somewhere to lie low and wait a day or two, then head to Penshaw and find an elf named Muriel. She'll get you to Eradore."

"Just get a horse and get back here," Gwen said.

"Yes, my lady." Tobias offered a mock bow and sprinted to the stable.

Gwen watched fretfully until Tobias entered one of the stalls. She looked around to make sure there were no soldiers, but the trees blocked part of her view. She crept closer to the edge of the tree line and stopped when she smelled urine. The scent was strong and burned her nostrils. A few more steps revealed the source of the smell.

A makeshift latrine had been dug in front of the trees. Gwen pinched her nose shut and finished surveying the area. It was quiet and she didn't see a single soldier, which she found odd. *Shouldn't someone be on watch or something?* she wondered.

The door to the stall Tobias had entered opened, its hinges creaking. Gwen flinched, expecting the entire garrison to come pouring out of the outpost. Instead, Tobias led a dappled mare out and then mounted it. He flicked the reins, and the horse took off with a burst of speed. Gwen turned and ran through the trees, breaking free of the copse and ending up on the road.

She saw Tobias approaching quickly, but she noticed another horse following him. A black-clad soldier rode on its back and lifted something up. A moment later, there was a whizzing sound and Tobias let out a cry of anguish. He remained on the horse, and as he neared Gwen, he leaned over the side and stretched out his arm.

Gwen jogged toward him and grabbed ahold of his hand, using her momentum and his strength to shoot upward and land on the saddle behind him. She wrapped her arms around him and felt something wet and warm against her arm. Tobias flicked the reins again and rammed his heels into the horse's flanks, urging the beast to go faster. Gwen looked back and saw the mounted soldier wasn't following them.

Roughly a mile down the road revealed why as Tobias grunted and slouched forward, almost falling off the horse. Gwen jerked the reins from him and slowed their pace, giving the horse a reprieve but also allowing her to look over Tobias. She found a crossbow bolt lodged in his side and an alarming amount of blood soaked into his shirt.

"Tobias, can you hear me?"

The man was unconscious. Gwen considered removing the bolt, but she didn't know if that would help or further injure him, so she left it alone. She had seen the results of barroom brawls before, but this was something entirely different. He needed a healer, and they weren't anywhere near one.

Gwen managed to pull Tobias into her lap and got the horse to move faster, but nowhere near the breakneck pace Tobias had. She assumed they would have to ride through the night before they reached the nearest town, but when she spotted a farmhouse a while later, she whispered a heartfelt thanks to the sky and stopped the horse. Gwen laid Tobias on the horse's neck and slid off the saddle, then ran to the front door of the house and knocked loudly. The door opened and an older man peered out at her.

"My friend needs help! He's lost a lot of blood and needs a healer."

The man looked from her to the horse. "Me and Gail ain't healers, but she can stitch him up. Help me bring him inside." He stepped out of the house and shouted over his shoulder, "Gail! Get out here, woman!"

Gwen helped the man pull Tobias from the saddle, and they awkwardly carried him into the house. The man guided Gwen into the kitchen, and they laid Tobias on the table. It creaked under Tobias's weight, but it held firmly.

"What happened?" Gail asked, her voice low and frail.

"I'd say he was hit by a crossbow," the man said, pointing to the bolt in Tobias's side.

"Let me get my things. Errol, be a dear and get me a bowl of water and some cloth."

The two left the kitchen. Gwen looked at Tobias's still form. The bolt had pierced his right side, just above the hip. His cobalt-hued shirt was dark with blood, and more seeped from the wound, dripping onto the table. Gail returned first, holding a needle and thread.

"Have you ever tended a wound?" she asked.

"Never," Gwen answered.

"Some don't have the stomach for it, but when you've lived with animals long enough, you get used to some ugly sights."

Errol carried a wooden bowl half-filled with water and a bolt of cloth under his arm. He pulled a chair out from the table and set the bowl on it, then started unrolling the cloth, cutting it into strips.

"I'm not one to pry," Errol said as he worked, "but what brings you two out to the country at this hour?"

"We were on our way to see … a friend," Gwen said. "Before we were attacked."

Errol frowned. "The road used to be safe from brigands. Lately, though …" He exchanged looks with Gail. "Well, lately there've been problems."

"The soldiers?" Gwen boldly asked.

"Yes," Gail said. "They come through our land sometimes, picking from our crops and stealing our chickens."

Gail gently pulled Tobias's shirt away from the wound, then examined the bolt. "Errol—"

"Yeah, yeah," Errol muttered. "'Be a dear and pull the bolt out.' I got it, woman."

Gwen averted her gaze, unsure she could stomach the gruesome sight.

"There we go," Errol said, and Gwen looked back at Tobias and immediately regretted it. More blood flowed from the wound. Gail cupped her hands and dipped them into the bowl, then poured the water onto Tobias's damaged flesh. Tobias groaned and his head lolled to the side, but he remained unconscious.

Gwen felt faint. All the blood was making her queasy. Errol took notice and motioned for her to follow him.

"Holler if you need anything," he told Gail. She waved him off, focused on her work. He led Gwen out of the house and around to the back.

"He's not fit for travel, so you're going to need

somewhere to stay for the night. We don't have room in the house, but you can stay in the barn. The nights have been warm, so you shouldn't need a fire, but if you do, keep it away from the walls."

"Thank you for the offer, but I don't think we should stay here," Gwen said.

"I know the lodging I'm offering isn't the best, but it's all we have."

"It's not that. I just don't think it's wise to stay in one place too long right now." Gwen looked in the direction they'd traveled from. The road was empty, but something was telling her to keep moving.

Errol nodded wordlessly. "I understand. You're free to risk it, but I think your friend is going to need the rest. Jouncing around on a horse will likely break the sutures Gail's stitching."

Gwen was torn. She knew Tobias needed to rest, but she was certain the soldiers were going to come looking for them. "I guess a few hours won't hurt," she said. "I don't have any money to give you. I suppose I should have mentioned that earlier."

"There's no charge for kindness," Errol said. "Don't worry about payment. Just take care of your friend."

"Thank you."

After Gail had stitched Tobias's wound closed, the three of them carried him to the barn and laid him on a makeshift bed of straw. Gail covered him with a clean blanket, and Errol brought the stolen horse in, tying its reins to a post.

"If you decide to stay for the night, you should take the saddle off him," Errol said.

Gwen nodded and sat beside Tobias.

"He should be fine, so long as he doesn't tear the stitches," Gail said. "I know you want to be on your way, but I suggest letting him rest until morning."

"I'll keep that in mind," Gwen replied.

The couple left her a lantern and returned to the house. Gwen watched the light cast flickering shadows along the walls. She was suddenly overcome with exhaustion. Her muscles ached and her eyes were growing heavy. She stood up and paced around the barn, trying to stay awake.

Eventually, she grew tired of being on her feet and used some hay as a chair. She stared at Tobias and pondered the things he'd told her. If he wasn't lying, who were her real parents? Had they given her up because they didn't want her, or because they couldn't give her the life they wanted her to have?

Gwen's eyes shot open, and she realized she had dozed off. She stood up and looked around, trying to determine what woke her. Tobias was in the same position, his eyes still closed. A sound outside caught her attention, and she peeked out of the barn.

A group of mounted soldiers were outside the farmhouse. One of them was on foot, standing at the front door. Gwen saw Errol was talking with him. He pointed to the road, waving his hand westward.

Gwen held her breath, hoping the soldiers would leave. The one on foot shouted something and struck Errol in the face, knocking the man to the ground. Gwen covered her mouth in horror, stifling a scream. She looked at the horse, then at Tobias. There was no way she could lift him onto the saddle herself. That left only one option. She would have to—

"Where am I?"

It was Tobias. Gwen rushed to his side. She put a finger to her lips and shook her head, then mouthed the word 'soldiers.' Tobias's face scrunched in confusion. Gwen leaned down and whispered in his ear.

"The soldiers are here."

Tobias closed his eyes. "We need to go," he rasped.

"I'm with you on that, but you're injured."

"Better injured than dead. Help me up."

Gwen grabbed Tobias's hands and pulled with everything she had. A pained expression covered Tobias's face, but he only grunted softly. Gwen was impressed. She would have screamed in agony. Tobias hovered a hand over the bandage Gail had wrapped over the wound.

"Is this your handiwork?" he asked.

"Hardly," Gwen answered. "If I help you, can you get on the horse?"

"I think so."

Gwen retrieved the lantern and hung it on the wall near the horse, then struggled to assist Tobias into the saddle. A long moment of frustration gave way to victory, and Tobias was seated. The lantern illuminated his face and Gwen saw a haggard and pale complexion. Tobias grabbed the reins and turned the horse toward the barn doors.

"Take my hand," he said.

"I can manage," Gwen replied. She struck her foot in the stirrup and flung herself upward. The first two times she didn't get high enough to get her leg over the horse, but the third time she succeeded.

The horse clopped over to the doors just as they swung open. Three soldiers were there on foot, swords drawn. Gwen's breath caught in her throat, but Tobias kicked the horse and yelled, "Yah!"

The soldiers scrambled out of the way as the mare burst forth from the barn. Shouts rose, and Gwen saw the mounted soldiers were pursuing them.

"They're coming!" she shouted.

"We can lose them in the woods," Tobias cried back.

Gwen couldn't make out much detail of the landscape, but she did see tall shadows that rose from the ground and guessed they were trees. Tobias spurred the horse, and it sped across the farmland, the air whipping Gwen's hair about wildly. She kept looking back, hoping the soldiers would give up their chase, but there was no such luck. They were still there, but they hadn't gotten any closer.

They reached the woods and Tobias turned the horse to the right, guiding it to a brook. The water moved slowly and wasn't very high.

"This should throw them off," Tobias said, forcing the horse into the water. They headed upstream, traveling for a long while in silence. They left the woods behind and were greeted by rolling green hills. Once the water started to get deeper, Tobias took them back onto dry land and stopped atop one of the hills to stare back the way they'd come.

"I think we lost them," he said, his voice little more than a whisper.

Gwen wasn't certain, but she thought she saw movement down by the stream. "What's that?" she asked, pointing.

Tobias stared for a moment, then his eyes widened. "Impossible," he choked. "They're still tracking us."

CHAPTER 6

CONAL

Conal stared at the crossbow in his hands, the bolt notched and ready. Silence had smothered the forest as those surrounding him waited. He looked up to see the steward five paces away, cringing in abject terror, the two highwaymen gripping him by the arms, holding him up. His brilliant design of extricating himself had gone painfully wrong and he wondered if they knew he had never killed a man before. Not that he hadn't wanted to on more than a few occasions but wanting and actually doing were two vastly different affairs.

"Well, come on," Jock urged. "We don't have all day."

With a grin of false bravado, Conal shifted his gaze to him. "Hardly seems sporting. How can I miss?"

"That's the point," Jock answered. "You're not supposed to miss."

"I know, but where's the fun of killing an unarmed man held firmly in one spot?"

"You want to give him a chance?" Jock raised an eyebrow.

"Why not?" An idea blossomed along with his

confidence. "Give him a five second head start down the road. Make it interesting."

Jock sniffed a laugh. "Alright." Turning to the steward, he pointed down the road. "You've got five seconds. If he misses, you live." He looked back at Conal. "You ready?"

"Ready and waiting," Conal cheerfully replied, shifting position on the road and raising the crossbow to his shoulder.

With their attention focused on Conal and the steward, they didn't notice Pharyl's stern wave at another highwayman, demanding the man's crossbow. Despite initial misgiving and after repeated silent demands, the man handed the weapon to him.

"You can let go of him," Jock commanded the two men holding the steward. Staring directly at the steward, he pointed to the road behind the terrified man. "Let's see how fast you can run. Go."

The steward spun around and gave panic to his legs, churning as fast as he could, hearing Jock announce, "One… two… three… four…" pause, "five."

Conal took aim at the disappearing steward. Despite having never killed a man, he was more than proficient with a crossbow, this time aiming just to the left of the man's head.

In the interval between Conal's aim and squeezing the trigger-lever, Pharyl stood in the stirrups, aimed and launched his bolt, hitting the steward squarely between the shoulder blades, causing him to stumble enough to the left that Conal's bolt rammed into the back of the man's head.

"Ouch," Jock smirked. "That's gonna leave a bruise." Turning back to Conal, he complimented,

"Nice shot," adding, "and you too," to Lord Pharyl. "I will send a man to you to negotiate our bargain to eliminate Blayne."

Conal's mouth had dropped open the moment his bolt whipped the man's head forward. Now rooted to the ground, he fumbled with his emotions. In truth, the steward meant nothing to him. Had Conal continued in Pharyl's employ as a Cobra he would have had the man killed per Pharyl's instructions, but someone else would have done the killing. His hands would be clean. But was there a difference... really? Still, the steward was a traitor and needed to be dealt with. Besides, it was Lord Pharyl's bolt that killed the man.

Conal's introspection was interrupted when Jock circled his finger in the air and called out to his band, "Let's get ready to move out."

Conal hustled several steps to catch up with him. "What about the slaves?"

"What about them?"

"Manumission?"

Jock shook his head. "Not my problem, not my call."

Though disappointed, Conal understood. Now was not the time to press the issue. Looking back over his shoulder, he saw Pharyl waiting to speak with him.

"I am sorely disappointed I am losing your services," Pharyl gravely said.

"Who knows where the future lies, m'Lord. I still proudly wear your mark." He dipped his head towards the bandaged shoulder.

Pharyl sat back in his saddle, peering intently at the young man before loudly declaring, "To all who stand here now as witness, I declare Conal to be a free man." He narrowed his gaze at Jock. "When you send your man to see me, I will give him the necessary papers."

"Thank you, m'Lord." Conal bowed and inwardly grinned. He had yet again got himself out of a mess.

Gathering the reins, Pharyl nodded and resumed his march, two of his guards having already moved the steward off the road into the forest where carrion fowl and animals would feast upon the body.

Waiting until Pharyl was down the road, Jock wryly commented, "While he gave you your freedom, I notice he took your horse."

"It was his to begin with," Conal shrugged with a smile. "So. What's the plan?"

"We head on home. Walk with me." Jock led the way into the forest, Conal dodging trees and bushes to keep up. "Tell me about yourself. Where are you from?"

"Urve."

"On the coast?"

"Yes."

Jock tossed a quizzical glance at him. "How did you end up in Hamlyn?"

"My father decided I needed to be educated, so he sent me to the priory in Ecclesley. Not liking their method of education, I escaped when I was fifteen, knocked around for a couple of years refining my inept skill of thievery then threw in my lot with a man called Oscon."

"I've heard of him."

Conal scowled. "I hope to meet him again in better circumstances when I can plunge a knife in his throat. It is because of him that I wear this brand."

Jock glanced at him then quickly surveyed the men and women scattered around him. "How is it that you were branded a Cobra?"

"I'd love to say because of my formidable abilities, but honestly, I haven't a clue."

Jock chuckled. "You think fast on your feet, which is a good thing. We'll need that where we're going."

"I thought we were going to help Pharyl," Conal said.

"We are… but not yet. I'll explain later."

Accepting the response for the moment, Conal asked, "Who are you… when you're not Jock?"

Jock grinned, impressed once again with the young man. "I am Rhonyn."

Conal held on to his next question when he saw them, the horses, a man and a woman guarding them.

"You can either ride double or walk," Rhonyn said. "Your choice."

A man emerged from a thicket and languidly walked towards Rhonyn. He was tall, with a full dark-brown beard, thick hair that fell below his shoulders, and coal black eyes. He dressed like a huntsman with tight dark green leggings in calf-high leather boots, and a brown leather vest over a forest green long-sleeved shirt. A supple leather bag of lamb skin held by a shoulder strap bounced on his left hip as he walked. His right hand held a staff of polished oak topped with a dragon's head. As the man walked up, Conal couldn't tell if he was looking at Rhonyn or him for the eyes were solid and opaque. The man stopped and swiveled his head to gaze at Conal, at least that's what it felt like.

"This him?" The man's voice was an odd contrast to his dress for the voice had a resonant hum of tranquility, the softness of peace.

"Yes," Rhonyn answered.

"Where you from lad?"

"Urve," Conal replied, a bit unnerved by the sightless eyes. "Who are you?"

"This is Drustan," Rhonyn answered for him, "the half-druid."

"Which half?" Conal said without thinking, causing Rhonyn to giggle and Drustan to stiffen.

"He means no harm," Rhonyn soothed then turned to Conal. "You would do well to curb your quick tongue on occasion. Do you not know what a half-druid is?"

"Uh… no." Conal had heard of druids, but half-druids?

"A half-druid," Rhonyn explained, "is a druid bonded with an undead soul."

"Sounds painful," Conal quipped.

"Have a care, lad," the druid snapped, straining to maintain his soothing voice. "Do not mock that which you don't know or understand. Hold out your hand."

"Why?" Conal usually didn't dislike someone from the start, but this guy was an exception.

"Do it," Drustan commanded.

"I say again," Conal stubbornly replied, "why?"

"Because I told you so." The half-druid's voice morphed to a brittle harshness.

"Just do it, please," Rhonyn said, carefully watching the interaction.

Figuring they weren't going to let it go until he obeyed, Conal reluctantly stuck out his hand.

The half-druid grasped Conal's hand and closed his eyes.

Conal felt a searing pain shoot throughout his body, and he yelped as he worked to pry his hand free, but the druid's strength was far too strong. It was like Conal had gotten his hand stuck in a rock crevasse and despite his wild flailing, the rock never moved. The pain increased along with an intense heat until he felt he was going to explode and melt at the same time.

The druid let go and Conal careened backwards, tumbling onto the ground.

"What the hell," Conal yelled, clutching his hand.

"Well?" Rhonyn said, looking at Drustan.

"I could not see the birth-mind," the half-druid answered, looking at Conal who shook his hand, trying to cool it off. "His other memories are of Urve and a sense of despair at the separation from his father." He bent forward slightly to focus on Conal. "Are you telling me the truth?"

"I haven't said anything," Conal snarled. "You nearly killed me."

"I know," he nodded. "That's what bothers me." He brusquely turned to Rhonyn. "He has strength far beyond a mere wharf-rat."

"I'm not a wharf-rat," Conal growled. "My father is a jewelry merchant and a very successful one. So get your story straight."

Drustan tilted his head to look at the bulge beneath the shirt on Conal's shoulder. "You wear a brand. Shall we look at it?"

"Why?"

Drustan chuckled. "To see how it heals."

Though curious himself, Conal didn't like the thought that this half-wit… uh, half-druid wanted to see it.

"Tell me," the druid said. "Does it still hurt?"

Conal frowned in thought, realizing that the pain had stopped as soon as the branding iron lifted from his arm. "No, not really."

Drustan nodded. "Come. Let us see how well it

heals."

Conal hesitated then unbuttoned his shirt and reached up and unwrapped the thin cloth surrounding the brand.

Drustan reached out to touch it and jerked his hand back as though stung. "A Cobra head." He stepped back, shaking his head. "This is all wrong. It doesn't fit."

"Doesn't fit what?" Conal demanded before glancing down at the brand, not surprised that his scar had completely healed and the brand itself looked quite good.

Instead of answering, the half-druid spun around and stalked off.

"What's with him?" Conal sniffed.

Rhonyn bent down to study Conal's brand, looked up at Conal then swiveled his head to watch the half-druid flop down beneath an oak tree. "Your scar has healed."

"So it seems." Conal nonchalantly replied.

"You were branded this morning?"

"Yes."

Rhonyn stood back up. "Do you not find this unusual?"

"I was always a fast healer," he shrugged.

Rhonyn shook his head. "Not this fast."

"You mind telling me what's going on?"

Rhonyn stared at him a moment before saying, "We are searching for someone."

"Who?"

"A king's son."

"What does that have to do with me?" He put his shirt back on.

"You are the right age."

Conal paused to button his shirt and barked a

disbelieving laugh. "Me? Are you daft? My father's a jeweler. I've been a highwayman for these past several years. I've just been branded as an outlaw. What's wrong with you people? You round up guys my age and let Grip and Grin over there roast them to see if they might be a king. What's wrong with this picture?"

"I know it sounds strange," Rhonyn grinned, "but there are reasons behind it."

"So, who is this king anyway?"

"His name was Kamron."

"Was? So sometime along the way, this guy loses his kid then dies and now you're trying to find the kid?"

"Kids. There's a girl too."

Conal shook his head in disgust. "This is the stuff of fairy tales. Next, you're gonna tell me that you guys work for some evil king who wants to kill the kids because they're the rightful heirs to the throne."

When Rhonyn remained silent, Conal threw up his hands. "I was making a joke. Please tell me you're not serious."

"We are," Rhonyn quietly replied, "and you can help us."

"How? I don't know any royalty, let alone any king's kids. And why would I want to throw in my lot with an evil king? By definition he's bad. You actually think something good is going to come of this?"

"There's far more going on than I can explain or that you would understand," Rhonyn said. "Besides, you got something better to do?"

"Yeah. I could go learn to be a Cobra."

"Maybe later," Rhonyn firmly said. "For now, you're one of us."

"Just great," Conal fumed and stomped off to mingle with the horses who were probably the only sane creatures around here.

Rhonyn watched him trudge away before turning to walk over where Drustan sat. "What did you see?"

"He is a conundrum. He has the aura of the one we search for, but he has too many inconsistencies. His birth-mind is blank before nursing. That alone gives me cause to suspect. And his healing. Another factor. And he endured the limits of my strength. However, he bears the Cobra Head."

"So?"

Drustan lifted his eyes to stare at Rhonyn. "The eagle will bear the vipers in its claws, yet from the west a cobra will rise and strike down the eagle."

Rhonyn shook his head. "That means nothing to me."

Drustan curled a lip. "The eagle is King Torian. The vipers are Kamron's children. The cobra is the unknown assassin who will claim the throne as his own."

Rhonyn looked back over his shoulder at Conal who was nuzzling one of the horses. "What do you want to do?"

"We can take no chances. We must kill him."

CHAPTER 7

GWEN

"How are they still following us?" Gwen asked, shouting to be heard above the mare's thunderous galloping.

If Tobias replied, Gwen didn't hear him. She held onto him tightly as they covered more ground and was careful not to touch near his wound. They rode until the hills flattened into grassland, and Gwen constantly looked back to watch their pursuers.

The sun was beginning to crest over the horizon and Gwen spotted a walled city up the road. She'd never been this far from home and was officially lost. Without Tobias, she probably wouldn't have made it this far.

"She doesn't have much left in her," Tobias said, patting the mare's neck comfortingly. "Good thing we're almost there."

"Is that where Eradore is?" Gwen asked.

"Yes. So long as we can reach the gates before the soldiers catch up to us, we can lose them for good in the city."

"Are you sure? Your little water trick didn't help."

Tobias was silent for a moment, then said, "I

think they're using magic. That's the only explanation for how they've kept on our trail."

"Magic?" The world suddenly seemed much larger than Gwen had ever imagined. Plots to overthrow a king, soldiers chasing commoners across the countryside, and magic. It was too much at once.

"Do you always repeat what people say, or do you just do it to annoy me?" Tobias asked.

Gwen bumped him with her shoulder and then realized her mistake when Tobias hissed in a breath. "Sorry," she said. "I forgot."

"Don't worry about it. I'll get used to the pain. Besides, I've had worse injuries than this. I just need a few days to rest, and I'll be back to myself again."

"So what happens when we meet with Eradore? Will you tell him what happened at the inn and then organize the rebellion to attack the outpost?"

"Something like that," Tobias said evasively.

"Can you get the horse to move any faster?"

"Only if you want to kill her," Tobias replied.

"If it's between her life and ours, I say do whatever you need to. The soldiers are getting closer."

Tobias twisted in the saddle, his face scrunching in pain, and looked behind them. "Blast it," he grunted. "I'm sorry, girl," he told the horse, then snapped the reins. The mare picked up the pace, but not by much.

As they drew closer to the city of Penshaw, there were more signs of life. Cottages and livestock dotted the landscape, and they passed a few slow-moving wagons filled with vegetables. Gwen's stomach growled as if telling her it was time to eat. *Safety before food,* she told herself.

The city gates were wide open, allowing anyone

free access in or out. The horse slowed down to a tired trot, and they passed through the wall without issue. Gwen looked up at the raised portcullis and pictured a morbid image of it closing down on them. She chalked it up to her lack of sleep and turned her attention to the vast array of vendors, stalls, and people that filled the streets.

Gwen smelled so many wonderful scents drifting on the air, and they all made her mouth water. Tobias guided the horse down a street to the left and stopped outside a building with several horses tethered to wooden poles.

"We need to get rid of the horse and find somewhere to hide before the soldiers find us," Tobias said. "I'm going to need your help dismounting."

Gwen slid off the side of the mare and offered her hands to Tobias. He accepted one and tried to ease himself down but ended up slipping out of the saddle and landing on the ground with enough force to cause his bandage to stain with fresh blood. He grimaced and bit his lower lip.

"Wait here with the horse," he grunted.

"Where are you going?" Gwen asked, glancing around uneasily.

"Inside to sell the horse. Weren't you listening?"

Gwen rolled her eyes at Tobias as he went inside the building. She turned to watch the gates and fidgeted with the horse's reins. The Seven Stars was one of the largest buildings in Dawsbury, but it paled in comparison to ones around her now. Everything was big, from the buildings to the wall that stretched around the city.

Tobias returned and tossed a small bag to her. She caught it, the coins inside clinking together.

"Is this for me?" she asked.

Tobias laughed, then grimaced and clenched his fists. He took a breath. "No, it's *ours*. I just want you to hold onto it."

Gwen shrugged and hid the bag in the waistband of her pants. "Where to now?"

"We need somewhere to hide until we can get word to Eradore that we need a meeting. There's an inn nearby we can rent a room from."

"What about the soldiers?" Gwen asked.

"They're going to have a rough time searching for us. Penshaw is the city that never rests, so people are always coming and going. Once we're holed up in the inn, their search will be almost impossible."

"What if they're using magic?"

"That's why I said *almost*. Eradore will know if they are using magic. He's some sort of rare type of wizard or something. Anyway, let's get moving."

Tobias led Gwen along the backstreets where there were few people. He explained to her that it would have been easier to take the road at the gates straight down the middle of the city, but they were more likely to be spotted.

After a half hour of walking along cobbled stone streets, they reached an inn with a wooden sign that read *The Burrow*. It was tall like the buildings around it and music could be heard playing inside. Gwen felt a pang of sadness, thinking about the bard from the Seven Stars. Had he been imprisoned too?

The interior of the inn was radically different than the Seven Stars. A massive hearth sat in the center of the room, the façade crafted of white square stones stacked atop each other and lined with lime mortar. The floors were birch wood, which reflected the light that poured in from the many windows.

Tobias headed for the bar and Gwen followed, pausing briefly to look around at the host of people who were enjoying breakfast and the music. The people were lively given the hour, and Gwen spotted plates full of steaming eggs, fresh bread, and sausage.

"Gwen!"

She looked at Tobias. He was motioning for her to come to the bar.

"Stop gawking and get over here."

She joined him, and he held his hand out. "The money, please," he said. Gwen pulled the bag out and handed it to him, then continued looking around the inn. The place was packed with all different races. Gwen saw mostly elves, dwarves, and humans, but there was also a single gnome sitting by himself.

"We just need one room," she heard Tobias say.

"One?" Gwen asked, turning to the barkeep. At first glance, she thought the stocky dwarf behind the counter was a male, but then the dwarf spoke, and the voice was feminine.

"I'll sleep on the floor if it makes you feel better," Tobias said.

"We've only got one room available anyway," the barkeep replied.

"We'll take it," Tobias confirmed.

"How many nights will you be staying?"

"I'm not sure yet. Two, maybe three." Tobias opened the bag and poured half of the coins onto the counter. "Will that cover the room and some food?" Tobias pulled his sleeve up and flashed his wrist at the dwarf. It was subtle and Gwen almost missed the move. She looked at Tobias questioningly, but he ignored her.

"That's plenty," the barkeep answered. She set a key on the counter. "Third floor, last room on the left.”

"Much appreciated,” Tobias said. He passed the key to Gwen, and they took a seat at the only empty table available, which was next to the gnome. Gwen stared at the curious creature from her periphery until she saw Tobias frowning at her.

"What are you doing?” he asked.

"Nothing.”

"Didn't Boris teach you that staring is rude?”

"Sorry. I'm curious is all.” Gwen rubbed her eyes and stifled a yawn.

The barkeep delivered two plates of food to their table along with two tankards of ale. Gwen wasted little time in eating. She devoured everything on the plate and offered a contented sigh.

"That was good, but it's too early for ale,” she said.

"I'll drink yours, then,” Tobias said. The color had returned to his face, and he didn't look like he was on the brink of death anymore.

"How do we get word to Eradore?” Gwen asked.

"Keep your voice down,” Tobias admonished. "You never know who might be listening.” He took a long drink from his tankard, then leaned forward over the table. "There's a network of people here in Penshaw who move messages for the rebellion. We'll leave a message for one, and when Eradore gets it, he'll find us.”

"Where do you find these secret messengers?” Gwen asked.

Tobias smiled. "You're eager, aren't you?”

"I want my father rescued,” Gwen replied. "Once he's safe, I'll feel better.”

"I know. One step at a time.” Tobias turned around to look at the gnome and offered a slight nod.

The gnome rose from his chair and came over to their table. He stood a little over three feet in height and wore spectacles that kept sliding down his enlarged nose. His head was bald, but he sported a long white beard.

"The swan flies low and the alligator draws near," Tobias said.

Gwen's brows creased in confusion. The gnome scratched his bulbous nose and pushed his spectacles up high, which made his eyes appear to grow in size. He shuffled on his way and disappeared through the inn's door.

"Did he understand what you said? —because I didn't."

"It's a coded phrase," Tobias replied. "In the event a messenger is interrogated by our enemy, the message won't make any sense."

"That's clever," Gwen said. "I would never have thought of something like that. So, do we wait here for him to return?"

"No. The return message will be delivered by someone else. We can go upstairs and get some rest while we wait."

"How will the new messenger know where to find us?"

Tobias inched his sleeve up to reveal a small tattoo of a swan. "Everyone part of the rebellion takes the mark. It's how we identify our allies. The room we've been given is specifically for people like us."

"Wait. I saw you flash your wrist to the dwarf. The barkeep is part of the rebellion?"

"Valmutrude isn't technically part of the rebellion. She plays a part much like Boris, allowing us to funnel information and other things through the inn. In some ways, she takes more risk than we do."

Gwen watched Valmutrude bustle about the inn and viewed her with a newfound respect.

"Come on," Tobias rose from the table. "I'm sure you could use some sleep."

Gwen got up and followed Tobias up the stairs located in the back-left corner of the inn. They reached the door Valmutrude had specified, and Gwen unlocked it and pushed it open. The bed called her name, and she rushed inside and threw herself on it.

"If you need anything from me, you might want to tell me now. Once I close my eyes, I'm out."

Tobias chuckled. "I'm fine. Get some rest. I'll wake you when we get word from Eradore."

Gwen closed her eyes. The next thing she knew, Tobias was gently shaking her shoulder. Hadn't she just fallen asleep? She blinked a few times, fighting off the sleep that tried to reclaim her.

"What is it?" she asked.

"Eradore wants to see us."

"Is he here?" Gwen sat up and wiped the sleep from her eyes. Her muscles no longer ached, but she was still exhausted.

"No. He said he can't leave his tower, so we must go to him."

"Oh." Gwen stretched languidly and climbed out of the bed. "How do we get there? Is a carriage coming to get us or something?"

"Or something," Tobias replied. He held out his hand to reveal a clear stone.

"What's that?"

"It's a key."

"That's an odd key," Gwen said, the skepticism evident in her tone.

"It's a magical key," Tobias clarified. "I don't

suppose you've ever traveled through a magical gateway before?"

Something about his words jarred Gwen's mind, and she started to recall a distant memory, but then it was gone.

"Are you all right?" Tobias asked.

"What? Yes, yes, I'm fine. I think I'm still a little tired."

"If you say so," Tobias replied. "Anyway, have you?"

"No," Gwen said. "I've never seen magic before, unless you count the old man who came to Seven Stars that did card tricks."

"That's not real magic," Tobias chided. "You're going to love this."

A slender mirror hung on the wall, roughly four feet long and two feet wide. Tobias walked over to it and pressed the stone to the glass, then traced a symbol over its surface. There was a scratching noise as he slid the stone around, but the mirror remained untouched. When he finished, the glass surface rippled like liquid.

"After you," Tobias said, motioning to the portal.

"You can go," Gwen said, feeling nervous.

"Ladies first," Tobias insisted.

Gwen gave him an unamused stare, then stepped up to the mirror and hesitated. It looked like a normal mirror aside from the constant rippling. Gwen took a deep breath, then touched the glass. Her hand slowly disappeared, and she quickly pulled back.

"I don't know if I can do this."

"You'll be fine," Tobias said. "Trust me."

Gwen wanted to ask him what his obsession with trust was, but instead she kept her mouth shut. She thought about her father imprisoned, and that bolstered her courage enough to force her to step into the portal. Tobias's words echoed in her mind briefly, and then …

… the world erupted in fire and pain.

CHAPTER 8

CONAL

Pretending to scratch the horse's cheek, Conal peered over the muzzle to watch Rhonyn and the half-druid, noting their not so surreptitious glances in his direction. He particularly didn't like the cold look on Drustan's face, the experience of the intense pain bursting from the man's simple handshake still fresh. The rest of Rhonyn's group spread out and patiently waited, lounging against trees and chatting quietly amongst themselves.

Instinct told him he needed to scoot while he still had a chance. A quick glance at the others showed that those with crossbows had released the bow string and removed the bolt, slipping it into the leather holders with the rest of their bolts.

"You like my horse," a woman said, walking up. She was half a head shorter than Conal, with dirty blond hair and a pert nose. Though dressed as a supposed highwayman in dark leggings and tunic, she had the aura of one in costume. A quiver filled with arrows dangled at her left hip, an unstrung bow in her right hand.

"Yes. I've always loved horses." He smiled at her, but his focus slipped past her face to where

Rhonyn nodded at something the druid had said and shot a quick glance at Conal before calling an archer over. It was the way Rhonyn turned his shoulder so that Conal could not see the hand gestures.

Call it intuition or whatever, but warning alarms erupted inside him along with the overwhelming need to flee.

"Uh… if you'll excuse me, I need to find a place to… uh…" He smiled self-consciously.

The woman grinned in understanding and pointed to a thick copse about ten paces beyond where they stood. "That's the men's spot, just on the other side."

"Thanks." With a quick backwards glimpse at Rhonyn, he nonchalantly made his way to the copse. Once hidden from view on the other side, he fled deeper into the forest, running like a man possessed.

It wasn't until Rhonyn looked up to check on Conal that he saw him missing, calling out to the woman, "Where is he?"

She hooked a thumb to the copse. "He's in the privy."

Frowning, Rhonyn hesitated between not wanting to give away his intentions and the feeling that Conal was a lot cleverer than anyone gave him credit. "How long's he been there?"

"Not even a minute," she replied, an eyebrow cocked, wondering why he was so interested.

Rhonyn's patience quickly waned, and he caught a male bowman's attention and pointed to the copse. "You. Go check on our guest. Make sure he's OK."

The man knitted his brows at the command. "He's probably just takin' a piss. Leave the man in peace."

"Do it," Rhonyn growled.

Rolling his eyes, the man stood and sauntered over to the copse, stopping at the edge. "You OK back there?" When he heard no response or sound, he stepped around then whirled back around. "There's no one here."

Though he had a head start, Conal heard the shouts, which sent a pulse of wild and reckless fear within him. Dodging trees and hurdling fallen logs, he plunged headlong, praying he had enough of a head start that it would take them too long to find his trail, though it wasn't like he was taking care to hide his tracks. He pressed on, swearing he could hear them on his heels. Crashing through a strand of young trees, he grabbed a tree just in time to stop him from falling into a river thirty feet below. Rapidly scanning the terrain, he saw the river was far too wide to leap across, even on a horse. The river had cut a deep channel and the current was quick. Believing he heard them almost here, he inhaled a deep breath and leaped, praying there weren't any rocks below.

His feet felt no bottom and by the time he emerged, the swift current had propelled him well beyond the point of his entrance. The initial shock of the cold water was momentarily forgotten as he turned onto his back to surveil the place where he dove in. Yet no one broke through the trees and a few moments later, the river curved, and he was out of sight.

Inhaling a sigh of relief, he turned back around, positioning his feet to his front, letting the river carry him along. Despite the cold water, his adrenaline flowed as he assessed his present situation.

It wasn't as bad as it might appear. He had always lived by his wits and had been in worse scrapes before. He always managed to come out OK. This wasn't any different.

After a while, the current slowed as the river

widened and became shallower. All too soon, Conal was forced to stand and walk in mid-calf deep water. The late afternoon sun cast long shadows, but Conal was thankful for the warmth as his soaked clothes clung to his body, chilling him.

Conal trudged along in the river, knowing no one could track him. A half hour later, the river started to narrow and deepen. Soon Conal was again floating, shivering and more than ready to get warm and dry.

Then he saw it, where the river did another bend, a weathered clapboard shack thrust out over the edge of the bank, held up by two pillars made of layered stone. In strong measured strokes, Conal swam to the shack, grabbed hold of a pillar and listened. When sufficient time passed with no sounds, he clambered up the bank and silently stepped onto the deck.

Looking behind him, the path leading to the shack was overgrown indicating no one had been here in quite a while. Pressing the thumb latch on the door, he entered the one room hut. A single shuttered window sat in the middle of the far wall that jutted over the river. In the corner to the left of the door was a small fireplace, a small stack of wood next to it. In the center of the hut was a small table with two chairs. A low pantry chest sat in the right corner next to the door. Above the chest were two shelves, empty except for four pewter mugs. A straw mattress lay on the floor by the window. All were covered with a thin layer of dust.

Conal shivered again and rummaged through the chest and hut, searching for a flint or igniter, finding a flint, striker and tuft down by the wood pile. Having much experience in starting fires, he soon had a fire roaring, his clothes peeled off and draped over the chairs next to the fire.

The grumbling of his stomach reminded him that despite having lunch hours ago, it had been his only meal since yesterday's breakfast. Yet the thought of putting on still wet clothes to search for something to eat was enough to ignore the hunger pains. Once his pants were dry, he would slip out the hut and see if he could find some berries or something else to stave off the appetite.

Standing by the fire, his hands splayed above the warming flames, he glanced down at the brand on his left shoulder, surprised, though not really surprised, that the burnt skin had healed. When he told Rhonyn that he was a fast healer, he was merely relaying what had happened in the past. One time not long after he had joined his first band of outlaws, he had fallen from a roof during an escape and broken his leg. His supposed friends left him there. When the constables came upon him, he had concocted a story that the outlaws had kidnapped him and tossed him off the roof because he was purposely slowing them down. As a bonus, he willingly gave them descriptions of several of the outlaws, even remembering some names they called each other.

They carried him to a barber-surgeon who had set the leg and handed Conal a bill of such an outrageous amount that after his initial shock, he confidently told him that his father had the exchange shop in the market square and if he would be so kind as to take the bill to him. Naturally, the quack's eyes lit up and he bustled out. No sooner had the man left that Conal peeled and chipped off the plaster made of bee wax and sheep lard. By the time he had removed the plaster, the leg had mended.

When he showed up at the outlaw hideout, they were more than surprised, especially knowing he had broken his leg. Eyeing him with overt suspicion, it wasn't long before he decided to move on.

Exhaustion suddenly draped over him, and his eyelids became very heavy. Testing his clothes, he was pleased that they had dried, and he slipped them back. He then wedged a chair against the front door before stretching out on the straw mattress. A few moments later, he was fast asleep.

Dawn crept over the mountaintops when a kick at the door bolted him awake. A male voice from the outside grumbled, "Put your shoulder into it again. Maybe it's stuck"

"Of course it's stuck, you moron. There's somebody in there," another male voice said. "I smell smoke from a fire."

"Don't call me a moron."

"Well, you are. Maybe it's stuck," the voice imitated. "If it's not locked and it doesn't open what else is it?"

"That still doesn't make me a moron."

"It doesn't take much to make you a moron."

"Spoken like one with experience."

Conal furrowed his brow, concentrating on the voices. He was pretty sure they were male, but there was something about the pitch that was a bit off. Though his first inclination was to leap out the window into the river, the thought of being wet and cold first thing in the morning was unappealing.

He yanked the chair away just as the individual outside thrust a shoulder against the door, sending a dwarf crashing into the table.

"Good morning," Conal cheerily greeted them.

The second dwarf craned his head back to take in the stranger. "Who are you?"

"Name's Conal. This your place?"

"No –" the dwarf replied before being interrupted by the dwarf on the floor who had quickly recovered and stood behind Conal.

"Yes."

"Is it 'no' or 'yes'?" Conal grinned, knowing the truth.

"OK, OK, mebbe it's not ours," the dwarf admitted.

"Your names?"

"I'm Torgreth," the dwarf at the door said with a friendly grin. He was stout like most dwarves, with thick curly long brown hair and a beard that dropped to the middle of his chest. He wore the clothing of a hill dwarf: brown woolen trousers tucked into heavy knee-high leather boots, long-sleeve tan cotton shirt, and a light brown sleeveless tunic of deerskin. He hooked a thumb at the other dwarf. "This is my brother Voldar."

Voldar was about the same height, which was mid-chest on Conal. His hair was a darker brown and his brows thicker and dark, almost black.

"Didn't expect to see anyone here," Torgreth commented.

"I didn't expect to be here."

Voldar glanced around the room then scrunched his face at Conal. "You travel pretty light."

"Long story."

"We got time," Torgreth said, turning around to pick up two very large packs.

"Aren't you two a bit far from home?" Conal prayed they had food in those packs and were feeling generous enough to share some.

The two dwarves exchanged a quick guilty look before Torgreth said, "It's a long story."

"I got time," Conal grinned, causing Torgreth to

snort a laugh.

"Then open up the windows and stoke up the fire whilst we set the table."

"We don't got enough," Voldar groused.

"Don't mind him," Torgreth apologized. "Early mornings always make him grumpy." He cast a humorous eye at his brother. "In fact, late mornings make him grumpy as does early and late afternoons… and evenings too."

"What are you blabbering about," Voldar complained, opening the pack.

"I'm just telling our friend here that you're not the sociable type." He cupped a hand by his face and leaned in to loudly whisper, "Mister Chuckles there doesn't like anyone, so it's nothing personal."

"Will you shut up and help me," Voldar snapped, setting three pewter plates on the table.

Before long, the two dwarves had bread, cheese, and sausage on the table along with bottles of mead. Conal retrieved three mugs and rinsed them out in the river, surveilling the area in the process. Satisfied, he returned to the smell of scrambled eggs.

"You two travel well. I thank you for your hospitality. Hopefully one day I can return the favor."

"Hopefully," Torgreth grinned, ladling eggs onto the plates. "Enjoy."

Needing no urging, Conal scooted a chair out. "So why are you two so far from home?" He sighed in contentment, the food tasting particularly delicious.

"The gist of it is that we got tired of digging," Torgreth explained. "Yeah, we're dwarves and we're supposed to be miners –"

"We're some of the best," Voldar interrupted. "Got noticed by the king himself. But you know what that meant?"

"No?" Conal sipped the mead. Though warmer than he liked, it was still good.

"Meant we had to dig even more. And it's just not digging a dwarf does. It's the carving too. That's what put us off." He suddenly grew morose and plunged a fork into a slice of sausage.

"Dwarves are supposed to be the best carvers in the world," Conal said by way of compliment.

"They are," Voldar huffed. "It's when you ask them to carve totems and strange words and symbols that makes the hair on the back of your neck stand up."

"So we left, sort of snuck away one evening," Torgreth continued. "Been gone ever since."

"They sent someone after us," Voldar sneered. "Didn't even have the guts to send a dwarf. No. They sent a human, no offense."

"None taken. Why would they want you back so badly?"

Voldar paused to study the stranger, suddenly aware that he had already revealed too much.

Sensing his hesitation, Conal sought to reassure him. "While you consider your words, I will reveal why I am here. I had thrown in my lot with a band of highwaymen who decided they no longer needed me and set me up. I was captured and branded."

"Branded?" Torgreth's eyes widened. "You're a runaway slave?"

"No. I was given my freedom shortly after I was branded."

Voldar cocked an eyebrow. "That makes no sense."

Conal explained the attack in the woods and subsequent attachment to Rhonyn's band. "It was when we went back to his assembly point that things went south. There back at the camp was a half-druid."

The two dwarves jerked back like they had been stung. Voldar snapped forward, peering intently into Conal's eyes.

"Was he a tall man? Dark-brown beard and hair, and eyes the color of coal?"

"Yes."

"By the gods," he wailed, leaping up. "He's found us. Pack everything up. We gotta get out of here." He gulped down the rest of his ale while trying to decide whether to finish eating or toss the food out the window.

"I say we finish eating," Conal calmly spoke

"You can stay here if you like," Voldar replied, wolfing down the breakfast, "but we're going."

"Why? I lost them when I jumped in and floated down the river."

"You don't understand," Voldar said, stuffing everything back in their packs while Torgreth doused the fire. "The druid part is bad enough. That part is still a man and has to sleep. It's the other part that never sleeps, roaming at will."

"You mean like some spirit?"

"Exactly."

"What about when he's awake?"

Voldar paused. "I don't know."

"And I don't want to find out," Torgreth added. "You coming?"

"Might as well."

Voldar pushed the door open and froze, the shadow of the imposing man spreading over him.

"Well look who we found," the half-druid taunted.

CHAPTER 9

GWEN

Gwen's flesh burned with intense heat and a migraine pounded at her skull, threatening to send her into unconsciousness. Her sight was gone, nothing but darkness everywhere she looked. Amidst the swirling pain and confusion, she felt betrayed.

Tobias had tricked her.

She crawled in a circle, trying blindly to backtrack into the mirror, and bumped into something. A hand touched her shoulder and she flinched away.

"What's wrong with her?" Tobias asked. His concerned words echoed oddly as if he were far away.

"You didn't tell me she was a Prestige," another voice said.

"I didn't know she was," Tobias replied.

"She must be. Her body is trying to defend itself from the residual magic of the teleportation."

Gwen heard someone approach her. Despite the worry she heard in Tobias's voice, the sting of betrayal was still present. She assumed the other voice was Eradore, but he sounded insane. She was no wizard.

"Take a deep breath," the assumed Eradore said. "Focus on the sound of my voice."

Gwen tried to do as he asked, but the pounding migraine made it almost impossible. "I can't," she gasped.

"Hand me the bowl with the mint in it," Eradore said. "It's on that shelf." There was a pause.

"Which one is that?" Tobias asked.

Eradore made a scoffing sound in his throat. "It's the third bowl from the right."

A moment later, the strong smell of mint mixed with something less desirable stung Gwen's nostrils. She gagged, but the pain in her head quickly faded.

"Now can you focus?" Eradore asked her.

Gwen's vision was still dark, but she turned her head in the direction of his voice. "Yes," she replied.

"Good, now listen carefully. Within the darkness of your mind, there are runes. Point your mental gaze toward your inner self and focus on the first rune that you see."

"I don't understand what any of that means," Gwen said.

Eradore gave a frustrated sigh and muttered something about humans and magic. "Let's try something else. Stare straight ahead and envision a mirror before you. What do you see?"

"I see a shadowy figure wearing a crown."

"Interesting," Eradore whispered. "Focus on the figure."

Gwen did so, and suddenly her viewpoint changed. It was as if she rushed up to the mirror and exchanged places with the shadow. She looked out into the blackness and saw faint glowing symbols floating around. She fixated on the nearest one. It was flowing and had many curves, yet at the same time it resembled an animal, a bird. It reminded Gwen of a dove.

She wanted to say that she found one, but she was afraid she'd lose her focus on the rune. Instead, she nodded her head slowly, hoping that Eradore would understand the movement.

"Speak the name of the rune," Eradore told her.

As she was wondering how he expected her to do that, the word formed in her mouth and she said, "*Bunús.*"

An invisible force inside her aligned with her spine, straight and taut. The burning of her skin stopped, and her vision returned. She was on all fours and the face of an elf was staring back at her. His flesh was tan, his hair a honey-brown hue. Piercing blue eyes watched her intently.

"What happened to me?" Gwen asked, pushing herself into a sitting position.

"Tobias failed to mention your magical inclination, which caused issues with your body. Most wizards have defensive spells woven into their portals. It keeps enemy wizards from entering their domains."

"I'm not a wizard," Gwen said.

"Not yet," Eradore clarified. "But you will be. These things take time."

"No, I mean I don't have magical powers. And I don't want to be a wizard, anyway."

"Have you ever cast a spell?" Eradore asked.

"No."

"Then how do you know you don't want to be a wizard?"

Gwen was silent, unsure of how to answer. She looked at Tobias, who shrugged. "I'm not here to talk about magic," Gwen said, turning back to Eradore.

"I'm here to talk about rescuing my father."

Eradore stood and turned his attention to Tobias. "Let us discuss this opportunity you mentioned, then we will talk about magic. Does that please everyone?"

"That works for me," Tobias replied.

Eradore looked back at Gwen.

"Yes," she answered.

Tobias helped Gwen to her feet, and they followed Eradore through a door that led to a curved terrace. There was a sitting area protected from the sun by a long awning that stretched out from the side of what Gwen realized was a tower. She peered over the side of the railing and saw a city sprawled out below them.

"Where are we?" she asked, cutting off Tobias and Eradore's conversation. "Sorry," she added, frowning, and took a seat.

"It's all right," Eradore replied. "We're still in Penshaw. This tower is my home, but this portion of it does not exist in the seen world."

Gwen blinked, the explanation going over her head.

"What he means is that if you were standing in the street down there and looked at this place, you would only see part of the tower," Tobias explained. "The rest is hidden by magic."

"Can other wizards see it?" Gwen asked.

"It's possible, though highly improbable," Eradore answered. "Why do you ask?"

"The men that are chasing us … Tobias thinks they are using magic to track us."

"Ah, yes. The men you speak of have a sorcerer with them. He's using an item that belongs to one of you to keep track of your location."

"How do you know?" Gwen asked.

"There is little that escapes my notice," Eradore replied vaguely.

Gwen didn't like his answer and asked another question. "Any idea why they are following us all this way over a stolen horse?"

"That will take some digging," Eradore said. "I have some people looking into it as we speak."

"I thought we agreed to talk about magic after?" Tobais asked, looking at Gwen and raising his brows questioningly.

"Yes, I'm sorry. I have a lot on my mind." Gwen cast her gaze back down at the city.

"That's understandable, but we must sort one thing at a time," Eradore said. "Firstly, you said Boris was captured. Where did the king's men take him?"

"To the outpost outside Dawsbury," Tobias answered. "Him and several others were chained and taken prisoner."

"What are you asking for?"

"Enough men to raid the outpost and rescue the prisoners. We need members of the rebellion who don't mind spilling blood, because we're going to make a statement with this attack."

A grin tugged at the corner of Eradore's mouth, but he remained silent for a moment. Gwen turned her attention to the elf. He wore pale blue robes that were thin and loose-fitting. Gwen thought she could see the material shimmer every so often, but figured she was seeing things.

"It's risky," Eradore finally said.

"It is," Tobias confirmed. "Gwen wants to see her father freed before she'll throw in with us."

A knowing look passed between the two men and Gwen pretended not to notice, but her curiosity was piqued. There was something more going on and she was determined to find out what it was.

"I'll send word through the city," Eradore said. "We'll gather men and weapons. Do you want to take the lead on this?"

"No," Tobias replied. "I don't think I'm ready to lead men into battle yet."

"Most leaders are never ready to lead. Moments like this are thrust upon them, and they do what is needed. Regardless, I'll put Roland in charge. You'll be his second in command."

"I can handle that. There's one more thing. Gwen wants to help free Boris."

Eradore looked at Gwen. She returned his stare.

"It's not safe," the elf said. "I'd prefer that you stay here."

"I won't," Gwen replied, her tone defensive.

"I'm not going to force you to stay, I was merely stating my opinion. You are free to go if you want, but I think there are far more pressing matters to deal with."

"Such as what?"

"Your training," Eradore said.

"I told you, I don't have any interest in being a wizard."

"We don't choose the magic. It chooses us."

"It can choose someone else, because I don't want it," Gwen huffed.

Eradore laughed, a melodic sound. "I'm afraid it doesn't work that way. Now that you have given life to the *bunús,* you will become aware of magical things. It's important that you learn to control your power, lest you hurt those around you."

"What is a *bunús?*" Gwen asked. At the mention of the word, she felt something pulse against her spine. It wasn't painful, just … different. It was akin to a muscle spasm.

"You felt it, didn't you?" Eradore smiled. "You'll get used to it."

"What is it?" Gwen repeated.

"It is like a key to a door, the door being you. You are a vessel, and the *bunús* opens you to the magic outside of yourself. With time and practice, you will see life in a different way, a *better* way."

Gwen wasn't so sure about that, but she was becoming more curious as Eradore explained things. If this magic could help rescue her father, then maybe it was something she should explore. That, and if she was going to join Tobias and Eradore in their quest to overthrow the king, the more she had at her disposal, the better.

"What can you teach me?" Gwen asked.

Eradore looked at Tobias. "Go seek out Roland. He's probably at the brothel on Desire Street, the Canary. I'll get word spreading to the others."

"As you wish," Tobias said, his excitement obvious. He rose from his chair and looked at Gwen. "I'll be back soon. You're in good hands with Eradore. Listen to what he has to say. You might change your mind."

"I doubt it," Gwen said, but as Tobias left, she felt like she was on the verge of making a decision already.

"The first thing we need to determine is what kind of magic user you are."

"There are different kinds of wizards?" Gwen asked.

"Anyone who can use magic is called a Prestige. Wizards are at the top in terms of power. They are the rarest type of Prestige and can do things most people can't fathom."

"That's what you are?"

Eradore nodded. "Yes. Sorcerers are people who can summon magic, but they require spell components. The items needed depend upon the type of spell and sorcerers can only memorize a certain number of spells. The more powerful the sorcerer, the more spells they can retain."

Gwen was afraid his explanation was going to take a while, and she wanted to avoid being bored. "How many types of Prestiges are there?" she asked.

"Three," Eradore replied. "The last type are mages. They are able to summon certain abilities through the runes they gather. Some abilities you'll learn on your own, but most of them will require someone to teach you. Once you've gained a rune, it will be displayed on your flesh."

"What do you mean displayed on my flesh? Like a tattoo?"

"No, like a brand. The rune will burn itself into your skin."

"Where?" Gwen asked, getting worried.

"It depends on what the rune does. Some mages are able to turn their skin into stone, deflecting arrows. A mark like that would appear on the chest, most likely. Other runes will appear on your hands or feet."

"So, a mage could potentially have their entire bodies covered in these runes?"

"Potentially, yes," Eradore answered. "Though that is really up to the individual. You don't have to take every rune that you find."

Gwen found some relief with that knowledge. The image of her entire body being covered in brands, whether they offered power or not, wasn't something she was keen on. Perhaps that was a bit vain of her to think, but she didn't care.

"How do I know which Prestige I am?" she asked.

"By taking a pilgrimage to the Obsidian Altar."

"A pilgrimage? I can't take time to travel … wherever. How long does it take to get there?"

Eradore snapped his fingers. "We're already here."

CHAPTER 10

CONAL

Hearing the half-druid's voice, Conal whirled around and dove through window and into the river below, swimming as low to the bottom as possible, letting the current carry him along. Arrows pierced the water above him. Feet furiously fluttering and his lungs desperate for air, he felt the current sweeping him down river. When he could no longer hold his breath, he popped up, gasped a lungful of air and plunged back down, never bothering to check if they were still there. Yet no arrows drilled into the water.

With the current picking up speed, he prayed he was now far enough downstream to be free of pursuit. Throwing caution to the wind, he raised his head far enough above the water to inhale a deep breath while scanning the riverbanks. His luck held as he saw no one on either side.

Yet the current was beginning to move him along at a faster pace. Deciding he'd had enough of this river, he worked his way towards the left bank, coming upon a bend where the river's course had deposited a layer of sand ankle deep below the surface.

Trudging across the submerged sandbar, Conal scrambled up the gentle slope and stood in the middle of a small meadow getting his bearings. The morning's sun felt good, and he peeled off his shirt, twisting it in his hands and wringing out the wetness then laying it out on the grass. His hearing on edge, he listened to the sounds of the gurgling river and leaves rattling in the morning breeze.

Hesitating to take off his boots to let them dry, he decided worst case would be someone coming upon him and him diving back into the river, his clothes left behind. Yanking off boots and trousers and underclothes, he wrung out the clothing and laid them next to the shirt then lay back in the grass, letting the sun dry his body.

After two hours of nerve-wracking imagined sounds, he was ready to move on. The clothes were dry enough to wear, though the leather boots were still damp. Judging from the direction of the sun, the river was meandering south. Conal figured the river's course would eventually lead him to a town, so he worked his way along the edge.

By the midafternoon the forest gave way to farmland. Though still cautious, he decided a stranger traveling the edges of farms would draw more attention than someone walking the main road. Edging the low stone walls bordering a pasture, he scanned both directions before stepping onto the rutted road.

With little traffic on the road, he relaxed, pondering what the next town was and whether he had been there before as a member of Oscon's gang. The area looked vaguely familiar, though in truth so many of these farming communities looked the same.

The road crested and he saw the fortified city in

the near distance. A branch of the river he had spent so much time in these past two days ran between a tall circular barbican and the crenelated granite walls. Conal frowned for it did look familiar though it had been a while since he had been here.

Trying to remember the name of the city, a sudden premonition pulsed within him, and he looked back over his shoulder to see a large group of riders in the far distance cantering towards him, a tall man garbed in huntsman clothing leading the group. Fear gave strength to his legs, and he fled up the road. A voice behind him shouted something he couldn't distinguish, but he knew what it was.

They had recognized him.

His legs churning, lungs screaming, he raced for the gates.

The closer he came the more he had to weave around merchant wagons, farmers carrying produce on their backs, children gamboling in and out of traffic, and indifferent soldiers heading out to patrol the surrounding area. Casting a quick furtive glance behind him, he saw them gaining on him.

One soldier connected the approaching riders with the breathlessly fleeing runner and attempted to intercede and question him, only to be stiff armed and knocked down. By the time he jumped up and gave chase, Conal was at the gate. The gate guards, seeing the altercation, stepped in front of him, their halberds crossed.

"Lemme through," Conal pleaded.

"Not so fast," one guard threatened.

"Artek," a voice behind the guards called out. "You made it."

The guard turned to see a handsome, well-built man in merchant's clothing, smiling at Conal. "You know him?"

"Of course I do. He's my cousin." The man pushed his way between the guards, placing an arm across Conal's shoulders. "I hope the trip wasn't too exhausting."

"Good to see you too… cousin."

The indignant guard Conal had stiff armed came fuming up just as Conal turned and pointed at Drustan and Rhonyn now at the edges of the crowds on the road. "Highwaymen. They robbed me."

Startled at the accusation, the guards' attention narrowed on the approaching riders. With their attention diverted, the man propelled Conal past them and bustled him through the barbican and onto the bridge leading to the gate to the city

Conal heard the raised voices, especially one belonging to Rhonyn who cried out, "Stop him. The man's a thief."

"Don't look back. Keep walking," the man urged.

"You there," a guard's voice called out. "You two. Stop. I said 'stop.'"

They were halfway across when the man said, "When I say 'run,' you run. Stay close."

Conal ticked his head, wondering if he was being led into greater trouble.

The man nodded as though responding to something Conal had said, while sliding his eyes to see several guards hustling towards them.

"Run!"

They bolted across the remaining portion of the bridge, Conal doing his best to keep up for despite the merchant's clothing, the man was fast. Once through the gates, the man swerved left, dodging people and livestock with the skill of an acrobat, Conal hard pressed to keep pace. Three intersections later, he ducked right. By the time he slowed the pace to a walk, they had turned left, right, and double-backed so many times that Conal was quite lost.

"Thank you," he said, catching his breath. "I owe you… cousin."

The man grinned. "You looked like a man who needed a friend. What's your name?"

"I am called Conal," he replied with a heartfelt smile.

"I am Bryok. Tell me Conal, why were those men chasing you?"

Conal twisted his head to regard his deliverer. Bryok was half a handspan taller, clean shaved, with silky smooth dark auburn hair tied in a ponytail. He had the face and body that made women look twice and Conal noticed the frequent stares and smiles that he elicited. It was apparent to him at least that the man was not a merchant for he walked with the strut of a warrior, and his eyes were constantly watching, taking everything in.

"It's sort of a long story."

"I'm a patient man, besides… you have someplace else to go?" Bryok chuckled.

"Not really," Conal shrugged.

"When's the last time you ate?" Bryok led them down a side street that emptied onto another side street.

Conal cocked an eyebrow at him. "I'm running for my life, and you want to know when I last ate?"

"By the way you were running away from your pursuers and the fact that you have no travel bag in addition to not being from around here, I made the assumption you might like something to eat before you moved on." He stopped below a carved wooden sign of a cleric's head and an ale stein suspended from a metal rod high above a door.

Conal silently read the name drawn in calligraphy on the glazed window in the door, *The Bishop's Head*. Thoughts of a warm meal and a cold ale caused him to salivate. "I had breakfast early this morning with two dwarves."

"Sounds like an interesting start of the day," Bryok acknowledged, opening the door.

In contrast to the bright sunny day outside, the tavern was dark even with the candles on the tables and wall sconces. Conal blinked trying to adjust to the dim light.

Bryok moved with accustomed ease, weaving around tables, patrons, and serving girls to a table in the corner, sitting where he could see who came in the door. Conversations, momentarily paused when he and Conal had entered, resumed at the same levels, the clatter of eating and drinking mixed in.

A pretty serving girl a year or two younger than Conal approached the table, favorably eying the two handsome men. "What'll you have, gentlemen?"

"Meat, cheese, bread if it's fresh and ale that's cold," Bryok replied with a smile.

"Right away." She sashayed back to the kitchen.

"Pretty girl," Bryok commented.

"Yes, she is," Conal agreed, his eyes finally adjusting to the low light.

The tavern had twenty or more tables, half of them occupied mostly with male patrons. The women who sat at the tables were the usual wives, lovers or business partners. Conal noticed a table closer to the door where an attractive older woman dominated the conversation, the men nodding respectfully.

"You were telling me about breakfast with two dwarves," Bryok said. "Where was this?"

Conal waited as the serving girl deposited the two mugs of ale. Lifting the ale in salute, he swallowed a deep satisfying draught, licking his lips. "This is good," he sighed, finally relaxing. "It was… uh… upriver a ways. By the way, where am I? I mean what town is this?"

"Monkreth."

"Ah," he nodded. "Thought I recognized the place. It's been a while."

"You've been here before?"

"Yeah. About two, three years ago."

"What were you doing here?" Bryok frowned, puzzled.

"Uh… let's just say that I was here on, uh… business." He grinned.

"Is that why they were chasing you? Business?"

"Ah, no." Conal paused again as the serving girl placed platters of cold meat, cheese, and warm bread on the table. When she ambled off to another table, he asked, "Why did you stick your neck out for me? You don't even know me."

"Like I said, you looked like a man who needed a friend," he cryptically replied, slicing a piece of cheese. "You were telling me about the two dwarves."

"Back to the dwarves again, eh? Why do I get the feeling these two dwarves are important to you?"

A middle-aged man with thinning hair sauntered up to their table, hands on hips, staring at Conal. "You look familiar."

Conal paused mid-bite, returning the gaze, the memory of swindling the man out of 40 gold regals suddenly crystalizing. "You ever been to Hemlyn?" he parried.

"No."

Conal shrugged and impishly grinned. "I get that a lot, though usually from the ladies, especially the pretty ones and sometimes even the married ones." He winked knowingly. "I've been here before, visiting my cousin." He ticked his head at Bryok. "I've been known to enjoy the company of an attractive lady, but I stay away from the married ones. Too much trouble, if you know what I mean."

Conal's answer didn't seem to satisfy the man. "I've had dealings with you. I know I have."

"I doubt it," Conal affirmed. "Other than my cousin and the ladies, there's not much else here that interests me."

Recognition swept through the man, and he thrust a finger at Conal. "I remember you now. It was almost three years ago. I don't forget a face, especially of a man who swindled me."

"You've made a mistake," Bryok interrupted, his eyes flashing. "Why don't you go back to your table and let us dine in peace."

"Not on your life," the man fumed. "I'm reporting the both of you to the authorities." He stood full height, folding his arms in self-righteousness.

"That would be a grave error," Bryok replied, his voice cold and hard. "I will ask you one more time to leave us alone."

"Ha," the man sniffed in derision. "I know my rights and I know that man is a thief. And you're probably one too."

He started to turn when Bryok's hand shot out and grabbed the man by the wrist, causing him to waver and grunt in pain. "Why don't you sit down with us."

Conal scooted over an empty chair from the nearby table as Bryok guided the man to sitting.

The man's face turned ashen, and his lips

quivered when his eyes abruptly glazed over.

"You need to finish quickly," Bryok warned.

"I'm done," Conal answered, downing the last of his ale.

The serving girl came up, smiling at Conal and Bryok then looked at the man. "What's wrong with him?"

"He's fine," Bryok said, "just a little over come with the news that his sister died."

"O how horrible," the serving girl commiserated. "The poor man."

"Give him a few minutes. He'll be fine." He placed several coins on the table adding a generous tip.

The girl's eyes lit up. "Thank you." Looking directly at Conal, she lowered her voice and said, "I'm Brigit. Come back real soon."

Conal smiled, wishing he could but knowing it would be a long time before he set foot in Monkreth again.

"C'mon, cousin," Bryok urged. "We have places to go."

Once outside, Conal asked, "How'd you do that?"

"Magic," Bryok chuckled then held up his hand displaying a small, inverted ring on the tip of his middle finger. Flipping the hand over revealed a small sharp barb. "It's coated with a numbing drug. When I grabbed his arm, I made sure the tip punctured the vein in his wrist. It works very quickly." He started walking. "It'll last long enough to us to get out of here."

"Where're we going?" Conal's senses were again on edge, as though they were being watched.

"I've got a place close by where we can sequester ourselves for a day or two. Now tell me about the two dwarves.”

“What is it with the dwarves?” Conal demanded.

“Just answer the question,” Bryok snapped. “Sorry. There’s a lot happening, and you may be stuck in the middle of something you have no idea about.” He turned down an alley.

Conal shook his head. Nothing made a whole lot of sense these past few days. “Their names were Torgreth and –”

“Voldar,” Bryok answered with an exasperated breath, “which means Drustan probably already has them.”

Conal stutter-stepped at the name. “You know Drustan?”

“Yes. He’s my brother.”

Conal sucked in a breath. “He’s a half-druid.” As soon as he said it, a terrible foreboding filled him. He shifted a look at Bryok whose attention remained focused forward. “Does that mean…”

“Yes. I am also a half-druid.”

CHAPTER 11

GWEN

Gwen looked over the railing and the city of Penshaw was gone. In its place was a sight unlike anything she'd ever seen before. Where the city had been far below, this place was level with the terrace. White marble floors and walls created a massive empty space except for the black altar that stood in the center.

"Where are we?" Gwen asked, awed.

"This is the Chamber of the Altar," Eradore answered. "And that," he pointed a slender hand, "is the Obsidian Altar. This is a sacred place among Prestige. This is where every Prestige begins their path. They come here to learn of themselves. Once you know where your path leads, you can fully embrace the magic."

Movement caught Gwen's attention and she spotted a few people, mostly human, walking through the chamber. There was an elf among them, but he was quiet and aloof while the humans chatted amicably.

"Do you want to know who you truly are?" Eradore asked.

Gwen stared at the altar, struggling internally.

Just a short time ago, she was serving the patrons of her father's inn. Now, she was with a strange elf in an even stranger place contemplating becoming a Prestige. She still wasn't quite sure what that meant, but the mystery was alluring. The image of the shadowy figure wearing a crown flashed in her mind, and she turned her gaze from the altar to Eradore.

"I do, but I'm afraid," Gwen said.

"Afraid of what?"

"I'm afraid of what I might find out about myself. I'm not sure I'm ready for things to change so drastically."

Eradore leaned forward, and Gwen caught the aroma of woodland scents. Trees, flowers, and an earthy smell that reminded her of freshly plowed farming ground all swirled together, adding to the exoticness of the elf.

"Change comes whether we want it to or not," Eradore said softly. "We can embrace it, or we can fight it. I've lived long enough that I've learned the latter brings only pain and heartache. Come, let us see what Prestige you are."

Eradore walked around the table and offered Gwen his hand. She accepted it and stood, doubt still tugging at her mind. The railing vanished before her eyes, and Eradore stepped down onto the marble floor. Gwen followed and released his hand but remained close to his side. They walked slowly toward the altar, and Gwen's heart began pounding within her chest.

When they were a few paces away, Gwen stopped. Eradore turned to her, his face expressionless. Gwen wondered how the elf was able to mask his emotions so well, but the thought was quickly drowned in the deluge of her anxiety. Eradore waited patiently until Gwen worked up the nerve to continue. She inhaled deeply and closed the distance to the altar.

"How does this work?" Gwen asked. Sitting atop the altar, she spotted a polished dagger that looked like it was forged of silver and immediately regretted asking.

"The altar requires blood. Not much," Eradore added, seeing Gwen's face pale. "Just a small amount. You'll cut your palm and touch the altar. The rest is different for everyone, but you will know which Prestige you are."

Gwen looked at the dagger. It was clean, not a trace of any blood or finger smudges on the hilt. The altar, too, was devoid of anything that would imply its purpose. Gwen was nervous, but her curiosity prevailed. She gingerly grabbed the dagger and pressed the tip against her palm. Her hand was trembling, but Eradore laid his hand on hers, steadying it. His touch helped calm her. She drew a breath and held it.

In a quick movement, she pressed the blade hard against her skin and slashed down, slicing a gash down the middle. Her flesh spread apart, and blood welled within the wound. Gwen hissed in pain and touched the top of the altar. She saw Eradore touch the side of the altar before a vision engulfed her.

Someone screamed, and Gwen turned to look. She was rooted in place, her hand attached to the altar, but she saw the carnage. Bodies littered a long hallway, pools of blood growing beneath them all. A figure disappeared into a doorway and there was another scream, this one a man. Despite her desire to flee, Gwen couldn't avert her eyes. The scenery moved around her of its own accord, and suddenly she was standing in the doorway.

A man wearing a crown was crumpled on the floor, clutching at his wounded neck. Blood spurted between his fingers, staining his garments and his hand. Another man stood over him, a sword held tightly in his grasp. It was evident that the one standing was the culprit of the grisly crime.

"Long live the king," the man sneered. He stiffened suddenly and turned around. His face was masked by moving shadows, but Gwen was certain the man could clearly see her. "You!" he exclaimed with disbelief. A blue outline began to glow off the man, though he seemed oblivious to it. He stepped toward her, but the scenery pulled her away and began to fade. Before the vision was gone completely, Gwen spotted a woman among the bodies in the hall also wearing a crown.

Gwen blinked and exhaled slowly, not sure what to make of what she'd seen. Eradore was staring at her.

"You're the ..." He paused, then said, "... a mage."

"How do you know?"

"Look at me. What do you see?"

"An elf?" Gwen said quizzically.

"Look closer," Eradore replied. "Do you see anything out of the ordinary?"

Gwen squinted, but that didn't help. Then she noticed it. A faint glow around him, this one green.

"I see a green light," she said, but that explanation didn't seem right. "Well, not a light, but something glowing."

Eradore smiled. "You have the gift of Sight," he said. "All mages have it. The color you see is called the Aspect. Everyone gives it off, but no one is sure of its purpose."

"Who were those people in the vision?" Gwen asked.

Eradore shrugged. "Who knows?"

"Were they real? Did that slaughter really happen?"

"It's possible, but we can't know for certain. The altar the vision gives is different for everyone. Some people see loved ones and others see things that have no meaning at all. The important thing is that we now know what you are. A mage."

Eradore was looking past Gwen at something behind her. She looked over her shoulder and spotted a black-haired man that gave her chills. He was flanked by three soldiers on either side, and they were heavily armed.

"What is the meaning of this?" Eradore demanded as they approached.

Gwen looked the man up and down. His clothing looked expensive. A navy shirt was tucked into black pants, and his boots shone with fresh polish. The man wore a flowing purple cape as well, and the gold clasps on his shoulders were fashioned into the shape of wolf heads. It was obvious to Gwen that the man viewed himself as important. His demeanor was borderline pompous.

"By order of His Majesty, the Chamber is now closed and off limits. Please disperse immediately or suffer the consequences."

Eradore stepped past Gwen and intercepted the man. "King Torian holds no sway over this domain," the elf said.

"He does now." The man retrieved a scroll case from one of the soldiers and withdrew a rolled parchment. He unfurled it and held it out for Eradore to see. Gwen's mother had taught her to read at an early age, and she scanned the flowing script. It detailed how the king had revoked the treaty with the Order, and the Chamber of the Altar was now property of the crown. At the bottom was the signature of the king and a stamp with his emblem.

"Torian goes too far," Eradore said.

"That's *King* Torian," the man retorted. "Now take your servant girl and leave this place before I have you arrested."

Gwen could tell by the anger on Eradore's face that he wanted to say something more, but instead he spun around and grabbed her hand, tugging her along back to the terrace of the tower. They crossed the threshold, and Gwen glanced back at the man. He stared after her, his gaze haunting her even after Eradore snapped his fingers and the Chamber disappeared.

"Who was that?"

"That was Viktor," Eradore replied. "He's one of Grimmar the Mage-Breaker's lackeys."

"Mage-Breaker? That sounds ominous," Gwen said.

"Given what just transpired, it will be soon. He hates magic and those who practice it. I'm certain he's behind this move. The king has never taken issue with us before." Eradore stared off at nothing for a moment, and his face became devoid of any emotion. "No matter. The Order is likely dealing with the situation already."

"What's the Order?"

"It is the governing body of the Prestiges. There's a hierarchy of leadership, but it's mainly for show. Most Prestiges live solitary lives, but there are a few who serve their communities or hold positions of power within the court. I suspect that's about to change. I'm sorry to overwhelm you with these things, but it took me by surprise. Please, let's get back to the task at hand."

"All right. You said I'm a mage?" Gwen asked.

"Yes. Now that you have the Sight, you can see people's Aspects."

"How many colors are there? The man in the vision had blue and yours is green. That's two, at least."

"Each race has the same color. Human Aspects are blue, elves are green, and dwarves are brown. There are others, but those are the main ones you'll see."

"Can I stop seeing the Aspects? It's a little odd seeing colors coming off people."

"Unfortunately, no. You'll get used to it with time. Most mages don't even notice the Aspects after a while. It becomes normal."

Gwen was disappointed to hear that, but it was too late to change her mind now. She peered over the railing and saw the city again. Dusk was beginning to creep over the landscape and Gwen looked at Eradore, puzzled.

"It was mid-afternoon when Tobias and I got here. It looks like it's getting dark now. Is that some sort of illusion?"

"No. Traversing vast distances by magic makes travel quicker, but the time still passes normally. Perhaps we should take a break to eat, then we can continue."

"How much is there to cover?" Gwen asked.

"I can only provide the basics, since you are a mage. Magic works too differently for me to train you, and I can't see runes. There is a mage here in

Penshaw that is part of the rebellion. She can show you your first rune, but if you want more of them, you'll have to seek out other mages."

"First things first," Gwen said. "We need to rescue my father and the others from the outpost. When he's safe, I'll decide what I want to do."

Over the next hour, the two ate a meal and Eradore showed Gwen some of his spell books. She couldn't read the magical texts, but he explained in more detail how magic worked for him. Once darkness fell and Tobias had yet to return, Eradore showed Gwen to a room where she could spend the night.

"We have a room at the inn," Gwen told the elf, but he shook his head.

"It's safer for you to stay in the tower. The soldiers can't track you here, and there's no telling what else Grimmar is plotting now that he's got the king's ear in his hand."

Gwen's stomach was full, and she was getting sleepy, so she didn't argue. Eradore retired to his own room and Gwen climbed into bed, stretching out on the comfortable feather mattress. She yawned and closed her eyes, only intending to rest them for a moment.

The next thing she knew, Eradore was looking down at her. Morning light filtered in through the room's sole window and the elf smiled.

"I've sent word to Aimil. She's coming here to meet you."

"Who's Aimil?" Gwen asked, rubbing the sleep from her eyes.

"She's the mage I told you about. I've also heard from Tobias."

"Is everything all right?" Gwen sat up, worry for

Tobias's safety forcing her wide awake.

"He's fine," Eradore replied. "But I have some bad news. Our spies at the outpost say that the prisoners have been tortured. Boris isn't doing well."

CHAPTER 12

CONAL

Conal's heart skipped a beat and his eyes roamed the surrounding doors and alleyways for a route to escape.

"You do not need to fear me," Bryok reassured him. "I am not like my brother."

"How do I know that?" Conal retorted.

"You don't. You'll have to trust me." He turned right into an alleyway and stopped when Conal didn't follow. "You can take your chances on your own or you can let me help you. I will not force you." He continued down the alleyway.

His mind racing, Conal knew he wouldn't last on his own with Drustan looking for him. And once the man in the tavern spilled the news that he was in the city, it would be even harder. Noting that Bryok hadn't bothered to wait for him, Conal decided he was his best option at the moment. Jogging to catch up, Conal matched strides with him.

"How do you know I'm not leading you back to Drustan?"

"I don't, but at least you fed me."

Bryok chuckled. "Let's hope your friend in the tavern decides it's not worth the effort to search for you." Stopping before a nondescript door, he quickly glanced up and down the alley before opening the door. Once inside, he turned and bolted the door and placed a crossbeam across it. "Makes it hard to get in."

"And almost as hard to get out," Conal pointed out.

"I have other ways of getting out."

"Figured."

Bryok led him through the dark interior hallway to a set of stairs then up two dimly lit flights to a door midway down the hall. Silently opening the door, he locked it behind them and slid a crossbeam into the holders.

The room was inky dark until Bryok held up a glow crystal that revealed an empty room with four hallways leading away.

"Follow me."

Bryok headed to the second hallway on the left. "This place is all interconnected, so it's easy to get lost, sometimes even when you know where you are."

Conal frowned, puzzling out how one could be lost if he knew where he was?

At the end of the hallway, a spiral staircase descended. Without hesitation, Bryok curved around with the steps, the light lowering with each step, Conal close on his heels. After a far longer time than it took going up two flights, the stairs emptied into another large dark empty room with more hallways.

"This is crazy," Conal complained. "Where are we?"

"Patience, my young friend. We're almost there." Bryok took the second hallway to the right this time.

By the time they reached the solid oak door at the end, Conal swore they had to be somewhere far beyond the city walls. Past the door was another set of spiral stairs that led up.

"How much farther?" Conal huffed.

"Top of the stairs."

Several minutes later, they emerged onto a platform surrounded by solid granite. Conal watched as Bryok pressed a stone and a section of the wall swung open, light from a fireplace spilling through the opening.

"Where are we?" Conal gazed around the spacious room, the walls carved from stone.

"We are inside the mountain behind the city."

Bryok retrieved a taper near the fireplace and walked around the room lighting sconces and candelabras, revealing a room far larger than Conal's first impression. Except for a wide ornate desk near the fireplace, a reading chair close by, and several bookshelves against the walls, the room was devoid of any decoration or personal touch. A single door adorned the wall to the right of the fireplace.

"You live here?"

"Yes."

Conal walked around the room, nearly stumbling over a small chest by the desk. Skirting the chest, he pointed to the door. "I assume that leads to the kitchen, bedroom and other rooms?"

"I don't cook," Bryok grinned. "But yes, there is a sort of kitchen... and other rooms. But let's get down to business, shall we?" He scooted out the chair behind the desk and sat. "Tell me why my brother was chasing you."

"I thought you wanted to know about the dwarves." Conal sat in the reading chair.

"Now that I know their names, I know all I need to know."

"Like what?"

Bryok studied him a moment then relented. "I suppose it's only right that you know, now that you're involved. Torgreth and Voldar are brothers, as you probably already surmised. They are from the dwarf kingdom of Gurim-duhr. They are master stonecutters and carvers, probably the best at their craft."

"Those two?" Conal scoffed. "How can that be? They're too young."

"How old do you think they are?" Bryok said.

"Probably my age."

"Try doubling that, maybe even tripling it."

"What?" Conal's jaw dropped. "That's impossible. I've seen dwarves before, and they don't look like they're in their fifties."

Bryok shook his head. "I don't know your experience with dwarves, but dwarves live longer than humans. And then there is the little consideration of what they were carving."

Conal knitted his brows, and he recalled what Voldar had said. *It's when you ask them to carve totems and strange words and symbols that makes the hair on the back of your neck stand up.* "What were they carving?"

In a calm quiet voice, Bryok said, "Rorkyn Orefell, the King of Gurim-duhr has fallen under the spell of the silken tongue of Havyrd."

"Who's he?"

"Havyrd is a devoted acolyte of Grimmar the Mage-Breaker."

"Grimmar the Mage-Breaker? Who's he?" Conal scrunched his face hoping he wasn't expected to remember any of this.

"He's the advisor to King Torian. Grimmar is

named the Mage-Breaker because he has been relentless in tracking down and killing anyone even suspected of being a mage or having any magic skills. The truth is that he only kills those he can't control. Those willing or forced to submit themselves to him are rune branded."

"Rune branded?" Conal was suddenly aware the Cobra brand on his upper arm.

"I'll explain about runes in a bit. Grimmar needed someone who could carve runes and totems without understanding what they meant. That's where the two dwarves, Voldar and Torgreth, come in. At first, Rorkyn was fine with them carving runes, never suspecting the runes were incantations. But then he got curious as to what the runes said and asked Grimmar about them. Immediately recognizing he had a problem, Grimmar sent Havyrd to work his influence over the king. Havyrd's gift, his power, is his voice. Few can withstand the lull and enticement of his words. Once he focuses his attention on you, you are powerless and will do what he commands. That is what happened to King Rorkyn. Though king, the man is consumed with the mundane, the trivial and the unnecessary. Havyrd actually rules, using the king as a puppet."

Conal pondered the story. "So, what does that have to do with me?"

"That's what I want to know. Let's get back to why was my brother chasing you?"

Conal shook his head. "To be honest, I haven't the faintest idea. All I remember is him clasping my hand and the pain nearly killing me. Then when I tell him I was branded –"

"You're branded?" Bryok stiffened.

"Yeah. I got a cobra burnt into my left arm. Here,

I'll show you." Conal peeled off his shirt and twisted his body to display the brand.

Bryok suddenly grew somber. "How long ago was this?"

Conal blinked in thought, surprised at how much had happened in between now and the branding. "Yesterday."

"Yesterday?" Bryok exclaimed. "That's impossible. The brand is healed." He frowned as he narrowed his gaze at the cobra head. "How did they brand you? This looks like a tattoo on top of a brand."

Puzzled, Conal bent his head to stare at his shoulder. To his surprise, the cobra head had color interwoven in the design. "That's weird. It wasn't like that last night."

"You say this happened yesterday?" Bryok asked, his disbelief obvious.

"Yeah. If you don't believe me, you can ask Lord Phayrl. He's the one who had me branded."

"Perhaps we should start from the beginning," Bryok said. "Tell me what happened."

Conal related the incidents from the time of the betrayal and his capture to the present. "Now you know as much as I do."

Bryok stood and began pacing, his hands clasped behind him. "So they admitted they were looking for the king's son and they suspected you might be him."

"Yeah," Conal sniffed. "I don't know what they were drinking, but the whole idea is absurd from the start. I know my parents. They live in Urve. I know what I've been doing these past twenty plus years, especially these last years with Oscon, the scum."

Bryok stopped pacing. "May I try something?"

Conal cocked an eyebrow. "Is it going to hurt?"

"Uh… maybe a little."

"What're you gonna do?"

"Clasp your hand like Drustan did."

"Not on your life," Conal loudly objected, shaking his head. "The last time was like the mother of all pain. It hurt worse than hell."

"But it's the only way I can determine the truth."

"What truth?" Conal folded his arms across his chest, his fists hidden.

"The eagle will bear the vipers in its claws, yet from the west a cobra will rise and strike down the eagle."

Conal glared at him. "What the heck does that mean?"

Bryok stood by the chair, gazing down at him. "It is the prophecy of our future. The eagle is the king of Isentol. The vipers are the children of the rightful king returned to reclaim the throne. That the eagle has the vipers in its claws means the children will be captured and powerless against the king until the cobra, whoever he or she is, defeats the king."

Conal blinked at him wondering what he had gotten himself into this time. "I still don't understand what this has to do with me."

"You have a cobra on your shoulder."

"So do lots of other folks."

"You are from the west."

"So are thousands of others."

"You're healing is beyond magical."

"Ah… OK, ya got me there," Conal sighed. "It still doesn't mean I'm some sort of conquering hero. Besides, I'm a lover, not a fighter."

"Self-image a little inflated?" Bryok smirked.

"Very funny." Conal cocked his head to the side. "By the way, what happens when you find this guy?"

"I protect him."

"So Drustan is chasing me because he wants to protect me?" Conal cocked an eyebrow in obvious doubt.

Bryok sat and leaned back. "I find that puzzling too. The only way I can find out is to see what he saw."

"How do you do that?"

"Hand clasp. It lets me connect to your memory."

"Uh-uh. We've been over this ground already. Besides, what will my memory tell you?"

"I don't know until I see. I can plumb the depths to see your earliest memories, some of which you don't know you have. But I can only do that via touch."

"Yeah, well, think of another way. Shouldn't there be someone who can vouch for what happened? Surely the kid wasn't sent away with no one knowing he was the king's son. Otherwise, he could grow up being a vagabond or a highwayman or a merchant or something quite un-royalty-like. And no one, not even him, would know it."

Bryok pointed to the papers scattered across his desk then to the books on the bookshelves. "There are signs and hints, but one has to study and discern. I am not the only one looking for the son. King Torian has his own wizards and scholars searching the writings and scouring the land tracking you down."

Conal's brow furrowed. "So in other words, if someone thinks I'm the one, my life is over."

"Yes and no," Bryok replied. "Yes, if you decide to go off on your own without protection. King Torian will want you dead, and not just you. He will destroy everyone who he suspects might even remotely be you or associated with you."

"So I'm pretty much screwed anyway I look at it."

His jaw clenched.

"Sadly, yes, for the moment. Will you let me determine the truth?"

Conal chewed his lip. "How long will it last?"

"It shouldn't take too long."

"That's not an answer. 'Not too long' is relative."

"The sooner we try it, the quicker we can decide what to do."

Heaving a frustrated and resigned sigh, Conal stuck out his hand, bracing for the pain as Bryok grasped it. At first nothing happened, and his guard dropped. Then the pain exploded, and he gritted his teeth, his body squirming in the chair, tears flowing down his cheeks. Just as he raised his other hand to pry the grips loose, Bryok let go.

Gasping for breath, he lifted his head to see a smile curl the corners of Bryok's mouth. "Well?"

"I have found you, my Lord."

"That's not funny," Conal snapped.

"It's not meant to be funny. It's true. You are the king's son." Bryok heaved a sigh of satisfaction. "I've been searching for years and years to find you. I can't believe you fell right into my lap. Of all the places I've been to, you end up here."

Finally recovered, Conal dismissively shook his head. "You sure you got this right? Shouldn't I feel sort of revelation, like 'O my God, I'm the long-lost Prince.'"

"It doesn't work that way. In time, you will come to accept it."

Bryok turned away, exhaling a slow sigh, silently chastising himself for the lie. The truth was he could only see so far back. There was a wall well before the birth-mind. The memories he did see were of a harbor town and his father and mother. Yet by all rights, with the power of the memory-probe, he should be dead. That in itself was enough to give him pause. But was it proof? That he had the strength to endure death-dealing pain along with his magical healing ability surely pointed to him as the one.

But he bore the mark of the cobra.

So which one was he – the king's son or the man who defeats Torian and claims the kingdom as his own? Maybe he was neither. Regardless, until Bryok was sure, he knew he had to keep Conal safe… until he didn't need him anymore.

CHAPTER 13

GWEN

We have to launch the attack now," Gwen demanded.

Eradore raised his hands placatingly. "We're working on it. Roland and Tobias have gathered enough men to overtake it, but I want you to have a rune before you go. If you are a quick learner, you'll be on your way to the outpost before midday."

"My father could be dead by then."

"You could die if you go to the outpost without some form of protection," Eradore replied calmly.

"I can carry a sword," Gwen said, but she knew he was right.

"Can you wield one? Have you learned to fight against trained soldiers?"

Gwen recognized she was on the losing end of the debate and sighed. "No. I've never even held one before. Well, one time I did, but it was to move it off a table at my father's inn."

"I rest my case," Eradore said. "I know it is difficult but try to be patient. We will rescue Boris, but everything must be in place."

"It's risky, I get it," Gwen huffed.

"That's not all. The rebellion isn't strong enough

to face the king's forces head-on. We must be strategic, calculating. Any loss we suffer will push us further back than we already are."

"Fine. I'll wait for Aimil, and when I've gained the rune, we go."

"Agreed." Eradore made an odd gesture with his hand, and a pile of folded clothes appeared on the bed beside Gwen. "I've taken the liberty of getting you some new garments."

"What's wrong with these ones?" Gwen asked, brow furrowed. Eradore opened his mouth to speak, then closed it. He lifted a finger into the air and opened his mouth again, then frowned.

"I'm kidding," Gwen said. "These ones are dirty, and I feel disgusting."

The hint of a smile pulled at Eradore's lips. "Funny. You can use the bathing chamber to clean up. It's on the floor below this one. When you're done, we'll have breakfast, and then Aimil should be here."

Gwen was relieved to hear that she could get clean and headed straight for the bathing chamber after Eradore left. She took her new clothes with her and set them on a side table. There was a wooden basin filled with water, and Gwen dipped a finger into it. To her surprise, the water wasn't cold. She stripped her dirty clothes off and climbed into the tub.

As much as Gwen wanted to relax in the water and forget her problems, there was too much going on. She felt guilty for not already going to free her father, but she couldn't take on an outpost on her own. Not yet anyway. If what Eradore said about magic was true, then she could gain the power she needed to stop any injustice.

Gwen got out of the basin and dried off with a

long cloth, then put on the clothes Eradore had given her. The black pants were soft and felt like silk, but the material was thick and clung tightly to her skin. The shirt was also black, but it was loose fitting. There was something about the shirt that made her skin tingle, and she made a note to ask Eradore about it.

When she returned upstairs, Eradore was sitting on the terrace with a dark-haired woman that Gwen assumed was Aimil.

"Ah, here she is," Eradore said as Gwen joined them. "Aimil, this is Gwen."

Gwen's eyes widened when she looked upon Aimil. Runes were branded from her wrists up the length of her arms, disappearing under the short sleeves of her leather armor. There were runes on her face as well, one under each of her eyes. Every rune was completely unique from the others. Gwen took a seat at the table and tried not to stare.

"It's nice to meet you," Aimil said. "Eradore says you have some hesitancy about being a mage."

"A little," Gwen admitted.

"I've been where you are, so I can relate. It was long ago, but I remember the emotions like it was only yesterday."

Gwen assumed Aimil was around her own age, just past twenty-two years. Her hair was brown and her skin as dark as night. The branded runes looked like scars, but Gwen didn't find them as abrasive looking as she imagined. The more she studied Aimil's arms, the more she started to like the runes.

"We're getting ready to strike the outpost outside Dawsbury," Eradore said.

"Truly?" Aimil asked, surprised.

"Yes. I confess it's a little premature, but Boris

and a few other members of the rebellion are imprisoned. They're too valuable to lose, and Gwen is Boris's adopted daughter."

"Tobias said the same thing," Gwen interjected. "I'm having trouble believing that."

"You can ask Boris about it when we rescue him, but I can assure you we have no reason to lie to you," Eradore said.

"I don't think you're lying. I just think you're mistaken," Gwen replied.

"There is a way to find out for certain," Aimil said.

That caught Gwen's attention. "How?"

"There's a place in the kingdom of Steepcross that can reveal a mage's true name. It's southeast of here, but if you want to know bad enough, the journey is worth it."

"I'll keep that in mind. Tell me about the rune you can show me."

"You're an eager one, aren't you?" Aimil asked, cracking a smile.

"I want to rescue my father, but Eradore won't let me leave until I've learned a rune."

"Eradore is wise, and I agree with him on this. There are many runes that you can learn, but the first one is the hardest and most painful."

"Painful?" Gwen asked.

"Yes. Once you learn the rune, it is burned into your flesh. The first rune has crippled many mages, but it's temporary. Even if it doesn't incapacitate you, it *will* hurt."

Gwen could feel her anxiety rising again, but she kept the thought of her father in the forefront of her mind and it kept her from giving in. "Is every mage's first rune the same?"

"No," Aimil answered. "Every mage can choose their first rune, to an extent."

"What do you mean?" Gwen asked.

"Well, most runes you learn will come from another mage teaching it to you. As you can see," Aimil lifted her arms for emphasis, "I have learned many. You can choose from my runes which one you want to learn."

"What if I want to learn more than one?"

"You can't. A mage can only give one rune to another mage."

"Why?" Gwen asked.

"No one is really sure," Aimil replied. "It's been a mystery for as long as there has been magic."

"So to get more runes, I have to find other mages to teach me?"

"Yes, but I would offer a word of caution. Not all mages are willing to share their secrets, so you will encounter mages who will refuse your request. They are few, though. Mages tend to favor academia, so most are open to teaching others."

"What kind of runes do you have?" Gwen leaned closer, looking over the numerous brands. There was one that caught her attention. It was shaped like a flower surrounded by a circle. "What is that one?"

"I want to try something," Aimil said. "Instead of telling you what my runes do, I want you to look at each one and tell me which you are most drawn to. Before we do that, though, I want to eat something. I'm famished!"

Gwen had completely forgotten about food in the midst of her curiosity. She had to force herself to be patient as they ate a small meal composed of eggs and roasted potatoes. Eradore and Aimil chatted about various things that Gwen found dull compared to magic. She cut a piece of bread from a fresh loaf and chewed on it as she agonized over how slow time was passing.

She had zoned out as she pondered who her real parents might be, assuming what Tobias and Eradore had said was true. Perhaps she came from a family of Prestiges? That would explain her magical inclination. Yet, why would they have abandoned her? Maybe she was born to a family that had an aversion to magic and feared having a Prestige as a daughter? Gwen was so deep in thought she hadn't noticed Aimil was looking at her.

"I'm sorry?"

"I asked if you were ready to pick a rune," Aimil replied.

"Yes, I'm ready."

Aimil laid her arms out onto the table. "Look at each one. Take in the details and point to the ones that stand out to you."

At first, Gwen thought the task would be easy. Yet as she studied the runes, it became apparent that it would take some time to see them all. Once she'd viewed all of the runes on Aimil's arms, the women stood and removed her upper armor, exposing her nakedness. Gwen's cheeks flushed with embarrassment, but Eradore's expression remained impassive.

"Keep going," Aimil said.

Gwen hesitantly continued perusing the runes. Aimil had more than Gwen could keep count of, and she wondered how long it had taken the woman to learn them all. The scarred brands continued from her arms and across her chest. Gwen made a pained look when she saw they were even on Aimil's breasts. Her stomach was smooth unmarred flesh, but the runes wound around to her back. There was one that looked like a wing that caught her attention. Gwen touched it softly.

"The Wing," Aimil said.

"How did you know which one I touched?" Gwen asked.

"I know my body," she said. It was all she offered as an explanation.

Gwen continued and touched one that looked like two cresting waves of water. She touched another that resembled what she thought was a fish, and the last one looked like a serpent, though its body was a zigzag. Aimil removed her pants, leaving her intimate area covered only by a loincloth. Again, Gwen blushed, but she knelt and examined the runes on Aimil's legs. There were none that drew her eye, and she stood.

"Is that all of them? Gwen asked.

"There is one more, but you don't need to see it. Its only purpose is for pleasure."

Gwen thought for sure that her cheeks couldn't get any hotter, but they burned more fiercely at Aimil's words.

"You've chosen four," Eradore said. "Yet you can only have one."

"Which one pulls at you the most?" Aimil asked.

Gwen looked at the ones she had picked again, and she was most drawn to the undulated snake. "This one," she said, touching it. "The snake."

"Interesting," Aimil said.

"What?" Gwen asked.

"Nothing. It's a good choice. That's a powerful rune, though. You're definitely going to feel this one."

That caused Gwen some concern, but she had

quickly come to realize from their conversation that power would come at a cost. "So how does this work? What do I need to do?"

"We need to go somewhere … higher," Aimil said, looking at Eradore.

The elf smiled knowingly and rose from his chair. "Follow me."

He led them to a stairway that only went upward, and they eventually reached the ceiling. A rectangular metal door rested in the center, surrounded by stones. Eradore pushed the door up, and they stepped out onto the roof of the tower. Gwen looked around, confused. Other than the tower, she could see nothing but thick gray fog.

"What is that?" she asked.

"It is the Ether," Eradore answered. "Remember, the top of this tower exists outside of the natural world."

"It's basically a pocket of space carved out magically, much like a cave," Aimil said. "Wizard stuff."

Gwen nodded, but it didn't make any sense to her. She walked to the edge of the roof and looked down. The city of Penshaw was nothing more than a speck far below. Gwen backed away, afraid she might slip and fall to her death.

"You're going to need some protection," Aimil told Eradore. He closed his eyes and muttered something. A sphere of shifting green energy surrounded him.

"I want you to close your eyes," Aimil said. "Clear your mind of everything. It might be difficult, but you must have no distractions."

Gwen did as Aimil asked and closed her eyes, but she was having trouble purging her thoughts. It took a long while, but neither Eradore nor Aimil rushed her. When her mind was clear, she saw the zig-zag snake rune floating in the darkness, similar to her experience with the *bunús* rune.

Speak it, a voice whispered in her mind. She recognized it as Aimil's. It sounded like an echo, and it repeated several times before fading. Gwen focused intently on the rune, but it was fuzzy, and the name evaded her. She envisioned her hand and reached for it. Intense heat assaulted her, and she jerked away.

You can do it, Aimil's voice echoed.

Gwen clenched her jaw and reached again. She ignored the heat and this time managed to grasp the rune. She pulled it closer until the fuzziness became clear and the name of the rune hit her like a blow.

"Tintreach," Gwen uttered aloud.

Searing light suddenly filled the darkness. Gwen opened her eyes, but the light was still there, blinding her, burning her. She screamed, but if any sound came out, she didn't hear it. Her heartbeat slowed, but each beat was excruciatingly loud. She'd gone blind, and deafness followed. Gwen had a feeling of weightlessness, like gravity no longer existed for her. The light faded, and as her vision cleared, she realized why she felt so light.

She'd fallen off the tower.

CHAPTER 14

CONAL

OK, suppose I accept that I'm the long-lost son of some dead king –"

"He was your father," Bryok gently scolded. "You should show some respect."

"Why?" Conal challenged. "I never knew him. I feel nothing for him."

"You don't know him because he sent you away to protect you."

"From whom?"

"Torian."

"Torian? The guy who wants me dead? How old is this guy?"

"Not as old as you'd think," Bryok cryptically answered. "Perhaps I'd better explain. Would you like something to drink?"

"Is this a long story?"

"I'll make it brief," Bryok replied, taking an iron poker by the fireplace and jabbing at the embers. "Your father, King Kamron, ruled the kingdom of Isentol. He had two children."

"That's right," Conal interrupted. "I supposedly have a sister. Where's she?"

"I don't know. She was not my concern."

"So there are others like you looking for her?"

Bryok turned to appraise the young man, brash yet quite intelligent. "Not only those like me, remember. Torian too has his henchmen looking for her."

Conal tilted his head in thought. "If he sent me as far west as possible, logically he would have sent my sister in the opposite direction, as far east as possible."

"A logical assumption," Bryok acknowledged with a nod, "though he might have thought his enemies would think the same thing."

"Good point. Forget it. You were saying?"

"Kamron sent his children to safety to be raised by noble-hearted parents, people whose trust and faithfulness were beyond question."

Conal bolted to standing. "My God, anyone who thinks I'm Kamron's son knows where my parents are. We need to go back. We gotta save them."

Bryok turned solemn. "It is too late to go back."

Conal's eyes hardened and his jaw clenched. "They're…"

"Dead."

Conal blinked tears away. "When?"

"Almost a year ago."

Conal sucked in a breath. "A year ago?" Guilt washed through him. Here he was complaining about Kamron when he was less than a dutiful son. He had justified his absence as necessary in order to accumulate wealth. He was going to surprise them, return the wealthy son and set up shop with his father. His parents would be proud. But wealth was elusive, and he had drifted farther away.

"There was nothing you could have done," Bryok soothed. "They knew the risk involved."

Conal's heart thumped, afraid of the answer to his next question. "What about my brother and sisters?"

Bryok shook his head.

Conal clenched his fists and snarled, "Someone is going to pay for this. Wait a minute. You said this happened a year ago. Why would you even know about it?"

"I was alerted when Torian's assassins descended on Urve. Not long after their arrival, a jeweler and his family were caught in a fire. Coincidence? Hardly. Though assassins are good, they are still human. I have a friend in Urve who stumbled on the assassins in the act. He was lucky to escape alive. It caused me to wonder why Torian would send his fiends so far? I've been waiting and watching ever since. Now that you are here, a piece of the puzzle has been solved… a very big piece."

Conal inhaled an angry breath. "Like I said, someone is going to pay for this."

"And so they should," Bryok agreed. "But we can't go off without a plan."

Conal folded his arms and stared into the fire. "My destiny is to reclaim my father's kingdom?"

"Yes."

"How can I do that? I have no army, no followers, and no resources. It's not like I can just walk in and shout, 'Hey. I'm Kamron's son. Get off my throne.' And how am I going to convince anyone if I'm not convinced myself?"

"Things are already moving. It's just a question of fitting in and adapting them to your needs. Still, there are a few things you need to know."

"Like what?" Conal crossed back to his chair and sat, slouching back, his arms folded. His anger still smoldering, his mind raced with the methods of pain he would inflict on those responsible for his family's deaths. He knew he should feel intense sadness, but the only emotion that swirled within him was vengeance.

"Well, for starters, Torian just happens to be your uncle." Bryok placed the poker in the stand and pulled the chair out farther from the desk and sat.

Conal's head flopped back as he stared at the granite ceiling. "Why does that not surprise me? What you're telling me is my uncle killed both my real father and my other father and family."

"Yes."

"Why?"

"You know the old saying, 'The more power a man has, the more he wants. The more he wants, the more he will do to get it.' Your uncle was not satisfied to be number two. And then there is Grimmar the Mage-Breaker. It seems that all the trouble started when Grimmar came to Torian's court."

"Back to my original question," Conal said. "How am I supposed to overthrow a king when I have no assets or resources?"

"We get them along the way," Bryok smiled, "starting in Gurim-duhr."

"The dwarf kingdom? I thought you said the dwarf king was under Grimmar's spell."

"He is. We must break the chain that binds him to Grimmar."

"How do we do that?"

"We must remove Grimmar's man, Havyrd Twin-Tongue."

"Twin-tongue?"

"Remember what I said. Havyrd is not one to be trifled with. He is called 'Twin-Tongue' because he has the power of words and voice. In one instant he'll convince you to follow him and in the next instant hand you a knife and tell you to kill yourself to prove your devotion… and you would do it. To defeat him, he must not be allowed to speak. Once anyone hears his voice, they are condemned to follow his words."

"By the gods," Conal marveled. "Had I that gift I'd be a rich man by now." *And maybe my family would still be alive…*

"Wanting wealth is oft times like wanting power," Bryok quietly reminded him. "The more one gets, the more one wants."

"Sort of moot at the moment," Conal grimly chuckled. "So where do we start? I mean, what's the plan? How do we get to this Havyrd guy without getting trapped?"

"Very carefully."

Conal shook his head in irritation. "I'm serious. Right now, there's you and me. Not overwhelming odds."

"Help is on the way. In fact, he should be here any moment."

"He? That's it? One more person?" His retort was interrupted by the sound of the hidden door scraping open, causing him to jerk upright and swivel around in time to see Drustan and Rhonyn enter.

Conal leaped up, his eyes darting to Bryok whose welcoming smile to the visitors told him he had been betrayed.

"I was hoping he was with you," Drustan smiled back. Seeing the panic in Conal's eyes, he soothed, "Perhaps I was hasty, my young friend."

"I'm not your friend," Conal shot back then turned to Bryok. "You bastard."

"It's not what you think," Bryok placated.

"You don't know what I think."

"Maybe if you shut up and listen," Rhonyn snipped, "you'd learn the truth."

At that moment two dwarves stepped into the room, the door closing behind them. "How about something to drink?" Torgreth grinned. "A nice cold ale would do."

Conal's mouth gaped wide. "Torgreth? Voldar?"

"At your service," Voldar replied with a sweeping bow.

Conal's brow bent in a deep furrow as his head twitched and his gaze flickered from one person to another. When none of them made any threatening gestures, he jammed his arms on his hips. "Will someone please explain what's going on?"

"That's better," Rhonyn said. "I'll let the two druids explain. I could use an ale." Without waiting for a reply, he headed for the door, turning to the dwarves. "You coming?"

"Wouldn't miss a cold brew," Voldar readily agreed, catching up, Torgreth on his heels.

Once Rhonyn and the two dwarves left the room, Drustan narrowed his gaze at Conal. "You're a hard man to keep up with." When Conal didn't reply, he said, "Perhaps I was hasty in my initial assessment. Why did you run?"

"You wanted to kill me," Conal retorted.

"I never said that," he lied

"Maybe not to me." Conal gave him a look that said he knew the man's intent.

Drustan warily studied the young man. How could he have known what was said to Rhonyn? "Like I said, I may have been hasty."

"So you admit you wanted me dead." Conal curled a lip. "Suppose you had succeeded?"

"I was wrong," Drustan huffed. "Can we move

on. You're not dead. What's done is done."

"Is that some sort of an apology? 'Gee. So sorry I meant to kill you. Nothing personal you understand. Just business.'" Conal flopped back in his chair, crossing a leg over the other.

"Yes, it was just business," Drustan answered, a smile curling the corners of his lips. "I made a snap decision that you might be in the way. I was wrong. Fortunately, you were faster than I expected. After I explained my purpose to Voldar and Torgreth they agreed to return with me to find you. Luckily Bryok was here to keep you safe."

Conal's look said he wasn't convinced. "So… do you think I'm the long-lost son of King what's-his-name?"

"He's your father," Bryok reprimanded, "and he has a name. Use it."

"OK, OK, King Kamron."

"Apparently I'm not the only one unconvinced," Drustan taunted.

"Look at it from my point of view," Conal said, rolling his eyes. "Going from highwayman to king's son is quite a stretch."

Drustan turned to Bryok. "Have you found anything?"

"I was about to try the naming bone when you arrived."

"What's that?" Conal asked.

"A name is an essence," Bryok explained. "When parents give a child a name, it connects who they are with what they intend their child's future to be. It is a future and a history at the same time."

"And the bone?"

"It will show us if you are who we believe you to be."

"Will it hurt?" Conal groused, remembering the two instances of pain.

"Not in the same way," Bryok answered. "It is not a physical pain."

"Sometimes there is no pain at all," Drustan added. "It all depends on the parents and child. The links are strongest between father and son or mother and daughter. Though rare, links can cross. When that happens, it means the dominant parent has implanted the child's future."

Conal exhaled an exasperated sigh. "All this is mumbo jumbo. The bottom line is what will the naming bond tell you?"

"It will tell us the truth of your connection," Bryok said.

"I assume I have a birth name?"

"Yes. Darrbie."

"Darrbie?" Conal blurted. "My father named me Darrbie? What kind of name is that?"

"It means 'one who is free from hatred and envy.' You don't like it?" Bryok asked.

"I am *not* going to be called Darrbie," Conal exclaimed. "I don't care who my father is."

"That is your choice," Drustan said. "But for now, consent to use the name so we can establish heritage."

"Darrbie," Conal sneered. "Sounds like a girl's name." Looking at them, he asked, "What's my sister's name?"

"Her real name or the name she is using?" Bryok replied.

"Both."

"We don't know what name she uses. Her birthname is Quinlee. It means 'woman of wisdom and insight.'"

Conal curled a lip. "Our parents named us Darrbie

and Quinlee? What is wrong with them? What kind of parent would name their kids Darrbie and Quinlee? This sounds like part of a joke."

"Can we proceed?" Drustan interrupted. "You can rant and rage later."

"Yeah, sure… but Darrbie? I mean, c'mon. Free from envy and hatred? Talk about way off the mark. First thing I'm gonna do when I find Oscon is torture the living stuffing out of him then kill him. How's that for being free of hatred?"

"Shall we begin?" Bryok said, ignoring him. Pulling out the bottom right drawer of the desk, he lifted out something wrapped in cloth. Placing it on the desktop, he unwrapped it, displaying an animal bone with runes carved into it.

"This is a naming bone," he explained. "It will give us the answers we seek."

"What animal?" Conal asked.

"It is from the femur of a stag."

"Is a stag required?"

"Yes. Now quit interrupting." He handed the bone to Conal. "All you need to do is hold the bone with both hands and say, 'I am Darrbie.' The bone will do the rest."

"That's it?" Conal regarded the bone in his hands. It was smooth, sliced clean at both ends. Engraved in black letters were runes and symbols he didn't recognize or understand. Inhaling a deep breath, he placed his feet shoulder-width apart and grasped the bone with both hands. "Might as well get this over with… I am Darrbie."

The bone grew warmer, and a faint orange glow surrounded the bone and his hands. Suddenly he was filled with overwhelming grief, like watching someone he loved executed before his eyes. His eyes slammed shut as the vision consumed him. Blood pooled beneath the body of a man on the ground, his purple robe stained. The jeweled crown that once adorned his head lay close by. Beside him, a lovely woman wearing a golden crown slumped to her knees, the hilt of a dagger protruding from her chest.

He cried out as she slumped to the ground. His hand involuntarily shot out as though trying to catch her. Her head slowly turned, and her eyes found his. With her last breaths, she smiled and mouthed the words, 'My son.'

Conal cried out and flung the bone from his hands. Opening his eyes, he felt hot and wiped away the sweat from his forehead and face. His hands felt even hotter, and he looked down to see runes slowly fading from his palms.

Shifting a look between Drustan and Bryok whose satisfied grin told him they were pleased with the results, he said, "Well?"

"What did you see?"

Conal related the vision and the pain he felt.

"You didn't see it because your eyes were closed," Bryok commented, "but the color surrounding your hands turned from orange to pure white, which means you are truly Kamron's son."

Stunned, Conal remained rooted to the floor, trying to make sense of everything. He had hoped it was all a mistake, that he could go back to the way things were before. But then he remembered that nothing was the same anymore. His family was dead... and he was now a king's son.

"I need a drink."

"That can be arranged," Bryok chuckled.

"By the way," Drustan casually said. "What do you know about dragons?"

CHAPTER 15

GWEN

Gwen's eyes widened in terror as she fell. She kicked her legs and flapped her arms as if that would help, and suddenly her descent ended, harsh and abrupt. Had she really just stopped her fall by flailing her limbs about? She flapped her arms again, and this time she rose through the air. Her body continued rising until she topped the tower, where she hovered for a moment before landing gently on the roof.

"How did I do that?" she exclaimed excitedly.

"You didn't," Aimil said, nodding to Eradore. "He did."

Eradore frowned. "I didn't expect the lightning to fling you off the tower. There will be better precautions in the future."

When Gwen realized it wasn't the ridiculous arm flapping that had stopped her fall, she laughed. She was thankful nobody had seen her lame impression of a bird.

"I thought that rune was a snake."

"No, it's a lightning bolt," Aimil replied. "Now that you say that I can see some similarity. Do you feel any pain?"

"A little."

Gwen lifted her left hand, cupping it with her right one. On the back of her hand, where the lightning bolt rune had been seared, the skin was swollen and bright red. Her flesh throbbed, but otherwise she felt like her usual self.

"She's strong," Aimil said to Eradore. "The last mage who took that rune couldn't walk or see for two days."

"How do I use the rune?" Gwen asked.

"She's also impatient," Eradore said. "I'm going to leave her with you for a while. I have some things to attend to that I've been putting off."

"She's in good hands," Aimil said. "Mind if I join the attack on the outpost? I'd love to strike at King Torian's soldiers."

"I'm sure Tobias and Roland would love to have you along. They're finalizing a few things, and they should be here within the hour." Eradore turned to Gwen. "I hope to see you again before I leave, but if I don't, please return here after the outpost is dealt with."

Gwen hadn't thought past the attack on the outpost, and she found herself suddenly reeling mentally. What would come after they rescued her father? He couldn't go back to the Seven Stars. If it was still standing, it belonged to the king. What would they do? *One thing at a time,* Gwen reminded herself.

"I will," she promised Eradore.

Eradore went back into the tower and Gwen looked at Aimil. The image of her nakedness was burned into Gwen's mind, and it was hard for her to look at the woman without feeling embarrassed.

"What?" Aimil asked.

"Nothing," Gwen replied quickly.

"Spit it out. There's no need for secrets."

"The runes on your … uh …" Gwen motioned to her chest.

"Yes?"

"What do they do? And why are they there?"

Aimil shrugged. "The magic puts the runes where it deems best. I've never questioned that. As to what they do?" Aimil looked around. "I suppose this is the best place to show you."

Gwen watched as Aimil lifted her right hand, arm extended. She tilted her hand back so that her palm was facing away from her and said, *"Guairneán."*

The gray clouds where Aimil motioned began to swirl. It started slowly but quickly increased until there was a powerful whirlwind spinning among the clouds. The wind whistled loudly, and Gwen's shirt lashed about. The force continued to grow until Gwen felt her footing start to slip. She grabbed onto Aimil for support.

Aimil looked at her. The woman's eyes held a wild look, like an enraged animal Gwen had seen once. It scared her and she released Aimil, more willing to be pulled into the whirlwind than to see what insanity Aimil might unleash, but the whirlwind slowed and faded altogether.

"The magic is addictive," Aimil said after the silence grew awkward.

"How so?"

"Have you ever been drunk?" Aimil turned around and Gwen saw the crazy look in the woman's eyes was gone.

"Yes," Gwen replied.

"After you've had a few tankards, you feel good, loosened up. And as the feeling grows, you like it and want more, so you drink more, yes?"

Gwen nodded.

"It's like that, only much more primal. Controlling the magic once a rune is activated can be hard. If you aren't careful, you can destroy everything around you. When you use the magic, it must be for a purpose. Wielding it at random will make you a danger to yourself and those around you."

"I understand," Gwen said. "I've never wanted to hurt anyone, even when I was angry. That won't change."

"It might," Aimil warned. "Power changes people."

Gwen decided not to argue with her. "How do I make the rune work like you did?"

"Do you feel the pulsing in your skin, where the rune is?"

"The pain?" Gwen asked.

"No. Search beyond the pain. You'll know the difference when you feel it."

Gwen looked at the rune on her own hand and mentally navigated past the stinging pain. Something pulsed softly. When she touched it with her mind, it zapped her, making her eyes water.

"You found it," Aimil said, stifling her mirth. "When you are ready to use it, you will focus on that pulse and speak the name of the rune. The magic will channel through you. Remember! Control is important. If you lose control, you may not live through the experience."

"I have a question," Gwen said.

"Ask."

"When I came through Eradore's mirror portal, my body was fighting the magic. It's a bit confusing, but I felt something inside me align with my spine.

The *bunús.* What is it?"

"The *bunús* is like the cornerstone of a building, the base that all runes are built upon. It enables a mage to become a vessel for the magic."

"Can a mage lose the ability to use runes? And do runes lose their strength?" Gwen asked.

"If a mage isn't in control of their mind, such as being drunk, the magic will be weaker. I've never heard of anyone completely losing the magic. Runes are as powerful or as weak as you allow. There are limits to magic, of course, but they are … high ceilings."

"You said power changes people. Did it change you?"

"Without a doubt," Aimil answered. "Believe it or not, I was once very meek. People pushed me around and I let them. Once I became a mage, I sought out every rune I could find. As I gained them and became stronger, I stopped allowing people to take advantage of me."

Gwen's eyes widened. "You were meek? You seem so …"

"Loud? Brash?"

"No," Gwen said. "Powerful."

Aimil laughed. "Maybe a little. Sometimes too much."

"What do you mean?"

Aimil grew serious. "I was married to a soldier. He would abuse me physically. Hit me, things like that. One day I decided it was enough. I'd gained only a handful of runes then, but they were sufficient."

"Sufficient for what?" Gwen asked.

"Sufficient to kill him. I called fire and burned him until he stopped screaming."

Gwen decided it was a good idea to never anger

Aimil. "That's … I'm sorry you had to endure his abuse."

"I'm sure he was, too, in the end. Let's forget about this. Remembering the past causes me to feel things I'd rather not."

"How did you meet Eradore?" Gwen asked, changing the subject.

"Ah, now that's a story. A host of goblins had somehow gotten into the city and began burning and ransacking. I was the first to show up and Eradore joined me. We put down the goblins together and ended up becoming friends."

"Is that how you got involved with the rebellion, too? Knowing Eradore?"

"I'm actually the one who convinced him to aid us. He wanted to remain neutral, but as Torian's soldiers continued to cause suffering, he changed his mind. His passion for the people is hard to rival. You'd think that since he's an elf he wouldn't care about humans, but that couldn't be further from the truth."

Gwen's respect for Eradore continued to increase the more she learned about him. Her hand still throbbed, and she traced the rune with her finger, careful not to touch the inflamed skin.

"When will the pain go away?" she asked.

"Considering how well you took the rune, I'd guess a day or so. I'm impressed you're even coherent, let alone conscious. Like I told Eradore, the last person I know who took the lightning rune was out for two days. You're made of tough stuff."

"I don't think so," Gwen said.

Aimil closed her eyes and muttered something under her breath, then looked at Gwen. "Tobias and Roland are here."

"How do you know?"

"Eradore told me." Aimil pointed to a rune on her left arm. It looked like two skulls with a thin string between them. "Let's get back inside. I'm sure you two have some catching up to do."

Gwen followed Aimil back into the tower and closed the metal door behind her. They found Tobias and Roland at the terrace and Gwen felt a flood of emotion when she saw Tobias. The night her father had been captured hadn't been long ago, yet it felt to her like weeks had passed. She wrapped Tobias in a hug.

"Everything all right?" he asked, awkwardly returning her embrace.

"Yes, I'm just glad you're back."

"Right. Well, everything is in place. Have you seen Eradore? I was going to let him know that the soldiers who followed us here have been snooping around, trying to get information on our whereabouts."

"He said he had to take care of some things," Gwen replied. "I find it odd they haven't gone back to the outpost."

"I'm sure it has something to do with you," Tobias said. "I don't think they chased us over that horse."

"Why would they have been chasing me?"

"Who knows? How's the time with Eradore been? Did you learn any—" He paused when he saw the rune on her hand. "So, you *are* a mage. I did not see that coming."

"Neither did I," Gwen said. "I wasn't sure about all of this. The rebellion, my father, magic … all of it, but now I think it was all meant to happen the way it did for a reason."

"Only time will tell," Tobias smiled at her. "You seem different somehow."

"What do you mean?"

"It's hard to put into words, but it's not a bad thing. It's just different."

Gwen gave him an odd look and shrugged. "When are we leaving? Eradore said my father wasn't doing well, and I want to get there as quickly as we can. It's already been too long for my comfort."

"Roland has organized everything, so we can leave now. I wanted to speak to Eradore, but I can talk to him when we get back. I found out an interesting bit of information while I was out."

"Oh? What is it?"

"I can't say. Not yet anyway."

"Then why did you bring it up to begin with? Now I'm curious," Gwen huffed.

"Let's get going," Tobias said, ignoring her comment. "I want to get there before nightfall."

They left Eradore's tower and wound their way down the maze of streets, ending at the main gates leading out of the city. As they walked, Gwen studied Roland. He was taller than her by a full foot and had black hair that was cut so short she questioned the purpose of even keeping it. A jagged scar ran the length of his right cheek. Roland walked with a confident bearing that showed he was a leader. A sword was sheathed at his side, the leather that covered the hilt well-worn from use.

Gwen looked from him to Tobias and could understand why Tobias didn't want to lead the attack. With someone like Roland at the head, people were probably more likely to willingly join the danger. Even then, attacking an outpost filled with trained soldiers sounded insane. And yet here she was, walking toward danger herself to rescue her father. Eradore had told her that she could ask Boris the truth about her relation to him. What if he corroborated what Tobias and Eradore said?

Again, Gwen found herself occupied with things she didn't need to focus on. They left the city behind and soon joined a small camp of men and women. Most of them were human, but Gwen spotted a few elves among their numbers.

"We're going to ride quick, but I don't want anyone pushing their animals too hard," Roland announced once everyone had gathered around him. "You were all told to keep your lips sealed about this little foray, and I hope you've all kept your word. Keep your eyes open, regardless. We don't want any surprises in case there are rats among us. Any questions?" Roland paused and glanced around. "Head out!"

There weren't enough horses for everyone to ride alone, so Gwen chose to ride with Tobias. The group of horses trotted along at a decent pace, but Gwen remembered their harrowing ride to Penshaw and found their speed to be much slower.

"So, what's this interesting bit of information you want to share with Eradore?" Gwen asked.

"You're going to keep asking until I say, aren't you?"

"Probably," Gwen said. "Probably meaning yes."

Tobias turned to look over his shoulder at her. She smiled at him, but his expression was troubled. "Listen," he lowered his voice. "I don't know if it's true, but the soldiers who followed us aren't from the outpost."

"They aren't? But that's the direction they came from."

"I know." Tobias glanced around to make sure no one had taken an interest in their conversation. "We already guessed they were using magic to track us, but we didn't know why. I think I know why now."

"Why?"

"They're looking for the daughter of the king."

"Torian has a daughter?" Gwen asked.

"Not Torian," Tobias clarified. "Kamron. There's always been rumors that his children escaped the slaughter, but the heat is picking up on those stories now. People are saying that Torian knows they survived and he's looking for them."

"What does any of that have to do with us?"

"Not us, Gwen. You."

"Me? What are you talking about?"

"I think you're Kamron's missing daughter."

CHAPTER 16

CONAL

Dragons?" Conal's face scrunched into a frown. "Where did that come from?"

"Just thinking of possibilities," Drustan said.

"Why don't you just wish for pixie dust and magical unicorns while you're at it?" Conal taunted. "Have you ever seen a dragon?"

"Yes, I have."

Conal fixed him with a sharp eye, waiting for the punchline. "You're serious."

"Yes," Drustan replied, "though it's been a while."

"A real dragon?"

"Yes." Drustan repeated. "Believe it or not, there was a time when dragons were rather common."

"Until the Hunting," Bryok sourly added.

"The Hunting?"

"That's what it was called," Bryok explained. "One hundred and fifty years ago, when Odhran was king in Tul Cragbyrn, he declared dragons an enemy to all the races."

"Why?" Conal asked, his thirst momentarily forgotten.

"Gold," Drustan answered, "and silver and other

precious things."

"Dragons had accumulated a vast amount of wealth," Bryok continued, "and Odhran wanted it. Isentol was once the dragon kingdom and Havengarde was the citadel, a sacred place for dragons."

"Why?"

"Does it matter why?" Bryok said. "That it was sacred to them is sufficient enough. Dwarves have their sacred mountains, humans their sacred burial grounds and elves… well who knows about elves." His smile quickly vanished. "It became open season on dragons. Celebrations erupted with each killed dragon."

"As you can imagine," Drustan said, "after a while it got harder and harder to find dragons. Finally, dragons disappeared."

"Yet you've seen one." Conal scoffed.

"Yes. Why do you persist in unbelief?"

"Because no one even talks about them anymore." Conal folded his arms. "Other than your supposed sighting, dragons might as well be nonexistent. Why bring them up now?"

Drustan shifted a glance at Bryok. "I raise the issue because dragons do exist, and it would be to your advantage to enlist their help."

Conal stared at him a moment before shaking his head. "First you tell me that I'm some dead king's son. Then you want me to get rid of some guy who can talk me into killing myself, but along the way, we're gonna look for dragons. Is that about right?"

"Pretty much," Bryok smiled. "Yet you fail to ask the important question, which is, 'Why are we so confident that we can find a dragon?'"

"OK… I'll bite. Why are you so confident?"

Bryok smiled. "Because we know where one is."

The door opened and Rhonyn breezed in, the two dwarves on his heels, each carrying two steins of ale.

"My compliments on the ale, Master Bryok," Torgreth commented, handing a stein to Conal. "Some of the best we've had in a while."

Conal hooked a thumb at Drustan. "I thought you two were on the run from him."

"We thought so too. Knew Rorkyn was lookin' for us and figured he sent him after us."

"Wasn't until he explained what was goin' on that we realized we were running from the wrong guy," Voldar added. "You were already down river by then. Nice reaction time by the way." He grinned and turned to Bryok. "No sooner had the door opened that he was out the window. Never seen anyone move so fast."

"Survival instinct," Conal shrugged then turned an accusing glare at Drustan. "If you knew then you were wrong, why all the arrows at me when I dove in?"

"Accidental," Rhonyn answered. "Had a few archers react before I could stop them."

Voldar took a draught of ale before asking Bryok, "So? Is he the one?"

"Yes."

Voldar slapped his thigh. "Excellent. Then we got us a chance."

"When do we start?" Torgreth enthused.

"Whoa, not so fast," Conal interrupted. "What's the plan?"

"Eliminate Havyrd," Voldar stated. "He's the cause of our problems."

"How?" Rhonyn inserted himself into the discussion. "We've been over this ground before.

Yeah, we have the king's son. So what? He's as human as the rest of us."

"Hey," Torgreth complained.

"I mean he's as susceptible to Havyrd's tongue as the rest of us are. How are we going to get to Havyrd without compromising ourselves? We've got to cross into Gurim-duhr then get into Morendir without anyone noticing us. Considering we've got two druids with us as well as the two dwarves he's been searching for, not to mention the 50 plus folks of my team, we're going to be easy to spot." He turned his attention to the two dwarves. "What did you two do that has Havyrd chasing you?"

"We got nervous making more rune bones and dice," Voldar answered, "and seeing more of our kin enslaved to Havyrd's foul desires." He shook his head in disgust. "It's bad enough Rorkyn is under his spell. What's worse is that Twin-Tongue isn't even a dwarf."

"He's not?" Conal sputtered, surprised.

"No. He's human, a mealy excuse of a man. If not for the power of his tongue, he'd be the kind you'd kick out of your way."

"This doesn't get us anywhere," Rhonyn complained. "We still have to get into Morendir undetected."

"I have an idea," Conal quietly announced. "We split up and meet inside the city somewhere."

"All of us?" Rhonyn raised an eyebrow in objection.

"No. You and your team head across the northern part of Gurim-duhr like you're heading towards Clagmoran. Word will get out and their attention will be diverted to you while the rest of us head south to Morendir."

"Then what?" Voldar cocked an eyebrow. "It's not like they won't be looking for my brother and me."

"And it's not like traveling with two druids will go unnoticed," Torgreth chimed in.

"We disguise ourselves and split up, one dwarf with one druid. No one's looking for me, so I'll be the third wheel with one group."

"Disguise ourselves as what?" Voldar asked, not much impressed with the idea, nor walking back into the proverbial hornet's nest in Morendir.

"Merchants or something," Conal huffed. "I don't care, just something so that no one recognizes you."

"OK," Torgreth mused aloud. "Let's say we make it into the city. What then?"

"We meet at some rendezvous place. Havyrd is human, right? That means he needs to eat and sleep. He probably has some sort of routine. He can't spend all his time next to the king. He's gotta pee sometime."

Torgreth frowned in thought. "Actually, he does have a peculiar habit of taking a walk around the king's palace right after lunch when most folks are getting back to work."

"That's right." Voldar's eyes brightened. "He does it every day. But we'd still have to get into the palace."

"I think we might be able to help," Bryok said, focusing on Drustan. "Rune bones." When Drustan hesitated, he narrowed his stare. "It's important."

"Fine," Drustan relented.

"Rune bones?" Conal repeated, gazing at the two druids.

"We have a collection of rune bones we've accumulated over the years," Bryok explained, "all imbued with magic. I think we have some we can use to help subdue Havyrd."

"Subdue? That begs the question," Conal pointed out. "Do you want him captured or dead?"

"Dead," both dwarves chimed in.

"Dead," Bryok repeated, Drustan nodding agreement.

"What do I do when… I mean *if* you are unsuccessful?" Rhonyn asked.

"Do what seems best to you," Conal replied, "but if this is our only option, we can't fail."

"Too easily said."

"You have a better plan?"

"Not at the moment." Rhonyn turned his attention to the two druids. "Let's say we get the dwarves to join the cause; there's still Clagmoran and the other kingdoms to deal with. What's your plan to get Kilmaryn to join?"

"Vanity," Drustan answered. "Look up the definition for vanity and you'll see a picture of Kilmaryn."

"Who's Kilmaryn? Conal interrupted.

"King of Clagmoran," Drustan said. "I've had dealings with him before. He's a good king, cares about this people. But his kingdom is all he cares about. He's fortified his kingdom and until someone breaches the walls, he won't budge."

"First things first," Conal reminded them. "Once we get Havyrd taken care of, we can worry about Kilmaryn."

"When do we leave?" Voldar piped up.

"What time is it?" Conal asked.

"Late afternoon," Bryok answered. "We leave at midnight. Gives us a chance to escape unnoticed."

"Gates will be closed," Torgreth pointed out.

Bryok smiled knowingly. "We have other ways to get out." He turned to Rhonyn. "You can leave whenever you're ready."

"We'll leave in the morning. I'd better go check on my team."

Rhonyn drained the rest of his drink and placed his stein on the desk when Conal suddenly remembered something Bryok had mentioned and turned to him. "What about what you said about the dra—"

"We can talk about that later," Bryok interrupted, speaking over him before addressing Rhonyn. "We'll send word to you in Merthyl-haven."

"Right. Good luck to you." Rhonyn nodded to the others, waiting for Drustan to guide him back out the way they came in.

While Drustan led Rhonyn through the maze, Bryok informed the two dwarves that, "There's plenty of food and ale in the kitchen and buttery. Help yourselves while Conal and I talk more about our plans."

"Sounds like yer tryin' to get rid of us," Torgreth grinned.

"I am," he laughed. "Conal and I have some other personal matters to discuss."

"No need to ask twice," Torgreth said, "especially when there's food and ale. C'mon brother. Let's see what's in the larder."

Waiting until they were through the door, Bryok motioned for Conal to sit. "You need to be cautious when you talk about dragons. First, not everyone is willing to accept the truth and second, not everyone can be trusted. And third, is that there are still those who believe the only good dragon is a dead dragon. So from now on, let's just keep this between us."

"OK by me. You said you know where one is,"

"We do, but we have to be exceedingly cautious. Remember what we said about the Hunting?"

The epiphany hit and Conal abruptly realized his mistake. "You think the dwarves or Rhonyn's people would try to kill it."

"Not necessarily them, but if word got out…"

"I'll keep my mouth shut."

"Good," Bryok said. "Now there's one more thing we need to talk about. Your brand. What do you know about the Cobra assassin?"

"To be honest," Conal shrugged, "nothing other than they're supposed to be a leader among assassins."

"You are partially right." Bryok walked over to stand by the hearth, placing his fingers under the brim of the mantel. A door appeared in the stone wall. Retrieving a candelabra, he beckoned, "Come with me."

Conal followed him into a large room filled floor to tall ceiling with shelves containing small boxes, each box labeled with the contents in a script that he didn't recognize. Bryok paused in front of a shelf and pulled down a box, opening the lid.

"Rune bones?"

"All the boxes in here contain rune bones. It's taken us a while, but we've probably accumulated more incantation bones than anyone else is all the kingdoms."

"Even more than Grimmar?"

"Hopefully even more than him."

"We've intercepted a number of his shipments," Drustan interrupted, "which means he knows someone is trying to stop him."

"Which is why he was so intent on capturing the

two dwarves," Bryok added.

Conal raised an eyebrow. "Why all the fuss? Why not simply have folks up wherever he is and have then carve runes right there?"

"Runes have to be carved exact," Bryok answered. "A misplaced serif on a letter or an incorrect angle of a line changes the rune and the spell with potential disastrous results. Dwarves are known for their expertise, Voldar and Torgreth being some of the best."

"So why not just kidnap them and bring them up there?"

"Too many problems with that," Dustan said.

Conal immediately understood. "They'd screwup a carving on purpose."

"Exactly."

Holding the box with one hand, Bryok picked a small bone out, holding it between thumb and forefinger at the ends. "This box here contains bones marked with incantations for agility and speed." He held it up so Conal could see the runes.

"What does it say?"

Bryok smiled paternally at him. "It is a language you will learn later. For now, be content that it is for your good."

"What do I do with it?" He went to reach for it, but Bryok pulled back.

"Patience. Do you not want to know what happens when you receive a rune bone?"

Conal frowned, suddenly apprehensive. "Is this like the naming rune?"

"Not quite," he chuckled. "Every rune bone has a power imbued in it. In certain bones, once the power is transferred, the bone is nothing more than a mere bone, not even good for a dog to chew on. What happens when a bone user receives the power depends on the bone and the imbued power. But what *will* happen is that the runes will be transferred to the user."

Conal glanced around the room at the number of boxes. "Have you used any of these?"

"Of course," he replied with a cryptic smile.

"Is it possible for one person to use all of them?"

"I suppose it's possible though it would not be prudent. Rune spells are not meant for everyone."

"Not everyone can use rune bones," Drustan pointed out, walking in. "Only individuals who are mage-marked can use rune bones. Anyone else who tries would suffer beyond description."

"And you think I'm mage-marked?" He cocked an eyebrow in doubt.

"Being mage-marked doesn't necessarily mean you are a mage," Bryok explained. "For some it means you are gifted with the ability to use rune bones to expand who you are."

Conal shifted his gaze around the room, noting the number of boxes and what must be thousands of rune bones. "Where did you find them all?"

"Various places. Here," he held the rune bone out to him. "Firmly grasp the bone so that the letters face your palm. The bone will get warm, maybe even hot. Whatever you do, do not let go of the bone until it cools."

Conal hesitated then took the bone in his right hand, rotating it so the runes faced his palm then griped it tightly.

At first, it felt nothing more than what it appeared, a bone with writing engraved on it. Then warmth radiated and he felt a tingling up his arm that radiated throughout his body. The bone grew warmer then hot, uncomfortably hot.

"Do not let go," Bryok warned then chanted a phrase that Conal did not understand.

The tingling turned into lightning charges and sweat dripped from his forehead.

"Keep holding it," Bryok encouraged.

Suddenly the burning and the pain stopped and whatever heat the bone had evaporated. Conal opened his hand and pulled the bone away, twirling it around only to discover the engraved writing had disappeared. He looked down at his hand and saw nothing. He looked up at Bryok who stood grinning at him like a proud father. "Where'd it go?"

"It has transferred to you. Check yourself."

It was when Conal checked his left forearm that he noticed it. The writing, in black runes the same size as on the bone, forever imprinted on his skin.

"What power do I now have?"

"Agility and speed. There are several other powers I suggest you take on."

"Like what?"

"Endurance and weapons. Speed is great, but if you grow tired after thirty seconds, what good it is to you?"

"Weapons?"

Bryok slowly nodded, inhaling a slow breath. "Just as there are more than one kind of weapon, there are more than one spell that will help. I suggest the normal sword and dagger but would also add throwing stars and nunchuks."

"Throwing stars? Nunchuks? What are they?"

"They are weapons every assassin needs."

Conal shook his head, furrowing his brows. "Just for the sake of argument, if I'm supposed to become king, why do I need to train to be an assassin?"

"How long will it take to become king? How many battles must you fight to claim the throne? What measures must you take to keep that throne?"

Conal blinked in understanding. "Point taken."

"You have natural leadership skills. You must now assume the role your brand has declared you. Do you wish to continue?"

Conal sucked in a deep breath, the heat and pain still a fresh memory. "Yeah. Might as well get this over with."

By the time Conal finished, seven sets of runes marked his body with the addition of strength and stealth runes. He was exhausted, glad it was over, yet intrigued with what other rune bones were there. Perhaps he would return and browse what was available... after he became king.

"Y'know," he said, still woozy from the spell transfers, and leaning against the door-jam, "What were those words you were saying when I held the bones?"

"Incantation words. In order for a rune to transfer, it needs to be unlocked. A rune can be unlocked one of two ways; either by the one holding the bone or a mage or wizard."

"Or a druid."

"Or a druid." He stared intently at him. "A word of caution. The incantation words must be pronounced correctly. Mispronounced words can result in some very unpleasant results… even death."

Conal eyes popped wide. "Point noted." His face morphed to a frown. "I always wondered why you're called a half-druid. What exactly does that mean?"

Bryok's smile faded. "It means what it says."

"I don't get it. Half of you is a druid. What's the other half?"

Bryok stood to full height. "It is something to be very afraid of. I have been placed into two worlds. Most of the time I live as a human, a druid, with the powers of a druid. The other world where I live is full of anger and hatred and resentment, spirit forces demanding to be unleashed. I have managed to keep them under control with the help of runes. I hope there will come a time when I can live in one world."

Conal noticed he didn't say which world. Glancing behind him, he noted that Drustan had gone to check on the dwarves. "What about Drustan? Is he like you?"

Bryok fixed him with a sharp stare. "Though he is my brother, be warned. The spirits have a greater hold on him. If he seems short tempered, it is because of the struggle of his worlds. I pray we can find an answer in time before he destroys us all."

CHAPTER 17

GWEN

The image of the slaughter from her vision came to the forefront of Gwen's mind.

"No," she said. "That's not possible."

"How do you know that for certain?" Tobias asked.

"Look at me. I'm nothing special. A princess would be ..." Gwen shrugged. "Better? She'd be beautiful and ... and, you'd just be able to tell. I don't know."

"You don't think you're beautiful?"

"Not really," Gwen replied.

"I do," Tobias said.

He turned his attention ahead, which Gwen was grateful for. Her cheeks were flushed, and she couldn't believe Tobias had complimented her like that. She did find him on the handsome side, but she had never looked at him in *that* way before. Yet as she thought about it now, it was possible that he was compatible with her.

Gwen debated with herself on what to say, but ultimately decided to keep her mouth shut. There were pressing issues, and a possible romance wasn't what she had in mind. At least, not yet.

The trip should have taken the better part of a single day, but as multiple problems arose, mainly with the horses, it took two days to reach the outskirts of the outpost. By the time the structure was within eyesight, they'd lost almost half their horses to a mysterious illness that caused the animals to weaken and collapse. Aimil had looked them over but was unable to find what caused it.

All of the rebellion members were still accounted for, and most everyone was in high spirits despite the setbacks. There were a few grumblers, but they were quickly reminded of their mission by their fellows, and the complaints were silenced. Roland ordered them to set up camp and called a handful of men to his side, including Tobias. Gwen stayed out of the way and watched the others methodically erect tents and build a makeshift stable for the horses.

Gwen walked to the edge of the camp and stared at the stone structure, wondering where the soldiers were keeping her father. Eradore had said he wasn't doing well, but Gwen wasn't sure what that meant. Had he meant physically or mentally? Gwen berated herself for not asking questions.

"Hang in there," she whispered pleadingly. "We're coming for you."

It was midday and the sun hung overhead, the heat beating down mercilessly. There was no breeze to offer any respite, and the black clothing Gwen wore made her misery increase. Tobias eventually joined her, standing there like a silent guardian.

"What's the plan?" she asked.

"Roland wants to wait until night to begin the attack. He said the darkness will work in our favor and allow us to get close before we're spotted."

"Do you think they can see us from there? If we

can see their walls, it seems likely they can see us."

"It's possible," Tobias admitted. "But they don't know we're coming, so they shouldn't be on the lookout for anything out of the ordinary. And if they do spot us, they'll probably assume we're merchants."

Gwen hadn't considered that. Given the season, that seemed a logical assumption. Merchants frequently passed through Dawsbury this time of year, so it wouldn't be odd to see a group of them camped out beside the road. Still, something didn't feel right to Gwen.

"I'm scared," Gwen confessed.

"So am I," Tobias replied.

"Really?"

"Yes. It's one thing to talk about rebellion, and something entirely different to actually do it, be part of it. There's so much uncertainty."

Gwen was relieved to know she wasn't the only one feeling that way. She'd mistakenly assumed her father had been wrong to tell her to find Tobias, but little by little she'd come to see the wisdom of his request. Tobias was a good man, and she was glad to have him at her side.

"When it gets dark, what are we doing?" Gwen asked.

"Roland is sending a few scouts ahead to make sure there are no surprises, then the rest of us will move in. The majority of us are going for the main building there." Tobias pointed to the largest part of the structure. "Smaller groups are going to hit the other two."

"Am I going with the largest group?"

"No," Tobias said hesitantly, quickly glancing at her from his periphery. "It's safer if you go with one of the smaller groups. They are less likely to encounter resistance. Once the main building has been secured, everyone else can join us there."

Gwen wanted to argue with him, but her fear convinced her it was probably the better option. Once they'd taken the outpost, then she could safely free her father. She nodded mutely, ready for nightfall.

The time passed slower than Gwen cared for, despite the fact that she tried to keep herself busy. She helped with food preparation, used whetstones to sharpen the blades of swords, and batched loose arrows together for quivers. After she'd assisted with everything she could, it wasn't quite dusk yet. She spotted Aimil standing alone near one of the tents and walked over to her.

"I'm guessing you're going with the main group?" Gwen asked.

"I am. Roland said I'm too valuable of an asset not to. What about you?"

"No. I'm going with one of the smaller groups."

"Is that what you want to do? I can convince Roland to let you come with us."

"No, it's fine," Gwen said. "I don't think I'm mean enough to fight my way into a fortress."

Aimil snorted, but she had a smile on her face. "Wait until life spits on you enough. Then you'll get mean."

"Other than your ex-husband, have you killed anyone?"

"Yes," Aimil answered without hesitation. "The world can be a brutal place. I've found it's always better to strike first."

Gwen thought that perspective was a bit harsh, but she didn't know everything Aimil had been through and didn't want to judge the woman.

"There are two things I value in this world," Aimil added. "Money and power. They rarely come one without the other."

"Why help with the rebellion, then? Eradore said their resources are limited compared to the king's."

"Some things are a mystery," Aimil replied, smiling again. "I'm going to rest until dark. I suggest you do the same."

Gwen was physically tired, but her mind was too alert to sleep. She watched Aimil disappear into the tent, then walked to her own and tried to sleep. Between the heat and her thoughts, it was impossible. She resigned herself to just lying there and let her mind wander until it was dark. The camp came alive with movement, and she stepped out of her tent.

"Gwen!" It was Tobias. He motioned for her and she hurried to him. "You're going to be with Tylindra's group. She's taking the building on the far left."

A tall elven woman with golden brown hair tilted her head in acknowledgment. "Greetings, Gwen. I've given my word to Tobias that I'll make sure you are safe."

Gwen felt her face flush again and hoped the darkness hid her unspoken response. "Thank you," Gwen said. "I'll try not to get in the way."

"Once we've reached the main building, give us a few minutes before you attack. We want to make sure we've drawn most of the soldiers to us."

"As you command," Tylindra said.

Tobias left them and joined the larger group. They began their quiet march to the outpost, and Gwen glanced around at those who remained. Tylindra's group had seven people, and the other group had five. The large force soon melded into the shadows until Gwen couldn't see any of them. She watched and waited, anxiety making her legs tremor. She shifted from leg to leg, trying to dispel the shaking, but it didn't help.

"They've reached the doors," Tylindra said.

"How do you know?" Gwen asked.

"I can see them."

Gwen looked at the elf, awed. "Really?"

"Yes. We elves have excellent vision in the dark."

I need a rune that does that, Gwen thought.

"Prepare yourself," Tylindra said. "We move in—"

A horn blared in the distance, followed shortly after by cries of surprise.

"Onward!" Tylindra shouted.

Gwen ran ahead, following the others of her group. Tylindra led them forward, then branched to the left. The distance didn't seem far to Gwen, but as they reached what she guessed was the halfway point, she was already panting, both her legs and lungs on fire. She and two other people fell behind, but Tylindra and the rest barely seemed affected and quickly outdistanced them. By the time Gwen and her two companions reached the outpost, the others had already made it inside.

"Should we wait out here for them?" Gwen gasped.

The other two looked at each other and shook their heads, then entered into the doorway. Gwen waited by the door as she tried to catch her breath, constantly surveying her surroundings. It was quiet around her, but the sounds of battle echoed from the main building. Gwen stepped into the doorway and listened intently.

A metallic tapping noise caught her attention, but

otherwise there was nothing. No screams, no one fighting. Curiosity convinced her to see what the noise was, and she crept down a long narrow hall. Several doors lined each side, most of them open. Gwen glanced inside each one, but there was nothing of interest until she reached the last door before a stairwell.

The tapping noise came from within, and Gwen risked a look inside. A dwarf, one of her party members, was trying to break a lock on a wooden chest. He glanced up at her and offered a nod, then went back to his work. Footsteps reverberated from the stairwell, and Gwen saw Tylindra and the others coming down.

"There's no one in this building," she said. "We checked everything. A source told us there should have been soldiers in here."

"What does that mean?" Gwen asked.

"It might be a trap."

"I thought Roland said everyone had kept quiet?"

"As far as we know, they did. That doesn't mean there isn't a spy in our midst. We need to get to the others and make sure they aren't being overwhelmed."

Tylindra led the charge out into the small courtyard and across to the main building. Gwen spotted a few bodies on the ground, both soldiers and rebellion members. She didn't see Tobias among them and breathed a sigh of relief.

Something whizzed past Tylindra's head and Gwen stopped in her tracks as an arrow struck the ground a few feet away.

"Archers!" someone cried.

Gwen rushed into the building, pausing at the doorway. Blood covered the floor, and there were more bodies. She looked back and saw three members of the group get hit with multiple arrows and collapse, including the dwarf she'd seen trying to break the lock. Tylindra made a hasty charge inside, half dragging a wounded man. The last member, another human, stumbled in behind them.

"If they've got archers up top, there's no way we're getting out of here without heavy losses," the man said.

"We need to find a way up there," Tylindra said, setting the wounded man against the wall. "Gwen, I need you to stay here with Braeden. I'll be back as quickly as I can, but we've got to take care of those archers."

Gwen resisted the urge to panic. "I'm not a healer," she said.

"None of us are, but I can't carry him up the stairs with me. Just keep pressure on his wound until I get back. Can you do that?"

"Yes," Gwen answered.

"Good. Stay here."

Tylindra and the other human left. Gwen knelt beside Braeden and pushed her hand over the wound on his chest. A piece of a broken arrow shaft stuck out, and Gwen had to spread her fingers around it to put pressure on the wound. Blood seeped out anyway and coated her hand. Braeden groaned weakly, his eyes closed. Gwen swallowed hard, hoping the man didn't die, but the wound looked bad.

"Where are they?" she asked impatiently. The sounds of battle were getting less frequent, and Gwen didn't know which side was winning. Braeden's body slumped a bit and went still, his chest no longer moving. Gwen removed her hand, wiping the blood onto his clothes. He was dead and she knew it.

She stood and went in the same direction Tylindra had gone. There were more lifeless bodies, and she stepped over them as she navigated her way along the hall. A hand grabbed onto her ankle, and she screamed, jerking her foot away. It was a soldier. The man was surrounded by a growing pool of blood.

"Help," he rasped.

"Where's the prison?"

"Down b-below," he stuttered. "Please help me."

Gwen shook her head and backed away from him. Everything inside her screamed at her to help the man. She silenced the internal voice by imagining the soldier as the one responsible for torturing her father. The guilt lessened and she ran ahead. Gwen found stairs leading belowground and hurried down them.

She reached the bottom and rushed through the dimly lit tunnel, glancing into every cell. They were all empty. Gwen's heart began to pound in her chest. Had the soldier's killed them all? Her eyes welled with tears as she neared the end of the tunnel. There were only a few more cells left. Gwen heard a voice and paused. It sounded like …

"Tobias?" she called out.

"Gwen?"

Tobias stepped out from the last cell on the right and waved her forward. Gwen closed the distance and wrapped her arms around Tobias.

"Where's my father? Have you seen him?"

"He's in there," Tobias replied.

Gwen released him and hurried into the cell. Boris was lying on the ground covered in blood. Countless lash marks covered his flesh, but he was still alive.

"Father," Gwen said brokenly. She dropped to her knees, wanting to hold him but knowing it would cause him pain.

"Gwen," Boris whispered, his voice strained. "Closer."

Gwen leaned over her father, her eyes scanning his pain-filled face. "You're going to be all right," she said. Her tears spilled freely, some of them falling onto Boris's cheek. "We're going to get you out of here."

"No," Boris said. "I'm dying."

"Don't say that," Gwen sobbed.

"Listen to me …" Boris struggled to speak, and he fell silent for a moment. Gwen touched the side of his face, running her fingers along his wrinkled skin. "You're not my … real … daughter," he managed to say.

"What do you mean? You're all I've ever known."

"You were brought to us … a stranger left you …"

"Who?"

Boris tried to speak, but he coughed feebly, and blood flecked his lips. "I … love …" His voice failed and his head lolled to the side. Gwen threw herself onto her father and sobbed. She didn't want to believe that he was dead and told herself over and over that he was going to hug her any minute, but he never did.

"I'm sorry, Gwen," Tobias said softly.

She sat up and spun her head around to look at him. "You're sorry? It's your fault he's dead! If you and Roland had gathered these people faster, we could have gotten here earlier!"

Tobias let her rage at him, his head lowered. Gwen got up and struck Tobias in the chest over and over. She was overcome with pain and pushed past him, rushing along the tunnel and back up the stairs.

Gwen could hear Tobias following her, and she ran as fast as she could, not thinking about anything except escaping her grief. She entered the courtyard and kept running.

"Gwen!" Tobias shouted from behind her.

She turned around to unleash her anger at him again and spotted the shadowy silhouettes of archers on top of the outpost. The archers that she had completely forgotten about in her anguish. Time slowed.

There was a click.

A whizzing sound.

A wet thud.

Tobias dropped.

"No!" Gwen screamed.

CHAPTER 18

CONAL

For two days, they traveled south through the mountainous dwarf kingdom. Conal teamed up with Bryok and Torgreth, leaving Voldar to travel with Drustan.

"They should get on well," Torgreth chuckled. "They're both grumps."

Before setting out on their journey, Conal had admired the walking staffs Bryok and Drustan had in hand. "Where did you find those?"

"Had these made some time ago," Bryok replied, holding out the smooth ebony staff crowed with a carved dragon's head, two emeralds set in place as the eyes. "Here." He handed the staff to Conal.

"By the gods," Conal sputtered, surprised at the near weightless heft to the staff. Yet the wood felt hard and dense. "What sort of wood is this?"

"It's called dragonwood," Drustan answered, shifting an irritated look at Bryok. "And before you ask, you can't find it anywhere anymore. When the dragons died out, so did their forests."

"But you said you knew –"

"We better get going," Bryok interrupted, shooting a 'keep-your-mouth-shut-about-dragons' look at him.

Giving Drustan and Voldar an hour head start, they had been careful to stifle the urge to catch up. They had eschewed horses as Voldar reminded them that, "Dwarves don't ride horses. We have ponies. And I don't know where we're gonna find dwarf ponies around here."

Though Conal had been through parts of the northern tips of the kingdom back in his highwayman days, he was impressed with the beautiful ruggedness of the land, the thickly forested mountains, the small villages of stone-hewn cottages, and the friendliness of the citizens. Even the border guards were friendly.

When they had approached the border station, Torgreth took the lead. "Let me do the talking."

While Bryok and Conal patiently waited by the border barrier, Torgreth ambled over to the two guards. Conal couldn't hear what was said, but saw the guards point at Torgreth and grin. After a bit of conversation, the barrier pole raised, and the travelers wished a good trip.

Once they were out of ear shot, Conal asked, "What did you say to them?"

Torgreth smirked and leaned over. "They're cousins of mine on my Mama's side. Pointed at my clothes and said it didn't matter what I wore, they knew who I was. Told me to be careful, 'cause they're still lookin' for me and Voldar. Said Voldar and Drustan were about an hour ahead of us. They'll keep good and quiet for us. They don't like what's been goin' on either."

That was two days ago. Since then, the trip had been remarkably uneventful. The inns had the usual one or two 'big people' rooms where the beds were larger, but the tables and chairs were lower and Conal felt like his knees were hitting his chest when he ate, though the ale was good.

They were an hour from Morendir when they met up with Drustan and Voldar waiting in a clump of trees by the road. The road curved around a low hill before opening up to a wide valley. In the distance, the city lay tucked against the mountains, a double gate in the middle of the tall sloping crenelated walls. Carved into the mountain behind the sprawling city was the citadel, the castle keep of the king of Gurimduhr. Flanking the wide iron doors stood two granite statues twenty stories high of ancient warriors in helmet and armor, their hands resting on their swords.

"We need to find a place to stay," Drustan commented. "If the inn is still there, let's meet at the Stag and Boar."

"You been here before," Torgreth said, surprised.

"A long time ago."

"The inn's still there. It's a good choice, out of the way."

"Give us an hour head start," Drustan said.

Two hours later, Conal experienced the critical stare of the guards who studied him and Bryok with overt mistrust.

"What's yer business here?" one guard gruffly asked, ignoring Torgreth.

"Now just a minute you," Torgreth bowed up. "Since when do you harass folks that want to do business in our city?"

"Business? Bah. If yer merchants, where's yer stuff?" He abruptly frowned. "You look familiar."

"Well, you don't," Torgreth retorted. "And who said we were merchants? We're traders. Now can we be on our way?"

The guard hesitated then flipped a hand waving

them through.

"That was quick thinking," Conal quietly complimented as they walked through the gates.

Torgreth chuckled. "First thing I could think of."

The dwarf led them through the crowded streets. Despite the obvious abundance of dwarves, there were enough humans and even a few elves among the cacophony that Conal's and Bryok's presence was not unusual though Conal noted the curious looks of some of the residents while others seemed quite indifferent.

Torgreth turned off to a side street well before the main market square. Another side street later and they stood under the hanging carved wooden sign of a stag and boar. Entering the inn, Conal glanced around the main room, seeing Drustan and Voldar seated in the corner.

"About time you got here," Voldar groused.

Conal had yet to pull the chair out when the inn's door opened, and a dozen guards burst in. Catching sight of the new arrivals, they swarmed towards them.

"Hullo Voldar, Torgreth," the sergeant of the guard said with an arrogant grin. "Nice of you to come home. Who're yer friends." The sergeant was a stout dwarf with his dark brown beard done up on braids.

"Hullo Bagrun," Voldar sneered. "I see they let you outta yer cage again."

"Aren't you the comedian. You dressed fer a part in a play? Which part you playin', the whiny little girl or the idiot brother?"

"I tried out fer those parts, but they said you were playin' both. It was a stretch of actin', but they said you were perfect for the parts." He sipped his ale, his eyes locked on his adversary.

Several of the guards did their best to hide their smirks while Bagrun, unable to think of a repartee, pursed his lips.

"You been missed," Bagrun said, "and the king wants you back."

"You mean Havyrd wants us back."

"Don't matter who. You comin' peaceful?"

"What about my friends?"

"He wants to see them too."

"Why? They're not dwarves. They're just merchants."

Bagrun barked a laugh. "Merchants? You all better get your story straight."

"We're not here to cause trouble," Bryok placated, spreading his hands as if to show deference. "Of course we will come with you, Captain."

"Sergeant," Bagrun corrected though flattered.

"Ah, my apologies. I naturally assumed you were an officer as my experience in other kingdoms is that a king always sends a person of high rank when wishing to personally see someone. It is obvious the king must hold you in high regard."

"Yes, well, of course he holds me in high regard," he preened before casting a condescending eye on Voldar and Torgreth, "unlike someone else here who chose to tuck tail and run."

"Does it have to be right this minute?" Conal pleasantly asked, his plan to sneak into the citadel crumbling like a house of cards. "I haven't ordered yet."

"Yer drink can wait."

"C'mon," Voldar said with a longsuffering sigh, scooting his chair back and standing. "Let's get this over with before Bagrun says the king is gonna make him a general."

Bagrun led the way through the city, the group receiving a mixture of stares, some curious others more of a scowl at the king's guards who chose to ignore the deprecating looks.

Despite apprehension, Conal took in the surroundings, especially when they emerged from the city dwellings to the narrow bridge that crossed a deep chasm separating the citadel from the city. Built from the granite of the mountains, the bridge gently arced across the gorge ending at the wide portico that shielded the tall oak doors. He craned his head to gaze up at the twin statues, stained and darkened by the ravages of time.

"Step lively now," Bagrun commanded, leading them across the bridge.

Halfway across, Bryok covertly tapped Conal's hand. When Conal looked up at him, he placed something soft in Conal's hands. Conal glanced down at his cupped hand to see a clump of cotton. Puzzled, he shifted a glance back up to Bryok who, though focused to his front, tapped his ear several times as though brushing something away.

Understanding swept through Conal and he slipped the cotton into his pocket.

Once through the doors, they stepped into an expansive foyer with a high ceiling supported by delicately carved columns left in place when the chamber had first been cut out. The granite floor, polished smooth from the centuries of foot traffic, glimmered in a dull patina.

Bagrun directed them through the foyer and into a wide hallway leading to an even wider set of grand stairs within a room so large Conal turned around to take it all in. The room rose four stories high with balconies and stairs and doors heading off in all directions.

Of a curious note was the eerie quiet, for no dwarves bustled about their various duties. No doors opened or closed; no dwarves swarmed the stairs or dawdled on the balconies. It was as if everyone had gone home leaving the room to whatever ghosts might linger.

"Awfully quiet in here," Conal commented.

"Shush," Bagrun reprimanded. "You are a guest here. Act like one."

"Guest? I was ordered here. I'd just as soon go back to the inn where I was enjoying myself."

Glaring at him, Bagrun picked up the pace as they marched up the stairs.

Another hallway met them at the top of the stairs. They were halfway down when Bagrun stopped.

"We're almost to the King's Hall. Here's the rules. When you step through the door, you will kneel, then walk to the middle of the king's chamber and kneel again. If King Rorkyn recognizes you, he will tell you to come forward. When Havyrd tells you to stop, you stop and kneel three times. You wait until the king speaks to you first. When you are allowed to speak, you will begin with the greeting of "Blessings and Peace upon you, Great King." You are to bow each time you are requested to speak. Do not avert your eyes but look at him directly as an honest dwarf would."

"What?" Voldar exclaimed. "What kind of crap is this? Who came up with this garbage? Who's he think he is, some sort of god? I'm not gonna do all that nonsense." He defiantly folded his arms.

"Then you will be compelled to do it. You have no choice."

"I do have a choice," Voldar snapped. He turned

around and started to walk back to the stairs before breaking into a run.

"Stop him," Bagrun ordered.

But it was too late. By the time the guards reacted, Voldar had sped away, taking four stairs at a time as he leaped down to the next floor. However, instead of heading for the main doors, Voldar led the guards on a wild chase through the citadel.

With half his troop chasing Voldar, Bagrun's smugness began to evaporate. Praying that Voldar would be quickly cornered and brought back, his patience frayed the longer they waited. Deciding he better get the others into see the king before they too made a run for it, he ordered the group to move on, silently rehearsing his excuse when they entered the king's chambers.

Looking up at the two druids, he said, "You two need to leave your staffs outside."

Bryok placed a gentle hand on Bagrun's arm, fixing him with an intent stare. "You want us to take our staffs with us. We're just old men and you know we need them."

Bagrun blinked as he stared back at Bryok, surprised he hadn't noticed how decrepit the man was. He shifted a look at Drustan, noting the same aged frailty. "Yes, yes, of course you may take your staffs with you."

"Thank you."

Conal frowned at Bryok who held a finger to his lips then pointed to a rune on his arm.

At the end of the hall, two guards lounged next to the doors of the king's chamber, chatting amiably though obviously bored. Unaffected by the approaching group, they languorously reached to open the doors, one guard stifling a yawn.

"Wake up you two," Bagrun growled.

Ignoring him, they swung the doors open, waited for the last dwarf to enter then closed the doors behind them and resumed their desultory dialogue.

The room was not as large or grand as Conal expected. Lit by too few sconces and candelabra, the room felt dull mixed with a heavy lethargy. Bored guards sat on both sides of the doors, quietly talking amongst themselves. With a passing glance at the visitors, they returned to their conversations.

What Conal could see was a room with a high ceiling supported by columns. Sconces attached to the columns provided a row of lights leading to a throne set on a platform, the rest of the room fading into shadows.

Rorkyn sat on the throne, an overly large high-back chair draped with animal pelts, his feet barely touching the floor. The brooding face, wrinkled with age, stared vacantly at the floor, his white beard flat across his protruding belly. The hairline had receded so that only the back and sides of his head sprouted close cropped white hair. Beneath the woolen mantel, a shirt of chainmail glimmered in the reflected light. The once powerful arms that had wielded a stout double-bladed axe in battle had grown soft. The sword he usually held in his hands now leaned against the side of the throne. Glancing up when the door opened, he readjusted his crown and beckoned them forward.

"Remember to bow," Bagrun stage-whispered, leading them to the middle of the room and stopping.

Having forgotten when, where and the number of times to bow, Conal waited to take his que from the dwarves who were themselves confused for some bowed while others kneeled. Seeing their comrades in different poses caused them to adjust resulting in something that imitated the bobbing ponies on a merry-go-round.

"Damn it all," Rorkyn barked. "Just stand still." Glaring at the visitors, his thick brows furrowed, he scratched his cheek through the grey flecked auburn beard. "You," he snarled at Bagrun. "Where's the other dwarf? And who are these men?"

Bagrun swallowed hard. "Uh, well, your Majesty, uh… it seems that, what I mean to say is that, while I had the two brothers as you requested, one of them escaped, leaped right away, he did, before I could stop him."

"Your Majesty," a warm voice cooed, interrupting the interrogation. Out of the shadows, Havyrd edged up the stairs to stand next to the king.

Conal felt a sudden tranquility flush through him, and he smiled as he relaxed and studied the advisor to the dwarf king. Watching Havyrd lean in and whisper in the king's ear, Conal was surprised at how short the man was, probably no taller than the dwarf he advised. Unlike the brawn of a dwarf, Havyrd was thin and pale, like one who feared the sun. His thin unwashed black hair hung in strands down to his shoulders. He wore the robe of a wizard with loose cowl and draping sleeves. Conal's peace was momentarily broken when Havyrd turned to smile at him, his teeth root stained.

Havyrd swiveled his bony face back to the king. "My Lord, are we not absent a dwarf, the very one causing us the most trouble?" When he spoke, the room filled with a sweet calmness infused with lethargy, and an overwhelming urge to float in serenity.

Conal felt Bryok nudge him and shot a quick

glance to see him rub his ear. Taking the hint, Conal separated a piece of the cotton and, pretending to scratch his ear, stuffed the wadding into hole. He paused plugging the other ear when he noticed Havyrd shifting his gaze towards him.

"Where is Voldar?" the king demanded, glaring at Torgreth.

"Don't know," he shrugged. "Could be anywhere."

"Why did they flee?" Havyrd coached.

"Yes," Rorkyn nodded. "Why did you flee?"

"Didn't like making witchcraft spells for him," Torgreth answered, beginning to slur his words.

Avoiding the subject, Havyrd leaned in to Rorkyn. "Who did he bring here with him? Are they spies? Have Voldar and Torgreth turned against you? Are these men really assassins come to kill you?"

"We are simple merchants looking to trade," Bryok spoke.

Conal struggled to place the other wadding in his ear as though some terrible force clamped his body in place. Straining against the force, he bent his head down closer to his hand just in time to hear Torgreth's detached voice say,

"They are not merchants. They are assassins come to kill you."

CHAPTER 19

GWEN

Something inside Gwen snapped.

She felt the pulse of the magic and threw herself fully into it. Power coursed through every inch of her, welling internally with nowhere to go. Gwen screamed in pain and fell to her knees. Her flesh burned and sweat collected on her forehead. She recalled the name of the lightning rune and said, *"Tintreach."*

A jagged bolt of lightning arced from her hand, snaking its way through the dark sky and striking the soldiers atop the outpost. Their dying screams were like fuel to the fire burning within her. She spoke the rune again and again, blasting the front of the fortress until the stones cracked and sent fragments airborne.

People escaped the building, running and ducking for cover. Gwen didn't know if they were friend or foe, and she didn't care either. She just kept hurling lightning at the outpost as she slowly rose back to her feet. Tobias hadn't moved yet. In any other circumstance, Gwen would have panicked. In her current state, her sole focus was on the power flowing through her. She was like a conduit, allowing the raw force of nature to channel through her body.

Gwen saw a flash, then a sphere of steadily glowing light formed around a group of people exiting the outpost. Aimil was shielding them from the lightning. One of Gwen's bolts struck the shield and bounced off, ricocheting into the doorway of the outpost. The stones of the upper portion gave way and the entrance caved in.

Destruction was everywhere, but Gwen wasn't satisfied. She stalked forward and stood guard over Tobias as she blasted away at the outpost. The people who had fled were no longer in the way, and she unleashed even more rage. The magic was taking every ounce of strength she had. She was aware that she had lost control. That meant nothing to her. Someone was shouting her name, but she ignored their calls.

Gwen's legs trembled and her focus was fading. Darkness was creeping toward her, bidding her to enter its embrace. She wanted to slip into the darkness, to lose herself completely and never feel pain anymore.

But it was a lie.

The darkness didn't want to comfort her. It wanted to suffocate her. Gwen pushed the exhaustion away and regained control, then cut ties with her connection to the magic. Her strength was gone, and she collapsed beside Tobias. She wanted to check his wound, but she couldn't move, and her eyes wouldn't focus. They were dry and her eyelids were heavy. Gwen called his name, but she couldn't hear her own voice over the ringing in her ears.

Her struggle to keep the darkness at bay became a losing battle. She closed her eyes and sailed away into oblivion.

When Gwen awoke, light was shining through the

fabric of her tent. She was on her side and laid there for a long while, trying to remember where she was and how she had gotten there. Her memories were disjointed and the pounding in her skull didn't help. A shuffling noise at her side startled her and she rolled over to see Aimil sitting cross-legged.

"You're alive," Aimil said. Gwen couldn't tell if she was being sarcastic or not.

"Should I be dead?" Her voice was coarse and sounded like someone else's.

"With what I saw last night, I'm surprised you aren't. You lost control over the magic and nearly killed innocent people. I warned you about losing control."

"I don't remember much," Gwen said guiltily. "What happened?"

Aimil picked up a wooden bowl and handed it to Gwen. It contained water and Gwen sat up to drink from it. The liquid was cool and eased the ache in her throat, but the movement increased the pounding in her head.

"You demolished the outpost," Aimil said. "And a lot of other things. It's a good thing you went unconscious. You might have died otherwise."

"What about the prisoners? Are they safe?"

"A lot of them were already dead or dying. We didn't save many of them, but this wasn't just about them. This was a message to Torian. The people have had enough and are going to fight back. We slaughtered all but two soldiers."

"Why?" Gwen wanted them all dead.

"If there was no one to run to the king and tell him what happened, then what good would ransacking the outpost have done? They serve as our messengers."

Gwen drank the rest of the water and laid back

down. Her headache eased a little, but not much. "I feel like my head is going to split open," she complained.

"Accept it as a lesson learned," Aimil said. "Never use magic when your emotions are in turmoil."

"I don't plan to do that again."

"Good." Aimil stood and pushed the tent flaps open, then paused and looked back at Gwen. "Despite our victory, we lost many. Roland has the others packing up, but you should stay in here and get some rest. I'll come back when they are ready to break down your tent."

Aimil left, and Gwen stared up at the tent's ceiling. She remembered vividly that her father had died, but everything else was a blur. Her eyes welled with tears. She didn't think their outcome was much of a victory. And then she remembered what Boris had told her, that he wasn't her father. Eradore and Tobias had been right.

Tobias.

Gwen sat up too quickly and immediately regretted it. The world spun around her, and she became disoriented, but she managed to crawl outside of the tent before she retched. The dizziness faded and Gwen found enough strength to stand and survey the area.

Roughly half of the camp had been broken down already, and the rebellion members had commandeered two wagons that had been outside the outpost's stable. One of them was filled with bodies. Gwen shuffled toward it but was intercepted by Roland.

"You shouldn't be moving around," he said. His tone was authoritative, but the look on his face was one of concern. "How are you feeling?"

"Like I was hit by a boulder."

"Would you like me to help you back to your tent?"

"No, I can manage," Gwen replied. "Where's Tobias?"

It was only there for a brief moment, but the pained expression that crossed over his face said everything. Gwen's legs gave out, and she crumpled to the ground. She wanted to cry, but no tears flowed. Roland knelt and picked her up, then carried her back to her tent. He set her down gently and heaved a sigh.

"I'm sorry. I know Tobias was your friend. He was mine, too. The world has lost a good man. We're taking our fallen with us to ensure they receive a proper burial." He paused. "If you need anything, let me know."

Roland left her alone. She didn't want to believe that Tobias was dead. As the realization set in, she blamed herself. If she hadn't been so insistent on rescuing her father, then he'd still be alive. This time the tears did come. She had failed to save her father. Tobias was dead. What did she have now?

When Aimil eventually returned, Gwen had barely moved. She hadn't slept either, but merely stared off at nothing.

"It's time," Aimil said.

Gwen got up and followed her in silence. They left the tent and Aimil made Gwen grab some bread and an apple, then watched her eat it.

"Loss is never easy," Aimil said, climbing onto a large black horse. Gwen mounted the horse beside her, a smaller speckled gelding. The animal was docile and began a steady trot at Gwen's flick of the reigns. The two rode together without speaking, leaving the others behind. Gwen wondered why they were leaving without them but assumed they would catch up.

The silence became too much, and Gwen said, "I feel like it's my fault."

"That's a natural response," Aimil said. "But you are not to blame. Tobias would have gone to the outpost and fought whether you were involved or not."

"I don't think so. If my father hadn't been taken, Tobias wouldn't have had any reason to be there."

"Whether it was this outpost or another, this battle was going to happen regardless. Trust me, there is nothing to gain by blaming yourself. It won't bring the dead back and it won't make you feel any better."

Aimil spoke so matter-of-factly that Gwen decided it was impossible to argue with the woman. She considered Boris's last words again. If he wasn't her father, who was? And who was her mother?

"You said before there was a place where a mage could learn their true name," Gwen said. "Have you been there before?"

"Yes, a few times. Why do you ask?"

"I need to know who I really am," Gwen replied. "My father confirmed what Eradore told me, but he died before he could say who brought me to him."

"There's a mage I know in Steepcross who could give you a rune. She's a little … eccentric, but she's harmless. She has many runes you could choose from."

"As many as you?"

"No," Aimil replied. "There are few like me. At least, I've only encountered a few. There may be others, but I have only traveled among the human kingdoms."

"I've never traveled anywhere," Gwen said. "Is the trip dangerous?"

Aimil turned to look at her. "There is little danger, but it's a long journey. On a quick horse with minimal stops, it could take a few days. The place is on the border of Steepcross and Auleavell, the elven kingdom."

"I want to go," Gwen said. "Will you come with me?"

"I think I can do that," Aimil said, offering a smile. "Who knows, maybe I'll find another rune while we're there."

The two stopped to rest and stretch their legs, allowing the horses to graze near a stream. The rest of the rebellion members caught up to them, and they traveled as a group back to the city of Penshaw. Gwen tried not to think about the horrible events of the night before, turning her thoughts instead to the future.

When they reached Penshaw, Gwen and Aimil returned to Eradore's tower. Aimil relayed the events to Eradore while Gwen sat quietly. Although they had just arrived, Gwen was ready to go. She wanted to find out where her real parents were and why they had left her to be cared for by someone else.

"This minor victory came with a great cost. I'm afraid it may have set us back further than any of us anticipated," Eradore said. "Even so, we will continue to undermine the king and his rule."

"As we should," Aimil said. "Gwen and I are going to Steepcross. She wants to know her true name."

Eradore frowned. "I assumed she would, but not so quickly. Are you sure this is what you want to do?"

"It's not about what I want to do, it's about what I *need* to do," Gwen replied.

"Very well. No one will stop you, of course. You are free to do as you wish, but I would ask a favor of you."

"What is it?"

"I need a message delivered to a friend in Auleavell. I don't trust anyone else to do it, and magical means are … not the best option right now."

"Who am I taking it to?"

"Her name is Lyra, and she is an ally of the rebellion. She's trying to drum up support within the court of Auleavell, but it's not easy. Auleavell's king, Falael, wants nothing to do with our struggles."

"He's a coward," Aimil said.

"That remains to be seen," Eradore replied. "There are rumors that Torian wants to expand his kingdom. If it comes to war, Falael will have no other option but to fight. Lyra is trying to convince him of that. This letter will help her argument."

Eradore handed Gwen a scrollcase. She took it and held onto it tightly. "I'll deliver it to her as soon as I'm done in Steepcross."

"Thank you. I know you must have a lot on your mind, and I admire your tenacity to continue onward through the pain and the grief."

Gwen offered a nod.

"Let's get on with it, then," Aimil said. "We'll see you when we return, old friend."

Eradore smiled and escorted them out of the tower. Aimil led Gwen back to the stable they had boarded their horses at and retrieved them, then went to the market to get supplies. Aimil purchased everything they needed, then they left Penshaw behind, traveling east toward Steepcross.

Everything Gwen knew had only been a half-truth. There were so many uncertainties ahead, but

Gwen was ready to face them.
    She was finally going to learn who she really was.

CHAPTER 20

CONAL

Guards!" the king roared, leaning forward and thrusting a finger at Conal and the others. "Throw them in the dungeon."

Conal was the first to react, whirling around and yanking the sword out from Bagrun's scabbard. Bryok and Drustan followed suit, using their staffs to whack the nearby guards so hard as to knock them sprawling to the floor

Startled, Havyrd tried to regain control, using his most persuasive voice until he saw Conal advancing towards him. "You will put down your sword. Put down your sword." Fear exploded in his eyes when Conal failed to respond to his commands. Backpeddling away from the king, he shouted, "Kill them!" before spinning around and racing away.

But Conal intercepted him before he reached the door, spreading himself across the doorway.

Shocked at the man's speed, Havyrd jerked his arms out to his front, his hands as though reaching for Conal's throat as he voiced an incantation. "You cannot breathe. Your throat tightens. You are choking."

Impervious to his conjuring, Conal raised his

sword causing Havyrd to flinch, only to have his stroke blocked by Torgreth who had somehow managed to find a sword of his own.

"What are you doing?" Conal flared, suddenly defending himself against Torgreth's attack.

"That's right," Havyrd cried out. "You must protect me. Kill him."

"Protect Havyrd. Kill him," Torgreth intoned, pressing the attack.

While Conal deftly avoided Torgreth's blows, a panicked Havyrd sped back to the king, a terrible foreboding pulsing within that he was losing control.

The druids, doing their best to avoid killing or maiming the guards, had managed to corral them to a far corner.

"Get more guards," Havyrd shouted when the doors opened and Voldar marched in surrounded by the other half of Bagrun's troop.

Immediately understanding the discord, Voldar broke free and made a beeline towards Torgreth only to be slowed down when Havyrd intervened.

"Kill the intruders. Protect me."

Voldar jerked to a stop, confusion clouding his senses.

Seeing Voldar stop, Conal knew the reason. "Don't listen to him, Voldar," he cried out, parrying Torgreth's attack.

But it was too late as Havyrd's power swept through the dwarf and he looked around for a sword as the remaining guard members attacked the two druids.

"We need to get out of here, Sire," Havyrd urged, grabbing the aging king's arm.

"What's going on?" he growled as though suddenly aware of the fray.

"Assassins, Sire," Havyrd pressed, tugging the king's arm. "We got to go."

"What?" Rorkyn thundered. "You think me coward that I cannot defend myself!" It was then he saw Voldar reaching for his sword. "What are you doing? Get away from my sword."

"Must protect Havyrd," Voldar chanted, wrapping his fingers around the hilt.

"Dammit you," Rorkyn barked. "Let go my sword." He grabbed Voldar's hand.

Refusing to let go, Voldar and Rorkyn struggled over the sword, both trying to pry the other's hands from the grip.

Havyrd frantically scanned the room. His hopes rose as he saw the guards swarming around the two tall men. Over by the door, the younger man was fending off Torgreth and two guards. Standing to full height, he held his arms up and spoke in the most entrancing voice he could muster.

"Listen to me. Stop. Put down your weapons."

The effect was instant, and the dwarves immediately dropped their swords to their sides. The two druids, staffs held at the ready, likewise paused, warily regarding the dwarves surrounding them.

His confidence returning, Havyrd cast a haughty glare at the druids when out the corner of his eye he saw movement. His head jerked to the right to see the young man leaping towards him, sword raised.

Though surprised at the sudden lull, Conal reacted with speed, his body moving without thinking as he slipped past Torgreth and the two guards. He was upon Havyrd before the man had a chance to defend himself. The last thing Conal saw was the abject terror in the man's eyes as his arms moved up to block the blow.

In a blinding swift arc, Conal's blade swung down with such force, it sliced through the man's neck. The head momentarily wobbled before flipping down to the floor, blood spurting out the neck as the body crumbled to the ground.

It wasn't until he stood over the decapitated body that the enormity of his act burst within, for he had finally killed a man. The first impulse was to retch. It wasn't that he hadn't seen men killed before. It's just that someone else was always responsible.

Fighting back the taste of bile, he flicked his head around to see the startled dwarven faces when a faint burst of reddish light filled the room for an instant then vanished.

The king was the first to speak. "What goes on here?" His thick brows furrowed in a deep 'V'. He stared down at the headless body of his former confidant and the pool of blood creeping around the still warm flesh. He blinked in lucid understanding.

He snapped his head up to give Conal a hard stare. "Did you do this?"

Realizing the king had spoken to him, Conal stood to full height and pulled the cotton form his ears. "Sire?"

"I said, 'Did you do this?'"

"Yes, Sire."

Rorkyn's attention abruptly shifted to the gloom of the room. "Why is it so dark in here?"

"That is the way he wanted it, Sire," Bagrun replied, flicking his hand at a guard to light more sconces.

As the room filed with light, the king returned his focus on Conal then the two druids. "Who are you?"

"I am Conal, Sire." He respectfully bowed.

"Why did you kill him?"

"He was evil, Sire."

Rorkyn's face scrunched as he struggled to remember, snippets of the past year gaining clarity. "Why was he evil?"

"He had the magic of the Rune Tongue, King Rorkyn," Bryok answered.

Rorkyn shifted his gaze to discover who spoke, seeing Voldar and Torgreth standing to the side. "You two! You ran away from here."

"Yes, Sire," Voldar boldly replied, stepping forward. "We ran because no one would do anything about him." He jabbed a finger at the crumpled corpse. Seeing the king returning to himself again, Voldar unbridled his tongue. "He had power over you. You did everything he wanted you to do. The kingdom is falling apart and all you did was sit on the throne and let Havyrd rule. He was destroying everything. Instead of mining and building like any respectable dwarf would do, he had us carving runes into bones."

As his memory crystalized, Rorkyn twisted his head to level a stare at the two druids. "Who are you?"

"I am Drustan, Sire." He bowed. "And this is my brother Bryok. We are half-druids." Seeing Rorkyn's stiffen, he hastily added, "We are not here to harm you. In fact, we are here to seek your help."

"Help?" Rorkyn placed a hand under his chin and twisted his head, cracking his neck before staring at Bagrun. "Get me something to drink… an ale."

"Yes, Sire," he replied before pointing a finger at a guard. "Get the king an ale."

"Where are all your servants, Sire?" Bryok asked, noting the absence of anyone except the guards.

"Don't need servants," he gruffly answered. "At

least, I don't think I do… do I?" The last was directed at Bagrun.

"No, Sire. We're dwarves, remember? We don't have servants."

"Of course I remember," he growled. "I'm a dwarf, dammit." His attention snapped back to Drustan. "Help with what?"

Wondering if Havyrd's spell still lingered in the old man, Drustan explained, "Your advisor was a servant of Grimmar the Mage Breaker, advisor to the king of Isentol."

"Torian?" he barked. "That man has the gall to send someone to infiltrate my court?" He pushed himself to standing, wobbling a bit before demanding, "Where's my ale?"

The doors burst open, and the guard returned with a pitcher of ale and an artfully carved pewter stein. "It's coming, Sire." With the help of another guard, he filled the stein and handed it to Bagrun who handed it to the king.

Rorkyn downed the entire contents in four swallows, smacking his lips. "Ah, Now I can think. Alright druid, speak. What is it you want?"

"Torian gains power, even as we speak. His army grows as does the strength of his magical arts."

"He's a magician, a wizard?" Rorkyn frowned, holding out the stein for a refill.

"No. He's gathered wizards and sorcerers and mages to his court. Their numbers grow daily."

With each passing minute, Rorkyn's clarity improved, and he blinked in understanding. "The man has been raiding my northern frontier for the past several months… and I've done nothing about it." He cast a disgusted look at Havyrd's corpse. "Now I understand why."

"We are racing to get the surrounding kingdoms to join together to stop him," Bryok said. "Will you join us?"

"Who is 'we'?"

"Already rebellion occurs near in and around Isentol. Rhonyn awaits in your north."

"Who is he?" Rorkyn sat and leaned forward, forearms on his thighs

"He is a friend who owes allegiance to no man or dwarf."

"Or elf?"

"Or elf," Bryok agreed. "He comes when he's needed and right now, he knows he's needed."

"He has an army?" Rorkyn leaned back and scratched his cheek.

"His army is small, but elite."

Rorkyn paused to think. "That's it? That's all you got?"

"Sire," Drustan patiently explained. "We don't know who else has agreed. Like us, our friends have spread through the kingdoms garnering support. We don't know who else has agreed."

"But we do know," Bryok interrupted, "that if nothing is done, this kingdom will fall to Torian, just like all the others."

Rorkyn pursed his lips, his head bobbing in a slow nod. Conal again caught his attention. "Who are you?"

Conal sucked in a slow breath of irritation, and repeated, "I am Conal, Sire."

"Are you a druid?"

"No, Sire."

His stare narrowed when he saw the rune markings on Conal's arm. "Then who and what are you?"

Deciding to keep his newly discovered heritage to himself for the moment, Conal opened his shirt and pulled it back to reveal the tattoo. "I'm a Cobra."

Rorkyn jerked back while the other dwarves stutter-stepped away in fear.

"Assassin." Rorkyn gripped the arms of the throne chair.

"Yes." Conal strutted to stand before the king. "But have no fear, Great King. My quest is to restore the Kingdom of Isentol to the House of Kamron."

Though flattered to be called 'Great King,' Rorkyn cocked his head to the side. "Thought the House of Kamron died when he did."

"It is rumored his children still live," Bryok said, shooting Conal an irritated look.

"We're wasting precious time," Drustan interrupted. "We need an answer. Will you help or not?"

"Forgive my impetuous brother, Sire." Bryok smoothly said, cocking an eyebrow at Drustan. "Yet he does have a point. Time is critical."

"Let me think about it," Rorkyn hesitated.

Before Bryok could entreat him further, Drustan said, "You have a bone room?"

"A what?"

"Yes," Bagrun answered for him, stepping up. "Havyrd had us carve runes into all sorts of bones then kept them in a room that only he had the key for."

Torgreth bent down and patted Havyrd's headless body, eventually turning him over. "Here it is." He lifted the key attached to a chain around the neck, wiping the blood off on Havyrd's robe.

"Where is the room?" Drustan asked.

"We know where it is," Voldar answered.

"Sire." Bryok's voice rose in volume. "The rune bones are dangerous. They need to be destroyed."

"But not by just anyone," Drustan joined in.

"You mispronounce the rune and you're dead," Conal added. "One can only imagine what Havyrd had in mind when he had these made." Conal hadn't a clue what he was talking about, but he figured if he sounded ominous enough, he'd be helping the two druids.

"What do you suggest we do with them," Rorkyn asked, assuming a regal air.

"With your permission," Bryok replied, "we will take them with us, away from the kingdom"

"Why?" Rorkyn said, suddenly suspicious. "We have mages and wizards here in Gurim-duhr. Perhaps they ought to look at them first."

"If you so wish, Sire. But remember, Havyrd was Grimmar's man. Grimmar pretends to hate magic when, in fact, he is merely eliminating the competition, keeping those loyal only to him."

"Do you trust all your wizards and mages?" Conal asked. "Be a pity if one or more turned on you and you'd be right back where you were with Havyrd."

Rorkyn snarled at the thought. "Fine. Do what you want with them. Just get them out of here."

"Thank you, Sire." Bryok bowed.

"Will you fight with us?" Drustan challenged.

Rorkyn scrunched his face and stared at Bagrun. "Where're all my generals?"

"Spread throughout the kingdom, Sire, far away from here," Bagrun boldly answered. "Havyrd didn't want anyone around who might sway his control over you, so he had you order them to patrol the kingdom."

"Who's in command around here?"

Bagrun thought for a moment. "I guess I am,

Sire."

"What rank do you hold?"

"I'm a sergeant, Sire."

"A sergeant?" Rorkyn sputtered. "That fool entrusted my safety to a mere sergeant? That's irresponsible. I can't allow that. You are promoted to captain. Find someone to replace you."

Bagrun's initial annoyance at the 'mere sergeant' comment morphed to surprise at the sudden promotion to captain, skipping over lieutenant. "Yes, Sire."

"What's your recommendation, captain?"

Bagrun closed his mouth and rapidly thought about the past year before saying, "Go for it, Sire. Be the first one to join, if that's the case. Let no one say that a dwarf wasn't at the front, leading the way."

"Well spoken, captain." Rorkyn turned to Bryok. "You have my answer."

"Thank you, Sire"

"The bone room?" Drustan urged.

"Go." Rorkyn flipped a hand at them, shooing them away. "You go with them, Captain Bagrun."

"Yes, Sire."

Voldar led the way to a room close by, adjacent to Havyrd's quarters, inserting the key into the padlock and opening the door.

The room was the size of a large walk-in closet, filled with crates of rune bones stacked on top of each other. Bryok and Drustan shared an apprehensive glance then walked in. Selecting a bone from an open crate, Drustan was the first to react.

"I hope we're not too late." He flipped it over to show Bryok then flung the bone back into the box.

Bryok selected another bone and turned it for Drustan to see.

The half-druid's head shot up to gape at his brother. "This does not bode well."

"What?" Conal asked, not sure he wanted to hear the answer.

Ignoring him, Drustan turned to Bagrun. "How often did Havyrd send the bones north?"

Bagrun swallowed hard. "Every couple of weeks, protected by dwarves until they got to the border. Then the man-guards took over. We haven't sent a shipment since Voldar and Torgreth took off."

"How long is that?"

"About a month," Voldar answered.

Bryok studied the number of boxes in the room. "Looks like he was keeping back quite a bit. Why?"

"What's on the bones?" Conal demanded.

"Incantations," Drustan replied.

"I know that," Conal huffed. "What kind of incantations?"

Instead of answering, Drustan turned to Bagrun, desperation in his voice. "We need to get these out of here, now. We need a wagon. We also need all these crates nailed shut."

As Bagrun whirled around to issue orders, Drustan leaned in towards Bryok. "We need to split up. I'll take the bones back to our place. You and Conal head back to Tir Manach."

"Why?" Conal interrupted.

"Because King Caldyr needs persuasion and you're the man to do it."

"Me?" Conal squeaked. "Why would he listen to me?"

"Because Lord Pharyl is favorably inclined to you," Bryok answered.

"Yeah, but he's not the king," Conal argued.

"He's close enough," Drustan firmly stated.

"Bryok will go with you to protect you."

"How about a dwarf?" Torgreth interrupted, causing the three men to twist their heads to frown at him. "What I mean is that I can help persuade King Caldyr. Tell him that Rorkyn is already assembling the dwarf armies."

Drustan nodded. "Good idea." Addressing Bryok, he said, "Once I get the bones safely away, I'll head up north to connect with Rhonyn. Meet me there."

Conal listened as Drustan gave further instructions. A thought popped into his head. *Wonder if we might bump into Oscon. Wouldn't that be sweet. I'd teach him a lesson he'd never forget.*

'Wake up, Conal," Bryok chastised. "We need to go. And you need to forget about Oscon."

Conal's eyes popped wide. "How'd you know what I was thinking?"

"I'm a half-druid, remember?" Bryok answered with a smile. "Besides, we don't have time to deal with the little fish."

"Little fish?" Conal scrunched a face in confusion.

"Didn't you know?"

"Know what?"

"About Oscon."

"What about him?"

Bryok studied him for a moment, realizing Conal had no clue. "Oscon is Caldyr's man, reporting back to him about what's going on in the kingdom."

"You mean…" Conal's jaw dropped.

Bryok chuckled. "Yes. The entire time you thought yourself a highwayman, you've been working for the king." Letting Conal stew for only a moment, he added, "But Oscon serves two masters. All the reports he sent back were conveniently intercepted by another whose master lives in Havengarde."

Conal's jaw tightened. He'd been played the fool more than once. It was time to become the Cobra he was destined to be.

RUNE MARKED

BOOK 2

CHAPTER 1

GWEN

Gwen could smell rain in the air.

Her mount's ears perked up as thunder rumbled ominously overhead, but otherwise, the animal continued trudging along the road undeterred. Aimil rode next to Gwen, her attention focused ahead.

"Should we try to find shelter?" Gwen asked.

Aimil shrugged. "A little rain never hurt anyone."

Gwen decided that was a fair point, but she didn't find the idea of getting soaked very appealing. Since she had no idea how to get to their destination, she was left with no other choice but to continue following Aimil.

The rain started as a gentle sprinkle and quickly turned into a downpour. The road was worn from wagon traffic and the indents left from the wheels quickly filled with water, tinted brown from the dirt.

Between the storms and the complete lack of civilization, Gwen was glad to have Aimil's company over the last few days. The woman had her quiet moments, but she never shied away from conversation. Any time Gwen started to think about her father or Tobias, she would divert her mind by asking Aimil a random question. If Aimil had grown tired of her, she did well to hide it.

They rode through the storm and the sun eventually returned, making the air feel thick and humid. Gwen's wet clothes stuck to her skin, irritating her and making her mutter foul curses under her breath. The two traveled a half-mile after the last of the rain fell before Gwen spotted a town ahead. A poorly made sign displayed the town's name: Woodpine.

"Have you been here before?" Gwen asked.

"I usually pass through without stopping. There's not much to see."

Gwen frowned in disappointment. Aimil hadn't set a breakneck pace by any means, but it was steady with few stops. Unless she had to relieve herself, Aimil barely left the saddle. As the road led them into the heart of Woodpine, Gwen found the place similar to Dawsbury. They even had an inn, which made Gwen question what Aimil meant when she said there wasn't much to see. There was always something interesting to see at an inn.

Aimil continued through the town without stopping and as they were about to cross over a small bridge, a group of armed men stepped into the road in front of them. They wore piecemeal armor and their weapons were more rust than metal.

"Halt!" One of the men shouted, pointing a spear at Aimil's horse.

Gwen pulled on the reins, forcing her mount to stop. Aimil continued ahead until the spear tip was inches from her horse before she directed the animal to stop. The man with the spear seemed uncertain and glanced around at his fellows.

"What's the issue?" Aimil asked.

"You've got to pay the toll," the man with the spear said.

"Yeah, pay the toll!" Another chimed in.

"Are you in service to the king of Steepcross?"

"Bah! The king is a fool," the spearman replied. "He's off in his castle ignoring all the problems around here. So, you know what we said? We said, 'we're going to make our own laws.' And one of those laws is you have to pay a toll to cross this bridge."

"And if I don't want to pay the toll?" Aimil asked calmly.

"Then we'll take it from you by force," one of the other men threatened.

"Move out of my way," Aimil said.

The group of brigands exchanged looks and whispers with each other, and Gwen assumed that they must not have received a reaction like Aimil's before. They seemed confused about how to handle Aimil. Finally, the spearman poked the horse and said, "Pay first, then we'll move."

Aimil looked at Gwen, then back at the brigands. Gwen saw the look in Aimil's eyes and guessed trouble was going to ensue. She was about to turn her horse around when Aimil lifted her left arm and said, "*Tine!*"

Flames erupted from her hand, catching the spear on fire and causing the group of men to stagger back from the heat. The apparent leader dropped the spear and threw his hands up in defeat.

"I don't like repeating myself," Aimil said.

"No need to," the man said hurriedly. "Let's go, boys. Clear the way!"

The brigands dispersed from the road and Aimil flicked her reins. Her mount continued along the road and Gwen urged her horse to follow. As they crossed the bridge, Gwen thought she could hear someone crying out for help. There was a shack on the left, old and dilapidated. She guessed the sound was coming from there.

"Do you hear that?" Gwen asked.

"It's probably a trap," Aimil replied.

"Maybe, but what if it's not?"

Aimil stopped her horse and turned her gaze on Gwen. "If it is, are you prepared to have the blood of these fools on your hands? We can easily leave right now, but if it's a trap and we have to fight our way out, these men will die. Swords and spears cannot overpower magic."

Gwen hesitated. The cry for help sounded genuine. She couldn't leave knowing someone might need help, but the thought of killing the brigands didn't sit well with her, either.

"I think we should check it out."

"Suit yourself," Aimil said. She dismounted and headed for the shack. Gwen slid out of the saddle and jogged to catch up. The brigands watched them until Aimil opened the door of the shack. The leader stalked toward them.

"Stop!" He shouted. "Don't go in there!"

Aimil ignored him and stepped inside. Gwen peeked through the doorway curiously, but she kept her focus on the men around them. Gwen lifted her arm, facing her palm at the approaching leader. He stopped in his tracks, but his expression revealed his anger. Aimil stepped out a moment later, followed by a young elf.

Despite his disheveled look and dirty clothes, Gwen thought there was something regal about the elf. His blond hair was matted and a smear of blood ran the length of his forehead. Twin pools of emerald green stared at Gwen and she averted her gaze, somehow feeling inferior.

"That's our elf," the brigand leader said.

"Says who?" Aimil questioned.

"Says me. We captured him fair and square. You aren't stealing our reward."

"Reward?" Gwen asked. "What do you mean?"

"That elf is the prince of Auleavell. He ran off and his father is offering a reward to anyone who returns him. Me and my boys are going to do just that."

"No, I don't think so," Aimil said. "He's coming with us."

"Are you deaf, woman? I just said you aren't stealing our reward."

"How much is the elven king offering?"

"A thousand gold astrals."

"How about a wave of flames and death instead?" Aimil asked.

The leader's bravado disappeared and he spat on the ground. "Blasted mage," he grunted.

"He'll ride with me," Aimil told Gwen, then she walked back to where they'd left the horses. The brigands eyed them with hatred, but none of them were brave enough to risk testing Aimil's promise of death.

Gwen mounted her horse and waited for Aimil to take the lead. She continuously looked over her shoulder to make sure the men weren't doing anything. Aimil's horse began trotting along and Gwen urged her mount into motion. They put a decent distance between them and Woodpine, then Aimil guided her horse to the left, off the road. They rode into a thicket of trees and Aimil dismounted, trying her reins to a tree branch.

"What are we doing?" Gwen asked. "It's still daylight."

"I want to make sure those fools don't do anything stupid," Aimil replied. "The last thing we need is to be surprised in the middle of the night."

"Good point," Gwen said, dismounting and tying her horse next to Aimil's.

The elf they'd rescued was subdued. He sat down on the ground among the trees. His eyes moved back and forth from Gwen to Aimil.

"Let me guess," he said. "You're going to take me back to my father and take his money."

"Possibly," Aimil replied. "Then again, maybe not. What are you doing out here, anyway?"

"I left my father's court willingly," he answered. "His closed view of the world around us is suffocating, at best. I've heard the gossip among my father's servants. King Torian is threatening our peaceful way of life. My father doesn't believe Torian is a menace, so he's ignoring the rebellion's pleas for help. I refuse to stand with my father on this."

"So, you ran off to a human kingdom?" Aimil asked. "You do know Auleavell and Steepcross aren't exactly on friendly terms, right?"

"I know that," the elf said. "I'm not a fool. I was on my way to Isentol to find the rebellion when those humans attacked me. Attacked me! Within Auleavell's borders, no less. How they managed to get past our patrols is a mystery that's been plaguing me for days."

"Well, it seems you are in luck," Gwen said. "Aimil and I are part of the rebellion against King Torian."

"Truly? Oh, thank the goddess. I was afraid I had

traded one captor for another."

"What's your name?" Gwen asked.

"Kirith of House Euldin."

"Well, Kirith, it seems your friends aren't quite ready to give up on that reward," Aimil said. "Stay low."

Gwen hid behind a large tree and peered around the edge. The brigands they'd left behind were coming up the road swiftly, all of them riding horses. Gwen guessed they had stolen them from the people of Woodpine.

The leader slowed his mount and whistled, pointing toward the thicket where Gwen and her companions were hiding.

"The tracks go that way," he said.

Gwen watched the men dismount and draw their weapons. She looked at Aimil. The woman had turned her attention behind them. She tilted her head to the side, listening to something Gwen couldn't hear.

"What is it?" Gwen whispered harshly.

Aimil held up her finger, a sign for Gwen to be quiet. Kirith's head jerked to the side and his eyes widened.

"Sentinels are coming!" he warned.

Aimil cursed and beckoned Gwen to come closer. The two women rushed to where Kirith was and Aimil closed her eyes. A moment later, one of the runes on her right arm began to glow with a sickly green light.

"Don't move," Aimil said softly. "I can hide us visibly, but noise can still be heard."

Gwen stood completely still. She didn't realize she was holding her breath until she started to hear her heart beating in her ears.

Kirith slowly lifted a hand and pointed. Gwen looked and didn't see anything at first, but then she saw movement. It was almost imperceptible. A tall elf wearing leather armor that mirrored his surroundings slipped through the thicket without a sound. He carried a bow in one hand and a quiver of arrows across his back.

The elf stopped when he spotted the brigands and raised his bow, slipping an arrow onto the string. He took aim and paused. Gwen wondered what he was waiting on, but then she spotted more movement. Three other elves, similarly dressed as the first, moved into position and readied their arrows.

At an unspoken command, the elves let their arrows fly at the same time. Each arrow struck a target, taking down half the group of brigands. The leader shouted a retreat, but the elven sentinels fired off another round of projectiles to finish the job.

Gwen swallowed hard and hoped the elves would disappear as quickly as they returned. Kirith closed his eyes and lowered his head into his hands. The elves investigated the bodies of the brigands and then left in the direction they'd come. Gwen looked at Aimil. The woman had her eyes open now, and she was watching the trees intently.

"Are they gone?" Gwen whispered.

An arrow whizzed past her face, so close she felt the wind stir against her lips. She jerked her head back belatedly in surprise and noticed an elf standing behind Aimil. She pointed wordlessly, her eyes widened in terror. The elf pressed the tip of a sword to Aimil's back.

"Tell me why I shouldn't end your life," the elf demanded.

CHAPTER 2

CONAL

One hand on top of the other, resting on the pommel of his saddle, Conal sat astride his steed on the crest of the road, staring at the city of Hemlin in the near distance, remembering the last time he was here. "Are you sure we have to go in there?"

"We need a place to rest," Bryok reminded him. "Besides, you're a different person than the last time you were here." He flicked his reins, urging his mount forward.

Conal ticked his head at the city. "Tell that to them."

"I'm hungry," Torgreth said, squeezing the flanks of his stout pony.

"Why'd we come this way when we're supposed to be heading to Denhelm," Conal complained, catching up to ride beside the dwarf.

"Like I've already said… several times," Bryok answered with a hint of frustration, "we need to meet with someone here." He scanned the road and the surrounding farmland. All seemed normal with the usual traffic headed in and out of the city gates.

"Who is this guy again?" Conal asked.

"He's a friend. He's the one who told me about you."

Conal raised an eyebrow in doubt. "If you knew about me, why didn't you come get me, *before* I got branded?"

Bryok paused then said, "Because there were other matters that demanded my attention."

"Like what?"

Bryok cast a glance at Torgreth. "Like two dwarves that needed immediate rescuing."

"Yer brother scared the piss out of us," Torgreth chuckled.

"Drustan can be intense at times."

"Ya think?" Conal snorted a laugh.

Merging into the ebb and flow of travelers, farmers, clerics, and merchants, Conal was surprised when the two guards at the gate paid them scant attention. "Something's not right," he quietly commented as they passed through the gatehouse. "They didn't even make eye contact."

"Maybe they're bored," Torgreth offered.

"They weren't bored the last time I was here," Conal countered. It wasn't until they were halfway up the main street towards the market square that he blurted, "They're not real guards."

"What?" Bryok and Torgreth replied in unison.

"They're not real guards," Conal repeated, spinning around. "Look at the uniforms. They're wearing the red jackets, but where's the rest of the uniform? The boots? The helmet?"

Bryok paused to cast a concerned glance over his shoulder. "We need to find my friend. Find out what's going on. Follow me."

Bryok set a brisk pace, taking streets and alleyways around the market square to the stables.

Once their mounts were settled, Bryok led them deeper into the back alleys of the city. At the corner of one alleyway, Conal grabbed his two companions' arms and dragged them into the shadows.

"Wha –" Torgreth began before Conal jabbed a finger to his lips and pointed across the street to a man pretending to be nonchalant, leaning against the wall by a residence door as he studied the passersby.

"That's Jestyn. Oscon has to be close by." Conal's sudden desire for revenge bubbled up as he silently deliberated how.

"Leave him," Bryok urged. "We'll deal with him later. We need to find my friend."

"I'm not going until I see what he's up to."

"We don't have time for this," Bryok fussed. "We'll come back for him."

Ignoring him, Conal lifted a foot to step out when the door opened and Oscon emerged, blinking in the sunlight. "There you are," Conal snarled.

He was halfway across the street before anyone realized. Jestyn was the first to see him.

"Well look who's back," he mocked until he saw the grim determination in Conal's eyes. Immediately interspersing himself between his boss and the approaching former highwayman, he placed a hand on the handle of the dagger by his side, a warning that he would not hesitate to use it. Remembering the young man's past with the highwaymen, he was neither intimidated nor worried that he could handle this young pup.

"Hold it right there," Jestyn ordered, a hand pressed forward.

Conal stared past Jestyn to see the smirk plastered on Oscon's face, a smirk that said he would repeat Conal's humiliation if necessary.

Oscon's arrogance grew when Jestyn slipped the blade out and pointed it at Conal. His smirk abruptly vanished when Conal smacked the blade out of Jestyn's hand then delivered such a blow to the man's chest that it cracked several ribs and sent him flying backwards to crash against the stonewalls of the building only to crumple into a heap on the street.

What followed next happened so fast that Oscon wasn't quite sure how he ended up with Conal's hand wrapped around his throat, his body lifted inches off the ground. What he did know was the vice-grip squeezing his throat hurt and he couldn't breathe. In desperation, he grabbed the dagger in his boot and swung up to stab Conal in the gut, only to have his thrust stopped short, Conal's grip so tight that he felt his hand grow numb, the blade slipping from his fingers to rattle on the ground.

"You set me up," Conal growled, his anger adding power to his strength. "You condemned me to be a slave."

He felt a calm hand touch his arm and heard Bryok say, "Let's not kill him quite yet. We still need information from him."

"C'mon Conal," Torgreth urged when Conal hesitated. "You can kill him later. I'll even help if you want. We can cut off his fingers then his toes, peel his eyelids off and even cut out his tongue."

Startled at the gruesome details, Conal twisted his head to gaze at the dwarf who returned his look with a loopy grin. "You are one strange dwarf," he chuckled, shaking his head.

"Mama said the same thing about me." Torgreth's grin widened.

Conal relaxed his grip and Oscon sucked in a deep breath.

Bryok stared down at Oscon. "You're coming with us. You make one false move and you're a dead man."

"What about him?" Torgreth hooked a thumb at Jestyn who hadn't moved, his hands clutching his ribs.

"Leave him," Bryok answered. "Doubt he'll be going very far anytime soon."

Torgreth bent down and picked up Oscon's dagger, twisting it around in his hands. "Nice dagger. Where'd you get it?"

Oscon shifted a wary glance at them, his hand rubbing his throat. "Bought it a while ago."

"Really?" Torgreth shot him a 'you're a liar' look. He held up the dagger so that his two friends could see. "This dagger is made from dwarven iron. The smith's mark is here." He pointed to a symbol beneath the quillon. "Note the crown in the mark? The maker was a king's smithy." He turned to give Oscon a hard stare. "There hasn't been a king's smithy in any dwarven land for over 150 years."

"How do you know that?" Conal asked, impressed.

"Because the last king's smithy was Gunnar Iron-hammer. He was my grandfather." Narrowing his stare at the man, his lip curled in anger. "I'll ask you once more. Where did you get it?"

Oscon looked down upon the dwarf, shrugging in feigned ignorance.

Torgreth turned to Bryok. "Can I kill him?"

"Not yet," Bryok answered with a curious frown. "What more can you tell us of the blade?"

"It was most likely a gift from my grandfather to the king in Isentol."

"Kamron?" Conal blurted.

"No, my young friend," Torgreth answered with an indulgent smile. "It would have been King Cered, Kamron's great-great grandfather." He turned back to Bryok. "This is a king's gift, which means it is also probably elven imbued." He twisted his head to give Oscon a look of disdain. "And this fool probably didn't even know it."

"Elven imbued?" Conal marveled before a curtain pulled back from nearby window diverted his focus and he suddenly noticed passersby slowing their stride to gawk. "We're beginning to draw attention."

Torgreth jabbed the dagger point into Oscon's side. "Start walking. Pray that I don't accidently stumble and stick this all the way in."

Oscon's arrogance returned as he moved away from the door and into the street. Catching Jestyn's eye, he ticked his head in a quick nod, receiving a nod of understanding in return. "You fools. You don't know who yer messin' with. When word gets out what you done, yer lives won't be worth a copper royal."

Conal noted the exchange between the two outlaws and calmly walked over to Jestyn who had struggled to his knees. Grabbing him by his shirt, he effortlessly lifted him up to dangle above the street.

"Don't think I've forgotten your part in all this. When I'm finished with Oscon, I'm coming for you. I will make you suffer like never before. Tell the rest of them. I'm coming for them too. You all betrayed me. I don't care where you run. I will find you."

His anger growing, Conal spun around, Jestyn whirling like a rag doll, and flung his former associate against the stone wall. Jestyn flopped to the ground, his arm broken.

Leaving Jestyn groaning in pain, Conal twisted

his head to glare at the passersby who quickly gave urgency to their steps.

"My, my," Oscon sneered with false bravura, "such violence. Pity I didn't know this about you before. I can use a man like you."

"We need to go," Bryok intervened.

Leading the way, Bryok led them through streets and back alleys as they moved single file, with Oscon behind Bryok, Torgreth behind Oscon, the dagger's blade firm against the man's side, and Conal bringing up the rear. At one nondescript door halfway down a deserted alley, Bryok stopped and knocked in a rhythmic pattern of three-two-three-one knocks. A peephole door slid to the side.

Bryok leaned forward and whispered, "Dragon home."

The peephole door closed, and the heavy oak door silently swung open revealing a hulking brute of a man whose intimidating scowl reminded those attempting to force their way in that he would personally inflict mayhem on them.

"Is he here?" Bryok asked.

The man nodded and lifted a thick arm to point down the darkened corridor.

By the tine Conal entered, Bryok was hallway down the hall. The door closed behind him and he squinted to see light coming from beneath the door at the end of the hall. Light spilled out into the corridor when Bryok opened the door then stood to the side as the others stepped into a large room sparsely furnished whose sole occupant stood close to the fireplace, reading a book on a tall book stand. Wall sconces surrounding the room provided more than ample light.

Conal startled for the tall individual behind the

book stand was an elf.

"Greetings, Galadyr," Bryok said with a respectful nod.

"Greetings, my friend," the elf replied with a warm smile, closing the book. Galadyr stood a little taller than Conal. He wore a sleeveless tunic of supple forest brown leather, and woolen breeches the color of faded crimson, tucked into stout leather boots that ended just below his knees. His long blond hair was held back by a braided leather cord wrapped around his forehead revealing the telltale pointed ears.

"This one," Bryok indicated Oscon, "needs guarding."

No sooner had he finished that the door opened and the hulking man at the outside door stepped in.

"Take that one," Galadyr said, pointing a slender finger at Oscon, "and see that he is well contained."

"What's going on?" Oscon demanded. "You can't treat me like this."

The hulking man growled and went to reach for Oscon.

"Easy Brunet," Galadyr soothed before addressing Oscon. "You have a choice on how you can leave this room. Choose wisely."

Oscon's eyes twitched from Brunet to Conal to the elf, knowing he had only one choice. Snarling, he jerked around to follow Brunet.

Once the door closed behind them, Galadyr shifted his devoted attention to Conal. "Is this he?"

"Yes," Bryok answered. "What's going on in the city? Who is guarding the gates?"

"There has been some unrest," Galadyr explained. "The men you saw were new recruits. They have not had time to be fully kitted."

"Unrest?"

"Rumors mostly… enough to make Pharyl exercise caution."

Accepting the answer, he nodded for Torgreth to show Galadyr the dagger. "There is also this."

"Well met, friend Torgreth," the elf greeted him, accepting the dagger. "The reasons for your escape have been made known to me."

"And who are you?" the dwarf boldly asked.

Galadyr raised a finger telling him to wait while he studied the dagger. "This is a king's dagger." Holding the dagger in both hands, he bent his head and closed his eyes, bringing the flat of the blade up and pressing it against his forehead. A thick silence filled the room as they waited and watched Galadyr's serene face morph to a heavy frown. Opening his eyes, he inhaled a slow breath.

"The dagger's name is 'Bloodthirst.'" He tilted his head to stare at Torgreth, his cobalt blues eyes boring into him. "Where did you find this?"

"Oscon had it," Torgreth replied. "It's elven imbued, isn't it?"

"Yes," Galadyr nodded, shifting his gaze to Bryok. "I will question the other in a bit. We must discern how he came by this."

"What's so special about it?" Conal asked.

"It is a king's dagger," Galadyr explained.

"Everyone keeps saying that," Conal interrupted.

"A king's dagger," Galadyr patiently continued, "can only be forged by a dwarf, and not just any dwarf." He tilted his head to narrow his gaze at Torgreth. "The dwarf must be from the lineage of the Iron Hand, like you. Once the dagger is crafted, it is carried to the eleven kingdom of Auleavell where mages imbue the blade with a special gift. Some are warning blades that glow or hum when danger is near.

Others are reactive blades that give additional strength to the man who wields it so that if attacked, he can defeat his enemies. Still others, like Bloodthirst here, were designed to wreak vengeance, thirsting for blood and death until the threat is no more. It is a blade to be fearful of, because in the wrong hands it can do much damage."

Conal's brow furrowed. "Then why didn't Oscon have this power?"

Galadyr looked at him as thought the answer obvious. "He is not a king."

"So only a king can use this dagger?"

"A king or one descended from a king."

Conal blinked at the revelation. "May I see it?"

Ignoring Bryok's look of fear, Galadyr handed him the dagger.

Grasping the handle, Conal felt a sudden surge of rage fill his entire body as the clarity of the room clouded so that only the dagger had any visible form. The blade in his hands felt like an extension of his own body and his head snapped up and the cloud vanished as his angry eyes locked on each one in the room, instantaneously measuring each individual's threat towards him. Then just as suddenly, the seething storm disappeared and he stood in the middle of the room, his heart pounding as though coming off the battlefield.

"What did you see?" Galadyr held his hand out for the dagger.

"I didn't see anything," he replied, catching his breath, reluctant to surrender the blade.

"What did you feel?" Galadyr fixed him with a firm stare, his hand still out.

With a disappointed sigh, he handed the dagger to him. "I felt anger, totally consuming anger, like I wanted to kill everything around me. But then when I looked at each of you, the anger went away."

"That's because we were not a threat to you." Galadyr slid a satisfied glance at Bryok.

"I have a question," Torgreth announced, looking straight at Galadyr. "Who are you?"

"I am Galadyr."

"Yeah, we know. Where are you from? Why are you here?" Torgreth folded his arms across his chest.

Galadyr paused as if deliberating how much to tell. "I am from Auleavell."

"Long way from home," Torgreth observed.

"Yes, that is true." Studying the dwarf then Conal, he placed the dagger on top of the book he was reading and cupped his hands behind his back. "I am a friend of Prince Kirith."

"Who's he?"

"Let him finish," Bryok chided.

"Sorry," Torgreth lamely replied.

"Prince Kirith," Galadyr continued, "is King Falael's son, one of the few who recognizes and understands the threat the kingdom faces."

Torgreth was about to say 'so you ran away' when reminded of his own flight from Havyrd and King Rorykn. Instead he said, "So you came here to look for help?"

"Yes, which leads me to ask how that fellow came by this dagger. Its original home was in Havengarde. How did it end up here? I think it's time we found out."

"He's not gonna say much," Torgreth warned. "We tried already."

Galadyr smiled. "I'm sure you have. Let's try again." He held up the dagger and cast a sly glance at Conal. "Perhaps I should give this to you when we interrogate him."

CHAPTER 3

GWEN

Gwen and Aimil marched wordlessly between the elven sentinels, their hands bound behind their backs with silken cord. Kirith wasn't bound, but the leader of the sentinels kept a close eye on him. Gwen knew that they had been traveling along the border between Auleavell and Steepcross, but she hadn't expected to stumble upon a group of elven soldiers, let alone their prince.

The Aspect of all the elves glowed green. Gwen remembered that Eradore had said that she would get accustomed to seeing them and he'd been right. It was there in the background, an incorporeal *thing*, but she didn't really notice it unless she focused on it. Aimil's was blue, like her own, and she unexpectedly remembered the dwarf from the attack on the outpost. His Aspect had been brown.

"Release them," Kirith said. It was a litany from him, repeated every so often.

"I cannot, my Lord," the lead sentinel answered, just as he had every other time.

Gwen found the sentinel armor intriguing. It was enchanted with magic, that much was obvious to her. The material was constantly changing to mirror the scenery around them, cloaking the elves in perfect camouflage.

"Am I not the prince of Auleavell?" Kirith asked. "Or has my father taken that as well?"

"You are still the prince, my Lord."

"Then why will you not heed my command to let them go?"

The leader remained silent.

"Blast you, Haladavar!"

Gwen repeated the name under her breath. It rolled off her tongue like honey. She looked at Aimil. The woman had been silent since they'd been captured, and she wore a scowl plastered across her face.

"I'm sorry I got you into this," Gwen said.

"Don't be," Aimil replied. "If I didn't want to be here, do you really think these ropes would stop me?"

Gwen had been wondering about that. She'd considered using her lightning against the sentinels, but since Eradore had asked her to deliver a message to someone in Auleavell, she didn't think that was the best idea. Apparently neither did Aimil.

"Then why do you look so angry?"

"Angry?" Aimil laughed. "This is my normal face out in the world. It keeps people from bothering me."

"Silence!" Haladavar snapped, looking over his shoulder at them.

Gwen glared at him but she didn't speak another word. They trekked through thick woodland for several hours and Gwen could feel blisters forming on the bottoms of her feet. Her throat was dry and all she wanted was to sit long enough for the ache in her legs to go away. She staggered a few times, almost tripping over tree roots. The air grew less humid the further they traveled, which Gwen was thankful for.

The sound of civilization drew Gwen's attention, and she perked up, looking ahead for the source of the noises. Numerous trees, many of them as thick as buildings, towered over the rest of the forest. Elegant archways were carved into their facades, providing natural entrances to the interior of the trees. Gwen's breath caught in her throat at the staggering beauty.

"There's nothing like it anywhere else," Aimil whispered. "And I've traveled to many places."

Standing outside some of the trees, guards holding spears and polearms watched everyone with an eye of suspicion. As Gwen and the others traversed the main path through the city, some of the elves looked at them distrustfully and others outright ignored their presence. Gwen noticed the tension among the elves and wondered what had happened recently.

Haladavar led them to the largest tree Gwen had ever seen. Its trunk was wide enough to hold six carriages end to end. It rose into the sky, the canopy lost high above. Gwen stopped walking as she admired the tree. The guard behind her shoved her roughly and she fell to her knees with a grunt. Kirith turned around and glared at the guard, then helped Gwen to her feet.

"I'm sorry," he said quietly. "I will right this wrong."

They continued into the massive tree and Gwen's mind spun at the intricate details that had been carved into the walls. Stags, unicorns, and odd symbols and shapes covered every inch of space. The area they entered was a large open assembly room with two winding stairways on either side that led up to the next level.

"Wait here with them," Haladavar told the other

guards, then he went up one of the stairways.

Gwen continued to admire the beauty around her until Haladavar appeared at the top of the stairs.

"Bring them!" His voice drifted down to them, filled with authority.

The guards prodded Gwen and Aimil, and the two climbed the ornate staircase. When they reached the top, Haladavar led them past an open balcony that offered a magnificent view of the forest-city, then up a smaller set of stairs. An ivory throne wrapped in vines sat against the back wall. Falael, king of Auleavell, sat in the throne, his hard eyes fixed on Kirith.

Two guards stood at either side of the king, armed and intimidating. Gwen found their demeanor so different from Eradore's.

"The lamb returns to the fold," Falael said. His eyes roamed the rest of the group and his attention paused on Gwen and Aimil, then he looked questioningly at Haladavar. "Why are there humans in my kingdom?"

"These are the people we found Prince Kirith with, my Lord."

"A fact you neglected in your report moments ago."

"My apologies," Haladavar said, bowing his head.

"Forgiven," Falael said. He looked back at Kirith. "Tell me, is my fist so iron-shod that you can't bear the weight of living under it?"

"I left because you refuse to see the threat that lies before all of us," Kirith replied. "King Torian is trying to expand his kingdom and he will stop at nothing until he rules every inch of land."

"Is that so? How would you know this? Have you

been to Isentol?"

"No," Kirith answered.

"Do you see King Torian's armies at our doorstep?"

"No," Kirith repeated.

"Then tell me how you know such things without signs of proof?"

Kirith bowed his head in defeat.

"Lyra has come here and poisoned the minds of our young generations. She spews lies and deceit about our neighbor with no proof. This is why she has been removed from my court."

Gwen perked up at the mention of Lyra's name. That was the person that Gwen needed to deliver a message to. She glanced at Aimil. The woman shook her head ever so slightly. Gwen wanted to ask the king where Lyra was, but her exhaustion took away her will.

"We need to find Lyra," Gwen whispered.

"We'll worry about that later. We have bigger problems right now."

"What problems?"

"Why do these humans speak in my presence without permission?" Falael demanded.

"I'm sorry," Gwen said loudly. "I meant no offense."

"And yet, like a wild dog, she continues to bay. Are these the humans you saw within our borders?"

"Possibly," Haladavar replied. "We did kill some others that were armed."

"Trespassing in Auleavell is strictly prohibited," Falael said.

"They weren't trespassing," Kirith spoke up. "They rescued me from the ones who captured me."

"A human doing a just deed? I find it difficult to

believe." Falael looked at Haladavar, who frowned.

"You dispel the rumors of King Torian's ill intent, yet you claim that humans are incapable of doing what is just? Do you not see your own madness?" Kirith asked.

"The poison in his mind seeps from his mouth," Falael said. "Take the humans away. Their trial will be held in the morning."

Kirith tried to protest, but Falael shot him a glare, silencing him. One of the guards grabbed ahold of Gwen's arm roughly and snapped a thin bracelet around her wrist. The faint pulse of magic that was always within her suddenly disappeared. She turned to Aimil in shock, her eyes widening.

Aimil jerked away from the guard trying to grab her and struck a blow to the side of his face. The elf collapsed in an unconscious heap, but another took his place. Aimil backstepped and lifted her right hand. Gwen winced, preparing for the flare of magic, but it never came. She opened her eyes to see Aimil frozen in place. She looked around, but no one else was affected.

"Must I do everything myself?" Falael asked. He was standing now, his left hand held out in front of him, fingers splayed wide. The other guards hurriedly snapped several bracelets onto Aimil's wrists and then Falael released his spell.

Gwen guessed by the look on Aimil's face that she was trying to use her runes, but nothing was happening. "What is this?" she growled.

"It is for your safety, as well as ours," Falael answered. "Now get them out of my sight. And take Prince Kirith as well. If he wants to wallow in the poison, let him."

Haladavar motioned the other guards to follow

him, and he escorted them up higher into the tree. Gwen looked back at the fallen elf, hoping Aimil hadn't killed him. Just as he was leaving her line of sight, she saw him sit up. She sighed in relief but was anxious about where they were headed. If Falael had such a dim view of humans, she assumed they were going to be taken to a nightmare of a prison.

As it turned out, the 'prison' was an extremely comfortable room with an open view of the forest-city. Gwen looked around, assuming that the room must be for Kirith. Since he was a prince, he'd be well taken care of. Yet as Haladavar left all three of them inside, she was glad to be proven wrong. The other guards closed the doors and barred them from the outside.

"So these trees do have doors," Aimil said.

"Only the personal chambers," Kirith replied. "This is a guest room for visiting nobles."

"And your father expects us to stay here all night, just to face a trial tomorrow?" Gwen asked.

"Sadly, yes. My father is a difficult man, as you have seen."

"No wonder you ran away," Aimil said. She pulled at the bracelets, but they didn't budge. "What are these blasted things?"

"Those are shackles. They will keep you from leaving the boundaries of the city by force of pain."

"They are also cutting off my magic," Aimil huffed. "How do I get them off?"

"Yes, they do restrict magic. Only the guards can remove them."

Aimil growled in frustration and began pacing back and forth across the room. She reminded Gwen of a wild animal. The woman couldn't handle being caged.

"What is this trial your father mentioned?" Gwen asked.

"He thinks you've trespassed into Auleavell. He closed our borders, which makes your presence here a crime. Tomorrow morning, he'll parade you before the nobles and they will judge whether you are innocent or not."

"There's a chance we'll be declared innocent?"

"That's highly unlikely," Kirith replied. "Many of the nobles share the same limited perspective as my father. They will find you guilty."

"What happens if they think we're guilty?"

"You'll be executed."

Gwen slumped into a nearby chair, exhausted and overwhelmed. Aimil was still pacing. Kirith sat across from Gwen, his expression downcast. That was another difference she noticed among the elves. Kirith was like Eradore, letting his emotions show on his face. Falael and the guards seemed emotionless, their hearts hard.

"Your father mentioned someone named Lyra. Do you know her?"

"Yes," Kirith replied. "She is a voice of reason among my people. Lyra has opened my eyes to the threat that Torian poses."

"I have a message for her from a friend." Gwen didn't necessarily consider Eradore a friend, but she wasn't sure what else to call him. Her leader? That didn't sound right, either.

"My father banished her from the court," Kirith said.

"What does that mean?"

"She's not permitted inside this tree, but she is allowed to stay in the city."

"Do you know where to find her?" Aimil asked,

walking over to join them.

"There are a few places she could be, but what does it matter?"

"It matters because we're going to sneak out of here."

"How do you propose that?" Kirith asked. "You have no magic, and my father has guards at the door."

"We're not going out of the door," Aimil replied. She looked away and Gwen followed her gaze to the open balcony.

"We're going out that way."

CHAPTER 4

CONAL

Oscon was tied to a chair when they entered the room, one eye swollen, surrounded by a purple bruise. Dried blood edged the corner of his lips.

"What happened?" Conal asked, amused at the change in the man's fortune.

"He was being uncooperative," Brunet replied with an unemotional shrug.

Oscon bent his head up to glare at them. "Yer wasting my time. I got nuthin' to say to you."

"Yes," Galadyr blithely replied, "we know. That's why we're going to let Conal torture you." He handed a set of iron pliers to Conal.

Conal looked over at Torgreth, furrowing his brow. "How did that go again? We cut off his fingers then his toes, peel his eyelids off then cut out his tongue?"

"Something like that." Torgreth grinned at Oscon. "This is gonna be fun. You're not going to enjoy it, but we will."

"Yer bluffing," Oscon snarled before turning his venom at Conal. "I shoulda dumped you long ago. You were nuthin' but a dead weight, good fer nuthin'.

That's why I got rid of you."

Conal stood before him, pliers in hand. "That's the best you got? Let's see if you sing the same tune." He pulled up his sleeve to reveal his brand. "Recognize that?"

Oscon's defiance wavered. "What the hell? You're a Cobra?"

"You've got eyes. What does it look like?"

"But… when did that happen?"

"I've been one all along," Conal lied. "You think I didn't know you were working for Caldyr? That you were also sending reports back to Havengarde? Why do you think I joined your band of fools? Because I was so impressed with your leadership?" He barked a derisive laugh. "Puh-lease."

"You gonna talk him to death," Torgreth interrupted, "or are we gonna get to torturing?"

"You're right," Conal said with a smile, squeezing the pliers several times. "The one thing I couldn't discover before my untimely departure was who your contact was. Let's start with the fingernails." He grabbed Oscon's hand and pried a finger back, jamming the pliers against the fingertip and clamping down on the fingernail.

"Wait a minute," Bryok intervened. "If you're going to torture him, what's the incentive for him to tell you anything?"

Conal frowned, pondering the question then shrugged. "I was more curious than anything else. I didn't think he'd tell us. Just thought I'd ask before we began."

"Suppose he agrees to tell us what we need to know?" Bryok ventured. "Do we need to torture him?"

"You mean not torture him if he tells us what we

need to know?" Conal stared at him like he was spoiling all his fun.

"That was the general idea."

Conal shifted a look to Oscon then back to Bryok. "How do we know he's telling the truth?"

"We don't."

"Then what does it matter what he says? Let's just get on with it." He started tugging on the fingernail. "Wonder which hurts more, just yanking it out or tugging slowly?"

"Pain lasts longer if you tug it slowly," Torgreth observed.

Oscon tensed, struggling to disengage his finger from Conal's vice grip. Sweat dripped down his temples and forehead.

"Before you rip that out," Bryok pointed out, "we still haven't determined where he got the dagger."

"Ah, that's right. I did ask, didn't I. Still, like I said, what does it matter? But... just to humor you, I'll play along." Conal relaxed the pressure just a bit then started tugging again, locking his gaze on Oscon. "You want to tell us about the dagger?" He tugged harder.

"Blayne gave it to me," he bellowed.

"Blayne? As in Brody's son Blayne?"

"Yes, yes. He gave it to me."

"Where did he get it?"

"I don't know. I swear it. I don't know."

"Really?" Conal tugged harder.

"O god, I swear."

"Was Brody your contact?"

"Yes, yes."

"He's lying," Torgreth sneered. "Yank it out."

"O god, O god, please. I swear it's the truth."

Conal slid a glance at Galadyr who dipped his

head in a quick nod. The door opened and a man slipped in, pretending to whisper something in Galadyr's ear.

"We'll need to continue this later," Galadyr announced.

Without a word, they slipped out the room, leaving Oscon sweating and breathing heavily, his imagination rampant with anticipated pain.

Back in Galadyr's room, Conal chuckled. "That was easier than I expected. For someone who was supposed to be so tough, I barely tugged on his fingernail and he started whining like a little girl."

"You all played your parts very well," Galadyr smiled.

"What do we do with him?" Bryok questioned. "We can't release him, and we can't leave him here."

Galadyr saw Conal's overt look at the dagger. "I don't think that's a good idea."

"What?"

"Remember your experience with it?"

"You afraid I can't control myself?" Conal folded his arms across his chest.

"Yes." Galadyr placed the dagger on the book on the bookstand, his hands resting on top.

"If that belongs to the king, by rights, isn't that mine?"

"You're not a king," Bryok calmly reminded him. "You're the son of a king."

"Huh?" Torgreth burst.

Realizing his indiscretion, Bryok heaved a sigh of irritation at himself. "You might as well know. Conal is King Kamron's son."

"So, it is true," Galadyr intoned.

"You saw for yourself when he handled the blade."

Instead of rejoicing, Galadyr's face tightened. Clasping his hands behind him, he stepped away to begin slowly pacing. "He will need protection."

"Is this joke, another game?" Torgreth demanded.

"It is no joke, Torgreth Iron-hand," Galadyr solemnly replied. "Our friend here is the son of King Kamron."

"How is that even possible?" Torgreth argued. "He was a highwayman and before that lived in some town on the coast." He cast a suspicious eye at Conal.

"It's a surprise to me too," Conal shrugged, "but I'm coming to terms with it."

Torgreth swung his hand in a deep sweeping bow. "My liege."

"Very funny," Conal deadpanned.

Torgreth tilted his head to stare at him. "Aren't you the same guy who jumped out the window and into the river to escape from Drustan?"

"You have to admit it was a good dive," Conal pointed out.

Torgreth smiled then looked up Galadyr. "You wouldn't lie to a dwarf, would you?"

Galadyr smiled despite himself. "No, I wouldn't lie to you. It is true."

"Can we get back to the issue at hand," Bryok chided. "We need to get to Denhelm, and we can't take Oscon with us."

"Why not?" Torgreth asked.

"Because he'll only slow us down."

"And they're probably already looking for him," Conal added before rethinking the problem. "But the longer he stays away, the more likely someone else will take charge… which means his position with his band of followers will have been compromised." A smile curled the corners of his lips. "The longer we can keep him away, the less necessary he becomes, which means my former companions will not want to spend their time looking for us." He shifted his gaze to Galadyr. "Is Brunet coming with us?"

"No. Your idea has merit. We will do as you have suggested."

Bryok narrowed his gaze at Torgreth. "No one else is to know of Conal's true identity, not even your brother."

"I can keep a secret," Torgreth emphatically stated, giving Conal a look that said he was still unsure he wasn't being played.

"We need to leave," Galadyr warned. "Rumors abound that all is not well in Tir Manach. We head for Denhelm and Lord Pharyl as soon as I explain our plan to Brunet."

It was early afternoon when they slipped out the alleyway door and headed to the city gates, stopping by a stable to collect their mounts.

"I'm sure no one will notice us," Conal wryly observed, making his way through the crowded streets, "a dwarf, an elf, and two men... just your everyday group of friends."

"There's nothing we can do about it," Bryok said. "Keep watch for any trouble."

Bryok led the way, Conal beside him, Galadyr and Torgreth behind, Torgreth receiving the most stares. Initially smiling at the overt staring, Torgreth quickly tired of pretending and replaced his smile with a scowl.

"North, north-west," Conal quietly warned. "I recognize the woman. She's one of Oscon's band."

Their eyes met and Conal gave her a smile of recognition, causing surprise and momentary confusion. Abruptly she melted into the swarms of pedestrians.

"She's gone to spread the word about me," Conal said. "We need to hurry."

"Slow down," Bryok countered, reaching for Conal's reins. "We don't need to draw more attention to ourselves."

Finally clearing the city gates, Bryok ordered, "Let's pick up the pace," and spurred his horse to a trot.

"Don't forget about me," Torgreth complained, his pony's rhythm more of a canter than a trot.

"She's a strong mare," Galadyr informed him, "and can keep this pace hours."

"Not sure I can," Torgreth grumbled, struggling to get comfortable in the saddle.

A half mile outside the gate, they crossed the intersection of the road leading north towards Urve and south towards Monkreth. Conal looked back over his shoulder.

"They're coming," he exclaimed.

Nearly twenty riders spilled though the city gates and gave chase. Urging their steeds to a gallop, they knew they could not keep this pace for long. And despite Torgreth's doughty steed, the little pony could not keep pace. Accepting that they could not outrun their pursuers, Bryok slowed their pace to a halt and turned to face the approaching riders who quickly caught up and surrounded them.

A tall man well-built man with a full rust colored beard stepped his horse forward. Leaning forward, he gave Conal a condescending smile. "Hullo Conal,"

"Hello Maldwic." With an indulgent grin, Conal scanned the group. "Sort of makes it hard to keep it a secret that you're all highwaymen when you're so obvious. Which genius thought it was a good idea to ride out all together?"

Maldwic's smug smile wavered as he suddenly realized not only had he compromised the band, but when Oscon found out, his life wasn't worth a copper royal.

"We came to rescue Oscon," he awkwardly said, Oscon's absence painfully obvious.

Conal snorted a laugh. "Let me see if I understand you correctly. You compromised everyone in the company because you wanted to rescue Oscon?" In exaggerated turns of his head, he looked to his left then right. "As you can see, he's not here. Further, wasn't it Oscon himself who said that anyone left behind is on his own? Didn't Oscon say that no one is more important than the company?"

"He's right, Maldwic," a female voice spoke up.

"Seems to me," Conal pointed out, "that if Oscon is on his own, he's no longer the boss anymore. That means someone else has to take his place."

Maldwic's face brightened until Conal added, "Isn't Jestyn next in command?"

"He ain't here," a male voice said.

Conal cocked his head to the side and narrowed his gaze at Maldwic. "I guess that means you're the boss now."

Momentarily startled at the elevation, Maldwic sat up straight, assuming to role of one in command. "Yer right. I'm the boss now."

"Well, boss," Conal smiled, "what are your plans? Are you going to sit out here where everyone can see you or are you going to fade away and regroup?"

"We're going to regroup," he replied. "Why don't you come with us? I can use a good man like you."

"Much as I'd like to," Conal replied with a

feigned sigh, "I'm committed to another venture. Perhaps you might like to join us."

"What're you doing?"

"We're going to Lord Pharyl's to enlist his aid to fight King Torian."

A heavy silence reigned for a moment before Maldwic laughed. "You're a funny one. What're you really doing?"

"It's true," Galadyr spoke up. "We seek alliances to fight against an evil king who, if he is not stopped, will one day rule this very kingdom."

"An elf." Maldwic observed, curling a lip.

"And a half-druid," Conal said, pointing to Bryok.

"And a dwarf," Torgreth chimed in.

There was a visible reaction to the revelation that Conal traveled with a half-druid.

"You travel with interesting companions," Maldwic said, regarding Conal's friends with a wary eye.

"So do you," Conal smiled. "I ask again, will you join us?"

"What's in it for us?"

"Everlasting fame and glory," Conal grandly answered.

Maldwic sniffed a derisive laugh. "Fame and glory don't put food in your belly."

"If that's all you seek, then I can promise that you will have plenty of food."

"We're wastin' time," the female voice scolded.

Conal turned his head to see the speaker, a pretty woman with thick blond hair held back with a leather ringlet. "You're right, Beca. We are wasting time." Addressing Maldwic, he said, "If you're not coming with us, then let us be on our way."

Maldwic frowned then slowly shook his head. "Can't do that."

"Why not?"

"Your friends have seen us."

"They can be trusted," Conal avowed.

"Sez you."

"You're making a huge mistake."

"You're the one making the mistake," Maldwic countered. Before he could command his company to attack, Conal spoke up.

"I challenge you."

"What?"

"I challenge you. By all rights, I'm still part of the company. Because I was captured doesn't change the fact that I am one of you. Even when they tortured me and tried to make me reveal names, I never said a word." Conal was on a roll and his story took on exaggerated proportions. "Even when Oscon set me up, I never said anything. When I was betrayed by my own boss, I never said a word against him or any of you." He fixed Maldwic with a sharp eye. "I am still a member of this company. By the rules established, I challenge you."

Maldwic's initial irritation faded when he sized up his opponent who was at least half a head shorter. "You want to challenge me?"

"Yes." Conal dismounted, handed the reins to Torgreth, and stepped into the cleared space in front of Maldwic.

"Suit yourself. Your funeral." Maldwic slid down from his saddle, handing the reins to the rider next to him.

"The challenge ends when the first person yields and the other is declared the winner," Conal said.

"I know the rules," Maldwic sneered, standing

two paces away.

"I don't have a sword, so it's barehanded."

"That's fine." He unhooked his sword and handed it to the opposite rider next to him.

"You ready?"

"Anytime you are," Maldwic boasted.

Conal stuck out a hand. "Let's shake hands before we begin."

Maldwic cocked an eyebrow. "Why?"

"No hard feelings. That's all."

Immediately recognizing that he could avoid a fight simply by squeezing Conal's hand so hard that he would beg for mercy, Maldwic grasped the offered hand.

A battle of strength commenced and Maldwic was shocked by the young man's grip. The cheers for Maldwic quickly diminished as the man began sweating, pouring out all the strength he could muster, his frustration surging for Conal seemed far too relaxed.

Maldwic's knees started to tremble then buckle as his companions watched in stunned silence. Excruciating pain pulsed up his arm and his face and body tightened in anguish, yet still he gripped Conal's hand, except it was Conal who gripped *his* hand, for try as he might, he could not reciprocate the power of Conal's strength.

And then he could take no more as he felt the bones grinding against each other, the pain wracking his entire body.

Crying out, "I yield," he dropped to his knees, cradling his limp hand, gasping in heavy breaths. Tilting his head to stare up at him, his mouth gaped open. "Who are you?"

"I am Conal, the new boss of this company." He

bent down to help lift him to standing. Turning to the rest of the highwaymen, he said, "Does anyone wish to challenge me?" None responded, more than a few looking at him with awe.

Swinging back up into his saddle, he waited as Maldwic struggled to pull himself up into the saddle then addressed the company. "Maldwic remains second in command. Obey him as you would me for eventually, he will become boss."

Surprised, Maldwic respectfully dipped his head.

"We ride for Denhelm. As of this moment, you are no longer Highwaymen, but respected members of an elite troop."

Thinking this a new hustle, they grinned and smirked.

Deciding it would be more trouble to tell them the truth, he returned their smiles. *Wait until they find out I'm a Cobra.*

CHAPTER 5

GWEN

Gwen was relieved when Aimil said they would wait until nightfall to escape. Her blistered feet were sore, and she needed to rest. The guards opened the doors and a young elven girl entered, carrying a tray of fresh fruits, cheeses, a loaf of bread, and some wooden plates. Kirith played host and divvied up the food onto the plates, then handed them to Gwen and Aimil.

"Is this a snack?" Gwen asked.

"No. It's dinner time here, and even prisoners get fed."

"This is what elves eat for dinner? There's no meat." Gwen didn't mind fruit and cheese, but she needed something more filling to sate her hunger.

"We don't eat meat. Not unless there are no other options," Kirith said.

"What? Why not?"

"We are one with the life forces around us, and we do not believe in taking another life unnecessarily."

Gwen found that perspective entirely foreign and didn't know what to say, so she kept quiet and ate. She looked around the room while she chewed, admiring the beauty of it. It didn't take long for her to realize that elves put intricate details into everything. Even the chairs they sat in had animals carved into the wood.

"You said this room is for visiting nobles," Gwen said. "How many elven cities are there?"

"Only a handful," Kirith answered. "Though there are many small communities across Auleavell."

Gwen plucked a few grapes from a stem and popped them into her mouth. They were perfectly ripe and flooded her mouth with sweet juices that excited her taste buds. Despite that, she was thirsty and wondered why the elven girl had neglected to bring something to drink.

"I need water," she said, looking at Kirith questioningly.

"My apologies," he replied. "I'm being a forgetful host." He rose from his chair and walked to a small table that had a silver pitcher and wooden cups. Kirith filled three of the cups and delivered two of them to Gwen and Aimil. Gwen drank deeply of the water. The cool liquid slicked her throat and she immediately felt more rejuvenated than she had in weeks. Her surprise was etched upon her face, causing Kirith to smile at her.

"The waters of the Thaestra River bring healing," he said.

"This water is magical?" Gwen asked, peering into the cup. It looked normal to her.

"Call it magic or the power of nature," Kirith said. "We care for the river, and it cares for us."

"I'd forgotten about the river," Aimil said. "I've heard that people who bathe in the water experience miracles."

"Not all who have, but there are many with such

stories. We elves are used to the water, so we do not notice the difference as much. Would you like to bathe in the water? There is a tub in the corner there." Kirith nodded toward the corner of the room.

"How do you get the water up here?" Gwen asked.

"Much of the Thaestra flows underground, but magic directs it into the trees through hollowed roots. The water flows continuously, keeping the bathing tubs fresh. Try it," Kirith motioned. "It will soothe your pains."

"I don't want to get my clothes wet, especially if we're going to scale down the tree," Gwen replied. She was curious, though.

"Then remove them."

Gwen gave Kirith an odd look. He'd said that so casually as if it wouldn't be awkward for her to disrobe in front of him. He was a complete stranger.

"Elves do not view nakedness the same way we do," Aimil said, as though reading her mind. She stood and walked over to the tub, then removed her clothes and stepped into the water. Gwen averted her gaze too late and caught a glimpse of Aimil's backside, but she had practically seen the woman naked before when she had chosen her rune from Aimil's body. Still, it was embarrassing to Gwen.

"Go," Kirith encouraged. "I can sense your exhaustion. The water will help."

He seemed sincere, but Gwen wasn't sure if he was just trying to get her naked. Her feet cried out for relief, and she finally relented and went to the tub. She cast a glance at Kirith, but he wasn't looking at her. She hurriedly removed her clothes and climbed into the tub, sinking below the moving water. The temperature was neither hot nor cold, but a perfect balance between the two, and she sighed in relief.

The throbbing in her feet faded and the ache of her muscles dulled until she didn't feel weary at all.

"That's incredible," Gwen said. "I feel … perfect."

"The stories I've heard don't do it justice," Aimil said. She leaned back and stretched out with a groan.

The tub was large enough to hold at least four people comfortably. Gwen decided if all elven nobles had baths like this one, they were blessed beyond measure. She looked up at Kirith as he approached the tub. He removed his shirt and Gwen's eyes widened.

"What are you doing?" she asked, trying to keep her voice calm.

"Partaking of the waters," he said simply.

Gwen turned her gaze as Kirith removed his boots and stripped his pants off, then joined them in the tub. She swallowed hard and moved away. Elves might view nakedness differently, but Gwen didn't.

The three of them sat silently. Gwen felt awkward but Aimil and Kirith were relaxed as if they weren't all naked in front of each other.

"The message you have for Lyra … what is it about?" Kirith asked.

"I'm not sure," Gwen replied, glad to have a distraction. "My friend just asked me to deliver it to her. He said she was an ally to the rebellion."

"She is," Kirith confirmed. "Support among my people grows for her daily, but my father ignores her warnings. He would be wise to heed her words before it's too late."

Gwen found Kirith's last few words odd, but Kirith's tone hadn't implied anything ill. She looked toward the balcony and saw that the sun had almost descended. The patches of sky that were visible through the trees were vibrant orange.

"It's almost time to go," Gwen said.

"A little longer," Aimil replied. She moved closer to Kirith and ran her fingers through his hair, tucking the long strands behind his pointed ear. Kirith looked Aimil in the eyes and Gwen felt even more awkward than before. She moved past them and got out of the tub, feeling self-conscious about her body. A glance over her shoulder revealed that Kirith and Aimil weren't even paying her any attention.

Gwen looked around for something to dry off with and found a long strip of cloth hanging on the wall near the tub. She grabbed it and dried off, then put her clothes back on. They were dirty, but she didn't care. Her eyes widened when she heard the sounds of lovemaking and hurried to the balcony, trying to get as far away from the sound as possible.

She peered over the railing and eyed the descent. The ground was far below and the thought of scaling down the tree caused a flutter in Gwen's stomach. It seemed like an impossible distance. And what if she fell? Gwen chewed her bottom lip in worry. She noticed the moans from the tub had stopped, but she didn't dare turn to look.

Aimil joined her at the balcony and Gwen was relieved to see the woman was dressed.

"What was *that* about?" Gwen whispered harshly.

"I was clearing my head before we do this," Aimil replied. "And don't act like you don't have needs."

Gwen ignored the comment and continued to peer down at the ground. Darkness had settled across the landscape, obscuring the view. Gwen's heart fluttered in her chest.

"Are you sure this is a good idea?"

"Not really," Aimil replied. "But what other option do we have? Unless we can find a way to get these shackles off, I don't see how we're going to get out of here. Besides, you have to get that letter to Lyra. I don't think Falael is willingly going to let you give it to her."

The woman had valid points. Gwen breathed in deeply several times, trying to calm her pounding heart. "Let's get this over with, then."

Aimil went first, tossing one leg over the railing. She adjusted her grip and the other leg followed, then she began a slow descent along the tree. Kirith stepped onto the balcony and Gwen's cheeks flushed. He didn't seem to notice or didn't care, and he motioned after Aimil.

"Do you want to go next?"

"Yes," she replied quickly, then climbed over the railing. Gwen locked eyes with Kirith for a moment and she could feel her face burning. She tried not to think about his muscled unclothed body and failed. *Focus,* she scolded herself.

She crept down the tree much slower than Aimil. Her footing was the hardest part since she couldn't see where to place her feet and her upper body strength was almost non-existent. Gwen struggled the entire way, scaring herself a few times when she slipped. After what she felt was an eternity, her feet touched the ground.

"Took you long enough," Aimil said, though she was smiling. Kirith stood next to her and Gwen scrunched her brows, trying to figure out how he'd beaten her down without her notice.

"Where are we going?" Gwen asked, brushing her hands off on her thighs.

"Lyra's usually at the temple at sunset, so we'll

look for her there first," Kirith said.

"What about guards?" Aimil looked around as if expecting a host of them to close in upon them at any moment.

"There aren't many at night. Since my father doesn't believe there are any threats to our safety, their numbers are minimal. We'll keep to the shadows regardless, just to be safe."

Kirith led them along a worn path, weaving among the trees. Gwen expected to see a few elves, but the night was quiet and no one else was out. They skirted along the edge of the forest-city, and Gwen bit back a gasp when she'd stepped too close to the border. The bracelet had grown hot against her skin, catching her by surprise.

"Watch your steps," Kirith said. "If you cross over the border, pain will be the last thing you know before you die."

Gwen was bothered by how nonchalantly he said that. How often did people get shackled? And how often did they die from trying to escape? She shuddered at the thought and intentionally kept a wider distance from the invisible border of the city.

A well-lit clearing was ahead and Kirith slowed his steps. They kept hidden in the shadows and he whistled a few notes, the sound disguised as a bird call. A moment later the same whistle echoed back.

"It's safe," Kirith said. He led them into the clearing and Gwen saw two elven guards standing at either side of the temple archway. Her heart skipped a beat, and she was about to sprint in the opposite direction when they bowed low to Kirith.

"My Lord," they greeted in unison.

"Good evening," Kirith replied, offering a tilt of his head. "The city seems clear tonight."

"Quiet as a den of foxes," one of the guards said.

Kirith looked over his shoulder at Gwen and Aimil and motioned them to follow him inside. Gwen looked up at the temple, surprised that it too was built within a tree. She'd foolishly expected a building of stone with columns. The interior of the tree was bright, and the walls were inscribed with designs just as detailed as the ones in the palace.

Pews lined the room on either side while a walkway stretched down the middle. The pews were formed from the tree itself and radiated magic that Gwen could feel even through her shackle. A few elves were present, their heads bowed. The place exuded peace and Gwen's worries were washed away in a wave of tranquility.

"What deity is this temple for?" Gwen whispered.

"Solara," Kirith replied. "Goddess of the Stars."

Gwen looked past him to where a large dragon statue resided. It sat upon a raised dais, a foot above the rest of the floor. Its wings were spread wide, each several feet long. The scaly body of the creature twisted back and forth from its head down to the tip of its tail. Kneeling in front of it was an elven woman. Kirith led them along the walkway and stopped a few feet behind the woman. They waited in silence until the woman finished her prayer, then she stood and turned to face them.

"Prince Kirith," she greeted warmly.

"Lyra," Kirith said. "This is Aimil and Gwen."

Lyra's slender brow rose curiously. "How did you get humans into Auleavell without your father knowing?"

"He knows," Kirith replied, pointing to the bracelets on Aimil's arm.

"Of course he does," Lyra said, a smile tugging at

the corner of her lips.

Gwen studied the woman intently. There was something about her that seemed … *off,* but she didn't know what it was. She was an elf, as tall as Kirith, and just as beautiful in appearance. Her hair was golden brown, and it reached down past her waist in a long elaborate braid. Her eyes were green, but they held a fierceness that Gwen found intimidating. Despite that, her voice was soft and melodic, adding to the calm atmosphere of the temple.

"Gwen has a message for you from a friend of hers," he added.

Lyra looked at Gwen expectantly. "Who sent this message?"

Gwen cleared her throat. "It's from Eradore." There was an entire speech she had prepared, but the words disappeared from her mind. She retrieved the scroll case and fumbled with it, then handed it to Lyra.

The elf opened it and unrolled the parchment, her eyes scanning over what was written. She lowered the parchment and looked at Kirith.

"If your father knows they are here, why did he let them come to me?"

"He doesn't know we're here. We snuck out of the palace."

"Clever. I assume there will be a trial?"

"Yes, tomorrow morning," Kirith replied.

"That is good. Take them back to the palace and ensure that they are present for the trial."

Gwen heard their conversation, but she wasn't listening. She was focused on Lyra. There was something … *there.* Lyra's Aspect. It wasn't green like the other elves. It was silver. She tried to get Aimil's attention, but the woman wasn't looking at her.

"Are you sure? The nobles will say they're guilty."

"I am sure," Lyra said.

Kirith was conflicted. "I promised them I would make things right. I don't want them to be executed."

"They won't be," Lyra replied.

"How do you know?"

"It's time."

"Time for what?" Kirith asked.

"It's time to implement our plan."

CHAPTER 6

CONAL

Riding beside Bryok, Conal inhaled the scent of the pine forest, a fragrance that always filled him with peace. Behind him, Galadyr and Torgreth engaged in friendly antagonism as to who were better carvers, elves or dwarves. The rest of the company rode two abreast tailing behind them.

"I've been wondering," Conal said looking over at Bryok, "when we were in Morendir and you and Drustan were looking at the rune bones, you nearly fainted when you saw one set of bones in a box. Then when we packed all of them onto the wagon to take back to Monkreth, you kept that box separate, carrying it yourself. Why?"

Bryok's placid face hardened. "They were dangerous."

"Aren't all rune bones dangerous in some form or other? You said so yourself."

"These were especially dangerous, evil." His jaw clenched and his nostrils flared.

Startled at his intensity, Conal asked, "What were they?"

Bryok paused before he replied, "Dragon-lock runes."

"Dragon lock? What do they do?"

Lips pursed, Bryok inhaled an angry breath. "They bind a dragon to an individual, one consumed with evil for no one of noble heart would ever bind a dragon to himself."

Conal furrowed his brow, wondering why Bryok was so angry. "It's not like they can ever be used."

"Don't be a fool," Bryok snapped.

"What's your problem?" Conal shot back. "How many dragons have you seen in your lifetime? Show me a dragon and maybe I'll worry about it. Until then, let's remain focused on the job at hand. Besides, didn't you burn those rune bones?"

"That's not the point," Bryok retorted. "Someone had those bones carved, someone with a deep knowledge of magic, someone who could ruin your chances of reclaiming a kingdom. That alone should worry you."

"Like who?"

"How should I know? But if there are Dragon-lock bones, trust me, there are worse ones already carved."

Conal suddenly realized the glaring flaw in his quest: if he could use magic, so could the enemy. Truth was, he hadn't given it much thought, assuming that Bryok or Drustan could counter anything used against them. Ever since he was imbued with his extraordinary strength and other traits, he'd begun to feel invincible. Now he wasn't so sure.

Giving voice to his thoughts, he said, "So you and Drustan are going to need help if we're to defeat Torian and his wizards."

"Drustan and I are half-druids, remember? Which means that we have only half the power of a true wizard or mage. But we are not without resources for we have friends who more than make up for our limited abilities."

Conal rode in silence for a bit, smiling at the ongoing debate behind him. Torgreth had scored an advantage when Galadyr admitted that no one carved stone like a dwarf, but quickly added that elves were without equal when it came to wood carving, causing Torgreth to begrudgingly admit that elves were mighty fine wood carvers, probably among the best.

An idea blossomed and he gazed over at Bryok. "Can I learn magic?"

Bryok shook his head. "It doesn't work that way. You either have the gift or you don't. Remember what I said back in Monkreth. Only individuals who are mage-marked can use rune bones and being mage-marked doesn't necessarily mean you are a mage."

"How do I know I am not a mage if I'm never taught how to be one?

Bryok narrowed his gaze at him. "When you look at me, what do you see?"

"Huh?"

"What do you see when you look at me?"

Puzzled, Conal studied the man riding next to him and shrugged. "I see a half-druid named Bryok with his reddish-brown hair tied behind his head." He purposely left off the 'handsome' part, not wanting to inflate the man's vanity.

"What about colors?"

"Colors?"

"Yes, do you see any color?"

"Of course I see color," Conal indignantly replied. "I can see the color of your hair, the color of your clothes, even the color of the horse you're riding. What does that have to do with anything?"

Bryok nodded with satisfaction. "You are not a mage nor a wizard and will never become one."

"How do you know?" Conal snapped, insulted by the curt dismissal.

"Do not be offended," Bryok soothed. "In fact, be thankful. Being a mage or wizard isn't without its problems. No matter how hard you try, once people find out you're a mage, people treat you differently, at arms' length, never trusting you. They call upon you when they need something then want nothing to do with you once they get what they want. You are different. You are not meant to be a mage. You are meant to rule."

Assuaged at the backhanded compliment Conal mulled the uncertain future. Casting a sly look at Bryok, he quietly said, "Have you really seen a dragon?"

"Yes," he answered, looking over his shoulder to check no one else heard the conversation. Leaning over towards him, his voice low so that only Conal could hear, he said, "There is one not too far away. If we are close enough when we stop for the night, I will take you to him."

Conal's heart skipped a beat. "Really?"

"Shhh, not so loud," Bryok grimaced. "And yes, really."

"What's he like?"

"I think it best we drop the subject for the moment," Bryok cautioned, settling back in his saddle. "There will be enough time tonight to answer your questions."

Frustrated at the reply, Conal changed topics to divert his own distraction. "Are there other runes that would be good for me to have?"

"Most runes deal in the physical realm, like

increasing strength and stamina, or special weapon abilities. Thus, if you want to add to the abilities you now have, you need to think in terms of the physical. What other physical skills would you want?"

Conal pondered only a moment. "I was thinking along the lines of what would a Cobra need? Things like stealth, maybe a knowledge of poisons, stuff like that."

"Stealth is possible," Bryok replied, "but knowledge of poisons is something you'll have to learn yourself. Remember the restrictions concerning the physical."

"But you said *most*," Conal countered.

"I know where you're going with this," Bryok objected, holding a hand up. "Making the leap to the spirit world requires the person be some type of magician, like a mage or a wizard. That's why the Dragon-lock rune bones are so dangerous."

"Because only a mage can use them?"

"Only a very powerful mage," Bryok corrected.

Conal frowned. "So why were they in Morendir? All Havyrd had was his voice. Once that was taken away, he was nothing."

"I know," Bryok said, slowly nodding. "That's what concerns me. Why would someone put such powerful rune-bones there?"

"Maybe they thought it was a safe place, away from prying eyes," Conal offered.

"Hey you two," Torgreth called out. "We need an unbiased judge. Who's the better carvers, elves or dwarves?"

"They're both good," Conal replied without thinking.

Torgreth snorted a laugh and leaned towards Galadyr. "That's what my Mum used to say when me and Voldar brought carvings to her to tell us which one was the best. Never did choose a winner. Stopped asking her after a while."

"That's because you both carve in different media," Conal explained. "To make value judgment, we'd need to see a stone carving by an elf and a wood carving by a dwarf. Then we could judge fairly."

"That was profound," Torgreth teased. "I'm impressed."

Ignoring him, Conal asked Bryok, "Where should we spend the night?"

"About halfway to Denhelm, near the ruins of Glaston," Bryok replied, understanding the reason for the question. "At this pace we should get there after dark."

"We need to pick up the pace then," Conal suggested.

"Your call," Bryok replied.

Increasing the pace to a trot and taking occasional rests, they arrived at the outskirts of the ruins in the late afternoon. Conal was more than ready to get off the saddle.

"We camp here tonight," he announced.

"Here?" several voices nervously complained.

"Here," Maldwic asserted. "Where do you want us to set up, Boss?"

"You decide, Maldwic," Conal answered, sitting on his horse, surveying the ruins of what had once been a thriving city.

Centuries of war had ravaged the city. Lichen and ivy covered the walls, broken in places, a testament to the battering rams and trebuchet stone missiles. The gates, ripped from their hinges, lay inside the barbican. Weeds and trees had reclaimed much of the city streets and parks. The present residents consisted of rodents, coyotes, and the occasional bear. When the last assault had slaughtered the remaining living defenders and citizens, the city was pronounced accursed. Stories grew of the dead roaming the homes and castle, unsettled and unable to find rest.

Though dismissing the stories as fabled imagination, the place still gave Conal the creeps.

"It's still a little bit of a ride," Bryok quietly relayed.

"Maldwic," Conal called out to his subordinate.

"Yes, Boss?" Maldwic guided his horse to come alongside him.

"Bryok and I have some business to attend to. We'll be back after it's dark. Don't worry," he added, seeing the doubt on the man's face, "Bryok's a druid. We'll be safe."

"OK, Boss."

"Where're we setting up?"

"In the barbican. It's big enough for all of us and gives us better protection."

"Fine. See you in a bit."

"Take this." Maldwic handed him a short sword encased in a leather scabbard. "I had it as an extra. Figured you might need it."

"Thank you, Maldwic." He buckled the sword around his waist. "Give the company a name. Something strong and noble. Something like 'Maldwic's Marauders.' That has a punch to it."

"But you're the boss," he countered, though flattered with the suggested name.

"Only for a little while. Besides, I have bigger plans in mind. I'll be back shortly."

While Maldwic reined his horse around to give instructions to the company, Torgreth piped up, "Where you going?"

"We have some things to discuss," Bryok answered, giving Galadyr a knowing look, receiving a nod of understanding in return.

"You can't discuss them here?" Torgreth cocked an eyebrow.

Galadyr placed a gentle hand on the dwarf's shoulder. "It is something that needs to be discussed far enough away from prying ears."

Torgreth twisted his head up to give him a curious stare. "How do you know?"

"I don't," he blandly replied, "but I trust them enough not to interfere."

Torgreth blinked at the revelation and grinned. "Point noted. Guess I'd better find a place to settle before all these thieves get the good spots. Come along elf. I've got extra leaf if you got a pipe."

Conal followed Bryok as the druid rode the edges of the city walls to the north-east where the heavily forested mountains rose and then onto a little used path that snaked its way through the evergreens and hardwoods, repeatedly curling back on itself as it ascended.

"Can you tell me anything about the dragon?" Conal finally asked, his curiosity bursting.

"His name is Krag," Bryok answered, "Krag the Patient One or sometimes Krag the Wise, though now, he is merely Krag. He is a Forest Dragon."

"Forest Dragon? How many kinds are there?"

"At one time there were many," Bryok explained, a great melancholy in his voice, "all different sizes. Some were small, the size of the largest draft horse. Others were large, like the Mountain Dragons, and some even larger, like Rock Dragons."

"So how big is a forest dragon."

"You will see when you meet him."

"What's he like?"

Bryok frowned in thought. "He can be gruff at times, but you have to understand all that he has seen, all that he has endured."

"Do you think he will help us?"

"That will be up to you to convince him."

"Me?" Conal blurted. "Why me?"

"Because you are the king's son. While I think about it, I would not mention that you bear the Cobra brand… at least not yet."

"Why not?

"Remember the prophecy?"

"The eagle will bear the vipers in its claws, yet from the west a cobra will rise and strike down the eagle," Conal intoned. "Yes, I remember. So what?"

"So, let's just keep quiet about that for now, shall we?" Bryok sternly replied.

"Why?"

Bryok heaved a long-suffering sigh. "Because the Cobra part implies that the vipers, or the king's children will be dominated by the Cobra."

"No, it doesn't," Conal argued. "All it says is that the Cobra will strike down the eagle. It says nothing about ruling or anything else."

Bryok flipped an inpatient hand at him. "You just don't understand."

"What's to understand? And how do you even know this prophecy is about me and Torian?" Conal said with a dismissive shake of his head.

"Can we drop it for now?" Bryok snapped. "Just don't mention it, OK?"

"OK, OK, mum's the word."

Silence ruled for a few minutes before Conal asked, "What else can you tell me about him?"

"Be respectful when you talk to him. Though you are a king's son, he too is royalty, a prince at one time. And remember, we need his help."

"Why? How can he help if he's spending his life hiding?"

Bryok shot him a look of irritation. "He is waiting, like the few remaining survivors, for a true king to rise up, one that will establish peace, a peace where dragons are free to live without fear of being hunted."

Conal pondered the answer. "Seems to me you're putting a lot of faith into a tiny fraction of our effort. Dragons have been hiding because they've been hunted almost to extinction. And now you think they're going to want to help us?"

Bryok jerked his horse to a halt. "Do you want to see this dragon or not? I have half a mind to turn around and not waste my time." He thrust a finger at Conal. "Dragons were hunted to near extinction because no one saw any need for them. It's hard to stay alive when everyone is out to kill you. Would you feel the same way if humans were the target of extermination?"

Conal held up his hands in defeat. "OK, you win."

Prodding his horse forward, Bryok huffed, "Use your brains. Dragons have great powers. How can we best use them to achieve what we need?"

Fading sunlight rimed the mountain tops as Bryok led them into a wide clearing. Conal glanced around at the pleasant meadow. Wildflowers undulated in the gentle wind. The cloudless sky above added to the aura of peace. Securing their mounts back down the path, Bryok led Conal to the middle of the field.

"You wait here while I go see if Krag is willing to show himself."

"Why can't I come a long?"

Bryok heaved a sigh of exasperation. "Have you not been listening? They don't trust anyone. Just stay here."

"OK."

Conal watched Bryok stalk across the field then disappear into the woods. For some reason, Conal expected an immediate appearance, as though the dragon was hiding in the forest at the edge of the meadow. When minutes passed and the daylight began to fade, Conal grew concerned. What if something had happened to Bryok? Suppose they were in the wrong place? What if the dragon was hiding somewhere else and was no longer there?

Knowing it was futile to go look for him, he debated calling out when a gigantic, winged creature filled the darkening sky above him, circling slowly before plummeting to the ground to stand towering over Conal, causing him to stumble backwards.

"So, you're the one," Krag said, his voice rich and resonant. He sat back on his haunches and folded his wings behind him, his tail curling around him. "Tell me human, why should I trust you?"

CHAPTER 7

GWEN

Gwen spent most of the night tossing and turning, her anxious thoughts making her mind run wild. It didn't help that Kirith hadn't answered her questions about the plan that Lyra mentioned.

Lyra.

Gwen knew there was something more to the woman. Her Aspect alone was an oddity, but it was more than that. She wished she could figure it out, but whatever *it* was, it continued to elude her. Aimil hadn't seemed to notice anything out of the ordinary, but Aimil had traveled to many places. Gwen considered the possibility that she was overthinking things.

When dawn came, she hadn't slept much. She was surprised to find that all of her aches and pains were gone, a blessing from bathing in the Thaestra water. The same young elven woman from the previous day made another appearance, bringing a tray full of food for breakfast. The options were the same, mostly fruits, and Gwen forced herself to accept that she would have to wait for meat until they returned to human lands.

If they returned at all.

"The nobles are arriving for the trial," Kirith said from the balcony. "It won't be long now."

Gwen thought back to when they found him with the vagabonds. His hair was matted with dried blood and he'd looked ragged. Even so, Gwen had still seen his beauty, had felt his regality shine through the roughness. Now that he was cleaned up, it shined doubly so. His hair had a natural glow to it and his eyes held an excitement she didn't understand. And he and Aimil shared something now, didn't they?

"Are you still refusing to tell us what this plan entails?" Gwen asked, trying to stay focused.

"Trust me," Kirith said, stepping back into the main room. "I would never allow you to enter the path of danger in my homeland."

Trust him. Those words reminded Gwen of Tobias and a twinge of pain pulled at her heart. She closed her eyes for a moment and gritted her teeth against the hurt, waiting for it to pass, then opened her eyes again.

"I'm sorry if I have angered you." Kirith was staring at her.

"It's not that," Gwen replied. "Or you. It's nothing."

Kirith bowed his head, but Gwen could tell he was curious about her reaction. She picked up an apple from the tray and bit into it. The crisp skin broke under her teeth, showering her tongue with a rush of sweet juice. She devoured the rest of the apple and waited.

The young elven woman returned, this time bearing a purple robe. Kirith let her put it on him, then said something in another language to her. Gwen assumed it was elvish. It sounded musical and tickled her ears. The young elf bowed to him, a smile playing at her lips, then left.

"Who is that?" Aimil asked.

"That is my sister, Talahna."

"She's a servant?" Gwen asked.

Kirith laughed loudly. "Talahna is not a servant," he replied. "She's—"

His words were cut off as the doors opened fully and a host of guards, including Haladavar, strode inside.

"My Lord," Haladavar greeted Kirith. "The court awaits your presence."

"Lead the way," Kirith replied.

The guards were wearing extravagant capes and their chainmail armor gleamed as if it had been polished. Their demeanor was solemn, their expressions serious. Gwen felt as though the trial was some sort of sacred ceremony judging by the change of atmosphere. Kirith stepped into the hall, followed by Aimil, then Gwen. Haladavar took the lead and the host of guards moved into position around the three prisoners.

Gwen didn't recognize anything they passed, but their arrival and detainment had been such a blur. She admired everything about Auleavell. Everything except King Falael. Kirith was so different from his father that she was tempted to question whether Kirith was truly from Falael's loins. The fact that they were so similar in appearance was the only reason she didn't.

They walked down the stairs, all the way to the bottom floor. It was crowded with elves, both nobles and commoners, and guards lined the walls around the entire room. Falael was at the center of the room seated on a chair made of tree roots. It curved gracefully up from the floor and Gwen marveled at it, but she didn't think the chair looked very comfortable. It appeared to be more for looks than functionality.

The crowd was gathered around the center, but a ring of guards around Falael kept everyone from getting too close to him. Apparently, Falael didn't trust his own people. Haladavar escorted them through the crowd and stopped outside the ring of guards. Falael stood up and the room went silent.

"Welcome, nobles of Auleavell. Today we must decide the fate of two criminals, but we must also choose a punishment for our wayward prince."

The ring of guards parted and Haladavar led Kirith to Falael's side. Gwen scanned the crowd, looking at the faces of the nobles. They looked proud and haughty just like their king. She looked at Aimil and had to hide her smile. The woman wore an expression that dared someone to test her anger.

"What are the charges against them?" one of the nobles asked.

"Trespassing," Falael answered. "And as everyone here knows, that means they must be executed."

There was a general murmur of agreement throughout the room. Gwen turned her gaze to Falael, her anger rising at his words.

"They weren't trespassing," Kirith said loudly. The room went silent again, but this time Gwen noticed it was from shock. "They rescued me from bandits who thought to collect a bounty on my head. A bounty put out by my father, no less."

"He speaks out of turn despite knowing the law," Falael said. "Lyra's poisoning of his mind, and the minds of our children, must end. She has already been banned from this court, but clearly, that is not enough. We must force her from Auleavell."

"Excommunication!" someone shouted.

The word was repeated by others until the room echoed with it. Falael raised his hand, calling for order.

"I agree," Falael said. "Every noble who votes in favor, raise your right hand."

Gwen was surprised to see how many arms went up across the room. Lyra was odd, sure, but that didn't mean she should be removed from her own home.

"It is decided. Lyra Talinos has been excommunicated." Falael looked at Haladavar. "Find her and remove her."

The tone in his voice sent a shiver down Gwen's back. His command sounded more like an order for death. Haladavar bowed low and motioned to a few guards, who followed him out of the chamber. Gwen wasn't sure how any of this fit into some sort of plan.

"Now, back to the humans," Falael said. "They were caught trespassing with Prince Kirith as their prisoner. Haladavar himself found them and brought them here for trial. Every noble who votes them as guilty, raise your right hand."

Gwen's heart sank into her stomach as every noble in the room raised their hand into the air. Aimil turned to the elves closest to her and shot them stares of death. A few of them stepped further away, but others ignored her.

"We need to escape," Gwen said to Aimil. "Whatever Lyra and Kirith had planned isn't happening now."

"Where do you plan to go?" Aimil asked. "We're bound here as long as we have these bracelets on, remember?"

Gwen had forgotten. She tugged on her bracelet futilely while she looked around the room, trying to plot out the best route of escape. There were too many guards and too many obstacles between them and the exit.

"It is also decided," Falael's voice echoed throughout the room. "The humans are guilty and will be executed by nightfall." There was a low rumble of approval from the nobles. "Lastly, we must decide upon a just punishment for our prince. He has allowed the lies from Lyra's mouth to pollute his mind and has even spoken evil in my presence. Who here would like to suggest his chastisement?"

Several nobles raised their hands and spoke at the same time. Falael smiled and it made Gwen's stomach churn. He was enjoying the spectacle. The fact that he found delight at the prospect of his own son's torment was something Gwen couldn't fathom.

"There will be no such punishment issued," an angry voice said. Gwen turned to see who had spoken and gasped when she saw Lyra striding through the archway. The crowd of elves parted to let her pass, but some of the guards along the wall rushed to stop her.

"Halt!" she demanded. The guards hesitated and even Gwen felt the authority in her voice. She wanted to obey Lyra and she wasn't even moving.

"Stop her!" Falael said. "Remove her from this chamber!"

"Guards!" It was Kirith shouting. "Nobles! It is time to rise!"

The room erupted in chaos. Guards turned on one another, as well as the nobles, snapping the magic negating bracelets onto their wrists. Gwen drew close to Aimil for safety, but the elves were too preoccupied with their fellows to care about them. Kirith rushed his father and put a bracelet onto Falael's wrist as the clang of steel rang out. The factions of guards struggled, those loyal to father and son pitted against one another.

"It's a coupe," Aimil said, a hint of surprise in her voice. "Kirith is taking the throne."

Gwen wondered if they were the cause of it all, but then she remembered Lyra's plan. This must have been what she meant. She looked for the woman in the crowd and saw her heading for Falael.

"I think it's about to get bloody in here," Gwen said. "We should get out into the open."

"No," Aimil replied. "I want to see what happens."

Before Gwen could make up her mind about fleeing the tree, Lyra grabbed Kirith's hand and lifted it.

"Hail your new king, Auleavell!"

A cheer ran out and Gwen realized the battle was over just as quickly as it began. Kirith's supporters had subdued the others.

"I excommunicate you!" Falael snarled at Kirith. "You are banished from this court!"

"No, father," Kirith replied calmly. "It is *you* who is banished from this court. The people have spoken this day. You and those loyal to you are hereby stripped of your titles and powers. As king of Auleavell, I rescind the excommunication of Lyra and grant Gwen and Aimil their freedom. They are friends of Auleavell and are welcome in our lands at any time, with or without invitation."

"You can't do this," Falael said. "You have no authority!"

"Your age must be getting to your mind," Kirith replied. "I just did it." He motioned to one of his guards. "Take him away."

Falael was led up the stairs first, then the other nobles were escorted from the room. Those nobles loyal to Kirith remained and he bestowed the titles and lands of those arrested to them.

"May it be remembered that the king of Auleavell is the voice of the people. When that voice fails in its duty, another will speak in its place. Let everyone here never forget this lesson."

As the crowd began to disperse, Kirith joined Gwen and Aimil. Two guards stayed at his side.

"Thank you for trusting me," he said. "Lyra and I laid this plan out before I was captured. I knew my father would never realize that Torian is a threat, so I did what I had to for my people and yours."

"I am sure Eradore and the rest of the rebellion will be proud to call you an ally," Gwen said. "I'm sorry that you had to usurp your father."

"It is my hope that my father will come to see reason while he is locked up. If he can, then I may be tempted to step down and let him rule again."

"Though I do not believe he will, it is a heartfelt sentiment," Lyra said as she approached them.

Gwen looked at her and saw the silver glow of her Aspect. She wanted to ask her about it, but it didn't feel like the right time. Instead, she offered Lyra a smile and then turned her attention back to Kirith.

"Can we have these removed?" Gwen asked, lifting her arm and nodding at the bracelet.

"Of course," Kirith replied.

One of his guards removed the bracelet from Gwen and the other freed Aimil. Gwen felt the magic surge back into her mind, its steady pulse thrumming in the rune on her hand. It reminded her that she might find another rune before she left for Steepcross.

"Are there any mages here?" Gwen asked.

"There are a few," Kirith said. "Would you like to meet with one?"

"Yes. I was hoping to gain another rune if anyone is willing."

"You and Aimil are my honored guests. Nothing will be kept from you."

"Nothing?" Aimil asked. Her tone reminded Gwen of the previous night when she and Kirith had … Gwen's cheeks flushed in embarrassment at the memory.

"Nothing," Kirith confirmed.

"I would like to see the Thaestra River."

Kirith's eyes widened briefly. "It is forbidden to outsiders … but I will make an exception for you. I must attend to a few things, but I will meet you back here in an hour. Do you plan to come as well?" Kirith asked, looking at Gwen.

"I would love to after meeting with one of your mages. Is that all right?"

"That is agreeable. Lyra, would you mind showing Gwen to the mage you think best suited for her?"

"I know just the one," Lyra replied. "And since it is still early, I know exactly where to find him."

"Thank you," Gwen said to Kirith.

"It is I who should thank you. The both of you. If you hadn't rescued me, I think we'd find ourselves in a completely different place right now." Kirith looked at Aimil. "Feel free to wander until I return."

"I'll occupy myself," Aimil smiled.

"Follow me," Lyra said, heading for the archway that led out of the tree. Gwen hurried after her, staring uncertainly at her Aspect. She had noticed that Lyra was the only elf she'd seen with one that wasn't green. They left the tree and followed a path that forked to the left. Lyra slowed her pace so that Gwen could match her strides.

"I'm not blind to your mistrust," Lyra said.

"I didn't say I don't trust you," Gwen replied.

"You don't have to. I know why you stare at me so."

"Why is that?"

Lyra lowered her voice. "Because you see that I am not an elf."

CHAPTER 8

CONAL

Conal craned his head back to stared into a pair of coal bright eyes high above him. "Uh… where's Bryok?" he managed to say.

"He keeps watch over my hiding spot while I am here," Krag replied. "A wise precaution, don't you think?"

"Certainly," Conal answered, still in awe as he took in the size of the beast, "especially from the way things have been going around here lately."

"Lately?" Krag snorted a dismissive laugh.

"Well… maybe longer than that," Conal sheepishly admitted before blurting, "what kind of dragon are you?"

The question surprised, yet pleased Krag. "I am a forest dragon."

"Wish it was daylight so I could see you better."

"I can see you just fine," Krag replied with a hint of humor.

"That's because you can see in the dark."

Again, Krag was surprised. "How is it that you know this?"

"I used to read about dragons when I was young," Conal answered.

"Young?" Krag laughed. "In dragon years, you are still a baby."

"I know," Conal chuckled.

"Tell me then, if you have read so much about dragons, why did you believe they did not exist?"

"How did… ah, Bryok told you that." Conal stepped closer. "I suppose I was swayed by the absence of dragons for so many years. As is our habit, when something is missing for so long, we believe it no longer exists. Then the so-called experts begin writing about dragons of the past and it doesn't take much effort to believe there are no dragons anymore."

Krag bent his head down to within inches of Conal's face, his large glowing eyes staring directly at him. "I sense something different about you. Place you hand on my forehead."

Conal reached a hand up, feeling the smoothness of the hardened scales and bumps on the dragon's forehead then flattened his hand.

Krag closed his eyes and darkness swallowed the meadow.

"I feel an imbalance in you," Krag said, "something about who you are." He opened his eyes. "You are unsure of who you are. Deep inside you, you know, but you are unconvinced. It's like you are waiting for something to happen that will settle it once and for all."

Conal jerked his hand back. "How can you tell that? I didn't feel anything."

"You were expecting our connection to hurt, like some rune bone?" He sniffed a laugh. "I am a dragon, not some incantation scratched into a dried brittle bone. If I wanted, I could have bound you to me for the rest of your life."

Startled, Conal stepped back.

"It's not what you think," Krag reassured him.

"You don't know what I think," Conal retorted.

"First," Krag asserted, his voice firm, "bonding with a dragon is a rare privilege that very few experience. Second, humans being violent creatures by nature, what makes you think I would want to bond with you? Third –"

"I get it," Conal snapped. "You're a powerful dragon who could impose his will on me. In fact, you're so powerful you've been hiding like a scared rabbit for the past 150 years." It came out before he could stop himself. Already he was imagining Bryok cringing at his stupidity.

"Scared rabbit," Krag thundered, rising up on his rear legs, his wings unfurling.

Refusing to be intimidated, Conal folded his arms across his chest. "Yeah, a scared rabbit. I'm still trying to figure out why Bryok was so keen on enlisting your help. If you're so powerful, why are you hiding? Why not just come out and assert yourself? Demand to be accepted."

Wisps of smoke puffed out from Krag's nostrils. "Easy for you to say, human."

"I have a name," Conal tartly reminded him.

Krag's eyes flamed then settled as he sat back down and folded his wings. "Tell me, Conal, what would you do when everyone went out of their way to try and kill you? Suppose elves and dwarves suddenly made a pact to destroy humans and you found yourself one of the last humans left. Would you be so bold as to stand out in public and 'demand to be accepted'?"

"But I'm not as powerful as you are," Conal countered.

"When the forces of evil are marshaled against you, it doesn't matter how strong you are. When the odds are tens of thousands to one, what are your chances of winning? We few who remain know that our time is running out. In time, dragons *will* be a thing of the past. I and a few others have gone into hiding because there is no one who will join us, no one who will stand firm and say, 'No more.'"

"I will."

Krag gazed kindly at the young man. "You? Who are you that I should place my hope?"

"I am a king's son, *the* king's son," Conal stoutly affirmed.

Krag paused and smiled. "So, you now accept who you are?"

"Not you too," Conal groaned.

"Someone else remind you to accept who you are?"

"Bryok. The man's infuriating because he's always right. Don't tell him I said that."

Krag chuckled. "So, Conal, king's son, what is your quest?"

"Odd as it sounds, I'm going to reclaim my throne."

"Which one is that?"

"The one Torian now usurps."

"Torian?" Krag jerked upright. "You are Kamron's son?"

"So they say."

"Are you or not?" The bright eyes flickered.

Conal hesitated. He had said it once already. Why was it so hard to say again? He was being noble when he told Krag that he would stand with him. If he said it now, it meant that he had to accept it, believe it, embrace it.

Inhaling a slow breath, he answered, "I am he."

Krag rose to his back legs and flapped his wings. "It's about time."

"About time for what?" Conal asked, raising an eyebrow.

Krag settled and stretched out before him, his huge face several feet away. "What you seek to do is fraught with danger. Do you know the prophecy?"

"Yes." Conal remembered Bryok's warning to say nothing about his Cobra brand.

"Then you know you will fall into Torian's hands. Your fate will depend on the one who is the Cobra."

"Wouldn't that be *our* fate?"

Krag nodded. "A wise answer." He abruptly jerked his head back, twitching side to side, sniffing the air. "Someone's coming. They're close." He thrust himself into the air, calling out, "Bryok knows where to find me."

As Krag rose into the air, shouts bellowed from the opposite side of the clearing.

"There he is. Shoot him, quick! Aim fer the heart."

Arrows shot skyward as half a dozen men burst onto the meadow, firing madly at the dragon swirling and rising above them. Some arrows bounced harmlessly off Krag's thick skin, others arced and fell back to the earth.

Enraged, Conal raced across the field, unsheathing his sword as he ran. Too late, the attackers shifted their efforts as the dervish burst upon them. The speed and precision of his attack as he cut and slashed sent five men to their quick deaths.

Seeing his comrades cut down one and two at a time, the last man took to his heels, jettisoning his bow and quiver and racing back into the woods.

Conal stood in the middle of the carnage, his chest heaving as his anger dissipating. Looking up into the sky, he prayed Krag was unharmed and secure in his hiding place. A rising three-quarter moon gave light to the meadow. Glancing back down, he counted the bodies of the men he had just killed. Five. Five bodies lay mangled at his feet. It was then he noticed long hair on the body closest to him. Using his foot, he flipped the still warm corpse over revealing the tortured face of a young woman.

His first reaction was overwhelming guilt. Not only had he killed again, he had killed a woman.

"Conal?" Bryok called out, pushing a man ahead of him into the clearing. "You OK?"

"I'm fine," he responded, forcibly pushing his remorse aside.

"I intercepted this one on the way back here," Bryok explained, frog-marching the man to where Conal stood.

Once again Conal was surprised for the man turned out to be a woman, a little shorter than he, lithe with sharp features. Yet there was something odd about her. Though she had the look of a cornered hare, there was a fascination with Bryok, bordering on slavish wonder.

Bryok looked down at the bodies. "Watch her," he commanded as he knelt down to examine a body, picking up a limp hand to scrutinize it. He repeated the process with the others before standing to confront the woman. "Show me your hand."

When the woman didn't respond but grinned stupidly at him, he grabbed her hand, causing her to yelp. He thrust the hand towards her face and twisted it around so she could see the back of her hand. "What is this?"

The loopy smile still plastered on her face, the woman stared at her hand then at him. She reached a hand out to touch his face.

Batting the hand away, he twisted the other around for Conal to see and jabbed a finger at the tattoo of a dragon's head with a lance through it. "She's a dragon hunter."

"At one time I might have thought that an absurd occupation," Conal said, "but not anymore. Seems sort of strange that after all these years of no one ever seeing a dragon they suddenly show up here at this very moment." He frowned at the woman. "What's wrong with her?"

Bryok twisted her arm to show the runes on the inside of her forearm. "She's been rune-marked." He heaved a sigh of disgust. "Haven't seen these in a long time. It marks the person as a dragon hunter, but the person is spirit bound to the owner of the rune bone. Back when dragon hunting was all the rage, there were lots of these kinds of people, all chasing the elusive dragon, reaping large rewards, only to discover too late that their lives were inextricably linked to their rune master. They spent their days searching for something they could never find, eventually dying out until there were no more dragon hunters. In the end, all the riches they thought they had belonged to the rune master, for they were compelled to search, never finding rest."

"So why now?" Conal asked. "Why the sudden appearance of dragon hunters?"

Bryok glanced back towards the mountain where Krag lived in hiding. "I think someone has discovered that dragons still exist and that they're on your side."

"Torian?"

"Seems logical."

Conal gazed at the woman. "What do we do with her?"

Bryok gripped the woman's wrist in his hand. In a speed almost too fast for Conal to see, Bryok jerked the woman's arm causing her to lurch forward. At the same time, he delivered a chop to her throat before spinning around with a slicing knife-hand to her neck with such a force that it broke her neck.

"My God," Conal startled as the woman wobbled as if suspended in midair before crumpling to a heap. "You killed her. Why'd you kill her?"

"She's a dragon hunter," Bryok coldly answered.

"Yes, but –"

"But what? She came here to kill Krag. She failed because you were here. You killed the others and now you're shocked because I killed her?"

"But she didn't have a chance to defend herself," Conal objected.

"She ran as soon as she saw which way the battle went," Bryok reminded him. "Had she lived, she would have told Torian about Krag and about us, about where we were and then returned to the hunt again. She was rune-bound. She had no other choice. What you should be worried about is how many other dragon hunters are out there?"

Conal knew he was right. The woman was a threat. One thing puzzled him. "Why are you so keen on enlisting dragon help? Seems to me that they're going to be more of a problem because we have to protect them."

"Did you learn nothing in your talk with Krag?" Bryok sourly asked.

"Actually, no," Conal replied. "We barely got talking when they arrived. Speaking of 'they,' what do we do with them?"

"Leave them. It's obvious they were not killed by a dragon. Anyone coming up here will be on guard and want to move on through as quickly as possible. We should go back." He led the way across the field and down the path to their horses who were calmly waiting for them.

"Surprised they didn't take fright," Conal commented.

"They know when there's danger," Bryok answered, "and when they're safe."

"One thing still puzzles me," Conal said, swinging up into the saddle. "How did they know Krag was here? If a dragon is so good at hiding that everyone thinks they no longer exist, how is it that they knew to look here?"

"That too concerns me," Bryok grimly nodded.

They rode back in silence, each lost in his own thoughts. As they approached the ruins, Conal sniffed the air. "I smell campfire smoke. Not very smart for security."

"Hey Boss," a female voice called out as the woman stepped from behind the gate pillar before the barbican.

"Hullo, Seren," Conal quietly replied, dismounting then leading his horse to the gate.

"Horses are over there." She pointed to the opposite end of the barbican. "Everyone's sleep 'cept for me and another roving guard."

"Why is there a fire?" Conal pointed at the circle of stones surrounding the rippling embers of a fire.

"Maldwic thought you might need some help returning in the dark."

"That was a good idea," Bryok interrupted.

Deciding he was tired and ready to find a spot to stretch out, Conal started to lead his horse to the tether line when the woman spoke.

"Had some folks come by not long after you left," she said. "Four men and two women."

Conal jerked to a halt. "Who were they?"

Seren started snickering. "Called themselves dragon hunters. Can you believe it? Who'd they think would fall for that? And they were serious as can be. Got mad when we laughed at 'em. And when they said there were dragons close by, we knew they were loony."

"Where are they?"

"Oh," she chuckled, "we sent them off. Maldwic sent an escort with them to make sure they got as far away from here as possible. Haven't seen 'em since. And that was just after you left. You didn't see 'em did you?"

"No," Conal answered, a little quicker than needed.

"One odd thing though," she commented. "They said they were looking for you."

"For me?" Conal sputtered.

"No, not you Boss, him." She pointed a finger and narrowed her gaze at Bryok. "They were looking for you."

CHAPTER 9

GWEN

"You're not an elf?" Gwen asked. She stopped walking and stared at Lyra suspiciously. "What do you mean?"

"Keep quiet," Lyra snapped, glancing around to see if anyone had taken an interest in their conversation. The few elves nearby were going about their business and Lyra turned her eyes back on Gwen. "It's not important."

"I think it is," Gwen replied. "Especially if you want me to trust you."

"There are many things in this life that you will never be privy to. If I trust *you,* then I will reveal what I mean. In time. Now come along."

Gwen felt the power of Lyra's authority like she had in the trial and followed her. She'd never been one to argue, and this day proved no different. They wound along the worn path that twisted through the forest-city, past the temple they had met at the night before, and stopped at the natural entrance to what Gwen assumed was a garden.

"Virion tends this place," Lyra said. "He is a wise mage and many elves come from afar to seek his advice."

"Will he grant me a rune?" Gwen asked.

"That is yet to be seen. If he thinks you are fit for one, he will grant it."

"Kirith said we would not be denied anything. Does he not rule over Virion?"

"You like to play with childish talk," Lyra said. "Do you not feel as dumb as you sound? Surely you hear your own words."

Gwen's face flushed with embarrassment and anger, but before she could recover her wits and offer a retort, a handsome elf came into view. She bit her tongue and watched him in silence. He knelt in front of a wooden lattice and lifted a wilting vine in his hand. A moment later, the vine was fully restored.

"How did he do that?" Gwen asked, her anger washed away under a wave of amazement and curiosity.

"Ask him," Lyra said.

Gwen stepped uncertainly through the entrance of the garden and approached Virion, stopping a few paces away. She waited for him to acknowledge her, but he quietly continued his healing work with the grapevines. Gwen could hear him humming lowly. At first, she thought it was an insect, but as he walked around to the other side of the lattice, she heard the sound clearly. Gwen watched him work and tried to remain patient, and even glanced questioningly over her shoulder at Lyra. The woman offered nothing in her expression.

"What is your name?" Virion suddenly asked.

Gwen snapped her head back around to look at him. His hands were still tending to the vine, but his head was turned in her direction. The first thing she noticed about him was his eyes. They were gray, close in color to his long hair, except his hair shimmered with life.

"You're blind?" Gwen blurted out. She immediately felt stupid for saying it.

Virion chuckled, not taking offense. "Yes, I am blind."

"I'm sorry. It ... surprised me. My name is Gwen." She wished Lyra would have mentioned something before she made a fool of herself.

"There is nothing to apologize for. Tell me, Gwen. What brings you here?"

"I'm seeking a rune," she replied.

"Ah, a fellow mage. Welcome to my humble garden," Virion offered a slight bow. "What kind of rune are seeking?"

Gwen paused. She hadn't given it much thought. She'd gained lightning from Aimil, but that wasn't necessarily her choice. She'd merely picked a rune from among hundreds on a whim, not knowing what it did.

"I'm not sure," she confessed.

"That's not necessarily a bad thing," Virion replied. "Perhaps I can help you decide. Come closer."

Gwen did as he asked, and Virion reached out a hand.

"Let me feel your runes."

"I only have one," Gwen said as she placed her hand in his. He ran his fingers over the outline of her rune and Gwen could feel power radiating from Virion. The elf was blind, but Gwen knew he wasn't helpless.

"Lightning," Virion said. "Your single rune is a weapon?"

Gwen couldn't tell by his tone whether he was impressed or bothered by that. "I didn't choose it," she replied. "Well, I did choose that rune, but I didn't know beforehand what it was."

"You chose at random?"

"Not really. I was asked to look over many runes and pick the one that stood out most. It turned out to be lightning."

"That's a fascinating way of choosing a rune," Virion said. "Are you disappointed with what you received?"

"No. It has helped me."

"How has a weapon of war helped you?"

"It helped me during a battle," Gwen answered vaguely.

"The rune fulfilled its purpose, as does all magic. Thank you for entertaining my questions, Gwen. Runes are powerful and should not be entrusted lightly. If you had to choose between a weapon of war and a tool for nature, which would you choose?"

Gwen considered the question carefully. Given what the future held with the plans of the rebellion, it would make sense that she should choose another rune that could cause destruction. Yet, if this was a test, Virion may refuse to give her a rune at all depending on her answer. She wanted more runes to aid in the struggle against Torian, and she didn't want to lie to Virion. If he chose not to give her a rune, so be it.

"I would choose a weapon of war," Gwen said.

Virion released her hand. "I am not surprised by your answer. I can sense turmoil around you. Is it fear that drives you to the arms of destruction, or something else?"

"I don't think I am headed to the arms of destruction," Gwen said, but as she spoke the words, she doubted the truth behind them. It was entirely possible that she was on the road to devastation by trying to take down a king. She'd already lost so much, and she felt as though her journey had just begun.

"Who can know whether that is true or not? I will grant you a rune, Gwen, but it will not be a weapon of war."

"Thank you," Gwen said. She was a little disappointed, but he had agreed to give her a rune.

"The rune I grant you is a tool that will help the world around you. Humans cause chaos wherever they go, but it is my hope that this rune will help balance you. You have seen Auleavell. What do you think of it?"

"It's beautiful," Gwen answered.

"I am glad you think so. To balance the chaos of lightning, I give you a rune of earthen power. Close your eyes."

Gwen did so. She flinched slightly when Virion's fingers touched her temples. A flood of green glowing energy filled her mind. It reminded her of the Aspect of the elves.

"You feel the rune," he said.

"Yes," Gwen replied. It swirled around her, whispering. She couldn't understand the words, but they gave her a feeling of renewal and growth.

"Speak its name."

"*Saol,*" Gwen said. There was a slight burning sensation on her right hand for a brief moment, then it was gone. Unlike her experience with the lightning, nothing else happened. She'd feared that she would be sucked into the ground or something similar, but there was only peace and tranquility. She opened her eyes and saw Virion staring at her. Although she knew he couldn't see, it made her feel awkward.

"What does the rune do?" Gwen asked.

"It attunes you to nature. Do you see that vine?" Virion pointed at one that was dried out. "It is on the verge of death. Help it flourish once more."

Gwen wondered how Virion knew the vine was damaged if he couldn't see. Instead of keeping it to herself, she voiced her question.

"Simply because I cannot see with these eyes, does not mean that I am blind to everything," Virion said. "I am in tune with the life forces around me and can feel when they are troubled."

"You must see the world in a very beautiful way," Gwen replied. She knelt and placed her hand gently under the wilted vine. The pulse of magic in her new rune made her fingers twitch and she tried to hold them still. She licked her lips and spoke the rune.

"*Saol.*"

A surge of green energy flowed from her palm into the vine. Gwen's eyes widened in surprise. The energy tingled as it left her skin. The vine accepted the flow, and its color slowly began to return. After a few more moments, the vine lifted off her hand and Gwen stopped the magic. She stood and looked at Virion.

"How does the rune restore life?" she asked.

"It doesn't restore life," Virion corrected. "Not in the way you think. Magic is in all things, but not all things can use it. When you channel the magic, it can invigorate things that have been lost. The vine was not yet dead. If it had been, the magic would not have done anything to help it. Magic can restore, and in rare cases create, but it cannot bring life to the dead."

"You said that you wanted this rune to balance me. Are you expecting me to use this rune to heal every wilting flower and tree I encounter?"

"Of course not," Virion replied. "I ask only that you use it for good."

Gwen didn't understand how she could use something inherently good for anything other than that, but she kept that to herself.

"Thank you again," Gwen said.

Virion opened his mouth to reply, then paused. A shadowed look appeared on his face and his eyebrows creased in concentration. He grunted and grabbed at his side, then crumpled to the ground.

"What is it?" Gwen asked, kneeling down and gingerly touching his shoulder. "Did I do something wrong?" She feared she must have done something incorrectly with the vine.

"Something dark has tainted Auleavell," Virion said between grunts of pain.

Gwen looked back at Lyra. She motioned for Gwen to follow her.

"Do I need to get help?" Gwen asked Virion.

"I feel what Auleavell feels," he said. "I'll be fine. Go if you must."

Gwen left the garden and followed Lyra. The elven woman walked hurriedly and kept glancing around at their surroundings.

"What is it?" Gwen asked. "Virion said something tainted Auleavell. Can you feel it, too?"

"I am not as connected to this place as Virion, but I sense something is amiss."

They reached the palace tree just as Kirith was coming out. Aimil followed behind him. Kirith looked troubled. "People are getting ill," he said. "It seems to have come out of nowhere. Not everyone is being affected, but we don't know what the source is."

"Caused by people loyal to your father?" Lyra

suggested.

"Maybe, but I don't believe so. My father is a hard man, but I don't think he would cause injury to his own people."

"Desperation can make people do unthinkable things," Lyra said.

Gwen felt something tugging at her mind, then pain lanced through her skin where her new rune was. She pressed her fingers to the back of her hand and suddenly she saw a vision of a river flowing underground.

"The river," Gwen said.

"The Thaestra? What of it?" Kirith asked.

"I think that's the source."

Kirith regarded her suspiciously. "What do you mean?"

Gwen lifted her hand to display the rune. "Virion gifted me with this. I think it's trying to tell me where the sickness is coming from."

"I must go and pray to Solara," Lyra said suddenly. "Forgive me, my Lord. I will find you when I am done."

Lyra rushed off and Gwen looked from Aimil to Kirith. It seemed the worst possible time to pray, but perhaps Lyra had some insight that wasn't evident to her.

"Let us go and see if the rune speaks truly to you," Kirith said.

He led them through the forest-city, heading north until they reached a large clearing. Five trees ringed the area, and between two of them was a glowing barrier. The barrier resembled a mirror, reflecting their appearances to them. Gwen tried to peer through it to see what was on the other side, but she only saw herself.

"This is the only way to the Thaestra," Kirith said. "You'll feel disoriented when you go through it, but it's only momentary." He wasted no time and stepped through, disappearing completely from view.

"Your turn," Aimil said.

Gwen stepped through and a powerful wave of nausea struck her. She staggered and almost fell, but Kirith grabbed her arm and steadied her. Aimil came through and stopped suddenly, looking past Kirith and Gwen, her mouth open in shock.

Kirith appeared confused and followed her gaze. He gasped. Gwen's queasiness subsided and she saw the startled look on Aimil's face.

"What is it?" she asked, then turned to look.

Standing beside the Thaestra River was a dragon.

CHAPTER 10

CONAL

They were looking for me?" Bryok frowned, avoiding Conal's questioning glance.

"Yeah," Seren answered. "Said you'd know where to find a dragon."

"Me?" Bryok exclaimed. "A dragon? What made them think that?"

"I know, right?" she smirked. "Like I said, they were all on the loony side."

"How about we worry about that in the morning," Conal suggested, yawning. "I'm tired."

"G'night, Boss," Seren grinned.

Tethering his horse next to Bryok's, Conal leaned in and in a tone only Bryok could hear, said, "They were looking for you. How would they know that about you?"

"I don't know," Bryok grimly replied.

"How would they know you were even here?"

"I said I don't know," Bryok snapped.

"Well you better figure out something fast, because they knew exactly where you were, where we were."

Bryok's lips pursed and he twisted his right forearm to reveal a small set of runes near his elbow.

Instead of the imprinted black ink, the runes gave off a very faint shimmer of crimson.

Conal saw it. "Why does that rune look weird? Never noticed it before."

Bryok slowly shook his head, his face grim. "This has never happened before."

"What's that rune for?"

"It is a special rune, one that I will not divulge at this time," he brusquely answered. "You will find out soon enough. Get some sleep. We need to get to Pharyl by tomorrow."

Though dissatisfied with the reply, Conal knew enough not to argue. He was pleased to see that Maldwic had set up a spot for him to stretch out next to his bed roll.

"Everything OK, Boss?"

"You still awake?"

"Wanted to make sure you were OK before I settled down."

"Everything's fine. Thanks for setting up a spot for me."

"Anytime. You run into those crazy fellas, the ones about the dragon?"

"No," Conal lied. "Why'd they think we'd know anything about dragons?"

"They were looking for that half-druid."

"So I understand," he yawned. "Talk about crazy."

Maldwic uttered a soft chuckle. "Know what I think, Boss?"

"What?"

Maldwic lowered his voice. "I think they might not have been as crazy as we think."

Conal twisted his head to stare at him. "Dragons? Do you believe in dragons?"

"I've never seen one or heard of anyone that has seen one. But… that doesn't mean they might not still exist."

"So, they've been hiding all this time? Think about it. A dragon has to eat and drink. In all this time, no one has even accidently bumped into one?"

"I know, I know," Maldwic agreed. "Still… that half-druid knows something."

"What makes you say that?"

"He's a druid."

Conal turned his head to see Bryok flipping a blanket off his shoulders. "Maybe you're right. Be nice to have dragons on our side."

"Have to find them first," Maldwic said.

"True," Conal drowsily answered. "In the meantime, we have enough things to worry about."

There was a heavy pause before Maldwic asked, "Are we still highwaymen, Boss?"

"Not anymore, Maldwic. We're mercenaries now."

Maldwic pondered the change. "Seems dangerous. Not everyone is a fighter."

"Doesn't have to be. Some are planners, some are better in logistics, some might be spies and those kinds of things. However, as we add more people to our company, we might want to emphasize the fighter part."

Maldwic nodded. "And I'm still going to become the Boss?"

"Yes. I have other things I need to accomplish."

"Like what?"

"You'll find out soon enough." *And now I sound like Bryok.* "Let's get some sleep. I want to be at Denhelm by tomorrow."

"G'night Boss." Folding his hands across his

chest, he was soon comfortably asleep.

Conal's thoughts wouldn't let him rest and by the time he drifted off to sleep, he felt his shoulder shaken and Maldwic grinning at him.

"Time to get going, Boss."

Rubbing his bleary eyes, Conal glanced around to see everyone else was awake, rolling up bedrolls while munching on jerky, day old bread, apples or anything else from their saddle bags. His stomach growled and he stood and stretched.

"Boss."

Conal turned and Maldwic tossed him an apple. "Thanks."

In short order, the company headed out the barbican, Conal in front, Bryok beside him. Galadyr and Torgreth had yet to settle their debate, but the topic had drifted from carvers to fighters and now to cooking. Conal wondered how soon it would touch on who were the better lovers.

The ride to Denhelm was uneventful. Conal figured the size of the company, all carrying weapons, was enough of a deterrent.

It was early evening by the time they arrived as the gate guards shooed people in or out in order to close the gates for the night. Seeing the size of the troop approaching the gates, one guard alerted the other guards who spread themselves across the opening.

"What do you want?" the guard sergeant demanded, inserting himself through two guards to stand defiantly before them. He was a middle-aged seasoned soldier with the air of one used to being obeyed.

"A place to spend the night," Conal replied with a smile. "This town does have inns, does it not?"

"Of course it does. What is your business here?"

"Not that it's any of your business," Conal coolly said, "but we are here to see Lord Pharyl."

"What do you want with him?" The sergeant folded his arms across his chest and stared at Conal.

"Like I said, it's none of your business." Conal leaned forward in the saddle. "But to assuage your inquisitiveness, send a runner to notify Lord Pharyl that Conal from Hemlyn is here to see him. I'll wait." Conal watched the man frown, deliberating on how much trouble he'd get into if he bothered the Lord versus how much trouble he'd be in if he didn't report what was going on.

Deciding instead to dodge the responsibility, he turned to one of the guards. "Get the captain."

"Ah," Conal chuckled, "let someone else take the blame. A wise decision, especially if one wants to safely move up the ranks."

The sergeant shot him guilty-as-charged sour look.

Several minutes later, the captain arrived in ill humor at being disturbed. He was a short man working his way towards plump, with an unruly shock of red hair that gave him the appearance of having just woken up.

"What goes on here?" he demanded.

"Like I told your sergeant, I've come to see Lord Pharyl." Conal waved at the company behind him. "I promise my friends will be good."

"I recognize 'im cap'n," one of the guards spoke up.

The sergeant snapped his head around to glare at the man. "Why didn't you say something?"

"You'd already sent Fergud to go fetch the cap'n."

"Well out with it, man. How do you recognize him?"

"I was with Lord Pharyl when we went to Hemlyn this last time… to collect slaves. I saw him then. He's Pharyl's man," the guard replied with a hard swallow. "He's a Cobra."

The effect was instantaneous. All those within hearing distance stiffened.

"I'm sorry," the captain said, his voice almost a grovel. "Please, please, come in." He swept his hand and bowed in a grand gesture.

"Thank you," Conal affably replied though irritated at the revelation. The way things were going, everyone would know he was a Cobra. Urging his mount forward, he led the way through the gate.

Maldwic threaded his way between the others and came up alongside Conal. "Is it true, Boss?"

"Which part?"

"Both."

Conal frowned in thought. "I *was* Pharyl's man for about half a day. My guess is that he still thinks I am. That's all about to change. And yes, I am a Cobra."

"No wonder I couldn't defeat you," Maldwic marveled.

"You're a good man, Maldwic and a far better leader than Oscon ever was. I have great plans for you."

"Yes, Boss. Thank you." Not wanting Conal see him grin with pleasure, he turned to nonchalantly gaze around at the parting crowds. Most people seemed unaffected by the visitors and simply stepped aside and went about their business. It was as he started to turn his head around to make another comment to Conal that he noticed something odd.

Acting as though he hadn't noticed, he turned back to Conal and smiled. "There's at least half a dozen working their way through the crowd following alongside us, more interested than normal."

Conal smiled back. "I know. I saw them when we came into the city. Pass the word to the others." As Maldwic drifted back, Conal leaned towards Bryok and raised a hand, pointing down the street. Pretending to comment on something ahead, he said, "We're being followed, and I have a feeling they're more interested in you than the rest of us."

"I noticed," Bryok grimly answered, slipping a glance down at his arm at the shimmering rune. Abruptly halting, he slid down from his saddle.

"What are you doing?" Conal demanded.

"Harder to ambush me with an arrow," he answered.

Immediately understanding, Conal ordered everyone to remain mounted and surround the druid. Galadyr and Torgreth flanked Bryok while Maldwic and others added to the protection, causing some consternation as they took up most of the street.

Yet their quick thinking thwarted the danger, though Conal knew it was temporary. Still, despite the complaints and snide comments by the citizens scrambling out of the way, they managed to safely arrive at the barbican leading into Pharyl's castle. Once they were past the portcullis, Conal breathed a sigh of relief. Entering the courtyard, he scanned the grounds. To his surprise, Lord Pharyl, flanked by half a dozen retainers, was waiting for him at the top of the steps leading to his apartments.

"Conal," Pharyl called out with a guarded smile, watching as his courtyard filled up. "I was wondering if I was ever going to see you again."

"Lord Pharyl," Conal grinned. Twisting his head to catch Maldwic's eye, he said, "Find a place close by to stay. Let me know where. Also, see what you can dig up on those who were following us."

"Got it, Boss." Maldwic circled his finger in the air and pointed out back out through the barbican.

Once Maldwic and company headed out, Conal slid down from the saddle, handing the reins to a stable boy.

"Let me introduce my friends," Conal grandiloquently said as three more stable boys appeared for the other two horses and Torgreth's pony. "This is Torgreth, as fine a dwarf as there ever was one."

"Ach, you're much to kind, m'Lord," Torgreth flipped a hand at him, though pleased with the compliment.

"The tall handsome elf is Galadyr, and the other handsome brooding man is Bryok, a half-druid."

They both dipped their heads in acknowledgment.

Pharyl recognized a not-so-subtle change in his former slave. The man appeared far too sure of himself, bordering on arrogant. He would need to be brought down a notch. Taught his place. The dwarf calling him 'my Lord' was too much. Assuming his most regal demeanor, he said, "What brings you here?"

"Urgent matters that we need to discuss in private." He started up the steps, the others in tow.

A retainer, sword drawn at his side, stepped forward to interpose himself between the ascending Conal and Lord Pharyl. Without breaking stride, Conal's fist shot out, catching the man squarely in the chest and propelling him into the air over the two startled guards behind him, who simultaneously turned their heads to follow their compatriot's rapid rise and crash onto the smooth granite stones of the portico floor.

"Hold," Bryok commanded, his hands raised, as the other guards scrambled to protect their Lord. "We are not here to harm his lordship. In fact, we come to seek his aid."

Pharyl's jaw had dropped when he saw his guard sailing overhead. He had not even seen Conal's hand move when the guard was lifted off his feet.

"Who are you?"

"I'm not one to be trifled with," Conal calmly replied. "Like Bryok said, we didn't come here to cause you harm. Matters are occurring that require your involvement. May we come in?" Conal stood two steps below Pharyl.

Pharyl frowned as he appraised the man who had so recently been a mere slave. What had happened that he now traveled with an elf, a dwarf and a druid, not to mention his own company? That alone warranted his interest. But it was Conal's overt lack of knowing his place that irritated Pharyl. He had half a mind to tell him to go bother someone else. For a moment, he regretted giving him his freedom. *Still... he did exchange his life for mine. I do owe him that.*

"Yes," Pharyl finally nodded, "come inside."

Pharyl led the way through the doors, the one retainer limping as he collected himself off the floor. Pharyl's steward joined them as they entered.

The steward was an austere man with a fawning smile reserved for his lord. "The hall is ready for you, m'Lord."

"Our discussion needs to be private," Conal reminded him.

Ignoring him, the steward addressed Pharyl.

"With m'Lord's approval, I've taken the liberty of providing some ale."

"That's fine Arnel," Pharyl replied. Wanting to remind Conal who was both boss and royalty, he tersely added, "The hall will be fine."

Conal jerked to a halt, causing the retainers to awkwardly stumble to avoid bumping into him. "Lord Pharyl. What we have to say is for your ears only. I chose you because I believed that you can be trusted. If after what you've heard you decide to share it, that is your choice. However, if this is more than you can accommodate, then we will leave and see if Lord Brody is more receptible."

Pharyl bristled at the man's insolence. Whirling around, he glared at his former slave. But Conal had anticipated the man's anger.

"I am not who you think I am."

"Really?" Pharyl snidely replied. "You're not the same vagabond I found in the goal in Hemlyn?"

"No," Conal confidently answered. "I'm not the same vagabond you had branded. Because you did not know, I will not hold it against you."

"Hold it against me," Pharyl exclaimed. "Now you've gone too far."

"Before you do something stupid," Conal shot back, "you may want to hear what we have to say. I traded my life for yours once before. Will you trust me enough to listen?"

Though Pharyl scowled at him, out the corners of his eyes he caught the surprised looks of his steward and retainers. Not wanting any further revelations, he twisted his head to look at the steward. "Leave us."

The steward turned an imperious gaze at the retainers. "You will wait outside."

"You too," Conal said.

"Me?" The steward cocked an eyebrow in umbrage. "But I'm his Lord's steward."

"I know," Conal drily answered. "I don't trust you like he does."

"Go Arnel," Pharyl said.

"As you wish, m'Lord." Arnel respectfully bowed then shot Conal an evil look.

Once the room was cleared of Pharyl's men, he folded his arms and cast an imperial gaze at Conal. "Well?"

Conal smiled then turned to Bryok. "You tell him."

"As you wish, m'Lord."

"What's with this m'Lord crap?" Pharyl snapped.

Bryok stood to full height. "The vagabond you had branded just happens to be the son of King Kamron of Isentol."

CHAPTER 11

GWEN

"Holy Solara," Kirith whispered.

The dragon's head perked to the side and it spotted them. Gwen expected to die. She'd heard stories of dragons breathing fire, destroying entire towns from existence. Granted, before now, she'd always assumed they were just stories, myths even, but here was one of the legendary creatures in front of her.

It was twenty feet long from head to tail, and its silver scales glittered under the rays of sunlight that filtered through the trees. Gwen didn't realize she was holding her breath until her lungs started to burn. She exhaled softly as if any sound would bring the dragon's wrath down upon them.

"Are you going to stare at me all day?" the dragon finally asked. Its voice was deep and throaty, and the words echoed among the trees. Gwen looked at Kirith and Aimil, not sure who the dragon was speaking to. The fact it spoke at all was enough to make her question her own sanity.

"You there," the dragon said.

"Me?" Gwen asked.

"Yes, *you*. Come near."

"I think it would be best if you did what it said," Kirith said lowly.

"No," Aimil said. "Dragons are sly, dangerous beasts. We should go."

Gwen was torn on whose advice to follow until the dragon narrowed its eyes on her. She felt obligated to obey the dragon and took a few tentative steps forward.

"Closer than that," the dragon huffed. "I'm not going to eat you."

Gwen looked over her shoulder. Aimil shook her head, but Kirith was motioning for her to continue. Gritting her teeth against her anxiety, Gwen closed the distance to the river and stopped when she was standing at the bank. On the other side of the river stood the dragon. She had thought the creature was massive from afar, but now that she was standing so close, it was even larger. Its scales looked smooth and when the dragon peered down at her, Gwen saw its eyes were a brilliant shade of blue.

"What's your name?" the dragon asked.

"G-Gwen." Her voice broke as she answered, and she cursed herself in her mind.

"Gwen." The dragon stared at her for a long while before continuing. "This river is the source of life for Auleavell."

Gwen looked down at the rushing water. It flowed from the north, weaving among the trees until it reached where they stood. The ground curved in a natural arch and the water disappeared underground. Gwen spotted a black liquid, thick and bubbly, on the archway. It was slowly dripping into the water. As the drops fell, the water turned dark and murky.

"What is that?" Gwen asked, wrinkling her nose as a bitter smell filled the air.

"Poison," the dragon answered. "It's fouling the river."

"Who would poison the river?"

"Who indeed? Given the events that occurred today, it was probably one of the disgraced king's supporters. This is an unimaginable crime."

"How do you know what happened?" Gwen looked up at the dragon.

"Haven't you heard the saying, 'dragons see everything'?"

"No," Gwen admitted.

"We do," the dragon said.

Gwen thought that was nonsense, but she didn't want to argue with a dragon and risk being killed, so she changed the subject. "What is your name?"

The dragon eyed Gwen warily, then said, "Venia."

"That's a beautiful name."

"Thank you," Venia preened at the compliment, standing tall and flicking her tail behind her.

"I can reach that stuff with a stick," Gwen offered, bending down to grab one from under a nearby tree. She walked onto the archway and held the stick out over the water, then moved it upward to catch the black liquid. As the liquid touched the stick, the wood sizzled and popped, then caught fire. Gwen jumped back a step, then hurriedly dipped the burning end into the river to kill the flames.

"That didn't go as planned."

"The poison has a bit of magic in it," Venia said. "Hold out your hand."

Gwen lifted her left hand.

"The other one," Venia clarified.

Gwen switched hands and Venia peered at the rune on her skin.

"You have the *Saol* rune. That can help."

"How?"

"I will teach you," Venia said. "Put your hand in the water, but not near the poison."

Gwen walked back to the bank and knelt beside the river, then lowered her hand into the water. It was cool against her skin and soothed the faint burning sensation that tingled around the rune. She watched Venia's reflection on the water's surface, admiring the dragon's beauty. The creature was obviously dangerous, yet Gwen was inexplicably drawn to the dragon.

"Channel the energy of the rune into the water and speak its name."

Venia's blue eyes seemed to glow in the reflection on the water. Gwen closed her eyes and mentally visualized the green energy that pulsed within the rune. She willed the energy from herself, and glowing green tendrils snaked from her palm. She opened her eyes and saw the tendrils knit themselves together, spreading through the water and obstructing the black liquid. Pain flared through Gwen's mind and hand, but she pushed through it, refusing to give in to the discomfort.

The tendrils of green energy spun around a glob of poison, circling it until the blackness faded and the water was clean. Gwen watched as the tendrils continued from spot to spot, clearing the river of the poison, but it was taking a toll on her. Weakness was creeping into her muscles and her vision started to blur. Venia said something, but Gwen couldn't make out the words. She sounded far away. Gwen tried to cut the magic off, but it continued to pour from her into the water, ignoring her frail command.

She started to panic and pulled her hand from the

water. The green tendrils weren't fazed. They continued to enter the river and destroy the poison. Gwen fell onto her back and stared up at the canopy overhead, a whirring distortion of color. She felt ill and thought she was going to vomit until darkness claimed her, sharp and sudden.

When she came to, her entire body was trembling. Venia was looking down at her. Gwen didn't consider concern to be a normal emotion for a dragon, though she didn't know what normal was anymore, but she thought that's what she saw in Venia's blue gaze.

"You're alive," Venia said, a statement more than a question.

"I am," Gwen rasped, then forced herself into a sitting position. She looked around and noticed that Kirith and Aimil were gone.

"Your friends fled in fear. You shouldn't hold any ill will against them for it. Not many have seen a dragon these days."

Gwen's first instinct was to be angry with them. The dragon could have eaten or maimed her, and her allies had left her for dead. Venia's words rang with truth, though, and Gwen dismissed her anger.

"I didn't know dragons were real," Gwen admitted. Her throat was parched, and her voice sounded odd in her own ears. She looked to the river, wanting to drink of the water but unsure if it was safe.

Venia followed her gaze. "You can drink," she said.

"Did we get all of the poison out?"

"Most of it," Venia answered. "You pushed yourself hard, perhaps too hard. The magic could have drained your life."

"But it didn't," Gwen said, then crawled to the edge of the bank. She cupped her hands and dipped them into the water and drank her fill, then turned her attention back to Venia. "What about the rest of the poison? Do you want me to try again?"

"No," Venia replied. "What remains will be washed away. You have done a great service for Auleavell. Not many would risk their life for a stranger, yet you risked yours for many. Perhaps there *is* hope, after all."

"Hope for what?"

"For this world. The darkness of Isentol grows daily and there are few who stand against it."

"I'm with the rebellion," Gwen said. "We're working to remove Torian from the throne. As long as there is someone fighting against tyranny, there is always hope."

"Wise words for someone so young." Venia stared intently at Gwen for a moment. "Where will you go now?"

"Aimil and I are going to Steepcross," Gwen said. "I go to learn my true name."

"The Great Library," Venia said. "I know the place, though I have not seen it in many years. The librarians are guardians of ancient tomes of power, as well as the world's history. You may be surprised at what you learn while you are there."

Venia's snout flared as she sniffed the air. "I must go," she said. "I will be watching you, Gwen. When the time comes to battle Torian, know that I will go with you."

Before Gwen could reply, Venia turned and vaulted herself into the air, her majestic wings carrying her into the sky. Gwen stood in place, watching until Venia's silver form was gone from her view. She left the river behind and headed back the way she had come. The barrier that protected the entrance to the river shimmered and pulsed. Gwen prepared herself as best as she could, then stepped through it.

A dizzying wave of sickness washed over her, but it wasn't as bad as the first time. Her vision cleared quickly, and Kirith and Aimil were there waiting for her.

"Are you all right?" Aimil asked. "Did the dragon curse you?"

"What? No," Gwen answered. "I'm fine."

"You spoke with the Guardian of Auleavell," Kirith said, awed. "She hasn't been seen by my people for over a hundred years. What did she say?"

"Someone poisoned the Thaestra," Gwen said. "She helped me cleanse the water. Well, most of it."

"You have been highly blessed." Kirith's wonder was still etched on his face.

"We need to get moving," Aimil said. "If we leave now, we might reach Steepcross by nightfall tomorrow."

"Are we in a rush?" Gwen asked. "I wouldn't mind staying another night here."

"As much as I would love to allow that, I'm afraid Aimil is right. There are already nervous whispers among my people that you two are responsible for poisoning the Thaestra. I know it's not true," Kirith added hastily, seeing Gwen's surprised expression. "I think it would be best for you to continue your journey, and I will work to quell the rumors."

Gwen decided Kirith made a valid point, especially since she was eager to learn her true name. "I can understand your people's fear," she said. "It's justified, though unfounded."

"Thank you," Kirith said. "I will ensure you leave well supplied."

"May I see Lyra before we go?" Gwen asked.

"Of course. I'll escort you there."

Kirith led them back to the forest-city and they stopped at the temple.

"I'll wait out here," Aimil said.

"And I shall get your supplies in order. Lyra should be inside praying to Solara." Kirith offered a bow and left.

Gwen stepped inside the temple and spotted Lyra kneeling in front of the dragon statue. She was the only one present aside from the guards outside and Gwen waited patiently for Lyra to finish her prayer. She enjoyed the peacefulness the temple exuded, and much like the water of the Thaestra, she felt renewed by it.

"Have you come to pray?" Lyra asked as she rose to her feet.

"No," Gwen replied. "I've come to say goodbye. Aimil and I are leaving."

Lyra walked along the pathway between the pews and joined Gwen at the doors. "Auleavell is indebted to you for rescuing Kirith from the vagabonds."

"There is no debt to be paid," Gwen said. "I did what was right."

"If you say it, then it shall be so," Lyra said. "Yet, I heard that you also healed the Thaestra."

"Who told you?"

"The Thaestra did," Lyra replied. "The waters are alive as you and I are, and they speak to those who listen."

Gwen remembered the vision she'd had and realized that the river had spoken to her through the *Saol* rune. Lyra said Auleavell was indebted to her, but she felt indebted to the elves. "Thank you," Gwen said. "For everything."

"There is much more to be done if we are to defeat Torian. I will pray that Solara guides and protects you."

"I will see you again," Gwen said, but as the words left her mouth, they felt more like a question.

"The future does not reveal its secrets, but I hope we meet again."

Gwen smiled and offered a bow, then left the temple. Aimil was gone and Kirith hadn't returned yet. She guessed that the two might have slipped away to enjoy each other's company again, but Aimil stepped into view from the side of the temple. She hopped over a large tree root and something shiny fell into the shrubbery.

"I hope you like cheese," Kirith said cheerily as he returned. His sister was with him, carrying two leather sacks. "Your horses seem eager, too."

Gwen had almost forgotten about the horses. She was glad they wouldn't have to travel on foot. While Aimil talked with Kirith, Gwen walked over to where Aimil had dropped something and spotted a glass vial. She picked it up and was about to tell Aimil she had dropped it when she spotted what was inside. It was almost empty, but there were a few drops in the bottle and the liquid was unmistakable. She quickly stuffed the vial into her waistband and covered it with her shirt.

Aimil wasn't acting any differently, but Gwen now knew who had poisoned the river.

CHAPTER 12

CONAL

Pharyl stared at Bryok, waiting for the punchline. When none came, he deadpanned, "You're serious."

"As a heart attack," Torgreth chimed in with a snort. "I know. Took me a while to get used to it. He such a loveable oaf, but it's true."

"Which brings me to another point," Bryok elaborated. "You may have unwittingly triggered the prophecy."

"What prophecy?" Pharyl asked, suddenly apprehensive.

"The eagle will bear the vipers in its claws, yet from the west a cobra will rise and strike down the eagle."

"How was I to know?" Pharyl blurted. "Are you sure he's the one?"

"Beyond all doubt," Galadyr said, not totally convinced himself, though there was something different about Conal that made him want to believe.

"How is this possible?" Pharyl argued. "He's from Urve. I remember him telling me that. Said he spent his whole life there."

"He and his sister were secreted out of

Havengarde when they were quite young," Bryok explained, "during the turmoil when Torian killed Kamron. Do you remember Torian sending messengers looking for traitors to the crown, supposedly traveling with two children, one a babe and the other perhaps a year older? You had just assumed the demesne here."

Pharyl blinked at the recollection. An emissary from Torian had arrived at Rexfyrd demanding Caldyr turn over any citizens of Isentol who had recently entered the kingdom, especially those traveling with two children under the age of two. To his credit, Caldyr told the emissary to "Get the hell out of my kingdom."

"I do vaguely remember that," he acknowledged.

"What Torian failed to perceive," Bryok said, "was that the children were split up. Conal went to Urve and his sister somewhere else. As time went on and his searching proved unsuccessful, he shifted his attention to his true desire – subjugating the surrounding kingdoms: elf, dwarf, and human. He has patiently gathered an army of wizards and mages to his cause. When he unleashes his forces, kingdoms will fall, one by one. Tir Manach will not be spared."

Bryok looked back over his shoulder, making sure the door remained closed. Turning back, he continued. "However, much to his shock, he recently discovered that both children live. To Conal's good fortune, Torian never suspected that he would end up with a bunch of highwaymen. However, his agents are again looking for his brother's children. In Conal's case, Torian discovered his family in Urve. That Conal never told them where he was is the only reason he is still alive."

"But it didn't save my family," Conal said

through clenched teeth.

Bryok solemnly nodded. "Torian knows the prophecy. He knows Conal still lives. We believe that his sister is also alive. We have friends looking for her. That said, it is imperative that we gain Caldyr's support to stop Torian."

Chagrined, Pharyl stared at Conal. "I… I didn't know."

"Of course you didn't," Conal said, placing a hand on Pharyl's arm. "Even I didn't know."

Pharyl's first instinct was to yank his arm away and castigate the offender, but he remembered he was now dealing with a potential king.

"We need to focus," Galadyr interrupted. "Time is of the proverbial essence."

"He's right," Torgreth added. "We got to get to Caldyr, and we need to protect him in the process." He hooked a thumb at Conal. "Though if you've ever seen him fight, you might think he don't need our help."

Conal frowned and cocked his head to stare at Pharyl. "Whatever happened to Blayne?"

Pharyl curled a lip into a snarl. "I've yet to deal with him. Brody claims ignorance yet refuses to do anything about it."

"Who's Blayne?" Torgreth asked.

"My brother-in-law's bastard son," Pharyl replied.

"He set up an ambush to kill him," Conal explained. "Didn't quite work out the way he wanted."

"Caldyr?" Galadyr reminded them. "You can deal with Blayne later."

Pharyl slid a caustic glance at him then relaxed, admitting to himself that he would deal with Blayne and Brody on his own terms… maybe even get Conal to help. "I will go with you."

"We were hoping you would say that," Torgreth grinned.

"We leave first thing in the morning," Bryok announced. "We will need a safe place to spend the night."

"You will stay here," Pharyl grandly offered, crossing the floor to open the door and curl his fingers at his steward. "Prepare lodging for our guests. Add four more places for the evening meal."

"Yes, m'Lord." Arnel dipped his head, hiding his dislike of Conal.

"I need to check on my friends," Conal stated.

"They're staying at the Stag's Head," the steward answered with an overt tone of condescension.

"And where might that be?" Conal ignored the man's conceit.

"I can have one of the servants show you," he replied without looking at him.

"How about I come with you?" Torgreth said to Conal.

"Good idea," Bryok nodded. "Galadyr and I can further enlighten Lord Pharyl."

Stepping out into the hallway, the steward address one of the servants, a young man in his early teens. Ignoring the two visitors, he commanded, "Show these two where the Stag's Head is."

"Yes, Steward Arnel." The teen reverently dipped his head.

Turning his back to Conal, the steward felt a sudden vice grip on his neck as he was physically lifted off the ground.

"The next time I come in here," Conal growled, "I expect to be treated with respect. Do you understand?"

Arnel flailed as he felt the grip tighten, and finally squeaked, "Yes."

Conal released his grip and the steward dropped to the floor and stumbled forward. Turning his back to him, Conal motioned the servant to lead the way, leaving Arnel gasping for breath.

The Stag's Head was a large respectable tavern two streets away from Pharyl's castle. When Conal and Torgreth entered, Maldwic and company had spread out and positioned themselves in strategic locations so that they could monitor who entered the tavern, who went upstairs with one of the girls, and who worked the tables, as well as keeping an eye on the taverner.

Seeing his deputy, Conal scooted the edges of other tables before pulling out a chair at Maldwic's table.

Torgreth ignored the not-so-subtle looks and yanked out a chair to sit next to Conal. "Think they've never seen a dwarf before," he groused.

Conal leaned back and gazed around the room, meeting the eyes of those too curious who quickly turned away. Shifting his attention back to Maldwic, he asked, "Find out anything?"

"Nuthin' yet, Boss. I just –" Maldwic stopped as he frowned and narrowed his gaze at two men who slipped in through the front door. With a satisfied nod, he caught the attention of two attractive members of the company and ticked his head at the newcomers. Immediately understanding, the two women got up from their table and started edging their way over to where the two men sat at a table near the far wall.

Conal nonchalantly leaned back, his gaze

sweeping the room, lingering briefly on the two men. He recognized the one. Leaning forward, he lowered his voice. "Let me know what you find out. See how many others there are."

"You stayin' the night at Pharyl's?"

"Yes. He and I still have a lot more to discuss. We leave first thing in the morning."

"We'll be ready."

"You do realize when they see me leaving, they're gonna know something's up," Torgreth pointed out, scooting his chair back.

Maldwic shot a glance over at the two women who were amiably chatting with the two newcomers whose rapt attention was focused nowhere else. He motioned to another company man, a stout man with full beard, who came to the table. "Escort our dwarf friend to the door."

"Let me know if you find out anything. Otherwise, I'll see you in the morning." Conal stood and together with the stout man, they blocked the view of the newcomers as they escorted Torgreth to the door.

Once outside, Conal scanned the streets, noting the usual bustle of merchants returning home, revelers heading to another pub, and the street urchins darting in and out among the crowd, begging for coins or racing away after failing to snatch a man's purse. What surprised him was the absence of soldiers or other security until he noticed a man standing near the street corner, pretending to be waiting for someone, a nondescript man who took more than a passing interest in them.

Catching the man's eye, he gave him a half-smile before crossing the street to head towards Pharyl's castle. The man immediately gave up pretense and openly followed them. Conal slowed his pace, causing the man to likewise slow his pursuit. Abruptly turning the corner, he grabbed Torgreth and shoved him against the building wall, placing a finger to his lips before sticking a foot out just as the man raced around the corner to catch up.

The man sprawled headlong onto the street. Conal was on him before he had a chance to react, reaching under his armpit and jerking him to standing.

"Looking for me?"

The man squinted at him, his eyes momentarily glassy as though having imbibed too much. A moment later they cleared. "Uh, no, no," he stammered. "I… I thought you were someone else. My apologies. An honest mistake. So sorry to have troubled you." He tried to escape, but Conal's grip was too strong. "You're hurting me," he whimpered as he squirmed.

"You were following me when I came into the city," Conal said, smiling with only his lips. "Why?"

"I thought you were someone else. Honest."

In one quick motion, the man lifted a knee up and pulled a stiletto out from inside his boot. But Torgreth's hand was quicker and the dwarf's grip, firm from years of carving stone, grasped the man's wrist with such strength that the stiletto dropped from his hand.

"Now that wasn't nice," Conal chided, looking down at the blade. "And here I thought we were going to be such best friends." Conal's other hand went for the man's throat and the man started gasping, feeling suddenly weak as Conal squeezed the carotid arteries. "I'll ask you one last time, why were you following me?"

The man's eyes bulged as he struggled to pry

Conal's fingers from his throat. "Not… you," he rasped.

"Who?"

"Other… man," he slurred.

Conal felt him weakening and he relaxed his grip. "Why?"

Gasping for breath, the man stared defiant eyes at him. "He knows why."

"Tell me."

"He knows why," he stubbornly repeated.

"Boss," Maldwic called out, coming around the corner. "Need help?" He had two others from the company with him, a man and a woman.

"Just trying to determine why he was following us." He released the grip at the man's throat.

Maldwic scrutinized the man, narrowing his gaze at him. "You got some friends of yours in the Stag's Head?"

The man swallowed and nodded.

Maldwic rolled his eyes and shook his head, letting out a huff of exasperation. "He's one of them."

"Them?" Torgreth repeated.

"They're dragon hunters," Maldwic scoffed.

"Dragon hunters?" Conal pushed the man away from him. "By the gods, you idiot." He jabbed a finger into the man's chest. "You tell those clowns that if I see any of you fools following us or interfering with us, I will track you down and rip your throats out myself."

The man's hands went to his throat and before anyone could stop him, he scampered off like a frightened rabbit.

"What is wrong with people," Conal snarled.

"I know," Maldwic chuckled.

"Keep an eye out," Conal said. "If they get in the

way, we take them out."

"Why?" Maldwic asked, surprised. "They're harmless."

Conal remembered the fight in the forest clearing when Krag escaped just in time. "I don't want them tailing us or compromising us," he explained. "We don't need their crazy notions. You know as well as I do that crazy people are unpredictable."

"You are so right, Boss. Had an aunt once that was crazier than a cross-eyed smithy. Don't know what happened to her, but I always kept my distance"

Conal grinned and placed a hand on his shoulder. "Once we get things better settled, I'll bring you into the planning sessions. Right now, I'm having to flatter and grovel more than I can stand."

Maldwic laughed. "I understand, Boss. We'll be ready."

"I know you will. That's why, as of this moment, the company is yours."

Startled, Maldwic's chest puffed up. "Thank you, Boss. I won't let you down."

"I know. See you tomorrow morning."

"Right, Boss."

There were guards at the gate when Conal and Torgreth approached Pharyl's castle. Upon seeing Conal, they snapped to attention.

"Good evening, Sir," one guard said, staring directly at Conal, causing him to wonder at the overly polite and respectful greeting.

"Good evening," Conal replied.

"What? No 'good evening' for me?" Torgreth quipped.

"Uh," the guard sputtered and swallowed. "Yes, uh, yes… sir. Good evening."

"That's more like it," Torgreth smirked.

They found Bryok and Galadyr still in the Great Hall with Pharyl. Pharyl looked up when they entered. Upon seeing Conal, he crossed the floor to greet him.

"I believe I owe you many apologies, m'Lord."

Caught off guard at the change, Conal shot a look at Bryok who nodded that all was well. "None needed, Lord Pharyl. Neither of us knew. However, that was then. We need to convince Cáldyr to help us."

"Lord Pharyl has offered half his army for our cause," Galadyr said.

"Half? That is very generous."

"I believe it is necessary," Pharyl said, with an air of self-importance. He would have to get used to treating this youngster with respect, awkward as it might prove to be. "My army commander should be here any moment."

"Thank you," Conal replied as regally as possible. "Bryok. Might I have a word with you?"

Bryok frowned with a quizzical look then joined Conal as he walked to a corner of the large hall.

"Your arm," Conal said.

Bryok cast a surreptitious glance to where Pharyl and Galadyr chatted before turning back to Conal. He lowered his voice and pointed to his forearm. "It glows and I feel a slight burn."

"Those who followed us are dragon hunters, but then you already knew that, didn't you," Conal challenged.

"Yes."

"Are you going to tell me what's going on? Like last time, they knew you were here."

"I don't know how," Bryok answered through gritted teeth, "though that's not entirely true."

Conal said nothing, waiting for him to continue.

"No doubt all the hunters are rune-marked. My guess is that they are rune-bound to Torian or one of his wizards." He locked Conal with a cold hard stare. "They must receive no mercy, for they will never give any."

"So you're saying…"

"Yes." Bryok added a curt nod. "When we find them, we must kill them."

CHAPTER 13

GWEN

After leaving Auleavell, Gwen and Aimil rode until evening and then set up camp on the side of the road. The landscape was a long stretch of flatlands comprised of tall golden grass that swayed in the breeze. They ate a small meal from the supplies Kirith had given them, and Aimil offered to take the first watch.

Gwen laid on the ground and stared up at the night sky, counting the stars and trying not to think about her earlier revelation. Aimil had dropped a vial that contained what appeared to be the same poison that had infected the Thaestra River. Gwen was certain it was the same liquid, but she wanted to be able to confirm it. The problem was that she didn't know how. And even if she did, what could she do about it?

The most troubling thing to Gwen was *why*. Why had Aimil done such a horrid thing? It didn't make sense unless Kirith had snubbed her in some way. Even then, Gwen didn't believe that Aimil would go to such lengths. At least, she didn't want to believe the woman would do something like that. Yet, she had to consider how she barely knew the woman.

If Eradore trusts her, then so should I, Gwen

thought.

She struggled with her feelings until sleep eventually claimed her. When Aimil woke her for her turn at watch, Gwen felt like she'd only just fallen asleep. She rose and tended the fire until sunrise when she allowed the embers to go cold. They ate breakfast, mostly cheese and grapes, and then rode most of the day. They stopped only a handful of times, and only long enough to relieve themselves or to allow the horses to drink.

They kept a steady pace, with Aimil determined to reach the capital city of Steepcross, called Arbington, before nightfall. When the city was finally within sight, the sun was in the middle of the sky. Gwen was surprised at how quickly they'd arrived. Large braziers stood outside the gates to light the way for straggling travelers, but they were empty now. The guards at the gates were dozing at their posts and Gwen and Aimil entered the city without issue.

"The Great Library requires an appointment, so we'll bide our time at the Crow's Foot," Aimil said, guiding her horse along the main cobbled street. "I've stayed there before. It'll do for our needs."

"What about our horses? Will the Crow's Foot board them?"

"No, we'll have to leave them somewhere else, but I know just the place."

Aimil led the way through the city, keeping to the main streets until they reached the other end of the city where another gate, this one smaller than the main one, led out into the countryside. The area was quiet, but a pungent smell lingered in the air.

"Most of the stables are located in this part of the city," Aimil said. "It keeps the stench and the mess in one place."

"That's a good idea," Gwen replied. "Having to smell this," she waved her hand, "while eating or drinking in a tavern would be less than ideal."

"Exactly. It also provides an easy exit if we have to leave quickly."

Gwen wondered why they might have to make a hasty retreat, but she said nothing. Every little thing Aimil said came across as suspect now that she'd found the vial. They left the horses with a young boy and paid the boarding fee to an older man whom Gwen assumed was the boy's father.

Aimil and Gwen backtracked to the center of the city and entered a large building with a sign that hung from the roof that read *Crow's Foot*. Gwen felt more at home than she had in weeks. The inn was crowded, and a troupe of musicians was playing a lively tune. The atmosphere was one of camaraderie and the ale was flowing. Gwen found it all refreshing and allowed herself to forget her problems for a while. She was so enrapt with the music that she barely heard Aimil say she was going to get them an appointment at the Great Library.

Gwen was pleasantly surprised when she spotted a familiar face. A young man was moving through the crowded room, making his way to where the musicians were. Brown hair, clean-shaven, handsome.

It was definitely him.

He waited for the troupe to finish their final song, then took their place and struck up a tune with his lute. Gwen watched him intently, remembering his performance from the last time she saw him. That had been the night that started it all and had put Gwen on the path to joining the rebellion. The bard's fingers strummed over the strings, playing with practiced ease. He was just as good as she remembered. She smiled, happy to know that he'd escaped her father's inn and that nothing ill had befallen him. Other memories, darker ones, hovered at the edge of her mind, but she kept them at bay by focusing on the music.

Aimil eventually returned and sat across from Gwen. The bard played several more songs before another musician took over, and then Gwen turned her attention to Aimil.

"How did it go?"

"As well as can be expected for a last-minute request," Aimil replied. "But one of the librarians owes me a favor, so I was able to get us in. If you're done drooling over the handsome bard, we can go now."

"I wasn't—" Gwen sputtered.

"Whatever," Aimil interrupted. "Are you ready to go? We've got a limited amount of time inside."

Gwen rose from her seat. "I'm ready."

Despite her tone of confidence, she had a lot of trepidation about learning her true name. Tobias had once mentioned that he thought she was the lost princess of Isentol, but she doubted that was true. And while Boris had admitted that he wasn't her real father, she didn't think that meant Tobias had been right.

They left the Crow's Foot and headed west toward a stone structure that Gwen had mistakenly assumed was a castle. It was plain and unadorned. A moat surrounded the building and the two women had to cross a bridge to reach the grounds of the Great Library. The entrance wasn't guarded, but there were two great wooden doors that Gwen thought would be impossible to move without a small army.

Aimil knocked on one of the doors. A few moments passed, and then a small rectangular panel slid open and two eyes peered out.

"Yes?" It was a woman's voice. Gwen thought she sounded old, perhaps someone of sixty or seventy years.

"We have an appointment," Aimil answered.

The eyes shifted from Aimil to Gwen, then the panel slid shut and the door opened. Gwen had been right. The woman standing before them was in her later years. Her hair was long, gray mingled with white. Her skin hung loosely on her face, and she wore a flowing blue robe trimmed in silver.

"Very well," she said, stepping aside. "Speak your name and enter."

"Aimil Cirillo." Aimil stepped forward and crossed the threshold of the doorway.

"Gwen Wilmarth." Gwen stepped forward, hoping she didn't experience a wave of nausea like she had in Auleavell. To her surprise, an invisible barrier kept her from entering the library.

"Try it again," the old woman said. "And use your true name this time."

"That is my name," Gwen replied.

She cleared her throat and said her name again, louder this time. When she tried to enter the library, she was again held back by the invisible force. Aimil was smirking, but the old woman frowned and eyed Gwen suspiciously.

"Deception will not gain you access into the library."

"I'm being truthful," Gwen protested. "That is my name."

"No, it isn't," the woman said. "Else the ward would have let you in."

"I can vouch for her," Aimil chimed in. "She's a new mage, and it's possible her given name at birth isn't the same one she has today."

The old woman pondered over the information for a moment, then said, "I've heard of stranger things happening before." She snapped her fingers and traced a symbol in the air with her hand. There was a sound of rushing air, then the old woman motioned for Gwen to come inside.

Gwen hesitantly stepped forward and this time she wasn't hindered. The temperature in the library was noticeably colder than outside, and the smell of old parchment filled Gwen's nostrils.

"It seems you need to learn your true name," the woman said.

"Yes. That is why I have come here."

"I see. You could have said that to begin with. Follow me."

The woman led the way through the library, which appeared much larger from the inside than Gwen would have imagined. There were dozens of rooms down various hallways, and books were everywhere.

"I'm the Head Librarian," the woman said as they walked. "My name is Marjorie, but you will call me librarian while you are here."

"Thank you for seeing us on such short notice," Gwen said.

"I don't make the schedule, dear, I just adhere to it."

"Does the title Head Librarian mean you are over this entire place?" Gwen asked.

"In a manner of speaking," Marjorie answered. "Though we have the Council of Librarians, and we all collectively make decisions by a majority vote."

"They are also all wizards like Eradore," Aimil said.

"A common fact," Marjorie said. "We consider ourselves a magocracy, if you will."

"A what?" Gwen asked.

"Leadership run by wizards," Marjorie clarified.

"I thought wizards were rare?"

"We are. This is probably the only place you'll ever see more than two wizards together outside of the Chamber of the Altar. Though if the rumors are to be believed, King Torian has negated the treaty with the Order and his guards have barred access to the Obsidian Altar."

"It's true," Gwen said. "I was there when they cleared the place out."

Marjorie huffed under her breath, clearly upset by the news. She turned right down a hallway and stopped outside one of the doors. Reaching into her robes, she withdrew a brass key and slid it into the lock, turned it, and hid the key back within her robes.

"This room holds the Stone of Truth," Marjorie said. "It is here where your true name shall be revealed." Marjorie pushed the door open and stepped into the room, then closed it once Gwen and Aimil had entered.

Gwen expected something grandiose, like a giant diamond or some other precious stone. Instead, there was a wooden table that held a palm-sized violet-blue colored stone. It was smooth and polished. Gwen wasn't certain, but she thought the stone was giving off a faint light.

"I've never seen anything like that before," Gwen said softly.

"It's an azurite stone," Marjorie replied. "It's imbued with ancient magic, spells older than the

Great Library itself. Some say it was given to wizards by the goddess Solara."

"I can believe that," Gwen said.

"I wouldn't," Aimil rolled her eyes. "Solara is a myth."

"Have you ever seen Solara?" Marjorie asked, looking at Aimil.

"No."

"Have you ever been beyond the horizon, to the land of the Godhood?"

"Of course not," Aimil replied. "No one has."

"Then you should not dictate to another whether something is true or not. You shouldn't make absolute statements without absolute proof. This is a place of learning, and I will not tolerate half-truths."

"Fair enough," Aimil said, but Gwen could tell she didn't like being told what to do.

"Now then, you will hold the stone and connect your *bunús* to it, then speak your name. If you are lying, you will know. Set the stone down on this parchment." Marjorie slid a fresh sheet from a stack to the center of the table. "The truth will be revealed."

Gwen swallowed the lump in her throat and reached for the stone. She could feel magic radiating from it. The energy pushed against her hand, though Gwen couldn't actually see anything. She lifted the stone and held it in her palm, then closed her eyes and envisioned the *bunús* rune in her mind. She felt it join the stone, the force of the connection almost causing her to drop it.

"Gwen Wilmarth," Gwen said.

A shock ran up the length of her arm and she cried out in surprise and pain. Gwen opened her eyes and hurriedly set the stone onto the parchment, then massaged her arm with her left hand.

"The stone knows truth from deceit," Marjorie said.

The paper hissed as the stone burned something into it, small tendrils of smoke rising into the air before quickly fading. Marjorie removed the stone and looked at the parchment.

"What does it say?" Gwen asked eagerly.

"See for yourself." Marjorie held the parchment up.

In a graceful, flowing script was the name Quinlee.

"Quinlee?" Gwen's face scrunched in displeasure. "What kind of name is that?"

"A rare name," Marjorie said, her expression curious. "There's only one person I've ever known to have it."

"Who?" Gwen asked.

"The lost princess of Isentol."

CHAPTER 14

CONAL

Employing the benefits of his stealth rune, Conal lowered himself over the walls of Pharyl's castle, pausing to get his bearing. Though late, he knew the Stag's Head would still be busy. Slipping through the streets, he stood outside the tavern and listened to the cacophony of patrons enjoying another ale.

The door opened and light spilled out along with two revelers who, upon seeing Conal, greeted him as a long-lost friend. Giving them an affable grin and slap on the back, Conal brushed past them and into the tavern, rapidly scanning the room, surprised that Maldwic was still there. To his credit, the new leader of Oscon's company was sober and alert, immediately noting the new arrival. Conal weaved around the tables to finally scoot a chair out next to Maldwic.

"Surprised to see you here, Boss," Maldwic smiled.

"Surprised to see you still here, too." Conal returned the smile.

"We've tracked down four of them," Maldwic said, getting to the reason he believed Conal was here.

"Good. I've got one more job for you."

"Whatever you need, Boss," Maldwic confidently answered.

"Kill them."

While the smile on Maldwic's lips remained, what was in his eyes vanished. "Uh… we… uh, I mean I… you know we don't have people who are good at that. We rob and steal, but we don't kill. We have a few who are capable of cold-blooded murder, but I don't completely trust them."

"I understand," he nodded. "That was one of the things I liked about the group. We were motivated by greed, not violence. I expect to use those skills in the future. As for now, tell me where they are, and I'll take care of business myself."

"No, Boss," Maldwic quickly reconsidered. After all, he was in charge now. "I'll take care of it."

"You sure?"

"Like I said, we got a couple of folks who will be more than willing to satisfy their bloodthirst. Leave it to me."

"Thanks. I'll see you in morning."

Morning came way too early for Conal. Making use of his stealth skills, he had prowled the streets until the early morning hours, noting the only people out were burglars. Twice he had come upon thieves in the process of breaking into a home. Twice he had foiled the act by remaining in the shadows and gently coughing, scaring the intruders half to death and causing them to bolt. It had been great fun; but now he was paying the price for his late-night escapade.

"Pharyl is sending a cohort of his soldiers with us," Bryok announced over a breakfast of roasted venison, fresh bread, cheese and ale. Peering intently at him, he suppressed a smile. "You look tired."

"Busy night," he said, uttering a drawn-out sigh.

"That's what you get for staying out late and partying." Bryok chuckled at Conal's confused frown. He held his forearm out to show Conal that the runes were not glowing. "Thank you."

Conal immediately understood, silently thanking Maldwic for solving the problem.

"'bout time you got up," Torgreth greeted him as he and Galadyr entered into the dining hall. He cut two slices of cheese, offering one to Galadyr. "Pharyl's cohort is about ready."

"How many are there?" Conal stood, casting a wistful glance at the unfinished breakfast.

"Slow down," Torgreth advised with a grin. "I said 'about ready,' which means another half an hour. Finish your lunch."

"Very funny," Conal smirked as he sat and ripped off a chuck of bread, slathering it with warm butter. "How many?"

Torgreth shrugged. "Didn't bother to stop and count."

Lord Pharyl strode in, his usual arrogance forcibly suppressed. "My Lord Conal. I'm sending a cohort of my best with you. I had my steward compose a missive to Caldyr, urging him to action." With an overt flourish, he produced a sealed letter, placing it on the table.

"Thank you," Conal nodded, affecting as regal an air as possible. He blinked, thinking how stupid he must have sounded. Hoping no one noticed, he shifted a glance at Torgreth whose smirk said he too thought it was rather pompous. *Good ol' Torgreth. He's the one person I can trust to tell me when I'm getting too full of myself.*

'I believe they're about ready," Pharyl said, referring to his cohort. He was ready to be rid of his guests and the sooner they were gone, the sooner he could stop pretending to fawn over this upstart.

Once outside, Conal scanned the assembled troops, his eyes lighting on Maldwic who was hustling over towards him.

"Morning, Boss," he smiled then leaned in so only Conal could hear. "Took out most of 'em last night. One managed to escape. Sorry."

"Nothing to apologize for," Conal reassured him then placed a hand on Maldwic's shoulder. "Just thankful I've got someone here I can trust." He shot a meaningful glance at the assembled cohort.

"Good morning, my Lord," the cohort commander called out as he approached. He was a wiry muscular man adorned with breastplate and carried a feathered helmet in the crook of his arm. A short sword slapped at his thigh as he walked. He was clean shaven with short dark auburn hair. "I am Cadfyn."

"Good morning, Captain," Conal amiably replied. "You have met Maldwic, chief of these marauders?"

"I have not, m'Lord," he answered, giving Maldwic a reserved nod. "I am unfamiliar with your group."

"We like to keep it that way," Maldwic said with a polite smile.

"Are we ready, Captain?" Conal interrupted before Cadfyn could probe further.

"Yes, m'Lord."

"I want to get to Rexfyrd as quickly as possible. Your cohort will take the lead. Set a good pace."

"As you wish, m'Lord." He saluted and jogged

over to where his orderly held his mount.

"I want you close by," Conal whispered to Maldwic. "Not that I don't trust the man… I just like having a more responsive force close by."

"You expecting trouble, Boss?"

"Not sure. Let's just say I have a feeling."

Conal's jitters proved unfounded as the first day's travel proved quite uneventful. They camped outside the small town of Athgal, two hours travel beyond the border of Pharyl's demesne. At first the town's sole tavern was thrilled to have the increase in business. That lasted until just before the ale ran out when two of Captain Cadfyn's soldiers got into a shoving match that turned into a brawl, which ended up destroying most of the furniture inside the pub.

Things didn't get any better when Conal and Bryok were awoken in the middle of the night by the tavern owner who demanded immediate payment.

More than cross because he hadn't slept much the night before, Conal, along with Bryok, confronted Cadfyn who seemed unaffected by the destruction.

"They're just letting off some steam, m'Lord. You know how it is."

"Letting off steam," Bryok snapped. "They destroyed the man's pub. Are you going to pay for the damages?"

"I gave the man a chit in Lord Pharyl's name. He'll get paid," Cadfyn replied, wondering why they were so irritated.

"Paid? And how long will that take?"

Cadfyn shrugged. "Don't know. Not my problem anymore."

"Are you that stupid?" Bryok burst. "How is he supposed to gain support if you're destroying everything in the process?" He thrust a finger at the indignant pub owner who stood close by. "What will he tell King Caldyr when word gets out that the army marching through here destroyed his business?"

"He'll get paid… probably a whole lot more than the pub's worth. The way I see, he's come out better in the long run."

"Really?" Conal interjected. "When do you think Lord Pharyl will deliver good on *your* promise? Your soldiers caused the damage; your soldiers can pay for the damage."

Cadfyn blinked in surprise. "I don't think that's a good idea. If they spend their money now, they won't have enough for when we get to Rexfyrd."

"That's not my problem," Conal shot back, amazed at the man's stubborn stupidity. "No one is going anywhere until you have given this man satisfaction."

"With all due respect, my Lord," Cadfyn retorted, his voice dripping contempt, "I take my orders from Lord Pharyl. His orders were to escort you to Rexfyrd. What happens along the way with my soldiers is my concern, not yours."

Conal noted disrespectful use of 'm'Lord' in addition to the man's insolence. His face hardening, he narrowed a penetrating gaze at Cadfyn. "You are of no use to me. Take your ill-disciplined rabble and go back. I no longer have any need of you."

Cadfyn stiffened, standing to full height. "I repeat; I take my orders from Lord Pharyl."

A sudden premonition flooded within Conal. Controlling the urge to teach the man a lesson, he shook his head, spun around and marched off.

Startled, Bryok chased after him. "That's not the way to settle this. You need to show him who is in command here."

"I know," Conal answered in a hushed voice, stepping close to an unattended campfire. Pulling out the letter Pharyl gave him for Caldyr, he glanced up at Bryok then slid a finger under the envelope flap and broke the seal. Pulling the letter out, he flipped it open when a smaller folded piece of paper slipped out. He caught it midair. Tilting the larger letter to read it by the firelight, he scanned it then quietly read it aloud to Bryok.

My Lord Caldyr,
The bearer of this note is a man claiming to be the son of King Kamron. The friends he has with him will stubbornly vouch for this claim. I confess that, despite the clever story they've conjured, I cannot bring myself to believe a word of it. All to recently I had purchased this man as a slave and had him branded. Determining that he demonstrated an unusual level of intelligence, I decided to manumit him and retain his services. Events occurred where he was detained by highwaymen and I lost the use if his abilities. Imagine my surprise (and humor) when he showed up claiming to be a king's son
He likewise claims that Torian is plotting to overthrow Tir Manach and it is his intent to prevent Torian from accomplishing these supposed plans. I would normally assume these the rantings of a madman and would have imprisoned him here but thought you might enjoy a good diversion. I send him with an escort of soldiers under the command of Captain Cadfyn. Cadfyn is not the sharpest blade in the armory, but he is obedient to a fault.
One additional matter needs to be brought to your attention and that is the presence of dragon hunters. I was more than surprised to discover the presence of

at least a half-a-dozen of these strange individuals. Why they are here and now truly baffles me. I have questioned several of them and their response is uniform – the dragons have returned. I have one or two under surveillance but view them for the present as harmless fools. Still, I thought it might interest you.
Your obedient servant
Pharyl

Conal glanced up at Bryok. "Skillfully done. I carry the letter condemning me."

"What's the other one say?"

Conal unfolded the small page. The handwriting was tight and neat.

My King,
In accordance with your wishes, I submit my observations concerning Lord Pharyl's letter. The gist of his letter is correct. This individual named Conal is an arrogant huckster pawning an unbelievable fable. He has even hoodwinked an elf, a dwarf and a druid with his outlandish tale. He should be dealt with as your wisdom decides.
As to the matter with Brody's son Blayne, it is as Your Highness surmised. How Lord Pharyl managed to escape is certainly cause for consideration.
One further point - I do not trust the druid.
Your humble servant,
Arnel

Conal sighed in disgust. "And to think that I trusted Pharyl. The steward's an ass, so it's to be expected. But I really thought Pharyl was on our side."

"Interesting that Pharyl's steward is reporting

back to the king," Bryok observed.

"What should I do with these?"

"Burn Pharyl's and save the steward's letter. It might prove useful later on." Bryok turned to glance back over his shoulder to where Cadfyn strutted with self-importance, having frog-marched the proprietor back to town with the threat of physical harm should he continue his harangue. "We need to jettison ourselves from this excess baggage."

"I agree. How? It's not like we can just sneak away. He's got his security out patrolling the area." Conal tossed Pharyl's letter onto the fire, watching the paper curl as it burned. "We need a diversion, something to keep them occupied enough for us to break away." Movement to the right caught his eye and Maldwic emerged from the darkness with a man Conal did not recognize.

"Hey, Boss, Bryok," Maldwic nonchalantly greeted them. "Want you to meet a new friend of mine. Goes by the name of Lorkan. Thought you might find what he has to say very interesting."

Lorkan was a tall muscular man dressed as a woodsman, bow in hand and a quiver of arrows over his shoulder. He respectfully bowed then glanced around at the surrounding campfires where Cadfyn's cohort were peacefully slumbering.

"My Lord," Lorkan said. "Do not proceed to Rexfyrd. Caldyr is under Torian's control. He has issued orders to find you."

"Who are you?" Conal demanded.

Lorkan lowered his voice. "I am a friend of Drustan. He told me to intercept you before you got to Rexfyrd."

Conal turned to Maldwic. "Do you trust him?"

"I do, Boss."

"That's good enough for me." Conal shifted his attention to Lorkan. "How did you get past security?"

"What security?" Lorkan sniffed in disdain. "I passed through the cohort soldiers unchallenged. To be fair, once I got to Maldwic's area, I was immediately challenged."

"It's not like we can just pack up and leave without being noticed," Conal pointed out.

"I believe I can help with that, m'Lord," Lorkan grinned. "If you can assemble your force to the side towards the road, I can create enough disturbance to give you a chance to escape. Head down the road to the next town. I have people there waiting for you."

"Give me five minutes."

"Yes, m'Lord." Lorkan dipped his head in respect then spun around and disappeared into the darkness.

"Why do I feel like I'm on the open sea in a boat with no rudder," Conal sighed. Inhaling a deep breath, he rubbed his tired eyes. "Guess we better wake up a dwarf and an elf."

"Already alerted them, Boss."

Conal smiled. "Why does that not surprise me."

In less than five minutes, Conal and his loyal group had stealthily edged over by the road, separating themselves from Cadfyn's cohort who slumbered fitfully, impervious to anything but their rest.

An explosion rocked the night as a blast of fire and light burst from one of the campfires followed by a voice crying out, "We're being attacked."

Shaken out of their deep sleep, most of Cadfyn's cohort scrambled out of their bed rolls, reaching for swords. Another flash of light instantly followed by another explosion erupted on the perimeter opposite Conal.

"They're here," another voice cried out.

As Cadfyn's soldiers raced across the campsite, Conal and company vanished into the darkness.

345

CHAPTER 15

GWEN

Gwen stared at the name on the parchment. Could it be true? Had Tobias been correct in his guess about her heritage? No, it couldn't be. Yet here was a sliver of proof.

"I …" Gwen didn't know what to say. Words and concise thoughts eluded her.

"Take a deep breath," Marjorie said. "It's not every day someone learns they are born to royalty."

Gwen nodded, trying to wrap her mind around the idea that she, a lowly barmaid, was in reality a princess.

"It's not possible," she said.

"The term would be improbable," Marjorie corrected. "Nothing is impossible, especially where magic is concerned."

"But how? Wasn't King Kamron and the queen murdered by King Torian?"

"Yes, they were." Marjorie pursed her lips, which caused her wrinkled flesh to tighten and Gwen thought she could imagine how the woman looked when she was a bit younger. "There is something I want to show you."

"What is it?" Gwen asked.

"It would be less impactful if I told you, so I will show you." Marjorie glanced at Aimil. "Unfortunately, I will require you to refrain from following, but you are free to explore the library at your will."

Aimil shrugged indifferently. "Fine by me."

"Very well. Come along, Quinlee," Marjorie said.

"Please just call me Gwen."

The three of them left the room, and Marjorie turned to the right and continued down the hall. Gwen had to walk fast to keep up with her, which was surprising considering the old woman's age. Gwen glanced over her shoulder and saw Aimil walking in the opposite direction. It pained her to have Aimil out of her sight, but there was little choice in the matter.

"There was a sorcerer who frequented the library many years ago," Marjorie said, drawing Gwen's attention. "He was a recluse and always studied alone, spending much of his time learning herbology."

Gwen wondered where Marjorie was going with her story and assumed she was just rambling.

"Others told me he tended a garden at his home, cultivating rare herbs from across the kingdoms for his potions."

"That's interesting," Gwen said, humoring the woman.

"It's rather boring, actually," Marjorie said. "Unless you are into herbology?"

"Uh, not really."

"I thought not. Remember that I do not tolerate deceit here."

"I'm sorry," Gwen said with embarrassment.

"Forgiven. Now, where was I? Oh yes. Kha'gan went to Isentol to acquire a specific herb that only grows on the castle grounds. While he was there, Torian launched his coupe. He killed his brother for the throne." Marjorie shook her head sadly.

"I don't remember that being part of the story," Gwen said. Then again, until now, the story of Torian's betrayal had never really been important to her.

"They were siblings, yes. I think most people don't talk about it because they don't want to think that a family member could ever do something so terrible to another."

"It is hard to stomach," Gwen agreed.

"Even so, Torian took the throne by force and murdered anyone loyal to Kamron. And did you hear that Kamron's children were murdered?"

"Yes, I have heard that part of the tale before. That's wicked. And another reason why it is hard for me to believe I am Kamon's daughter." Gwen's stomach churned at the thought of someone murdering innocent children.

"I've said that I do not tolerate deceit in this library, and so I shall cast that lie from your mind. Kamron's children were *not* murdered."

"They weren't?"

"No," Marjorie said. "When Kha'gan realized what was happening, he was inside the castle proper in a guest room. He was about to flee when he heard the crying of a babe. It was your cries that stopped him in his tracks. He absconded with you and your brother."

Gwen knew the story of Torian's betrayal. Anyone not living under a rock had heard it, but it always ended with the murder of Kamron's entire family, solidifying Torian's rule and claim to the throne.

"Wait," Gwen said, suddenly realizing what Marjorie had said. "He rescued both children?"

"Indeed. You and your brother, Darrbie."

"Darrbie?" Gwen tried not to laugh, but the giggling erupted from her anyway.

"Kamron chose names that were … different, to be sure."

"I'd say mortifying fits Darrbie and Quinlee more than 'different.' I'll stick with Gwen."

"Do as you wish, but if you want to enter the library in the future, you will have to use your true name."

As they conversed, Marjorie led them down several hallways, traveling further into the depths of the library. Every time they passed another librarian, they would press their hand to their chest in reverence to Marjorie.

"Kha'gan," Gwen said, stumbling over the foreign name. "Does he still come here?"

"No," Marjorie answered. "He died a few years ago."

"Oh." Gwen felt an odd sense of loss even though she'd never met him. Well, technically she might have. Marjorie seemed so convinced that she was the princess, but Gwen still had many reservations. "He told you all of this, then?"

"Not verbally. He sent for me when he was on his deathbed and gave me a book. At first, I assumed it was a collection of his potions that he wanted to leave to the library. There were some recipes in it, but more importantly, it held a detailed account of Torian's actions and Kha'gan's escape. The only thing missing was where he took you and your brother."

"Did he share that information with you?"

"He did not share that information with anyone.

A few days after the coupe, Kha'gan came here, exhausted and looking like a man who'd walked over his own grave. He confirmed Torian's betrayal and said he rescued two children. When I pressed him for answers, he refused to divulge anything more."

"I wonder why he never told anyone their location?" Gwen pondered aloud. "Surely, he knew someday someone might need to know the information."

"Or he knew that someone who shouldn't have that information might come looking one day. I assume that's why he cut his own tongue out shortly after."

Gwen stopped mid-step. Marjorie paused and looked at her, noting the horrified expression plastered across her face.

"Kha'gan took that secret to his grave, and I don't envy him for the things he saw that night. Many of these books are filled with tales of heroic deeds, but Kha'gan is the only hero I've ever known. I trust that you'll treasure what he did for you and that you won't let his deed be wasted in vain."

"I have vowed to remove Torian from the throne and joined myself with like-minded company," Gwen said. "The more I learn about what happened, the more my hatred for Torian grows."

They reached the end of the hall and stopped at a door that looked identical to the one that guarded the room that held the Stone of Truth. Marjorie removed the same key from her robes and unlocked the door.

"This is where we keep our most fragile books."

Gwen followed her into the room. It was illuminated by several globes of light that rested upon pedestals every few feet. The pale light revealed the room was full of tall glass cases, all of them filled with books that looked like they would fall apart if a slight breeze rustled their pages. Marjorie walked over to one of the cases and opened it, carefully retrieving a plain leather-bound book and handed it to Gwen. The leather was worn from use, but it was in good condition compared to the other books.

"Read it," Marjorie said. "Take your time. I can't risk letting you take the book from here, so you'll need to read it in this room. There's a table over there you can use. I have a few tasks to do while I'm in here, so just call for me if you need anything."

"There is one thing I need," Gwen said. She pulled the vial from her waistband and held it out to Marjorie. "Would it be possible to figure out what was in this?"

Marjorie took the vial and held it up, peering at the small drops that remained in it. "It's certainly not good, whatever it is, but I should be able to discern the contents."

"Thank you." Gwen took the book to the table and sat down. One of the globes was placed in the center of the table, providing plenty of light to read by. She gingerly opened the book and started from the first page. It was a recipe for a healing potion. The next page had one for stomach illness. Gwen continued flipping through the pages until she found the entry she was looking for. She inhaled a deep breath and prepared herself for what she was about to learn.

In the final days of King Kamron's reign ...

Gwen read Kha'gan's firsthand account of the events that happened the night of the coupe. The details were intense, and Gwen had to pause a few times to wipe the tears from her eyes. So many people had lost their lives, many more than Gwen would have imagined. Guards, servants, nobles. Anyone with strong ties to Kamron had been hunted down and murdered outright.

Many doubts were fluttering around in Gwen's mind about whether or not she was really the princess. She had the same name, but that wasn't proof she was one of the children Kha'gan had rescued. And then she read the description of the children. The girl had a birthmark on the bottom of her foot. It was a random shape, a splotch of brown on the arch.

Gwen's heart lurched in her chest. She removed her boot and twisted her foot around to look at the mark she'd seen many, many times. It was the same as Kha'gan's description. Gwen swallowed hard.

It was true.

She was the princess, Kamron's long-lost daughter. She put her boot back on and digested the revelation. Nothing about it made sense, other than Boris's admission that he wasn't her real father. Gwen continued reading. Kha'gan didn't mention who he left the children with, but he did mention that each one went to a different home.

"I have a brother," Gwen whispered. She wasn't sure how she felt about that. A swirl of emotions overcame her. She was both angry and sad at having missed out on all the time with him, yet also jealous of how his life may have been. Was he raised by a wealthy noble, living a life of splendor? She would have loved a life of pampered living.

Guilt assailed her for thinking such selfish thoughts. Boris had been a great father to her, and she had never gone without. She offered a silent apology to Boris's ghost and closed the book. Gwen sat in silence for a long while and eventually Marjorie joined her at the table.

"I'm stunned," Gwen said. "It's difficult to believe, but there are so many things Kha'gan mentions that leaves little doubt as to who I really am."

"Life is about learning who you are. Every time you think you have it figured out; you find that you've changed again. The journey of self-discovery is one that never ends."

"I have a brother somewhere out there," Gwen said, motioning to the outside world. "The chances of finding him are …"

"Improbable," Marjorie said, smiling.

"Nothing is impossible," Gwen repeated Marjorie's earlier words. "I'll try to remember that."

"I know you have a lot on your mind now, but I must add to the burden. The vial you gave me … where did you get it?"

"I found it in some brush," Gwen said vaguely. Until she knew for certain that Aimil was responsible, she didn't want to reveal too much to anyone. It was a possibility that Aimil had merely found the vial, but Gwen wasn't sure that was the case.

"Hm." Marjorie obviously wasn't satisfied with the answer, but she didn't press the issue. "I was able to determine what that liquid was. It's a mixture of poison and dark magic. I've seen similar poisons before, but this one was slightly different. The spells that were adhered to the liquid itself are intended to destroy. Seeing as there were only a few drops left, I must assume someone used it. I fear that whoever or whatever it touched is likely dead."

Gwen nodded and kept her expression calm, but she was losing it on the inside. Magic was involved, which proved to Gwen that Aimil had indeed poisoned the Thaestra River. Now, she just had to figure out why.

"Thank you for looking into it," Gwen said. "What did you do with the vial?"

"I disposed of it, and the poison. It was too dangerous to return it to you."

That meant the evidence was gone. Gwen would have to find another way to offer proof of Aimil's wrongdoing. On top of that, she didn't know who to report Aimil's actions to. Eradore, perhaps?

"There's one more thing," Marjorie said.

"What is it?"

"The Council wants to see you."

CHAPTER 16

CONAL

Conal and company were a half hour down the road when Lorkan came riding up.

"We need to pick up the pace, m'Lord. Cadfyn finally discovered you're no longer there. He was still marshalling his cohort when we left. With your permission, I'll lead the way."

"Go ahead," Conal readily agreed, praying he wasn't being led into another problem.

An hour later, Lorkan veered off the main road onto a side road that led deeper into the forest, slowing the pace as the road narrowed and twisted. Drifting back to ride beside Conal, Lorkan raised himself up in the stirrups to look behind them. Though dark, he could make out the indistinct shapes of Torgreth and Galadyr and several others behind the dwarf and elf.

"We should be clear in a little while, m'Lord. I've a few of my friends acting as decoys. They'll lead them well past the point where we entered the forest."

"Thank you. Back to my original question. Who are you?" He yawed and rubbed his eyes.

"I am Lorkan ap Dafydd. My father was your father's exchequer. When Torian usurped the throne, he kept my father in that position up until a year ago. He was accused of treason and thrown in the dungeon. His only treason was to question Torian's choice of confidants, especially Grimmar who calls himself the Mage-breaker. The man is a liar. Once my father was arrested, my family was no longer safe. My mother and sisters fled just before Torian's thugs arrived to arrest them too. I managed to escape and joined the rebellion. That is where I met Drustan and Bryok. Drustan told me who you were."

He paused and looked directly at Conal. "I was ten years old when Torian murdered your family. When no one found you or your sister, everyone assumed you too were killed by that butcher. I can only imagine the shock that Torian suffered when he discovered you were not dead."

"Your father and your family?"

Lorkan shook his head and shrugged, gently rocking in rhythm with the horse's gait. "I do not know. I pray my mother and sisters are safe. My father?" His voice trailed off.

Conal understood. Most likely Lorkan's father was made to suffer then killed in retribution for his family's escape. Deciding to change the subject, he calculated that Lorkan was nine or ten years older than he. "You never married?"

"Torian decreed that any marital arrangement of a member of his extended court, including the children, had to have the king's approval, which usually involved a large sum of money. Add to that the directive that the king himself would arrange marriages. While that improved the prospects of the homely and awkward children, others were not as fortunate, especially those families seeking to arrange appropriate matches... or anyone wanting to marry for love."

"So you never married," Conal repeated, disgusted with the malevolence of his father's murderer... his uncle. *Torian is my uncle.* The realization startled him. Up to now, Torian was simply an evil king, a man who needed to be destroyed so that peace and order could be restored. But now... Torian was a blood relative, a close blood relative. The thought burst within that he was on a quest to kill his uncle. How was that different from a brother killing his older brother?

Conal's family in Urve crowded into his musings and he remembered the years growing up at the seaport and the unconditional love of a man and wife who placed his future above their own lives. *He didn't just kill my royal father... he killed my real father, the man who raised me and loved me. He killed my family, the only family I ever had.* Conal's resolve stiffened like cold hard granite, and he understood what must be done. No quarter would be given, nor mercy offered. Like a rabid dog, the man needed to be put down.

"No," Lorkan answered.

Conal knit his brows, struggling to remember the direction of the conversation. That's what happened when he was tired and needed sleep. Thankfully Lorkan continued.

"I managed to avoid Torian's marriage entrapment. I absented myself from Havengarde by joining the army, volunteering for border security, a job few wanted."

"Why?"

Lorkan chuckled. "It's boring. Up until a year ago, just before my father was arrested, border security consisted of checking merchant wagons and chasing the occasional brigand. The rest of the time is spent dealing with pub owners complaining about soldiers damaging their pubs or bonding soldiers out of goal for drunkenness and fighting, and the occasional father threatening to kill the man who got his daughter pregnant. But truth be told, I'd rather be there than Havengarde."

"And now?"

"Now? Now I'm part of the resistance, the rebellion to overthrow Torian before he enslaves us all. The rebellion is wider spread than many realize, and I think Torian is just now recognizing it." He again turned his head to look at Conal. "That you are alive and well, and now assuming command of the rebellion gives us great hope and a fighting chance."

Conal's jaw slacked open and then immediately clamped it shut, hoping it was dark enough that Lorkan didn't see the shock on his face. *Assuming command? Me? Now?* He suddenly felt overwhelmingly inadequate. *What do I know about grand strategy or leading an army? I thought Bryok and Drustan were in charge.* Yeah, he had talked a good game with Maldwic, but now the heavy burden of leadership was dumped on him.

Then just as suddenly, confidence filled him. He could do this. He knew he had leadership talent when he had chaffed under Oscon's domineering hand. More than once he had offered a plan only to be told to shut up and remember his place and then see Oscon use his plan and claim it was his idea. He remembered the last encounter with Oscon. It had felt more than good to show the man that Conal was now in charge.

Up ahead, a man stepped out onto the path, an arrow notched in his bow. "Good morning, Commander Lorkan."

"Good morning. All quiet?" Lorkan reined in his horse causing everyone else behind him to stop.

"Yes sir."

"Good. How did you know who we were?"

"We could hear you coming, Commander. By the conversation, we assumed you were talking with Prince Darrbie."

"That's Prince *Conal*," Conal sternly corrected. He shot an angry glance at Lorkan. "My name is Conal. Anyone calls me Darrbie, I'm gonna reach down his throat and rip his heart out."

"Yes, m'Lord," Lorkan soothed. "I'll put the word out."

"My apologies, m'Lord," the man said with a startled bow. "I didn't know."

"I understand." Conal turned to Lorkan. "Where are we?"

"We are at my camp, m'Lord. We are safe here. It's time for you to get some rest." He led the way past the sentries, staying on the path, the forest on both sides.

Expecting to see a campfire or two, Conal was surprised that not only were there no campfires, but he couldn't tell how many were encamped. Yet the longer they plodded along, the more he wondered how large Lorkan's force was.

"How many do you have here?"

"Almost 3000."

"3000," Conal exclaimed.

"Yes, m'Lord. I know it might not seem much, but with the dwarven force under King Rorkyn and the army of King Kilmaryn, we probably have over 10,000 soldiers ready to heed your command."

Once again Conal's mouth gaped open. 10,000 soldiers submitting to his command. *By the gods, what have I gotten myself into?* Overwhelmed, fatigue flushed through him, yet he knew he had to act like a leader, even when he was bone tired.

They emerged into a small clearing and stopped before a marquee tent with scalloped edging, large enough to house four or more individuals. Lorkan dismounted and waved a hand at the tent.

"This is for you m'Lord."

"The whole thing?"

"Yes, m'Lord."

Dismounting, Conal frowned at the size of the tent. Someone had to set it up, take it down, and pack it for travel. "This is too big. Where'd you find it?"

Lorkan hid a grin. "It was… uh, donated, m'Lord."

"What about the rest of my friends?"

"They're all taken care of."

"They can stay with me."

"If that is what you wish, m'Lord."

"Where are you bedded?"

"Close by, m'Lord." He pointed to a wall tent less than half as large to the left.

Maldwic strode up, leading his horse.

"With your consent, m'Lord," Lorkan said, "I've placed your commander in this tent here." He pointed to a tent similar to his on the other side of Conal's tent.

Once the arrangements were settled and three more cots brought into Conal's tent, Lorkan bid him 'Goodnight' and went to check his security. Conal pulled the flap aside to his tent and entered, followed by Torgreth, Bryok and Galadyr.

A small brazier on a field table gave dim light to the interior where four cots with cotton stuffed mattresses on top were positioned. The sight of a comfortable bed was all Conal needed and he made a beeline to the farthest cot, sat down, yanked off his boots, and flopped back, yielding a sigh of contentment and was quickly asleep.

It was late morning when he woke, his stomach growling. Sitting up, he noted with satisfaction that his tent mates were still asleep. Pulling his boots on, he quietly stepped between the cots and slipped through the tent flap into the warm morning sunshine. The camp was deceptively quiet, the sign of disciplined soldiers. That surprised him, for there were probably more civilians than soldiers in Lorkan's army.

He was about to go look for something to eat, if there was still anything left over from breakfast, when a young man approached carrying a tray with a mug of ale and a plate of steaming eggs and sausage.

"Good morning, my Lord," the young man said with a smile. "It's not much, but I hope it meets with your satisfaction." He was a slender lad in his mid-teens, with curly blond hair and bright eyes like he was on some wonderful adventure.

Conal's mouth watered and his eyes lit up. "This looks excellent. Thank you." Accepting the tray, he glanced around for a place to sit.

"I'll go get you a chair, my Lord." He started to turn Conal stopped him.

"I'm fine. Thank you." He strode over to sit against a thick oak tree, crossing his legs and inhaled the aroma of hot food. This was far better fare than when he was with Oscon. Even the sleeping arrangements far exceeded anything Oscon ever found.

"Are you sure my Lord?"

"I'm positive. Thank you."

The young man dipped his head. "I am Bedo, my Lord. If you need anything, anything at all, I will get it for you."

"Thank you, Bedo," Conal said with a chuckle. "I'm fine." The young man certainly had enthusiasm. When Bedo didn't wander off but simply stood to the side, Conal repeated, "I'm fine, Bedo. You can go about your work."

"I am, my Lord. I am your runner, your personal assistant, your servant." Bedo grinned like there was no better job in the world.

"You are?" Conal sipped the ale then sliced a bite of sausage. The ale was surprisingly good, especially here in the field.

"Yes, Lord Darr – uh… I mean, my Lord." Bedo swallowed hard at his faux pas.

Conal stopped mid-chew and pointed the knife at him, his eyes narrowing with an intense stare. "If I hear anyone calling me or even referring to me by that name, I will slice his throat and feed it to the ravens. My name is Conal, C-O-N-A-L. Got it?"

"Yes, my Lord," Bedo said in a rush. "I'm so sorry. I'll never do it again. I promise."

When Conal saw the fear in the man's eyes, he relaxed. "Apology accepted. Let's forget about it. Tell me Bedo, where do you hail from and how is it that you are here with Commander Lorkan?" He piled a portion of eggs on top of the bite of sausage.

"I am from just outside Havengarde, my Lord. I am here because King Torian murdered my family." The light briefly departed from his eyes.

Conal locked his gaze on him and softly intoned, "Just like he did mine… both of them."

Bedo frowned in puzzlement. "Both of them, my Lord?"

"Yes. First, he murdered my father and mother and usurped the throne. Then, he murdered the family who put their lives at risk to raise me in safety."

"So it's true," Bedo marveled. "You really are the king."

"Not yet," Conal replied with a smile. "But with the help of men like yourself and Lorkan and others, I hope to reclaim what is mine."

Lorkan walked up, looking refreshed and content. "Good morning, m'Lord. Sleep well?"

"Very," Conal said with a cheerful grin.

"Is Bedo taking good care of you?"

"Yes, thank you. He and I were just getting acquainted."

"He's a miller's son so he's not acquainted with the finer points of the role of a royal retainer. I'll search for someone more suitable as time goes on."

Out the corner of his eye, Conal saw Bedo put on a brave smile, though he was crestfallen. "Actually, I prefer we leave things as they are. Bedo strikes me as an intelligent young man and will fit the bill admirably. Besides, we have more important things to worry about than looking for retainers when we have one right here."

Bedo's disappointment morphed to hope that Conal's word outweighed Lorkan's.

"It will be as you wish, m'Lord." Lorkan smiled, pleased that Conal was not like so many other pompous asses of royalty whose disdain for the common man often revealed their own glaring shortcomings. "We did have an interesting incident during the evening, m'Lord."

"Yes?" Conal chewed the last bite and swigged down the last of the ale, handing off the tray to Bedo as he stood. "Thank you, Bedo."

"You are welcome, my Lord Conal." Accepting the tray, he turned to go clean the plate and mug.

"You've made him very happy, m'Lord," Lorkan observed as Bedo strutted away.

"I like him. He's… um, enthusiastic."

Lorkan chuckled. "That he is. Like I said, he's a miller's son. His parents were murdered when they couldn't pay the increased poll tax. They were supposedly used as an example to all the others who had second thoughts about sequestering enough to feed themselves. We picked him up on the road to Rexfyrd. How he managed to get that far is anyone's guess. He's resourceful."

"You were saying about an incident," Conal reminded him.

"Yes." He motioned with his hands for Conal to follow him. "We captured four individuals trying to infiltrate our perimeter. They're not soldiers and they're not local. When questioned, they claimed they were dragon hunters." He abruptly stopped and tilted his head to give Conal a look of disbelief. "They claimed we had a dragon with us."

CHAPTER 17

GWEN

Gwen stood before a crescent-shaped stone table, where seven people were seated and stared at her. Marjorie sat in the center, with three men to her right and three women to her left. When Marjorie had told her that the Council wanted to see her, she had no idea how intimidating it would be.

Each of the members was middle-aged, with Marjorie clearly being the eldest. They all matched her, wearing the same silver trimmed blue robes. Gwen felt naked under their eyes like they could see into her mind and read her thoughts. It was foolish of her to feel that way, she knew, but she felt so vulnerable in their presence.

"Quinlee rí Túath," Marjorie said. "Welcome to the Council of Librarians. As you know, we are all wizards. Like all Prestiges, we seek knowledge and power. The Great Library is a vast source for all who would seek to learn and grow, regardless of their pursuits and race."

The other members at the table nodded and murmured their agreement.

"Yet, there is an encroaching darkness coming.

King Torian thinks himself an emperor and is working towards invading every kingdom around him, including Steepcross. The rumors whispered are many, but we know for certain that Grimmar the Mage-Breaker is behind it all. He has corrupted Isentol, and we also believe he ensorcelled Torian into killing his brother, the rightful king."

"I thought Grimmar hated magic and all those who practice it?" Gwen asked. She thought back to the man who'd entered the Chamber of the Altar. He was an agent of Grimmar and didn't look at all like a Prestige.

"So he says," Marjorie replied. "It is all a ruse. He has gained the allegiance of many Prestiges who want to control magic. We cannot allow that to happen. This Council has long held a position of neutrality in the world, but it cannot be so anymore."

The members at the table looked at Marjorie in surprise. The woman had obviously not shared that information before this meeting. Gwen was hoping these wizards would pledge their cause to the rebellion and join the fight against Torian. If what Marjorie said about Grimmar was true, they would need all the magical help they could muster.

"I see that you have two runes. Do you want more?"

"Yes." Gwen didn't even have to consider the question.

"Those of us before you have mastered something no other wizard has. What I am about to share with you cannot be repeated outside of this chamber. Do I have your word?"

"I won't say anything."

"Swear it," Marjorie said.

"I swear."

"Good. You know that only mages can bestow runes to other mages, yes?"

Gwen nodded slowly.

"Did you also know that mages can become so powerful that they ascend in power and become a wizard?"

"No, I did not. I'm still new to all of this."

"I can promise you that even the most seasoned Prestiges do not know this. It is something this council has discovered through many years of research. Once, we were all mages."

"What does that mean, exactly?" Gwen scrunched her brows in confusion.

"We are wizards, but we can bestow runes," Marjorie said plainly.

Gwen's face lit up in understanding.

"You know that the process of receiving a rune can be painful, so I will not caution you with fluffed words. These runes are powerful, most of them meant to be wielded as weapons in battle. As Simon can attest, this power comes with a burden."

Simon was the man next to her. He stood and pulled his robes open, revealing a crisscross of black lines across his chest. They pulsed visibly like unholy veins, the darkness standing in stark contrast to his pale skin.

"What is that?" Gwen asked.

"It is the residue of dark magic," Simon replied, closing his robes. "Few are brave enough to truly delve into its practice, and fewer still are strong enough to survive using it."

"You can choose which runes you want to take," Marjorie said. "I only want you to see the … consequences … that might arise."

When Gwen had first envisioned being covered

in runes, she had found the idea appalling, fearing that she would be ugly. Then she met Aimil and decided that while she didn't want as many runes on her own body, they were not a blight upon her flesh as she thought. Gwen looked down at the runes on her hands.

Tintreach and *Saol*. Lightning and Life.

Gwen knew she would need all the power she could get. If her skin looked like Simon's in the end, then she hoped she could one day find someone who would love her despite the flaws to her skin. If she lived that long.

"I will accept them all," she said.

"Very well. Choose who your first rune will—"

A knock on the chamber door cut off the rest of her words. One of the women rose from her chair and hurried to the door. She opened it a few inches and shared a whispered conversation with one of the librarians, then returned to the table carrying a letter and passed it down to Marjorie. Gwen watched her open it and waited anxiously to continue with the runes.

"It seems a meeting has been called," Marjorie said. "The rebellion is requesting an emissary from the Great Library."

"Let us send one, then," Simon said. "As you said, we must cease being a neutral party."

"Does anyone object?" Marjorie asked.

None of the other members said anything.

"Once we complete our business with Quinlee, then we shall decide on who to send."

"Where is the meeting to be held?" Gwen asked, wishing that Marjorie would quit using that ridiculous name.

"Haddence," she replied. "It's on the border of

Isentol and Clagmoran."

"When?" Gwen figured that would be the best place to report Aimil's crime, but she would need to get there in time.

"It's in two days. Now, for the matter of your runes. Please choose who you would like to receive a rune from first."

"Perhaps it would be best to start from one end of the table," Gwen motioned toward the women and swept her arm across, "and work down."

"A good suggestion," Marjorie said. "Sophia, if you would."

Sophia, the woman at the end of the left side of the table, stood and came around to join Gwen. She was slightly taller than Gwen with shoulder-length brown hair that was tied in a ponytail. Sophia stretched out her hand, directing it toward Gwen's forehead, and closed her eyes. Gwen closed hers as well and focused on the *bunús*. The magic flowing around Sophia and the others glowed brightly, except for Simon. An inky cloud surrounded him, pulsing and flickering with flashes of dark purple. It reminded Gwen of a storm cloud, only more sinister.

The rune Sophia offered hovered at the edge of Gwen's mind. It was wholesome and pure and felt similar to the *Saol* rune.

"*Leighis,*" Gwen said, speaking the rune's name.

An arc of white energy penetrated Gwen's body, weaving through the strands of her being and knitting itself into her. Gwen gasped as the pain flooded her, but just as quickly as it had come, it was gone.

"*Leighis* is a rune of healing." Sophia's voice broke the silence and Gwen opened her eyes.

The familiar pain of a new rune throbbed in her right hand and she lifted her arm to view it. Her flesh was raised and pink, and just above the *Saol* rune was her newest addition. It was a circle, surrounded by a square, surrounded by a triangle.

"If anyone is injured, you can use the *leighis* to heal them."

"Thank you," Gwen said, lowering her arm. Sophia returned to the table and the next woman came to take her place at Gwen's side. This woman was shorter than Gwen by a foot, but her red hair, green eyes, and fiery expression spoke volumes about her fierceness.

"I am Tala," she said. "Lift yer hand and open yer palm."

Gwen did as Tala asked, but the woman shook her head. "No, do not show me your palm. *Open* it."

"I don't understand," Gwen said.

Tala's green eyes twinkled mischievously, and she drew a dagger from within her robes and handed it to Gwen. Realization dawned on Gwen, and she hesitantly accepted the blade. She glanced at Marjorie, concerned something was amiss, but the elderly woman nodded, a comforting smile tugging at her lips. Gwen pressed the tip of the dagger to her palm. She swallowed her fear and pressed down slightly. The blade was sharp and easily cut into her flesh.

"That will do," Tala said. She took the dagger back and wiped the blood on Gwen's shirt, then cut her own palm with the blade. Tala held her hand over Gwen's to align their cuts, then whispered something under her breath.

Gwen's palm tingled, lightly at first, then it grew in intensity until her skin grew uncomfortably warm.

"Speak the rune," Tala said, though her eyes were still closed.

Gwen felt for the *bunús* rune and connected her mind to it. She was startled to see roaring flames spinning around Tala's hand, but she quickly understood what the rune's power was.

"*Tine,*" Gwen said its name.

The flames from Tala's hand coursed into her, searing through the cut in her palm. Gwen's entire body grew hot, and she could feel droplets of sweat slide down her face. With a whooshing sound, the flames died, and her body's temperature returned to normal.

"Fire," Gwen rasped, her throat parched.

"Aye, fire. It's as wild and untamed as anything ye'll ever come across."

Gwen had only taken two runes, but her legs were starting to tremor, and she was feeling lightheaded. She felt the fire rune on her left side, just under her armpit. The sensitive skin ached with pain.

"Do you need to rest?" Marjorie asked. "You don't look so good."

"I think I can do another," Gwen said, stubbornly trying to force her legs to quit shaking.

Marjorie looked to the next woman. "Beloria."

Beloria bowed her head to Marjorie. She didn't leave the table but instead stared intently at Gwen. She said nothing and hardly moved. Gwen grew troubled under her gaze, but she matched Beloria's stare and tried not to blink. Something at the edge of her vision floated toward her, but when Gwen tried to focus on it, it faded from view.

"Focus," Beloria said. "Focus on the *bunús.*"

Gwen knew that the *bunús* was the key to unlocking the power of the runes, but each time she channeled into it, she felt herself grow weaker. She drew a deep breath and closed her eyes. The *bunús* rune was there in her mind and she mentally reached for it. The magic funneled in and out of her, igniting her runes but stealing her strength.

One more and I can rest for a moment, she told herself.

The floating thing she saw before was a rune. Now that she was connected to the *bunús,* she saw it clearly. It came toward her, guided by an unseen force, and landed on her chest.

"*Láidreacht,*" Gwen said.

The rune rested where her heart was and after she spoke its name, it fused to her skin. The power of the rune took the rest of her strength, but it also gave her some in exchange. The vigor it offered was different than what it took, but it was a reciprocal action and Gwen felt the tremor in her legs fade.

"This rune feels weird," Gwen said. "Weird, but …" she struggled for the right word, clenching her hand into a fist.

"Strong?" Beloria asked.

"Yes," Gwen replied excitedly.

"The rune grants might. When you tap into it, you'll find yourself capable of feats you never imagined."

Gwen channeled the rune and spoke its name. Her muscles flooded with renewed energy. The weakness she felt before was completely gone.

"I can do another rune," she said confidently.

"Are you sure?" Marjorie asked. "It would not be wise to push yourself too hard."

"I'm fine," Gwen replied. "I feel like I could do this all day."

Marjorie frowned at her, but she acquiesced. The old woman left her spot at the table and came to kneel in front of Gwen.

"This rune will leave two marks," she said. "One on each of your legs. It will require twice the energy, so you must be mindful when you use it."

"I understand."

Once again, Gwen closed her eyes and went through the process of linking her mind to the *bunús*. A ghostly falcon took shape and circled the room. It dived down, splitting into two, and each bird struck her outer thighs. Gwen's knees buckled and she dropped, cracking her kneecaps roughly against the stone floor. She could feel the runes searing her skin, but the flow of magic wasn't opening up. Gwen struggled against the burning pain, trying to focus on the name of the rune. It eluded her for a brief moment, but it was long enough that she started to panic.

"*Luas!*" she finally cried out. Her thoughts blurred and darkness claimed her.

When Gwen opened her eyes, her face was touching the cold floor. She forced herself onto her knees and then heaved herself to her feet. Marjorie stood nearby, a look of concern on her face.

"I warned you about pushing yourself," she said.

"I know," Gwen replied, rubbing the side of her face. "It just took me by surprise. I'm fine, I promise."

"I think we should take a break. Sophia, can you get Quinlee something to drink?"

Gwen was secretly glad that Marjorie called for a break. She didn't want to appear weak or unworthy of their runes, and it made her feel better that she wasn't the one temporarily giving in. She accepted a wooden cup from Sophia and drank its contents, expecting water and getting a taste of wine instead. Gwen coughed and cleared her throat, then drank the rest of it and wiped her chin on her sleeve.

"Please call me Gwen. It's the name I've known all my life."

"As long as you are in my domain, you will suffer my will. Quinlee is your true name, and it is the one I will use."

Gwen rolled her eyes when Marjorie wasn't looking. She gently rubbed at the fire rune on her side. Of all the ones she'd received so far, it was the most painful.

"Is the girl ready?" Simon asked. "I have many things that require my attention."

"Patience is a virtue," Marjorie said to him.

"And it's one that I lack," Simon replied, scowling.

Marjorie looked at Gwen. "Do you need more time to rest? We can continue later if needed."

Gwen shook her head. As much as she wanted to rest, she knew that time was running short if she was going to get Aimil to Haddence in time for the meeting.

"Don't be a fool," Marjorie lowered her voice. "Simon's rune can kill you if you aren't careful."

"I can do this," Gwen said, casting a glance at Simon. He drummed his fingers on the stone table impatiently.

"Very well. I warned you. If you die, my hands are clean." Marjorie returned to the table.

"My lord Simon," Gwen said, raising her voice. "I'm ready."

"Call me librarian," Simon replied, rising from the table. Gwen thought him the most intimidating. His head was shaved, and his scalp glistened with a thin layer of sweat. As he drew near, Gwen saw there were black lines around his blue irises. They resembled the ones on his chest and Gwen found them alluring in their own way.

"Power can be born from fear," Simon said, then grabbed Gwen by her throat.

She tried to break away from his grasp, but he was stronger than her. He clenched his fingers tighter, constricting her flow of air and she began to panic. Gwen clawed at his hands, raking his flesh with her nails. Simon was unfazed. He backed her against the wall and Gwen looked to the other members for help. They sat quietly, watching. Gwen didn't understand. He was trying to kill her, and they were doing nothing!

It was a trap.

Gwen's thoughts became a confusing swirl. It was because she was Kamron's daughter. Someone else had found out about her identity and threatened their power if they didn't do something about her. Or was Aimil behind this? Did she know about the vial?

Use your runes. It was Marjorie's voice in her head. *Simon's magic is dark. It requires a darker means of transfer.*

Trying to kill someone was a way of sharing a rune? Gwen wasn't so sure she wanted that type of magic now, but it was too late to change her mind. She summoned the power of the strength rune and choked out its name.

"*Láidreacht.*"

The magic flowed through her body, and she grabbed ahold of Simon's wrist. She squeezed hard and felt something crunch. Still, Simon didn't let go, but his grip weakened enough for Gwen to force his hand off her throat. She gasped in a deep breath and balled her hand into a fist, striking Simon directly in the chest.

He staggered back and his robes fell open,

revealing the dark lines on his chest. One of the lines had been damaged by her punch and the inky darkness dripped down his skin. It coalesced at his naval and then sprang into the air, splattering across her forehead. Gwen screamed though it was more in surprise than pain. The liquid dripped down into her eyes, blinding her. She tried to rub it away to no avail.

Gwen saw the rune in the darkness. It was twisted and jagged and looked nothing like the others. The rune reminded her of a thorn bush. There was nothing beautiful about it. It was nothing but pain and anger and death. Yet, she spoke its name anyway.

"Draein saoil."

Her vision slowly returned, but it wasn't the same as before. There was a murkiness to everything as if she were looking at the world through a dark lens.

"No more," Gwen begged. "No more runes."

CHAPTER 18

CONAL

A dragon?" Conal snorted a laugh. "You hiding something I should know about?"

Lorkan grinned in response. "I know. Still, I do find it odd that they were so intent to come into my camp."

"I assume you've interrogated them beyond the fact that they're dragon hunters."

"We've done a quick assessment and other than them saying they're dragon hunters, we can't get much out of them. They're strange." Lorkan pointed across the open field dotted with small individual wedge tents to four individuals, their hands tied behind them, sitting on the ground around a fire pit whose embers had long since cooled. Two guards kept careful watch over them.

"In what way?"

"It's hard to describe, m'Lord. I thought it best for you to see for yourself."

As Conal and Lorkan approached, the four captives jerked their heads around to gape up at them. Three of the captives were women, young attractive women like the woman Conal saw during his visit with Krag. They all had the wild look of a cornered hare, yet their eyes had the glassy glaze of drug induced stupor.

Conal pointed to a woman about his age, strawberry blond hair folding over a smooth face with blue eyes and a pert nose. Except for the almost rabid look in her eyes, she was very pretty.

"Stand that one up," he commanded.

She yelped as one guard yanked her to standing.

Conal walked behind her to gaze down at her hands. Reaching down, he gently twisted her bound hand to reveal the tattoo of a dragon's head with a lance through it. With a frustrated sigh, he turned to Lorkan. "You'll get nothing from them. They are what they say they are. Why they are here is odd." In truth, Conal knew it had it had something to do with Bryok and he wondered if Bryok's rune was glowing.

"Why do they all have that strange look?" Lorkan asked.

Conal ticked his head at him to come over. "See that?" He pointed to the tattoo. "They've all been rune-marked."

"What does that mean?"

"It means that someone believes that dragons are still around. This person is also a rune-master. He or she put these brands on these dragon hunters. What it does is bind them to the rune-master. No, it's not what you think," he said when he saw the fear in Lorkan's eyes. "These people wanted to do this, but it was all based upon a lie. They were promised untold riches for finding and killing a dragon. They were told stories of unimagined wealth, living the idle life of never having to work again, of having servants and slaves at your beck and call."

"But look at them," Lorkan said. "They look like they've been drugged. How can they expect to find and kill a dragon in that condition… providing a dragon even exists?"

"They believe it does and the rune-master behind them also believes it. They will persist until they either find a dragon and kill it or die in the process. The question is, what do we do with them? We can't allow them to hinder or compromise our operation."

The woman's stupor abruptly vanished, and she quivered with excitement. A burst of murmuring erupted from the three on the ground. Conal looked up to see Bryok approaching, his face tight.

The woman stared at him with glee. "Dragon."

Lorkan cocked an eyebrow and exchanged a look with Conal. "They're crazy."

"I know," Conal readily agreed, noting the low glow of the rune on Bryok's arm.

"What do we have here?" Bryok asked, doing his best to appear ignorant.

"Dragon hunters," Lorkan replied. "And apparently they think you're a dragon."

Bryok frowned at Lorkan then splayed his arms and slowly bent his head to look at his own body, his head twisting side to side. In a deliberate gesture, he looked behind him. "I don't have a tail or wings. Does that mean I can't fly? How disappointing."

"Can you breathe fire?" Conal asked with exaggerated hope.

Bryok loudly exhaled and shook his head. "No. Just morning breath, which some have accused as smelling like dragon's breath, which never made any sense to me because it would imply they'd actually smelled a dragon's breath." He fluttered a hand in front of his mouth.

Lorkan smirked.

"Dragon," the woman repeated, taking a step

towards Bryok and struggling to free her hands.

The other three jerked and twisted, trying to stand only to be held down by the guards whose threats did not stop their struggling. Yet the sole focus of the dragon hunters was on Bryok.

Conal realized that as long as Bryok stayed with them, the dragon hunters would be a problem, a big problem.

"This is all rather strange," Lorkan observed, staring at Bryok. "They didn't show up until you showed up."

"It's happened before," Conal explained.

"It has?"

"On the way to Denhelm. We had four of them come out of the woods hot in pursuit of Bryok."

Lorkan cast a suspicious eye on Bryok. "Why?"

"I am a druid, remember?" Bryok parried. "You'd be surprised at the number of lunatics I get chasing after me once they find out I'm a druid, everything from wanting their fortunes told to making it rain on their farm while denying rain to the neighbor they don't like."

"But why dragon hunters and why now?"

Bryok fixed him with a sharp gaze. "Torian seeks to rule over all the kingdoms and will leave nothing to chance. It is obvious that he believes dragons exist and has sent out these poor fools to find them. The problem is that anyone or anything magical attracts them like bees to a pollinating flower. I'm only a druid. Can you imagine what it must be like to be a mage or wizard and have to fend these creatures off?"

"You're a druid," Lorkan said. "Can't you do something to fix it?

"Were it that easy," Bryok replied rolling his eyes. "You see that tattoo? It's a rune-mark. If you examine it closely, you'll see the runes. But more importantly, once you are rune-marked, you can never go back." He slid a meaningful glance at Conal. "In their case, they are forever marked as dragon hunters."

"What should we do with them?"

"Do you want them following you and continuing to advertise where you are?"

Lorkan turned to Conal. "We can't have them following us, m'Lord. Torian has already sent warring parties across the borders of Tir Manach. Caldyr does nothing to stop him. Were it not for Commander Sorcha, Torian would be at the sea by now."

"Who is Sorcha?" Conal asked.

"She's a former regimental commander. She spoke out against Caldyr's submission to Torian and barely escaped with her life. However, she was much loved and before Caldyr realized it, a third of his army had deserted. Her operations are to our north in Brody's demesne."

"Caldyr allows this?" Bryok said, an eyebrow raised.

"Caldyr has sent urgent demands for troops," Lorkan answered, frowning at the dragon hunters who were staring at Bryok with uncontained fascination. "We intercepted two messages meant for Pharyl."

"And Pharyl doesn't know all this is going on?" Conal knitted his brow, wondering if he had missed the signals while he was in Hemlyn.

"I can't say, m'Lord," Lorkan replied. "What I can say is that I wouldn't trust him."

Conal swiveled his head to stare at Bryok. "He knows who I am. It's just a matter of time before he directs his attention here."

"We assumed that, m'Lord," Lorkan interrupted. "That's why we intercepted you on the way to Caldyr."

"Where's Drustan?" Bryok interjected.

"He's still with Voldar and the dwarf forces near the four corners where the kingdoms meet. That is where we are headed."

"Then you have a plan in place?" Conal asked, hoping someone smarter than he had thought this all out.

"Not completely, m'Lord," admitted. "We head down to connect with King Rorkyn. We're praying that the forces to the east have likewise mobilized."

"What do we know about them?"

"Not much, m'Lord. Drustan probably knows more."

"What about Sorcha –"

"We don't have time to chase her down," Bryok asserted. "We know we can depend on the forces she has. It's merely a question of coordinating the attack. We need to get south to Clagmoran and find out if Kilmaryn is with us. We're wasting time."

"What do we do with them?" Lorkan ticked his head at the dragon hunters.

"Kill them," Bryok flatly stated.

Lorkan's jaw tightened. "We're not murderers."

"Then give me a better solution," Bryok retorted.

"They're here because of you," Lorkan countered.

"And if Drustan were here, we'd have the same problem," Conal pointed out.

"Or any other person with magic powers," Bryok added then narrowed his gaze at Lorkan. "Will you have magic with you when you attack Torian?

Because if you don't, even the gods can't help you."

"We are not murderers," Lorkan stubbornly insisted.

"Is it because you disarmed them?" Bryok challenged. "Then give them back their weapons and I will fight them. I will do what you are unwilling to do."

"What's all the fuss?" Torgreth called out, walking over to where Conal, Bryok, and Lorkan seemed to be in an argument. Galadyr strolled beside him, casually taking in the encampment.

"They captured four dragon hunters trying to infiltrate their lines," Conal answered, "and we're deciding what to do with them."

"What is to decide?" Galadyr calmly answered. "They are rune-bound to the mage master who serves Torian. If you believe Torian to be good, then release them. If Torian is evil, then those who willingly serve him are likewise evil. When you defeat Torian, will you set him free?"

Lorkan immediately understood, but the sour expression on his face said he still didn't like it. "Is it your wish, m'Lord?"

"Trying to absolve yourself?" Bryok tartly said.

"Everyone just stop," Conal commanded. "Arguing like this gets us nowhere. I'll do it." He started to unsheathe his sword when a voice stopped him.

"I'll take care of it, Boss," Maldwic boldly said, striding up, Seren and two others walking with him.

Conal slid his sword back in the sheath, both pleased and impressed with the man. "Thank you, Commander."

"You all go about your affairs," Maldwic said, "while we take care of business at hand."

Immediately feeling like his authority had been usurped, Lorkan held a hand up, exhaling a long-suffering sigh. "Thank you, Commander, but this is my responsibility. I'm the one who allowed them into my camp. I will deal with it."

Maldwic looked at Conal. "Boss?"

"He's right. It *is* his responsibility." Without waiting for a comment, he headed back to his tent where Bedo waited for him.

Maldwic hustled to catch up to him and matching strides as they walked. "Got some info for you, Boss. Overheard Lorkan's scouts reporting a large force crossed the border into Tir Manach and heading south."

Assuming Lorkan didn't know yet, Conal jerked to a halt and spun around to see the four captives kneeling and lined up in a row, Lorkan and three others standing behind them. Bryok stood two paces away in front of the captives, Torgreth and Galadyr behind him. With their attention devoted to Bryok, the captives didn't see or notice when Lorkan gave the command. In one uniform motion, he and the others raised their swords and in a fierce arc, sliced through the necks, separating heads from quivering bodies.

The deed done, Lorkan stood surveying the scene, reconciling distaste with necessity. Two women soldiers approached him.

"Those are the scouts," Maldwic revealed.

Though Conal couldn't hear what was said, he saw Lorkan straighten, question the two scouts then make a beeline towards him.

"M'Lord. Enemy troops about an hour away, heading south. We need to intercept them."

"Take charge. We'll follow your lead."

"Thank you, m'Lord. We leave in ten minutes."

Two hours of hard riding gave Lorkan's army time to set up an ambush. His scouts estimated the enemy strength at around 500, moving in cohort units of 50, each cohort led by a junior officer. The enemy commander, a large man with a perpetual scowl, sat upon a large steed, controlling his forces from the middle. Lorkan was impressed for the man moved his army as one with experience. Yet that mattered little for Lorkan's army outnumbered his opponent by 6:1.

Lorkan arranged his ambush in box pattern with the lid open, allowing the enemy to enter the box before Lorkan closed it with a rear guard. Much to Lorkan's distress, Conal refused to stay out of harm's way, firmly informing him that he intended to fully participate, positioning himself with Maldwic's small force blocking the road.

Lorkan had chosen the terrain well for the road the enemy followed undulated along the side of a mountain in a series of curves that blocked what was in front or behind. All they had to do now was wait.

"Never been in a real battle," Torgreth offhandedly commented, a double-bladed axe in his hand. "But I do know how to handle an ax."

"I am sure you will excel, my friend," Galadyr reassured him. The elf had chosen a longbow along with half a dozen quivers stuffed with arrows. Together, he and the dwarf stood inside the tree line beside the road where it sharply curved as it bent back on itself. Conal and Bryok stood opposite them across the road. Maldwic's small force, along with 300 of Lorkan's army filled in behind them.

Just as the enemy's lead scouts rounded the corner a ram's horn sounded and the shouts of battle filled the air.

Conal raced forward, easily outdistancing his friends and hurled himself past the scouts who had fallen, pierced with arrows from Galadyr's perfect aim. In short order, Conal came upon the main body already in the melee of battle as Lorkan's forces attacked from both sides. Trusting the power of his runes, Conal dove headlong into the fight, a crazed dervish destroying everything in his path.

All too quickly, the enemy gave ground, pressed hard from the sides, but especially from the vehemence of Conal's attack for he had cut a path through the enemy as he forged his way to the commander who by now realized that his position was lost.

In a vain attempt to rally his troops, the commander called for retreat only to find his escape route was blocked. Accepting fate that he and his army were lost, the commander dismounted and slapped the horse on the rear, sending him away then turned to do battle, surprised that he suddenly faced a man smaller than he, who had managed to carve his way here, the strewn bodies of the dead behind him.

"Who are you?"

Conal's eyes blazed and he felt a sudden surge of overwhelming strength as he answered, "I am Conal, the son of the true king of Isentol."

"That king is dead," the commander retorted.

"Just as you will be."

The commander raised his sword to block Conal's attack, immediately feeling as though a granite anvil had crashed into him. He felt a tingling in his arm as it weakened. Yet he hadn't counted on Conal's speed for no sooner had the downward stroke smashed into him, he felt a sharp pain and a sudden warmth across his stomach. He looked down to see his stomach sliced open. He raised his head just in time to see his last vision while still alive, a vision of a man whose cold angry eyes spoke of revenge before the world went black.

Once the commander went down, the enemy's will to fight withered and died. Throwing down swords and axes and bows, they stood in place and surrendered.

His berserker's rage draining away, Conal inhaled a deep breath, surveying the bloody battlefield of broken bodies and the cries of the mortally wounded. Movement out the corner of his eye caught his attention, and he twisted his head in time to see Bryok lurching into the forest, an arrow through his chest.

CHAPTER 19

GWEN

Gwen sat alone in Marjorie's personal chamber, nursing her pained flesh and bruised throat. Her experience with Simon had been violent and unexpected. Again, she lamented accepting the rune before knowing fully what it would require to accept it—and what it would cost her.

The door to the chamber creaked open and Gwen jumped involuntarily.

"I told her she needs to rest, but she refuses to," Marjorie was saying to Aimil as they walked into the room.

Gwen stood up and clenched her jaw to keep her teeth from chattering. Simon's rune was making her body thrum with power. And she was burning up, her flesh hot to the touch.

"We need to get on the road," Gwen said.

"We can leave tomorrow," Aimil replied, frowning at her. "You look like the gods stole your soul."

"I feel like they did," Gwen replied. The fingers of her right hand started tremoring and she balled them into a fist, her nails digging into her palm and reopening her cut. She didn't even feel the pain, barely felt the blood slicking between her fingers.

"Are you all right?" Aimil asked. She stepped closer, looking Gwen up and down. When their gazes locked, Aimil's eyes widened briefly, but it was long enough that Gwen saw the surprise in them. And possibly fear.

"You took a dark rune?" Her tone was on the border of incredulous.

"I didn't know," Gwen muttered.

"No one warned her?" Aimil asked, turning to Marjorie.

"I tried to, but she was adamant in her decision. Simon even showed her his lines."

Aimil made a noise in her throat, clearly displeased. She shook her head and grabbed Gwen by the hand and led her out of the room.

"Where are you going?" Marjorie asked, following after them.

"We're leaving," Aimil said. "And you can't stop us."

"I won't stop you. You are free to come and go as you choose. Gwen said she wanted all of the runes we offered, and I want to make certain she's changed her mind."

"I'm certain," Gwen said. "Thank you for everything, but we need to reach Haddence and we're already short on time."

"Very well," Marjorie said. "Farewell Quinlee. May we meet again."

Gwen offered a tired smile before Aimil continued pulling her down the hall. All Gwen wanted to do was sleep, but she knew she didn't have time to rest. Not yet. Aimil led her through the library and then suddenly they were back at the stable. Gwen looked around, confused as to how they got there. She had no recollection of anything other than being in the library.

"How did we get here?" she asked.

Aimil gave her an odd look. "We walked," she said.

"The whole way?"

"You need to sleep," Aimil said.

"I can't. We have to get to Haddence."

"Why? What's in Haddence?"

Gwen's jaw quivered against her will and she waited for it to subside before answering. "The leaders of the rebellion are holding a meeting. It's in two d-days," she stammered.

"Even if you were rested, we couldn't make that trip in two days."

"We have to try," Gwen said pleadingly. "We *have* to."

Aimil shrugged. "Fine. It's your funeral."

No, it'll be yours, Gwen thought.

The stable boy brought their horses out and Gwen struggled to climb into the saddle. Her muscles were like jelly. With the help of the boy and Aimil, she was able to get situated and Aimil led the way out of the city, following the wall until they reached the main gates, then taking the road northwest.

Gwen weaved in and out of consciousness, her eyes refusing to stay open. She swayed in the saddle and almost fell off her horse several times before she leaned forward and laid her head against the horse's neck and succumbed to her exhaustion. When she came to, they were still riding, and the city behind them was long gone.

"I thought you died," Aimil said from beside her. "I had to check your pulse to be sure."

"How long was I out?"

"About an hour."

Gwen was surprised to hear that. She felt like she'd been asleep for days. Despite the shortness of her nap, she felt invigorated. The strength had returned to her muscles and the tremors were gone. Her body still thrummed with magic from the dark rune, but her body temperature was back to normal.

"I can't believe you took a dark rune," Aimil said. "Most mages don't survive the process."

"It was pretty sadistic," Gwen confessed. "I thought Simon was going to choke the life out of me."

They rode in silence for a short time, then Aimil asked, "Who gave you the runes?"

Gwen opened her mouth to reply, then caught herself. Marjorie had sworn her to secrecy regarding the Council's ability to bestow runes despite the fact they were wizards, and she didn't want their wrath coming down on her.

"The council members had some of their assistant mages give me runes," Gwen lied. She could feel Aimil's gaze on her and suspected the woman knew she was lying.

"Simon is one of the assistant mages?"

"Yes."

"Interesting. That's also the name of one of the council members," Aimil said casually.

"And?"

"You're hiding something," Aimil accused.

"It's funny that you should think that," Gwen replied. "Considering I know what *you* did."

"I've done many things. You'll have to be more specific."

"Just forget it," Gwen huffed. She wasn't in the mood for this, nor did she want to confront Aimil yet. She wanted the rebellion leaders present when she laid out the events of Auleavell.

"Are you afraid you'll upset me?" Aimil laughed. "Spit it out already."

Gwen ignored her until Aimil brought her horse closer and grabbed ahold of her wrist. "What is it you want to say?" Aimil asked. Her tone was serious, menacing almost.

"Let go of me," Gwen demanded, trying to jerk free of Aimil's grasp. When Aimil didn't release her, Gwen got angry. Her face flushed with heat and she looked Aimil in the eyes.

"I know you're the one who poisoned the Thaestra River."

Aimil's expression barely changed, but she stiffened slightly.

"What are you talking about?"

"You dropped the vial that held the poison," Gwen said. "I saw it. And Marjorie confirmed it was a magical poison."

"You told Marjorie it was mine?"

"No."

They stared at each other as the horses continued to trot along the road. Gwen's heart was racing in her chest. She was afraid. Aimil wasn't one to be trifled with.

"Why did you do it?"

Aimil shrugged. "Just following orders."

"What? Eradore told you to poison the river?" Gwen's mind couldn't fathom that.

"Of course not. Eradore is weak."

"Then who?" Gwen asked.

"I suppose there's no use in lying now that you know," Aimil said. "The order came from Torian."

Gwen almost fell off her horse in shock. "You … you're working for that tyrant?"

"Your surprise is cute. I told you before that I work for the highest bidder. Who do you think has more money? The rebellion? Don't be ridiculous."

Aimil was a traitor. She'd just admitted it. Gwen knew she was in trouble now. There was no way Aimil was going to let her continue living after revealing that. Gwen swallowed hard, her eyes going from Aimil to the road ahead. There was nothing but fields around them. Aimil would kill her and get away with it. Gwen snapped the reins and her horse sped forward.

"You can't run!" Aimil shouted after her.

"Yah!" Gwen cried, urging her mount faster but the horse shrieked and staggered, its legs buckling. The animal collapsed, tipping to the side. Gwen threw herself from the saddle at the last moment, hitting the ground and rolling out of range. She got back onto her feet and saw the horse was dead. Blood seeped from its eyes and nostrils. Gwen turned to face Aimil as she approached. The woman was insane. She needed to be stopped, but Gwen had a fraction of the runes Aimil did. The odds were against her.

Three globes of green light appeared in Aimil's hand and she hurled them at Gwen. They struck the ground around her and the dirt and grass sizzled and melted. Gwen summoned the power of her fire rune and stretched out her arms, hoping the blast didn't harm the horse. She spoke the rune's name and released the magic. A wave of crackling fire poured from her palms. The rune on her side grew warm and tingled her skin.

Aimil cursed and spoke the name of a rune, erecting a magical shield around her and the horse. Gwen's flames struck the shield and fizzled out of existence. Aimil's mount came right at her, forcing

Gwen to cut off the magic as she jumped over her fallen horse to get out of the way. Gwen was thrown to the ground as something heavy struck her from behind. Rough hands rolled her over and she looked up at Aimil. Had she jumped off her horse?

"What were you planning to do? Turn me over to Eradore?" Aimil punched her in the mouth and Gwen could feel warm blood on her lips. She licked it off and winced as her tongue touched the wound.

"Yes," Gwen replied. "You will pay for your crime."

Aimil laughed and punched her again. "I thought you had potential, but I was wrong. You're like the rest of them. Weak and foolish."

"Because I want freedom from oppression?"

"No, because you want to upset the order of things. If Torian wasn't meant to be king, Kamron would have fended him off and defeated his brother. Things always work out as they are intended to."

"You're insane," Gwen growled. She tried to buck Aimil off her but failed. Aimil punched her again and Gwen's vision blurred for a brief moment. She grabbed onto Aimil's wrists and tried to gain control. Gwen knew she wasn't as strong as Aimil, so she reached for the power of the might rune. Before she could summon its magic, the dark rune called out to her. Gwen flinched away mentally from the darkness, but its pull was undeniable.

"*Draein saoil,*" she uttered.

The magic flared to life and Gwen felt an influx of energy entering her body. She didn't understand what was happening at first. Aimil gasped and tried to break away from her, but the rune held her firmly in place. And then Gwen realized what the rune's power was.

It was sucking the lifeforce out of Aimil. Gwen's stomach churned and she felt sick at the realization, but the rune continued to pull Aimil's energy away and filter it into Gwen. She wanted it to stop, yet she also wanted *more*. Her desires conflicted within her, a confusing whirl of dread and hunger.

"Stop," Aimil begged breathlessly. Her shoulders sagged and the life in her eyes grew dim. "Please."

Gwen wanted to stop, but she couldn't. The rune was directing her, bidding her to finish the task. "I … can't," Gwen panted.

A shadow passed overhead, but Gwen was too focused on the thrilling feeling of Aimil's life being sucked away to care what it was until something roared and broke her focus, cutting off the magic. Aimil slumped backward and Gwen crawled out from under her, looking around fearfully.

The shadow passed over her again and Gwen looked up to see a massive silver dragon. It spiraled lower and lower until it landed, stirring up dust and loose grass. Gwen immediately recognized Venia from Auleavell.

"What are you doing here?" Gwen asked.

"Saving your life," Venia huffed. "Foolish humans!"

"I had it under control," Gwen replied.

"Is that why you almost killed her? Dark magic should never be used so carelessly. If you had taken her entire lifeforce into you, it would have killed both of you."

Gwen's expression turned horrified. "I wasn't … how did you know what was happening?"

"Dragons see everything," Venia said.

Gwen remembered Venia saying that before, but she just assumed it was a figure of speech and not something literal.

"This isn't over," Aimil rasped.

Gwen looked at her in time to see a rune on her arm glow before she vanished.

"Where did she go?" Gwen demanded.

"Wherever she wanted, I suppose. That doesn't matter. Climb on my back."

"Do what?" Gwen asked.

"Get on my back. We're going to Haddence."

Gwen stared at Venia for a moment, thinking the dragon was joking, but Venia lowered her shoulder and waited patiently. Gwen slowly stepped closer and placed her hands on Venia's scales. She hesitated.

"We don't have all day," Venia growled.

Gwen climbed onto Venia's back and settled herself in a spot between the dragon's shoulders and neck. With a powerful flap of her wings, Venia launched into the air and Gwen screamed. Venia flew up, up, up, high into the air, then leveled out and headed northwest.

"Whatever you do, don't fall!" Venia roared into the air.

Gwen held on as tightly as she could and lowered her head against the wind. Aimil had betrayed her and the rebellion. She would tell Eradore everything.

And then she would track Aimil down and kill her.

CHAPTER 20

CONAL

Conal leaped across dead bodies to chase after Bryok.

Torgreth saw him race away. "Where you going?"

"I'll be back," Conal shouted over his shoulder, plunging into the forest. Up ahead, he saw the struggling Bryok weaving unsteadily up the mountain. "Stop. What are you doing?"

Ignoring him, Bryok pressed on, staggering doggedly forward.

"Stop. Where are you going? You need help." Conal dodged trees to catch up, surprised that the mortally wounded man could maintain such a pace. Conal's speed kicked in and he managed to overtake the druid as he struggled over a rock cropping.

"Help me," Bryok gasped, lifting a weak hand to point higher up to what appeared to be a cave opening.

"Where are you going?" Conal grabbed Bryok's arm and placed it over his shoulder, wrapping the other arm around the druid's waist to help him walk.

"Up there."

"Why?"

"I'm dying."

"What's up there?" Conal's face hardened, a sudden feeling of overwhelming loss flooding within him.

"Safe…" Bryok's breathing became labored.

By now Bryok's legs straggled with each step and by the time they reached the cave, his legs dragged behind him, the toes of his boots leaving parallel trails on the leaf cluttered forest floor. Inside the cave, Conal gently placed Bryok on his side on the dirt floor and kneeled beside him. The arrow had penetrated close to the heart and the barbed end protruded out his back. With each heartbeat, blood pulsed out of the wound.

Conal glanced around the darkness, wondering how Bryok knew a cave was here. It was larger than he realized with a tall ceiling and going back for some distance.

Bryok's eyes fluttered as he struggled for breath. "Listen… not much time…"

"Yes?"

"Dragons… will help… you… must return…" He inhaled a rattling breath. "Give it back."

"Give what back?"

"Haven… Havengarde… dragons' home. Give it back. Sacred." Bryok groaned. "Few left… promise me…"

"Sure, I promise. What, what?"

"Protect us." Bryok's eyes closed.

"Protect who?" Conal pleaded.

Bryok opened his eyes to gaze at Conal. "Dragons. Only twelve left…. Eleven now. You must save us."

"I will; I promise." Though not understanding, Conal was willing to agree to anything.

Peace settled across Bryok's face, and he smiled. "You are the one… I knew it… from the beginning." He closed his eyes and the tenseness in his body sloughed away.

Conal sat back, inhaling a mournful breath, feeling very much alone.

A dull silver glow enveloped Bryok's body and the rune on his arm began to glow, brighter and brighter. Suddenly the body began to stretch and grow, changing color and texture as it pushed out. Startled, Conal scooted back on hands and feet like a scuttling crab, watching as the body grew larger and larger, forming wings and a tail and the head of a dragon. The arrow, once protruding out Bryok's back, popped inside the dragon's chest though leaving a bloody wound behind, yet the feathered shaft remained visible near the dragon's heart.

Once the body stopped growing, Conal stood and gaped at the dead dragon stretched before him, his mind jumbled trying to comprehend what had just happened. Yet the all too obvious conclusion that Bryok was a dragon in human form was more than he could fathom. How was it possible?

Understanding began pushing its way through the overlapping and conflicting thoughts as the slavish pursuit by dragon hunters suddenly made sense. He startled as he suddenly realized that Drustan must also be a dragon in human form. Alarm vibrated within as Bryok's last words replayed.

"Dragons. Only twelve left…. Eleven now. You must save us."

His first instinct was to race back and urge Lorkan and the others to immediately head for Clagmoran or wherever Drustan was. But he remained and stared at the dragon who was once Bryok… or was this Krag?

He shook his head realizing the real reason Bryok wasn't there when Krag came to visit.

What did he mean by 'give it back?'

Conal frowned as he stared at Krag, wondering what he should feel. He had come to like and depend on Bryok and at first had been upset at the man's passing. Yet that Bryok was a dragon knocked that emotion off the pedestal. Sure, he was upset, but... the man was a dragon. Should he be more upset, especially as there were only eleven dragons left.

He needed to get to Drustan before anything else happened.

Conal turned and stepped to the edge of the cave, realizing for the first time how high up it was as he stood on the edge and gazed out over the tops of the trees of the vast forest. Casting a last look back, he descended into the forest, wondering what Drustan was going to do or say once he found out his brother was dead.

His return elicited more than a few polite, yet stern, rebukes.

"Don't ever do that again," Galadyr quietly chastised. "While you are a formidable warrior, you are not impervious to injury or capture. You need to let us know where you are."

Conal wanted to say that he could take care of himself, but instead said, "You are right. My apologies. Bryok is dead."

"I know."

"You do?"

"I was too late to stop the archer who slew him."

Conal peered at him, recognizing the pain of guilt. "It's not your fault. We all knew the risk that comes with battle."

"You're back, m'Lord," Lorkan said, his relief

obvious. "Please, m'Lord, don't run off like that again. I am responsible for your safety."

"You are right, Lorkan. And I apologize. I promise never to do it again."

Torgreth came strolling up, an impish grin curling the corners of his lips. "I told them you'd be back. Tried to get everyone to hide just to see the look on your face. Where's Bryok?"

"He's dead."

Torgreth's smile vanished.

Conal turned to Lorkan. "We need to meet up with Drustan and the others. What's our status here?"

"We're ready to move, m'Lord."

"Injured?"

"We lost eight, twenty-three wounded, two seriously. We've taken 156 prisoners. The rest are dead." He watched Conal glance around as if expecting someone. "He was one of the casualties, m'Lord," he gently informed him.

"Maldwic?"

"Yes, m'Lord."

Conal's shoulders slumped and his lips tightened. He had come to really like the man and knew he could count on him no matter the cost.

"Where's Seren?"

Lorkan hesitated. "They've left, m'Lord,"

"Left?" Conal stiffened, his nostril flaring.

"She said to tell you that they are not soldiers but highwaymen who only know how to steal and rob." His eyes softened. "Do not hold it against her, m'Lord. It is for the best. Maldwic was cut from a different cloth. He was a smart and loyal man who would obey without question. Yet he pushed his people beyond their level of comfort and abilities. Seren knows her limits. Still, she is loyal and will provide us with information regarding Tir Manach."

Conal grimaced and swiveled his head to glare at Torgreth. "I'm going to be mad at you if anything happens to you."

"Me too," Torgreth replied with a crooked grin. "How about we get going? I haven't seen that obnoxious brother of mine in far too long."

"We're ready to move out, m'Lord," Lorkan reminded him. "Bedo has your mount." He pointed back towards where the road curved around into the forest.

"Take charge, Commander." Conal stepped to the side to wait for Bedo.

They met up with Drustan and the dwarven army a day later just across the border into Gurim-duhr. Drustan took the news especially hard that his brother was dead.

"I am sorry." Conal stood inside Drustan's tent, gazing tenderly at the druid whose whole body ached with a sadness beyond comprehension.

"What are we going to do?" Drustan muttered, shaking his head.

Conal cast a glance over his shoulder at the activity within the wide encampment spread out over the surrounding countryside. Together with Rorkyn's army, there were close to seven thousand dwarves and humans in a combined force. Lorkan and the dwarven king were in huddled planning when Conal excused himself to talk with Drustan.

Drustan looked up at Conal, his eyes moist. "Did he say anything to you?"

"He said something about Havengarde and giving it back and sacred and dragons' home, and none of it makes any sense to me. But I do know one thing…

you are a dragon."

Drustan stiffened and shot a look past Conal to see if anyone heard. "Please keep that to yourself until I decide to reveal myself."

"Sure. Now explain to me what he meant." Conal scooted a field chair close to Drustan. "One thing I did notice was that anytime dragon hunters were close by, a rune on his arm would glow."

Drustan's eyes popped wide. "Dragon hunters? How many? Where?"

"We've eliminated them, at least all we know about," Conal reassured him.

Drustan flipped his arm over to glance down at the rune on his forearm. It was dark, revealing there were no dragon hunters close by.

"I swore to him that I'd protect you," Conal said, "but I need to know what I'm protecting. Tell me about Havengarde."

Drustan seated himself on the cot. "There was a time when dragons roamed freely. We lived in Havengarde and other locales, but Havengarde was our capital city, our refuge, our sacred place, for it was only in Havengarde that dragons could reproduce. I won't bore you with the history of why we dwelt in Havengarde, but know that we still hold the place sacred, especially now that our numbers have diminished to less than a dozen. If we cannot claim Havengarde again, then truly, dragons will cease to exist."

"How is that possible?" Conal argued. "Havengarde has been ruled by humans for hundreds of years."

"You forget how long dragons can live."

"OK, OK, point taken. But how did humans end up ruling Havengarde?"

Drustan exhaled a slow sigh. "Treachery. Dragons cannot work the earth like dwarves or humans. Our council met and decided to trust humans to build our refuge. It all seemed to be going well and we looked forward to the time when dragons would have their own city, a place sacred and holy where we could procreate. That lasted until almost the last stone was in place. Suddenly our friends became out captors, led by a man called Watcyn, a mason by trade, a wizard by reputation. The hunt for dragons began with him. Those who call themselves dragon hunters are bound by the same spells that that evil man created."

Drustan looked away for a moment then returned to his story. "Yes, dragons are powerful and in alliance with the right people would be quite the combination. But no one can fight everyone at once, for that is what happened. Humans and dwarves united to hunt us down."

"Not elves?"

Drustan shook his head. "No. Elves intuitively understand the balance in the world. It was because of the elves that we managed to save a remnant. It was the elves who discovered the runes of change that would allow us to appear in human form. Some of us called ourselves half-druids, because we were merely dragons in human form, albeit with the strength of dragons. Obviously, we had to be careful, lest someone discover the truth."

"And there are eleven left now?"

"Yes. They are scattered throughout the kingdoms. With Bryok's death, there are five males and six females. But time is running out. Just like humans, there comes a point in a female's life when she is no longer able to reproduce. Two of our females have reached that age. It won't be long for the other four. If we do not reclaim Havengarde, you won't need dragon hunters anymore, for we will die of old age, never to rise again."

Conal stood and started pacing. "Did my father know all this?"

Drustan shrugged. "The story of dragons and Havengarde is lost to memory, except for dragons and those scholars who spend their days studying the arcane. I'm sure had your father known, he would have done something. Bryok and I had decided to trust him, but by the time we arrived in the city, Torian ruled."

He closed his eyes in reverie. "How odd it was to walk the streets of our city again. It had been over a hundred years the last time I was there. It took a while, but we found the home where we lived. It's all changed now. The building has been bricked in and apartments built in levels. It's a very fashionable part of the city now." He smiled. "I had to laugh at the stories developed over the years as to why the streets were so wide. One such fable had it that the streets had to be wide enough for a four-team carriage to turn around."

He opened his eyes and pierced Conal with an intense stare. "Will you keep your promise… or do I place my hope in another?"

"You know who I am," Conal evenly replied. "I will repeat the last words your brother spoke to me. He said that he knew I was the one… that he had known it from the beginning. Nothing's changed. We go to reclaim Havengarde… before it's too late for all of us."

EMPIRE OF SERPENTS

BOOK 3

CHAPTER 1

GWEN

The city of Haddence was a flurry of activity. Gwen watched merchants pitch their wares, from brightly colored silks to food that permeated the air with their scents. Small children ran along the streets, playing a game and shouting at each other lightheartedly. It was almost enough to make her think that the impending darkness of Torian's madness was just a dream.

Almost.

Venia had landed outside the city and Gwen had walked from there. Despite traveling by air, which had been a living nightmare for Gwen, it had still taken two days to reach the city. Venia had a voracious appetite and continuously stopped to eat. She promised to be at the rebellion meeting, but Gwen wasn't sure how that would happen. Venia was massive, so unless the rebellion was meeting outside in a large open field, it didn't seem possible. The more pressing issue was that Gwen didn't know where the meeting location was, and it wasn't like she could ask someone, could she?

"Good day, madam! Wear the finest clothing this side of the border," a merchant said to her, producing an armful of elegantly sewn dresses. "I sew them myself." The merchant offered a grin that stretched his pockmarked face and revealed a mouthful of yellowed teeth. He was bald and slightly overweight, but his clothing was of high quality.

Gwen smiled and politely shook her head. "No, thank you. You haven't seen a group of people that seem out of place, have you?"

"I'm afraid not," the merchant replied, offering a wink. He tapped his waist where a bag hung from his belt. It clinked with coins.

The man's intent was obvious, and Gwen retrieved a coin from her purse and offered it to the merchant. He swept his hand over hers and the coin vanished, but Gwen hadn't felt his touch at all. Was he truly a merchant, or some sort of vagrant pickpocket?

"Go to the end of this street and you'll see the butcher shop on the right. Beside it, there's an alley that'll take you to a door. Knock twice."

"Thank you," Gwen said. She continued along the cobblestone street, but she could feel eyes watching her. A glance over her shoulder revealed the bald man was gone, replaced by an elderly woman. Gwen thought it was odd, but she followed the man's directions anyway.

At the end of the street was the butcher's building, and Gwen found the alley. She stepped into the darkened space and walked twenty feet to reach the door. Gwen raised her hand to knock and heard shuffling behind her.

"Don't move," someone said gruffly.

Gwen froze. Her heart skipped a beat.

"Who are you and what do you want?"

"I'm here to see my friends," Gwen replied

vaguely.

"Names, girl."

Gwen considered lying but decided not to. If this person was connected to the rebellion and she used a fake name, it could keep her from getting into the meeting.

"His name is Eradore."

"Never heard of him," the gruff man replied.

"Perhaps I'm in the wrong place. I'm sorry, I'll just be on my way."

"You aren't going anywhere."

Something sharp jabbed into Gwen's lower back and she sucked in a breath.

"Please—"

"Shut your mouth," the man said. He applied pressure on the blade and Gwen flinched. "Who sent you here? Torian? Grimmar? I'll gut you like a fish, you blasted spy."

Gwen barely heard his words. She was focused on the pulse of magic flowing through the fire rune. Her right hand grew warm as the flames started to form. The door in front of her opened and a robed figure stepped into view.

"What's this?"

"A spy. I was just about to show her what we do to spies."

"Gwen?"

At the sound of her name, Gwen cut off the magic and looked up to see Eradore. The elf was a welcome sight and she rushed forward and wrapped him in a tight hug. Eradore's surprise quickly faded and he patted her on the back, then pushed her at arm's length.

"Is everything all right? What are you doing here?" He looked down the alley, then back at her.

"Where's Aimil?"

"It's a long story," Gwen said. "Aimil's a traitor."

"Come in," Eradore bade. "Tell me everything. As for you," Eradore turned his eyes on the guard. "You almost got burned to a crisp and didn't even know it. Next time, check for runes."

"Yes, sir," came the gruff reply.

Gwen turned to look at the man and saw it was the merchant who'd given her directions. He tucked his dagger away and offered a bow to her. "My apologies. Just doing my duty."

"Don't worry about it," Gwen replied. She stepped inside the building, and Eradore closed and latched the door.

"Speak as we walk. The leaders of the rebellion are about to convene."

Gwen related the events at Auleavell and Steepcross, leaving out nothing. She even showed Eradore her eyes and the dark rune lines that started at her collar bone. His expression was unreadable, but Gwen had the feeling that he wasn't happy about the dark magic. The two reached a small room guarded by a handful of warriors and a mage. When she finished talking, Eradore was silent for a long while.

"Where's the vial?" he finally asked.

"Marjorie destroyed it. She said it was too dangerous to give it back to me."

Eradore frowned. "If what you say is true, Aimil poses a great threat. She's been privy to many things within the rebellion."

"She also knows about me," Gwen said.

"What do you mean?"

"She was in the room when Marjorie told me my true name. Aimil knows I'm Kamron's daughter. I doubt she'll keep that information to herself."

"I think you're right. She's probably already reported to Torian. I wouldn't be surprised if Grimmar himself comes looking for you. Come with me. The others need to know."

The guards stepped aside to let allow them through. There were many people Gwen didn't recognize. A few familiar faces stood out and she was relieved when she spotted Lyra. Roland was also present. He'd been there when Tobias had fallen during the fight at the outpost. Seeing him brought back a rush of memories. Aimil had been there, too. The feeling of betrayal stung Gwen's heart again and she forced herself to swallow her anger. Aimil would pay. Dearly.

"We've come together to devise our plans against Torian," Eradore said, raising his voice to be heard over the scattered conversations. The noise died down and Eradore motioned to Gwen. "These plans will be greatly affected by the news that we have a queen to lead us. This is Quinlee, the daughter of King Kamron."

All eyes went to Gwen. She wasn't used to being the center of attention and she could feel her face flushing.

"Hold on!" It was a dwarf. Gwen looked at him, glad for the distraction. It diverted everyone's attention from her. The dwarf had thick curly brown hair and a long beard. He folded his arms across his chest and glared at Eradore.

"We don't need a queen to lead us when we've got a king." He thumbed toward a man behind him. Gwen was drawn to the man for reasons she couldn't understand. He was handsome and fit, with thick auburn hair and intense brown eyes.

"Who are you?" Eradore asked.

"Name's Torgreth. And his name is Conal. He's the son of King Kamron, and the heir to the throne."

"What proof do you have?" Eradore asked. "We have proof from the Great Library that this is Quinlee."

"And we have proof of the naming runes," Drustan spoke up, "that this is Darrbie, Kamron's only son."

The others in the room began trying to talk over one another until it was a mass shouting match. Gwen rubbed her temples. All the noise was going to give her a headache.

"Stop!" she shouted. "Everyone just stop!"

The room went silent, and Gwen sighed in relief. "I don't want to lead us to war against Torian. I'm not a warrior and I know nothing of battle. I will defer to Conal. And if Conal is Kamron's son, that means he's my brother. There is no need for division among family."

Gwen looked at Conal and waited to see what he would say. She hoped he would agree to take the lead. If she were forced into it, she was afraid many people would die due to the mistakes she would make.

Conal gazed at his sister. She was very pretty. Part of him wondered had they met in different circumstances as strangers whether anything would have happened between them. He shuddered at the thought and refocused. Yet here she was, both a stranger and a sister. He thought he should feel something, some sort of elation at the reuniting with family. But his family had been murdered and what he felt now had nothing to do with family.

"I accept battle leadership," Conal calmly said. Though his words were full of confidence, his expression hinted that he had some doubts.

"Thank you… brother." Gwen felt weird saying that. She'd been an only child her entire life. Yet now her long lost brother was here, in the same room with her. It was difficult for her to fathom. "What's the plan?"

Eradore looked at Conal. "Torian has many Prestiges at his command, but the Great Library's emissary has informed us that they will join our forces. With their Prestiges on our side, we just might stand a chance against Torian."

"We also have a dragon on our side," Gwen said.

"A dragon?" Eradore asked. "You didn't mention a dragon."

"Sorry. I wasn't sure how I should bring it up, but the dragon that brought me here promised her aid. Her name is Venia."

"We also have a dragon," Conal said. "We had two, but one was killed by dragon hunters."

"Do these dragons know each other?" Eradore asked.

"I'll have to ask her," Gwen replied. "She said she would be here for the meeting, but obviously she isn't here."

"Don't be so sure," Lyra spoke up. "Dragons can do many things, and that includes shapeshifting."

Gwen looked at Lyra curiously.

"It's true," Conal agreed. "I've seen it myself."

"Are you… Venia?" Gwen was being surprised at every turn.

"I am," Lyra, really Venia, answered. "Though you should use my elven name. My dragon name is personal and only given to those I trust."

Gwen remembered asking the dragon for her name in Auleavell and Venia had given it to her. She was humbled by the trust that such a mighty creature had in her and felt indebted somehow.

"With dragons on our side, we should easily be able to take Isentol back," Eradore said.

"Don't place too much hope in dragons," Conal counseled. "Yes, they are powerful, but very few remain... less than a dozen. And Torian has dragon hunters tracking them down. We've killed those hunters we found, but there's no telling how many more are on the prowl."

"Then it's probably a good idea to keep them split up in case these hunters make it into our camp somehow. Do you have a plan?"

Conal slowly nodded. "We need to keep Torian off balance. It seems to me that Gwen has the weight of magic on her side. I know nothing about magic. Therefore, I propose that we divide our efforts. Gwen and her forces attack from the east with all the magic you can employ. Force Torian to concentrate his efforts and attention to the east. My forces will wait until Torian is occupied with battling in the east... then we will attack from the west."

"I'll take Gwen to Auleavell to meet up with Kirith and his forces," Lyra said. "They're ready to march with us, he just needs to receive word before we arrive."

"That's easily done through magical means," Eradore said. "I'll have a message sent to Kirith."

"That begs the question of how we coordinate our efforts once we are in position?" Conal asked. "We can't afford to wait for a messenger to get to us days after the fact."

"I have an answer for that, as well," Eradore smiled. "We have two mages that are connected magically by runes, but their bond is deeper than that. They're twins. Their sibling connection seems to have strengthened the power of the runes and they can communicate with one another over longer distances than usual. One of them will travel with Gwen and the other will travel with you."

Conal smiled. "Amazing things, these runes. That will work."

"What about the cities and towns along the way?" Gwen asked. "The people there are innocent and shouldn't suffer because we're marching through."

"I've thought about that," Conal said. "Anyone willing to join us is more than welcome. We can use all the extra bodies we can get. Everyone else can stay put and stay safe and out of the way. Most importantly, we buy everything we need along the way: food, supplies, even the ale. We are reclaiming a kingdom not punishing it. We want this to be as painless as possible."

Gwen was beginning to like Conal even more. He seemed to be a man of good intentions and she believed he would be a great leader in the aftermath of Torian's defeat.

"We can work out the minor details along the way," Conal added. "I think we should get moving. The quicker we are in position, the less time Torian has to prepare."

Gwen could feel excitement stirring within her. She wasn't a warrior but was ready to do what her people needed of her.

CHAPTER 2

CONAL

Ignoring the usual after-meeting conversations, Conal focused on Gwen. Crossing over to stand before her, the difference in height became glaring. He towered over her by at least two hand spans, causing him to wonder how one set of parents could produce two children of such different sizes. Yet she was very pretty, her green eyes inquisitive as she returned his stare.

"So you're my sister."

"It would seem so."

"Where've you been?"

"I grew up in Dawsbury, right under Torian's nose. It's on the edge of Isentol."

"What did you do?"

"My father owned an inn." She caught herself, remembering the man she had called her father. A lump formed in her throat, but she didn't cry. The tears didn't come as often as they did before. "I served tables for him."

"An inn?" Conal chuckled, slowly nodding. "An interesting place to raise a king's daughter."

Gwen smiled in return. "What about you? Where did you grow up?"

"Urve, a coastal town in Tir Manach. My father was a jewelry merchant."

"Was?"

Conal's casual demeanor vanished. "He's dead. My entire family is dead. Torian had them killed."

"Torian's men killed my father. And my friend. His name was Tobias," she replied.

Eradore walked up, a man and a woman tagging along. "I know you two have a lot to talk about, but unfortunately, we're running out of time. These are the mage twins I mentioned, Kalan and Korla."

Conal suppressed a grin for the 'twins' couldn't be more different. Kalan was a hand span taller with dirty blond hair and brown eyes. He wasn't handsome as far as eye-catching, but he wasn't unattractive either. Yet there was something about him that immediately put Conal off. The man exuded a not-so-subtle arrogance.

His 'twin' on the other hand was a very attractive buxom strawberry-blond with an hour-glass figure, a little taller than Gwen. In contrast to Kalan's smugness, Korla looked like she felt out of place, her emerald green eyes darting around the room, taking everything in.

Conal silently prayed that Korla was his 'twin.'

"One of them will –" Eradore began before Kalan cut him off.

"I'll go with her." He thrust a finger at Gwen then nudged Korla towards Conal. "You can have my sister."

"That's fine," Conal replied a little too quickly, hoping Gwen and Eradore thought he was covering Kalan's crass behavior.

"You'd better get moving then," Eradore said, giving the oblivious Kalan a look of irritation.

Conal turned to Gwen. "See you in Havengarde. Take care of yourself."

"You too." Her eyes locked onto his and she smiled at him.

For an awkward moment, Conal felt he should do something demonstrable, like a hug or something, to show he recognized he had family again. But it would be like hugging a distant cousin he had met once growing up. He was about to give her the noncommittal hand wave when she closed the gap between them and hesitantly hugged him.

"Watch yourself," she cautioned. "Our uncle knows we're alive."

She didn't need to say anything else, for Conal understood. "Let me know where you're in position."

"I will," she answered, releasing him. She felt like there was more to say, but whatever it was, the words eluded her. "See you soon."

"You too," Conal replied, ready to move on. All the questions he wanted to ask would have to wait. He turned to Korla. "You ready?"

"Yes," she shyly replied.

He searched the room and found Torgreth and Galadyr in conversation with Voldar and Lorkan, the elf with a bemused smile as he listened to Voldar relate some tale. Conal caught Torgreth's attention and soon the group was out in the streets and headed to the city gates.

"Where's Drustan?" Conal asked, suddenly remembering the half-druid-dragon.

"Last I saw him," Galadyr answered, "he was talking to Lyra."

Lyra… Conal remembered Drustan's words, *Two of our females have reached that age. It won't be long for the other four.* He wondered if Lyra was one of the female dragons who could still bear young.

"Speaking of which," Torgreth said, casting a sly look at Conal. "What's this 'we had two dragons, but one was killed' stuff? I've been with you for who knows how long and I've never even seen one dragon, let alone two… if they even exist."

"They exist, my friend," Galadyr replied.

Torgreth frowned at the elf. "You've seen one?"

"Yes."

"A dragon?" Voldar interrupted, cocking an eyebrow in disbelief. "You've actually seen a dragon? Simply saying 'I'm a dragon' doesn't mean you are one."

"If he says he has, then he has," Torgreth retorted.

"OK, OK," Voldar shot back. "What's with you?"

"He's an elf and elves don't lie. And even if they did, I still trust him."

"Thank you, Torgreth," Galadyr said, dipping his head in appreciation. "I pray that I always have your trust."

"Yeah, yeah," Voldar responded, with a little twinge of jealousy. "What about the dragons?"

"How about we have this conversation in private, once we're outside the city," Conal interjected.

"He's right," Korla said, her voice soft and delicate. "There are too many prying ears here."

Conal noted that she walked behind them, doing her best to keep up. Slowing the pace, he motioned her to walk beside him.

"So, you and your brother can communicate even though separated by great distances." It was a statement rather than a question.

"Yes." She gazed up at him, smiling pleasantly. "It's a trait we discovered when we were very young."

Conal returned the gaze and smile as they walked. "And you're really twins?"

She giggled with girlish charm. "Yes."

"Who's the oldest?"

"I am."

"Were your parents surprised that they were having twins."

"No. A mage midwife had predicted my mother would have twins a year before she was pregnant."

"She predict anything else?" Conal pondered how he could spend more time with her without it looking too obvious.

"Just that we would be mages."

"You'll forgive me if I say that I have a hard time picturing your brother as a mage." This caused her to giggle again and Conal was smitten.

"He never did want to be a mage. Wanted to be a warrior, a soldier. Pa wouldn't hear it, especially after the midwife said he was going to be a mage."

Conal thought about it a moment. "Is he a mage because that is what he's really supposed to be or because your father made him become one and therefore the midwife's prediction is true regardless of his desires."

Korla stared at him as though he had plumbed the depths of a divine mystery. "You are the first person ever to understand that. I've thought that all along, but never wanted to say anything because it would just make father angry. Besides, now it's too late for him to be anything other than a mage."

"I understand."

"I think we're far enough away from the city now," Voldar said with a knowing grin at Conal who glanced around, realizing they had passed through the main gates and he hadn't even noticed. "You can tell us about dragons now."

"Hold that thought," Lorkan announced, seeing a runner headed his way, a young man moving at a good clip.

"Commander," the young man greeted him, catching his breath. "Sorcha's intercepted a large force and is falling back towards us. She asks for immediate help."

"I thought she was at least two days north of us," Conal said. "We'll never reach her in time."

"We need to try, m'Lord. She's a resourceful commander, but she can't hold out against Torian and what remains of Caldyr's army."

Conal's lips pursed. "This is not how we intended to begin. We need Torian's attention in the east." Narrowing his attention on the messenger, he asked, "How did you get this information."

"Message hawk."

"M'Lord," Lorkan corrected.

The young man's eyes popped wide. "M'Lord."

"How long did it take for a hawk to get here?"

"A couple of hours… m'Lord."

"A couple of hours?" He was about to say that was impossible when he recalculated that a hawk could average 30 miles an hour. That would put Sorcha around 60 miles away. With a forced march, they could be there in two days.

"Your orders, m'Lord?" Lorkan asked.

Conal thought quickly. "This could still work. If Gwen can move her forces by the time we connect with Sorcha, it might still work." Turning his head to look at Voldar, he said, "Why wasn't the dwarf commander with us in the meeting?"

"He's a prickly one. Gets his felling hurt at the drop of a hat. Near as I can see, he was waiting for a royal invitation from you."

"We don't have time for games," Conal growled. "Lorkan, get ready to move. We go to help Sorcha. You two," he said to the two dwarves, "let's go have a heart-to-heart with Storri." Not forgetting Galadyr, he said, "Would you mind finding out where our druid is?"

"As you wish," Galadyr replied with a respectful nod.

"What about me?" Korla piped up.

"You go with – no, change that. You come with me." Conal increased his pace, the dwarves and Korla quickly marching to keep up.

As they made their way to the dwarven camp, Voldar leaned in to Korla. "The commander's name is Storri Broken-nose. You'll understand when you see him. One thing you gotta watch out though is not to slip up and call him 'Snorri.' As you can imagine, he doesn't like being reminded of his nose."

"It can't be that bad," she replied.

It *was* that bad when they stepped into Storri's tent and he looked up from behind the small field table he as using as a desk. Storri's nose looked like it had been hit with a smithy's hammer across the bridge for it was nearly flat, the nostrils like two eruptions on both sides.

"We missed you at the meeting, Commander," Conal said, doing his best to stare into the dwarf's eyes.

"I wasn't invited," he harrumphed.

"You don't need an invitation," Conal emphatically said. "You are an army commander. How am I supposed to plan and organize when the battle captain of half my force thinks he needs to be invited? When I asked King Rorkyn for support, he promised me he would send his best soldiers with his best commander. So you see, I need input from Rorkyn Orefell's *best* commander."

Assuaged, Storri cleared his throat. "Yes, well… all a misunderstanding, I'm sure."

"Good. We need to move out immediately. Sorcha is under attack and needs our support. If you will ride with me, I'd like to go over what we discussed in the meeting and get your input."

Flattered, Storri stood up and barked out orders to get ready to move then cast a look of authority at Torgreth and Voldar. "What are you two lollygagging around here for? Go find your regiment."

The two exchanged a worried glance as neither knew to which regiment they belonged. Besides, they had no clue what it meant to be a dwarf soldier. They liked where they were, hanging out with Conal.

"With your permission, General," Conal intervened. "I'd like to keep these two with me as liaison officers representing you. They know the operation and would be beneficial to me as the campaign proceeds, acting as messengers between you and me."

Storri harrumphed again and furrowed a thick brow at them. "Alright, m'Lord. If you can put up with those two, that works for me. Saves me the trouble of finding suitable liaison folks."

"Thank you. Well then, I'll leave you to get your army ready. I'll send one of the liaison officers to find you to let you know where I am."

Once outside, Torgreth sidled up to Conal sighing a big, "Thank you."

"That was very diplomatically played, m'Lord," Korla commented, impressed.

"We don't need personalities interfering with our

battle plans. I meant what I said in there. I need him."

As Conal led the way to where Lorkan's army was lining up, he turned his head to look at Korla. "Can you contact your brother and tell him what's happening?"

"What specifically, m'Lord?"

"That we've been forced into attacking earlier than we had planned. She needs to get her forces in place and engaged as quickly as possible." He turned his head to see where he was going. "And my name is Conal."

"I know, m'Lord," she replied, her voice almost a coo, "and I am flattered with your familiarity, but you are still a king's son, a prince, and I am just a mage."

Conal slid his eyes to the right to catch a glimpse of the beautiful woman striding next to him. *You are far more than just a mage. Are you playing hard to get? Is there a man in your life?* He was about to ask when she bent her head, staring at the ground as they walked.

She abruptly stopped, causing the others to stop.

She frowned in puzzlement and tilted her head to look up at Conal. "I don't understand. He's not responding. The only reason for that is that his mind is focused, concentrating on something else so much that he's not listening."

Conal's jaw tightened and he resumed walking, shaking his head. *What's the point of you being here other than as a distraction if you can't communicate with that idiot brother of yours?* "This is *not* good. If it doesn't work now, what makes you think it will when I really need it."

"I'm... I'm sorry, m'Lord," Korla fretted, taking three steps to his two to keep up.

"Forget it," Conal replied though his irritation

was evident. "You can try again later."

"Yes, m'Lord," she replied, lowering her eyes.

Conal was about to fuss at her to stop calling him 'm'Lord' when a runner from Lorkan raced up.

"M'Lord. Commander Lorkan says Sorcha's forces are a day out. She is surrendering ground faster than she can retreat. Commander Lorkan says that it is imperative that you give the order to march."

"Tell him to do so," Conal replied, breaking into a run. "Tell him we force march until we get there."

CHAPTER 3

GWEN

I've never seen a dragon before," Kalan said eagerly.

"If we don't defeat Torian, you won't see one again," Venia said. Her words sounded like a reprimand, but Kalan didn't seem bothered.

"Do we need to get supplies before we leave?" Gwen asked. "Food and water?"

"No need until we reach Auleavell," Venia answered. "We'll make several stops along the way, and I'll make sure it's near civilized places so you two can get what you need. I'll fly high enough that no one on the ground should see us, but that requires a lot of energy and strength, which in turn requires a lot of food."

They walked along the main street, headed toward the gates where Gwen had entered. The rebellion spy was at his vendor stall, calling out to passerby and holding his dresses out for visibility. Gwen locked eyes with him as they passed, and he offered a nod. When he'd cornered her and pressed a dagger to her back, her first instinct had been to kill with fire. As she considered that, it disturbed her. That wasn't her. She'd never wish harm on anyone except Torian and his lackeys.

And yet, she had almost taken the man's life without a second thought. Was she being swayed by the dark magic that coursed through her? Or had she changed more than she realized, becoming more like Aimil? She hoped that was not the case.

Venia led them out of the city and along a road that went northeast until they were far enough away that it was unlikely anyone in the city would see them.

"Stand back," she warned.

Gwen and Kalan backpedaled until they were several feet away. Venia closed her eyes and for a moment, nothing happened. Gwen held her breath and watched intently. The change began slowly. Venia's skin lightened until it took on a sickly pale color. She dropped to the ground on all fours, her body wracked with spasms so strong that her arms and legs trembled visibly. Venia hacked loudly. Her shoulder blades protruded from her back and Gwen flinched at how odd it looked.

A loud popping noise filled the air, then her shoulder blades elongated and morphed into wings. Her body lengthened and grew in size until she was easily twenty feet long. Her face extended into a long snout and her skin color changed again, from pale white to silver, and scales took shape all along her form. When it was over, Venia was breathing heavily.

"Does it hurt?" Gwen asked. "When you change, I mean?"

"Yes," Venia replied. "But the more I shift, the less I feel it. The first time I changed, I thought I was going to die."

"Absolutely fascinating," Kalan whispered. "A real dragon. In the flesh."

"Come," Venia said. "Climb onto my back."

Gwen had ridden on her once before, so she had little trouble getting onto Venia's back and settling herself into place. Kalan followed the same path up Venia's shoulder and stood over Gwen.

"Move back," he said.

"Why?"

"So I can sit in the front."

Gwen snorted. "No, you can sit behind me. There's plenty of room." She patted Venia's scales.

"I want the front."

Gwen glared at him and was tempted to pull rank since she was technically the queen, but instead, she shrugged and scooted back, giving him enough room to sit down. Once he was settled, she nudged up behind him.

"You'll want to get a good grip," Gwen said. "Or when she climbs into the air, you'll fall off."

Kalan felt along Venia's neck scales until he found spots that he could grab, then he clenched his hands tightly onto them. Gwen didn't have anything to hold except Kalan. She hesitantly wrapped her arms around his chest and hugged him close. He smelled of lilac, a heady sweet scent, with a touch of vanilla. She thought it odd he smelled so good. It made clinging to him less disagreeable.

Venia dug her claws into the ground and crouched low, poised much like a cat about to pounce. Unlike a cat, however, she sprang into the air and flapped her powerful wings. The air rushed around Gwen like the sound of a raging river and she watched the landscape quickly fade below them. Her stomach churned and her eyes teared from the whipping wind, but she exalted in it all. It wasn't every day she experienced something as miraculous as flying on the back of a dragon.

They flew for a long while and Gwen kept herself occupied by watching the countryside gradually change. The tracts of land were various colors and sizes, and all of them looked small enough that when Gwen held her fingers out, she imagined she could pinch them.

"We're heading down!" Venia roared.

Even though her voice carried, it was still hard for Gwen to hear her clearly over the wind. She leaned forward against Kalan. Venia began her descent and Gwen's stomach lurched again. She doubted she could ever get used to the feeling. They flew low over a wooded area and Venia landed softly in a clearing.

"I must feast," the dragon announced. "There is a town within walking distance if you are hungry. I don't think anyone spotted me, but we should be quick regardless."

Venia lowered herself closer to the ground and Gwen and Kalan slid off her shoulder onto the ground. Gwen felt odd walking on her own legs again, but the feeling was brief.

"I'm famished," Kalan said. "You coming?"

The sight of a dragon eating a deer or some other such animal wasn't an image Gwen wanted in her head. She nodded and they left Venia alone to hunt. The two exited the woods and walked through a wheat field until they reached the road that led to the town. As they drew closer to the boundary of the town, an older man was cutting the wheat down with a scythe while three younger men, whom Gwen assumed were his sons, collected the stocks and tied them into sheaves.

Sweat glistened on their tanned skin and one of the sons paused to offer an admiring stare at Gwen. She waved politely and hoped he wouldn't try to speak to her. He went back to work when one of the others shouted at him for taking a break. Kalan and Gwen entered the town and found a single tavern. It was a small wooden building with a thatched roof. Scrawled beside the door in red paint was the word *Foamy's.*

"A hot meal is calling my name," Kalan said. "And a cold ale."

"Ale sounds good," Gwen agreed.

The two went inside and were greeted with curious stares by the handful of patrons that were scattered across the room. One table, in particular, caught Gwen's attention. Four men in armor bearing Torian's crest were laughing and clinking their tankards together. Gwen's heart skipped a beat, but when the men didn't even look their way, her nerves calmed.

They don't know who I am, she told herself.

Kalan took a seat at a random table and Gwen followed him. Despite the presence of Torian's soldiers, the atmosphere of Foamy's was high spirited. As Gwen listened to the scattered conversations, she assumed the people were all locals. Except for the soldiers. They were minding their own business and the patrons seemed content to ignore their company.

A serving girl sauntered over, her skirt short enough that if she bent down, everything would be revealed. Her top was a loose-fitting piece of white material that barely clung to her ample bosom. Kalan eyed her lustfully and Gwen rolled her eyes at him.

"Typical male," she muttered.

"I'm Poppy," the serving girl said. "What's your fancy?"

"A night with you, Poppy," Kalan said with a not-so-innocent grin.

"Is that so?" Poppy placed her hands onto the table and leaned forward. Gwen watched Kalan's eyes lower to her cleavage.

"Yes indeed."

"Stick around long enough and you just might earn it," Poppy said, straightening. "For now, how does soup sound?"

"That sounds perfect. I want an ale, too."

"I'll take an ale also," Gwen said. "And some bread if you have any that's fresh."

"Coming right up," Poppy said. She strolled away to the kitchen and Gwen waited for Kalan to turn his attention back to her.

"You think we can spend the night?" he asked.

"I hope you're kidding," Gwen replied. "We don't have time for that. Try and keep your mind on what's important, will you?"

"You're no fun," Kalan complained. "Unless you're up for some … strenuous activities?"

"Have you ever been struck by lightning?"

"No," Kalan said confusedly.

"Talk to me like that again and you will be."

Kalan kept his wolfish grin, but Gwen could see the disappointment in his eyes. He shrugged and looked around the room, then set his gaze on the table of soldiers.

"What do you think they're doing here?" he asked.

"Nothing good, I'm sure."

Poppy returned, skillfully holding a bowl of steaming soup in her left hand and two large tankards and a plate of bread with the other. She set them down on the table and "accidentally" dropped a cloth napkin on the floor. Poppy knelt in front of Kalan seductively and peered up at him with a pouty face.

"Woman," Kalan hissed through his teeth. "I'm about to—"

Whatever he said was lost to Gwen's ears as the table of soldiers erupted into raucous laughter and one of them knocked over their tankard, spilling ale onto the table. A stream of golden liquid ran off the edge, splattering onto the floor.

"Poppy!" the drunk soldier shouted. "I need your hands!"

"That's not all you need," another soldier said lewdly.

Poppy rose to her feet and set the napkin in Kalan's lap, pausing with her hand on him for a moment before meandering over to the soldiers. She worked just as seductively with them, crawling on all fours to clean the ale off the floor. Kalan watched jealously.

"You know it's all for show," Gwen said.

"What?" Kalan looked at her, his face flushed.

"The way she's flirting. It's all an act. You do know that?"

"Of course I do," Kalan replied. Gwen knew he was lying.

He ate his meal in silence, but he continuously looked around for Poppy. Gwen sipped her ale, enjoying the familiar atmosphere while holding back the dreaded memory of the night at the Seven Stars where everything had begun.

Kalan finished his meal and downed what remained in his tankard, then walked over to a table of farmers. Gwen watched him curiously but couldn't hear what he was saying. A few of them nodded and looked at Gwen, raising their drinks in salute. Gwen's curiosity turned into suspicion. Was Kalan spreading rumors about her?

He left that table and went to another. Again, the people he spoke with looked at her and offered nods or raised their drinks. Kalan made his way to every table until only the soldiers' remained. As he walked past Poppy, he grabbed a handful of her buttocks and winked at her. He reached the soldiers and leaned down, speaking to the one who'd spilled his drink earlier.

The soldiers laughed at first and Gwen assumed he must have told them a joke. As Kalan continued talking to them, she noticed that their expressions were changing from amusement to glares of anger. Gwen rose from her chair and started walking toward them, intent on grabbing Kalan and heading back to Venia.

One of the soldiers said something, his tone getting louder as he spoke, but all Gwen heard was the word "treason."

"What are you doing?" Gwen demanded, grabbing Kalan by the arm.

"And here she is," Kalan said grandly. "The rightful queen of Isentol's throne!"

The soldiers all stood up at once and Gwen's heart sunk into her stomach. Kalan had betrayed her, just like Aimil had.

"That's enough of your nonsense," the soldier across the table growled. He drew his sword and pointed it toward Kalan.

Kalan looked at Gwen, a brazen look etched on his face. He pulled his arm free of her grasp, grabbed the edge of the table, and flung it into the soldier with the drawn sword.

And then all hell broke loose.

CHAPTER 4

CONAL

There was little grumbling during the night as the combined forces of Conal's army moved silently north, hoping to blunt Torian's incursion in time to save what remained of Sorcha's regiment. He was surprised at the determination and speed of the dwarven soldiers keeping pace with the taller human soldiers of Lorkan's army.

In the early hours just before dawn, the forward scouts sent word back that they made contact with Sorcha's rear elements and that Torian's forces had paused their pursuit to lay waste to the city of Blasingdon, allowing her to regroup and break contact with the enemy. Less than an hour later Sorcha strode up to Conal. Her small army, carrying their wounded, flopped down on the side of the road, receiving a welcomed rest.

Sorcha was a handsome tall blond with the strong and fit body of an athlete. She began to drop to her knee when Conal stopped her.

"Are you OK?"

"Yes, m'Lord," she answered, completing the obeisance.

"Don't do that," Conal moaned, bending down to

grab her arm and pull her up. "We can all be socially proper at some other time, but not here or now. We have more important things to worry about. What's your status?"

Sorcha brushed the grime from her cheeks, impressed with this prince who seemed unaffected by his position. "We've managed to delay them, but we couldn't do anything to stop them. We were able to break contact when they decided plundering Blasingdon was more important than pursuing us."

"How many?"

Lorkan walked up, nodding respectfully to Conal, "M'Lord," before addressing Sorcha. "I count seventeen walking wounded, six more gravely injured. I've physicians attending them."

"Thank you, my friend," she said, breathing a sigh of relief.

Conal turned to Torgreth. "Tell Storri I need him now."

"Right you are," he grinned and sped off.

"How many able-bodied do you have?" Conal asked Sorcha.

"I started with 757. I'm down to 702 with 32 dead and left behind. We're facing an army three times my size. I've managed to inflict twice my losses on them, but we were in no position to offer combat. I've managed to draw them south, hoping Lorkan would have sufficient forces to counterattack."

"Kilmaryn chose to retain his forces to block any southern probes," Lorkan explained. "Though I didn't like it for it reduces our western attack into Isentol, it makes sense. I pray that he has the good sense to join the battle when it all begins. That said, we number over 7,000."

Sorcha flashed a fierce grin. "More than twice the

enemy. It's time for payback."

"Do you know who commands Torian's forces?" Conal asked.

"No, m'Lord. Never got close enough to find out, though I did receive reports of a man of great size who appeared to be commanding. Though interesting, it does not tell me enough to know who it is."

"Do you still have scouts out?"

"Yes, m'Lord, but like all my soldiers, they need rest."

"I've already sent out some scouts to relieve yours," Lorkan said.

"I want to know where they are before we attack," Conal said, stating the obvious. Hands jammed on his hips, he scowled and glanced around. "Where's Drustan?"

"No one has seen him, m'Lord," Lorkan answered.

One of Lorkan's captains strode up with another man who was still catching his breath. "M'Lord, this man has information about the enemy."

At that moment Storri walked up.

"Good. Glad you're here. This scout has just arrived." Conal nodded at the scout. "Go ahead."

The man inhaled a deep breath. "M'Lord, the enemy remains in Blasingdon, continuing to pillage the city."

"Yes," Conal exclaimed with a fist pump. "How long will it take to get to the city?"

"It took me an hour to get here, m'Lord, but I pretty much ran the entire time."

Conal dropped to his knees in the middle of the road. Smoothing out a spot with his hand, he motioned for the others to kneel with him. Drawing a small square in the dirt, he explained, "Here's Blasingdon. Where are the city gates?"

"Here and here," Sorcha pointed to a front and rear gate.

"Have you been in the city?"

"No, m'Lord. We used it as blocking to help us get away."

"No matter. We approach from the south." He drew a line as he talked. "If we assume he's a good commander, he will have patrols even while the city is being ravaged. We need to eliminate any security he has so we can penetrate the city. We do this by dividing our forces to block both gates, dwarves to the main gate, the rest at the back gate. We need to get someone inside the city." He looked up at them. "We find someone who can handle himself and put him in the uniform of the enemy."

"We'll probably need more than one, m'Lord," Storri said, pleased that his army had the main attack through the main gate.

"I agree, General, but it will have to be someone other than a dwarf for obvious reasons."

"I know," Storri nodded.

"We assume that his army is expending their strength in drinking and chasing women –"

"Or men," Sorcha pointed out, self-consciously adding, "We like a good time too."

"Point taken," Conal smiled. "The point is that we want them to be wasted by the time we attack."

"If he's a good commander, he won't allow that," Lorkan countered.

"You are right," Conal replied, "but he *did* stop to allow his soldiers to pillage. That caused him to lose contact with his opponent. Not very smart. The spies we send in will alert us to the right time. When they give the signal, we attack from both sides."

"Challenge and Password?" Sorcha asked.

Conal thought for only a moment. "Challenge is 'Dragon' and password is 'Blood.' Make sure everyone knows it. Dwarves will be easy to recognize as friends. Let's not make any mistakes with the rest of us."

"Questions?"

"Assembly area after the attack?" Lorkan said.

"Operations security?" Storri added.

"Good points," Conal said, standing. "We need three-sixty security. I leave it to you two to coordinate. Suggestions for assembly area?"

"North of the city," Storri suggested.

"Sounds good. Let's get ready to move out. We need volunteers for spy duty."

"What about me, m'Lord?" Sorcha.

"You're in reserve." Seeing her disappointment, he said, "Don't worry. You'll get your turn. Your soldiers are tired and rest." He looked up at the sky that was beginning to lighten. "We got to go." Turning to the others, he said, "Oh, one more thing. I'm going with the spies into Blasingdon."

"What?" Lorkan exploded. "Are you crazy?"

"That's 'are you crazy, m'Lord'," Conal said with a half-smile.

"But... but," Lorkan stammered. "This is madness. You are the overall commander, the king's son. How can we protect you if you go in there?"

"I have stealth skills beyond what anyone else has," he replied.

"It's not a question of skills, my young lord," Storri said, his tone the voice of reason. "We all have no doubt that you can handle yourself. Yet all it takes is one misplaced word, one look of doubt, one misdirected arrow. We can't afford anything happen to you. It would destroy the rebellion. Surely you can see that."

Conal pursed his lips and looked at Voldar. "Well?"

"Really?" Voldar cocked an eyebrow. "You're going to possibly take the wind out of this rebellion because you want to show how stealthy you can be? Do you even have to ask?"

He slowly twisted his head to look at Sorcha who said nothing, merely shaking her head 'no.'

"Fine. You win. I'll be good. But when it comes time to fight, I want a piece of the action."

"If it becomes necessary, my Lord," Lorkan corrected him.

Conal let out an exasperated breath. "Fine."

It was mid-morning by the time they were in position. Lorkan's army had to work its way around the city through the forest. They had dispatched several enemy patrols before they had time to warn of Lorkan's army.

There had been no shortage of volunteers to sneak into the city. Conal settled on ten who donned uniforms from the dead enemy patrols. And there had been plenty of intel provided by fleeing citizens. Tales of rape and murder were the common themes.

Blasingdon itself wasn't a large city, perhaps some three to four thousand residents. Open fields about two furlongs wide separated the city walls from the surrounding forest. But Blasingdon was a fortified city with tall stone walls of grey granite and wide stout oak city gates, which were wide open. Dead bodies, some decapitated others with deep gashes sliced through various parts of their bodies, lay scattered in bloody lumps around the gate and archway across the moat. Several bodies lay where they fell, blocking the doors from being closed. Wisps of smoke near the center of the city curled and dissipated in the morning wind.

It was eerily quiet and Conal impatiently waited for his spies to give the signal, wondering if they had been spotted. Suddenly a man emerged from the rear gates and ran towards them. Lorkan recognized him as did Conal.

"M'Lord," he called out. "It's… it's unreal. They're dead, almost all of them."

"What?" Conal startled. How was it possible ten of his spies could accomplish such results in so short a time?

"We think it's the ale," the spy said, stopping in front of Conal and Lorkan. "We think it's been poisoned. There's still a few alive who are holding out in the center of the city, but for the most part, everyone else is dead. So is their commander."

"Show me," Conal ordered and started back with the spy.

Lorkan quickly issued orders, telling everyone to not drink anything in the city, as he randomly picked a bodyguard of twenty soldiers to protect Conal. "Do the dwarves know yet?"

"Yes, Commander. Heulyn went to tell them."

Conal's bodyguard preceded him through the city gates, stepping over bodies and fanning out and keeping watch.

Conal's mouth gaped open as he saw the multitude of soldiers curled up on the streets, their eyes glazed over in death. He closed his mouth and scrunched his nose at the stench of puke and feces. Stepping over body after body, Conal gaped as he saw their struggle. Some left claw marks on wooden posts or scrapes across the flaking stone walls.

"The last of them are this way, m'Lord," the spy said, directing them around a corner.

To their surprise, a crone of a woman stood in the middle of the street. She was shorter than Korla, due more to her bent of age that actual height. She wore the black of a widow, her silver hair tucked neatly under a black scarf.

"Yer too late," she cackled, her teeth root stained. "Did what I had to. Coulda used yer help yesterday. But now you shows up and late's better'n never."

The bodyguard reacted and began to surround her, weapons ready.

"Leave her alone," Conal commanded, and the bodyguards drew back, though still wary. Conal walked up and smiled at her. "Who are you, Mother?"

The woman's head snapped up to stare intently at him. "I know you." She glanced surreptitiously around and lowered her voice. "Yer the Cobra of prophecy. Looks like things're gonna heat up right soon."

Conal looked back over his shoulder at one of the bodyguards. "Fetch Korla." Turning back to the old woman, he smiled kindly at her, waving a hand at the dead soldiers. "So you did all this?"

"Yup." She tapped her nose and winked at him. "Knew they'd start drinkin' when they got here. Stupid soldiers got no discipline. Put poison in the ale. Not all of it, mind you, just the ones I knew they'd start with. Gimme time to do the rest. Slow actin'. Usual takes an hour or two. By then," she sliced a thumb across her throat.

"You've saved us a lot of trouble, Mother," Conal complimented.

"Name's Madlyn." She grinned a root-stained

smile at him.

"Madlyn," Conal repeated. "How do you know who I am?"

"Oh," she nodded, "I can tell 'cause you got a glow about you, like the one a dragon has."

Conal frowned. "Dragons have a glow about them?"

"Of course, dearie," she maternally replied. "Every living creature has a glow, a color. Some calls it 'Aspect.' Only a few can see it though." She chuckled. "Some spends their lives trying to discover it. It is what it is. Ya can't change it."

Korla walked up, giving the woman a polite smile. "You wanted to see me, m'Lord?"

"M'Lord is it?" Madlyn snickered, then awkwardly bowed. "Fergot my place."

Ignoring the jab, Conal spoke to Korla. "This is Madlyn. She is responsible for this resounding victory."

Lorkan strode up with Storri and Galadyr in tow. "There's no one left, m'Lord." He shook his head in amazement.

"We have a Chronicler with us?" Conal asked.

"Yes, m'Lord."

"Send someone to fetch him. I want Madlyn here to be forever remembered as the Champion of Blasingdon, for it is she who defeated our enemy. I want to make sure it is recorded correctly."

Surprised and flattered, Madlyn blinked in the sudden attention.

"We'll need to toss all the ale –"

"Don't need to," Madlyn interrupted. "Poison's already gone out of it. It don't last. Just long enough to do what I needed."

Conal nodded in understanding then noticed

Korla standing to the side, waiting for instructions. "Madlyn, this is Korla. She's a –"

"I know what she is," Madlyn replied. "I could tell it the moment she walked up."

"Because of her As –"

"Association with you, yes," Madlyn interrupted. "Figured you'd have a mage with you."

"Nobody said I was a mage," Korla said, her brows furrowed.

Madlyn grinned at her. "Takes one to know one."

"What? You're a mage?" Korla cocked an eyebrow in disbelief.

Madlyn's smile vanished followed by an intense frown at Korla. "'Course I am." She flipped a hand at the surrounding dead. "How'd ya think I did this?"

"A simple herbalist could have done the same thing," Korla argued.

"Bah." Madlyn turned to Conal. "She may be a looker, but she ain't got the brains to go with it. If yer finished with me, my Lord, I'll go tell the rest of them that escaped that it's safe to come back now."

"Will you come with us?" Conal blurted.

"Pardon?"

"I'm asking you to come with us," Conal said.

Madlyn was again flattered. "Why? I'm just an old woman."

"You're a mage," Conal corrected, "and we can use your help."

"Her?" Korla said, curling a lip. "She's no more a mage than I am a warrior."

Ignoring her, Conal repeated, "Will you come with us?"

"She's an old woman. She'll only slow us down," Korla argued.

Conal held up a hand for her to be quiet, though

his attention was on the old woman. "Well? Will you come with us?"

Madlyn looked at him then at the indignant Korla before grinning. "I'd love to, m'Lord."

CHAPTER 5

GWEN

"Treason!"

Gwen heard the word reverberate off the walls of the tavern as she watched the guard with the sword crash into the wall. The table bounced off him and struck the floor and broke, sending splinters flying in every direction. The other guards were momentarily surprised, but they quickly recovered their wits and drew their swords. Gwen grabbed onto Kalan's arm again and jerked him back just in time to keep him from being skewered.

"Blasted pigs!" Kalan shouted, trying to break free of her grasp.

"We need to go," Gwen said darkly. She summoned her strength rune and pulled Kalan across the tavern. Two of the guards hurried after them while the other one helped his fallen comrade. Gwen was considering using her fire rune next, but the patrons of the tavern blocked the soldiers and kept them at bay. She spotted Poppy behind the mob. Next to her was an older man who watched the unfolding chaos with an unamused expression.

"I'm sorry!" Gwen shouted, then hurriedly tossed a few coins onto a table and pulled Kalan outside, dragging him along behind her.

"I haven't had this much fun in a long time," Kalan laughed.

"You think almost getting stabbed is fun? I saved your life back there."

"Nah. Even if his blade would have hit me, it would have bounced right off. I've got the steel skin rune."

"The what?"

"If you stop pulling me, I'll show you."

Gwen glanced behind them. The guards hadn't gotten free of the crowd yet, but she doubted it would take much longer. "Show me when we get back to Venia." She released Kalan's arm and the two sprinted until they reached the wheat field, then cut across it and plunged into the woods.

"Venia!" Gwen called out. "We need to move!"

The dragon was in the clearing, her tail flicking back and forth. "What is it?"

"This fool started a fight with some of Torian's soldiers. We need to leave. Now."

Venia lowered herself so they could mount her and then she launched into the air. Gwen was angry at Kalan. What he'd done was stupid and irresponsible. She punched him in the back for good measure, then hissed in pain. Kalan wasn't lying. His skin was hard and her knuckles stung.

"Told you!" he shouted over his shoulder.

Venia's climb through the air plateaued and she continued flying northeast.

"Why did you start a fight with those guards?" Gwen demanded.

"Why not?"

"We have enough problems, and we don't need more. And what did you say to the others? Why did they look at me and raise their drinks?"

"I told them who you were," Kalan replied. "And that we were going to take the fight to Torian."

"Our attack is supposed to be a surprise. Or at the very least, have him looking one way while he gets crushed from the other. If you ever do that again, you'll need more than steel skin for what I have in store for you."

"Is that a threat or a promise?" Kalan teased.

Gwen bit her tongue. Kalan was hotheaded and didn't care if he crossed the line, and arguing with him would accomplish nothing. She avoided speaking to him until they landed. Gwen assumed it was so that Venia could eat again, but as she climbed off the dragon's back and looked around, there was a feeling of familiarity that came over her.

"Where are we?" she asked.

"On the border of Auleavell," Venia answered, glancing around uneasily. She sniffed the air.

"What's wrong?" Gwen also surveyed the area, but she didn't see anything.

"Kirith and his army should be here, but I can't smell them. Unless they are using magic to hide their presence, I don't think they are here yet."

"That's impossible," Gwen said. "Eradore sent word to Kirith before the meeting was over."

"Maybe the message never arrived," Kalan suggested.

"We're in trouble if it didn't." Gwen chewed on her lower lip, thinking. "We need to find Kirith. If his army doesn't march with us to Isentol, we don't stand a chance."

"I'll go," Venia said. "You two stay here. I can fly faster without having to worry about you falling off my back."

Gwen didn't like the idea of waiting around, especially not with Kalan, but it would take her too long on foot. That, and she didn't know where to find the forest-city.

"Go, but please hurry."

Venia sped off, the treetops swaying from the force of her wings. Gwen stared off into the woods. She tried not to think about what would happen if Kirith's forces didn't come through. Without an army to attack from the east, there would be no diversion from Conal's approach.

"Have you heard from your sister?" Gwen asked.

"She tried speaking to me before we left Haddence, but I ignored her."

"You *what?* What if it was something important?"

"I'm sure it wasn't," Kalan replied. "She probably just misses me. We don't separate very often, and when we do, she badgers me for attention. Honestly, it's exhausting. I enjoy getting away from time to time."

"That's fine and well, but next time she reaches out to you, answer her. I need to know what's going on with my brother." Gwen could feel her irritation rising again and she took a deep breath. There was something about Kalan's attitude that exasperated her to the point of rage.

Gwen paced in circles while they waited for Venia to return. Her nerves eventually calmed, and she looked at Kalan. He was sitting on a fallen tree, weaving leaves and thin vines together into a crown. He plucked a white flower and placed it in the center of the crown, then noticed she was staring at him.

"Here," he said, holding out his creation. "I made it for you."

"Is that an apology?" she asked, walking over to accept it.

"Hardly," he laughed. "I don't apologize for being myself."

Gwen looked away, a little embarrassed about her anger towards him. The man was infuriating, true, but maybe she had judged his character incorrectly. She took the crown and set it atop her head.

"How do I look?" she asked.

"Ridiculous," Kalan replied, but he smirked. "If you had pointed ears, you'd look like an elven queen."

"So you aren't always a complete idiot? That's a surprise." Gwen returned his smile. She felt that statement was somewhat true, anyway.

Kalan placed a hand over his heart, a mock look of pain on his face. "You wound me, Your Majesty."

Gwen rolled her eyes. "Show me the rune you mentioned."

Kalan reached down and pulled his pant leg up to reveal a rune that looked like a sword wrapped in ivy. "This one has saved me many times."

"What other runes do you have?" Gwen asked.

"Why? Are you interested in trading magic?"

"Possibly."

"I'll show you mine if you show me yours."

Things like that made Gwen want to punch him in the mouth, but now that she knew it wouldn't even hurt him, she just glared at him instead.

"You're too serious," Kalan said.

"Try having everyone you love be murdered and see how happy you are."

Kalan's smile faded. "I'm sorry," he said. "I didn't know."

"Don't worry about it."

The silence turned awkward, and Kalan suddenly pulled off his shirt, revealing several runes in random spots across his chest and even one on his stomach. Gwen didn't have any of them, which made her wonder just how many runes were out there.

"This one unlocks doors," Kalan said, pointing to a rune shaped like a key. Of all places, it was located over his heart. "Spiked ball, wind breath, shield, healing, animal manipulation, telepathic communication," he named them off as he pointed. "And this last one will be a real benefit when we encounter Torian's Prestiges."

Gwen peered closely. The rune looked like an open door. "What does it do?" she asked.

"It absorbs magical attacks."

"That will definitely help." Gwen expected Kalan's body to resemble Aimil's, and she was surprised to find that he didn't have many runes. "Are you searching for more?"

"Not really," Kalan replied, shrugging. "I like what I have." His brow furrowed and he tilted his head curiously. "I don't know how I missed it," he said.

"Missed what?"

"The lines in your eyes. How did you get a dark rune?"

"It's a long story," Gwen said. "I'd rather not talk about it."

"Give me the dark rune and you can have any of mine." His words had an eager tone to them.

"No."

"Just like that, huh? No counteroffer or anything?"

"No," Gwen repeated.

The silence resumed and Gwen went back to

pacing. Venia should have been back by now. Had she run into trouble? Were Kirith and his people under attack? Did Torian's arm reach this far? There were too many questions and not enough answers.

"There," Kalan said, shattering her thoughts.

Gwen looked to the sky and saw Venia returning. The dragon swooped down and landed. Kirith was on her back. When he saw Gwen, he leaped off and rushed to her, wrapping her in a hug.

"It is good to see you are well," he said.

"Same here," Gwen replied. "Where's your army? We're marching on Isentol now."

"Now?" Kirith sounded surprised.

"Yes. Did you get Eradore's message?"

"I didn't get anything."

A heavy weight fell onto Gwen's shoulders and she sighed. "I don't know what happened, but we need to go. Conal and his forces are heading for Isentol as we speak. We were to attack from the east and provide a diversion. Now we have a problem."

"I can gather my people, but I will need some time."

"That's the one thing we don't have," Gwen said.

"We'll raise an army on the way," Kalan interjected.

Gwen stared at him incredulously.

"What? You saw how those men responded in the tavern. In a small farming town, they gladly stood up to those guards to help us escape. People are tired of Torian. All they need is a little nudge."

Gwen looked at Kirith.

"He's got a point," the elf said.

Kirith was a male, so of course, he *would* side with Kalan. Gwen looked at Venia questioningly.

"I agree with Kalan," she said. "Kirith's army will

come, but not quickly enough. You'll have to convince your people to rise up against Torian."

Gwen thought they were all insane, but it did seem like their only option. "Where's the nearest town?"

"Wespin. It's a few hours from here," Venia said. "If I fly fast enough, we'll cut the time in half."

Gwen looked at each of them. Fate or destiny or possibly death was tightening the rope around her neck, suffocating her. She had to make a decision, but she didn't want to lead innocent men and women to be slaughtered. Conal's words echoed in her mind.

Anyone willing to join us is more than welcome.

"We'll leave our fate in the hands of the people, then," Gwen said. "Kalan, let your sister know what's happened and get me an update from Conal. We need to be in sync now more than ever."

Kalan nodded and stepped away.

"I trust you are still committed to this task?" Gwen asked Kirith.

"You have my oath," Kirith said.

Gwen turned to Venia. "What of the dragons? If there's eleven of you left, where are the others?"

"They're heading to Isentol," Venia answered.

That fact gave Gwen some solace, at least.

"We've got another problem," Kalan said. "Korla says that Conal and his army are attacking a city called Blasingdon because Torian's army has crossed the border into Tir Manach."

"It's one thing after another," Gwen complained. "Can you use your telepathy rune to contact other mages?"

"It depends on how far away they are," Kalan replied. "And I need to know their name or their general location."

"The Great Library is where she should be. Her name is Marjorie."

"I'll see what I can do." Kalan sat on the ground and closed his eyes.

"I hate to leave you with this situation, but I must gather my people. We will meet you in Isentol, Solara willing."

"I understand," Gwen said. "Maybe we'll stay alive long enough to see you again."

Kirith bowed his head and left, sprinting into the woods. Gwen watched Kalan, occasionally glancing at Venia. The dragon remained quiet but returned her gaze. Finally, Kalan's eyes opened and he stood.

"Marjorie says a force of Prestiges left the Great Library already and are headed to Isentol. She's going to tell them to meet us in Wespin."

"Thank the gods," Gwen said. "At least we have magic to battle magic."

"We should make haste," Venia said. "The faster you can spread word of the coming battle, the more people will join our cause."

Gwen motioned for Kalan to mount Venia first, but he shook his head. "Take the lead," he said. Gwen did so and Kalan sat behind her.

"Hold on tight," Venia said, then launched into the air.

Once they were gone, Aimil stepped out from the trees. She watched them fade in the distance and then opened the letter Eradore had penned. She'd intercepted the message hawk by accident while magically teleporting to Auleavell. Aimil read over it again, then tossed the parchment aside and activated her rune.

It was time to cut the head off the snake.

CHAPTER 6

CONAL

While Lorkan and Storri sent scouts out to patrol the surrounding area, ensuring none of the enemy had escaped, Conal, the two mages, his battle captains, and bodyguards set out to find the enemy commander. As they made their way through the streets Madlyn caught up to Korla, grinning confidently at her.

"Don't worry, dearie, I won't steal your man away from you."

"He's not my man," she huffed, "and even if he was, I doubt you would be a threat."

"Ooh, sure of ourselves, are we?" She smirked at her.

Korla stiffened. "I don't know why he wants to bring you along. I can handle it."

"Like how you helped when he attacked the city?" She parried with a feigned innocent grin.

"He didn't need my help," Korla tartly replied.

"Of course he didn't," she chuckled. "I'd already helped him."

Pursing her lips, Korla picked up her pace to catch up to Conal.

Conal was having second thoughts about inviting

the old woman, but she was resourceful and he needed a mage, someone unafraid to do what is necessary. That she seemed to enjoy picking on Korla might be a problem. He'd wait and see. Still, having two mages with him was more than he had expected.

They found the commander slouched in an imposing chair set on a platform in the reception room of the burgomaster's residence hall. His hands draped over the arm rests, a spilled drinking horn on the floor by his feet. The eyes, glazed over in death, stared at the far wall.

Conal was the first to notice it, a beautifully cut obsidian stone set in gold filigree on a necklace chain dangling from his neck. Reaching for it, he startled when Madlyn slapped his hand away, placing her other hand between him and the stone.

"You don't wants to do that, young Lord," she warned, "if you don't wants him to know yer here."

"Why?"

"Don't touch it," Madlyn commanded, glancing around the room. Retrieving a cloth napkin on a bureau by the wall, she wrapped the stone inside the cloth before casting a look back at Korla. "Go ahead. Tell 'im."

"Tell him what?" Korla replied confused.

"About the stone," Madlyn prompted.

"What about the stone?"

Madlyn frowned at her. "You sure yer a mage?"

"Yes," came the indignant reply.

"Enough," Conal interjected. "Why don't *you* tell me, Madlyn?"

Casting a suspicious look at Korla, Madlyn explained as she pulled the necklace over the dead man's head, "It's a Linking Stone."

"Linking stone?" Conal and Korla said in unison.

"Yes." She gave Korla a look of disappointment. "You have much to learn, dearie."

"I'm not your dearie," Korla shot back.

"Just stop," Conal commanded. "What does a linking stone do?"

"It's a connection, young Lord, between two people; usual a mage or wizard is at one end. The man holds the stone like this," she held the cloth in her hand, "and when he does, it tells the mage that he is ready to talk."

"How? They're too far apart," Lorkan said.

"That's why it's called 'magic,' dearie," she replied with a twinkle. "Once the connection is made, the mage then commands the man to do his bidding. If the mage is strong enough, he can use the man's eyes to see what he sees."

"By the gods," Storri snarled.

"No, dearie," she smiled with only her lips. "The gods got nothin' to do with this."

"What should we do with it?" Lorkan asked, shifting a worried look between the old woman and Conal.

Conal knitted his brow in thought. "Can the mage be fooled? I mean, supposed someone took the stone and pretended to be the commander. Could the mage be fooled into thinking he was still controlling the commander?"

Madlyn's eyes widened. "I know whatcher thinkin' young Lord."

"Answer the question."

Madlyn paused. "Yes. It is possible. But... it'll work only as long as the mage believes he has the right man. Pray that the mage is distracted for he can plumb the depths of the pretender's mind. If the mage discovers the deceit, the pretender is as good as dead for the mage with destroy him... from the inside out."

Conal nodded, inhaling a deep breath. "Where is the tallest building in the city?"

"We're in it," Lorkan said. "Remember? We saw the tower above the walls."

"Good." Conal turned to eh dwarven commander. "Storri, I need you to hide your army so that no dwarves can be seen."

"What're you gonna do?"

"I have a plan," he answered. "Lorkan. You take your army and assemble them outside the main city gates."

"What are you going to do, m'Lord?" Lorkan asked, his concern obvious.

"Gonna have a little chat with a certain mage," he replied.

"No," Korla burst. "You're crazy."

Conal's face hardened and he jabbed a finger at her. "You and Madlyn are with me. The rest of you, go do what I asked." Glaring at the bodyguards, he commanded, "And you all stay here."

"Are you sure you wants to do this, young Lord?" Madlyn peered intently at him.

"No, I'm not sure, but I have an idea and I have to try. Now please, we're wasting time."

"But, m'Lord –"

"No 'buts' Lorkan. I know what I'm doing."

"Do you?" Korla sharply replied.

"You go with General Storri and stay out of the way," he snapped, immediately regretting his anger when he saw the hurt in her eyes.

Madlyn led the way through the burgomaster's citadel. "Been here often enough. Always wondered what the view was like at the top."

Conal opened the door for her, letting her slowly lead the way up the spiraling stairs. Though chaffing to get to the top, he calmed himself, praying that his gambit worked.

"Anything I should know about working the stone?"

She paused on the step above him to look over her shoulder at him. "It is dangerous what you plan to do. If it works, fine. If not…" She shrugged. Resuming the climb up, she said, "Hold the stone loose in yer hands, just the fingers touching it. That way if he discovers who you are, it's easier to drop the stone. Tell him what he wants to hear. Butter 'im up real good, but don't overdo it. Remember who yer supposed to be."

She pushed through the door at the top of the stairs and stepped out onto the narrow walkway around the spire.

Conal stepped out behind her, immediately feeling vertigo causing him to firmly grasp the iron railing.

"Are you OK?"

"Yes… yes." He swallowed and forced himself to relax as he gazed out over the city walls to the forest in the distance then down at the streets littered with bodies.

"You sure you want to do this?" She gave him a hard stare.

"Yes," he resolutely answered.

Unwrapping the stone, she slipped it over his head, careful not to touch the stone. "Touch the stone with just the fingers of yer left hand. The mage will know you're there."

Obeying, Conal touched the stone and felt an

immediate tingle up the arm, into his shoulder and up his neck and into his head. His vision clouded to almost black. Then a voice spoke inside his head.

What? Ah, there you are. Where have you been?

I... I'm where I'm supposed to be, Conal replied.

Don't get smart with me. Did you do what I asked?

Conal paused trying to think of the right answer.

What's wrong with you?

Conal forced himself to relax, calling in the deception skills he learned as a highwayman. *I'm a little drunk*, he giggled.

Drunk? Where are you? the voice snarled.

Blasingdon.

Did you destroy the city?

Of course.

Let me see?

Conal bent his head to stare down at the streets. The weird feeling of someone else using his eyes sent a shiver up his spine.

Good, good. Yes. Stop. I see uniforms. Who are they?

They're the ones I been chasing. Managed to corner them in the city here.

Where are your soldiers?

Outside the town. Conal lifted his eyes to stare off in the distance beyond the city walls.

Why?

All the ale's gone. Conal snorted a laugh

Don't be a fool. I didn't send you here to lay around getting drunk.

My soldiers needed a break. Besides, the ale was free and so were the women. He snickered, conjuring up an image of woman he had met a year ago, hoping the vision would be convincing.

Focus, damn you. You're wasting time.

What's the rush?

Are you that stupid? I chose you because you were useful. Don't make me regret my decision.

Conal felt a flash of intense pain explode in his head. "Ow. OK, OK. I'm sorry."

Are you finished in Blasingdon?

Yes.

Then get moving.

Uh… Where am I going?

Has the ale befuddled you that much?

Conal felt the rising irritation in the voice. He needed to be cautious.

I… I am a little disoriented –

Disoriented? Now there's an interesting word. I'm surprised you were able to use it in a sentence.

Conal silently berated himself for forgetting who he was pretending to be. *I'm not stupid,* he indignantly replied.

Of course you aren't, the mage said with not so subtle sarcasm. *Calm yourself Firyn. You still have work to do. Go north. Hafgan waits for you. You will join her and attack Gorwick. I want that city destroyed. Let me know when you have succeeded.*

Which one of us commands? Conal demanded as though affronted he was not specifically named in charge.

The mage chuckled. *Vanity, vanity. Does it matter? She is a proven leader.*

So am I, Conal huffed. *Why must I submit to a woman? I didn't need her help laying waste to Blasingdon.*

I will acquiesce to your request… this time. Do not try my patience again.

Yes Master.

That's better. Say it again.

Yes, Master.

One more time. The mage sniffed a laugh of derision

"Yes Master," Conal droned, feeling an intense lethargy permeate his body.

Laying the clothe over her hand, Madlyn snatched the stone with one hand and slapped him across the face with the other.

"Yeow," he startled, a hand at his cheek. "What was that for?"

"You were starting to lose yourself."

"What do you mean?"

"The mage was beginning to exert control over you."

"How did you know?"

Madlyn peered intently into his eyes, examining them, finally nodding. "Yer fine now. I could tell by the voice you used at the end, like someone drugged. Well? Did you discover what you wanted?"

"Yes," Conal replied, reasonably sure he didn't want to try that experiment again. "The dead commander below is named Firyn."

Madlyn cocked an eyebrow at him. "I coulda told you that. You didn't need to do this." She held up the cloth wrapped around the stone.

"And I also learned that Firyn is on his way north to join Hafgan and attack Gorwick."

Madlyn grinned at him. "I didn't know that. What are we gonna do?"

"We're going to head north," he replied. He started to turn then abruptly stopped. "Who do you think was the mage at the other end?"

"Can't be sure," she thoughtfully replied. "Few mages got that power. My guess it was probably

Grimmar. You were lucky this time. Don't think ya oughta try it again."

"Not a problem," Conal agreed. "C'mon. I need to tell the others."

Twenty minutes later, he stood in the middle of the armies with Madlyn, Lorkan, Storri, Galadyr, and Korla whose insolent look told him she wasn't happy. Voldar and Torgreth, though not formally invited, stood at the edge of the group. Conal smiled at them and motioned them closer.

"The enemy here is supposed to be heading north to join forces with a woman commander named Hafgan for an attack on Gorwick. We will head north to join them."

"We're gonna attack Gorwick?" Torgreth blurted.

"No, my friend. We're going to destroy Hafgan and her army. I have an idea. It's going to require us making her believe we are Firyn's army come to help her. Once we destroy her army, we head into Isentol. It's about time Torian learns he is not in control like he thinks he is."

"Easier said than done," Storri commented. "What's your plan?"

"We'll need scouts well out in front so that she doesn't know who we are. The scouts, when confronted will need to play the part of Firyn's loyal soldiers. She won't suspect anything if she believes we are who she thinks we are."

"I like it," Lorkan nodded. "Gives us a chance to assess and deploy.

"We don't know how big her army is," Storri pointed out.

"I know," Conal agreed, "but, surprise is always to our advantage. Besides, we have two powerful mages with us."

While Madlyn preened, Korla's insolence vanished, replaced by a sudden feeling of overwhelming inadequacy.

CHAPTER 7

GWEN

Tell me again how this is going to work?" Gwen asked. She rubbed the back of her neck, trying to work out the soreness.

"We'll spread the word in the streets," Kalan replied. "Anyone you see is a potential ally."

"Won't that draw the attention of Torian's soldiers?"

"Probably, but unless you have a better idea, I think it's worth the risk."

Gwen knew Kalan was right, but she still didn't like it. She also didn't like being forced to change their strategy at the last minute. With a city as large as Wespin, there were bound to be problems they couldn't account for.

They had arrived less than an hour ago and were waiting near a well for Venia to meet them in her elven form. From the air, Gwen had seen that Wespin was shaped like a compass, with the city divided into four smaller sections by large waterways that dispersed water from the nearby river into the city.

"There's only three of us," Gwen lamented. "We could cover more ground if we had more bodies."

"And if a bard had four arms, he could play two

instruments. What's your point? Focusing on the problem doesn't get us anywhere."

Gwen looked at Kalan and he held his hands up placatingly. "I'm just saying, we should find the silver lining, no matter how thin it is."

"I know, but it's difficult," Gwen replied.

"Nothing of value is ever easy," Kalan said.

"You seem too young to have experienced many difficulties."

Kalan laughed. "You haven't met my father. He forces difficulty on me constantly."

"I'm sorry."

"Don't be. Maybe once this is all over, I'll be considered a hero and can choose my own path."

"What do you mean?" Gwen asked.

"I don't want to be a mage. Were it up to me, I would live by the sword, carving out glory and fame with my skill."

Gwen was surprised. Kalan was more like her in that regard. When Eradore had first told her she was a mage, she didn't want to walk that path. Yet, she had been forced upon it and walked it even now, unsure of what life would be like without magic. Lyra came into view at the end of the street, and she joined them at the well.

"We should split up to cover more ground," she said.

"I don't think we should," Gwen replied. "What if one of us gets into trouble? The others wouldn't know."

"Normally, I would agree with Lyra," Kalan said. "But in this instance, I must side with Gwen. We don't have enough people as it is. If one of us were to get caught by the guards, it would be impossible to free them. We should stick together."

Lyra frowned, but she acquiesced. "Very well."

Gwen waited for one of them to decide where to start, but they were both staring at her.

"What are we waiting for, Your Majesty?" Kalan asked.

"Stop calling me that," Gwen huffed. "It's just Gwen." She looked around at the various shops that lined the street, thinking. And then an idea came to her. "We could find bards to help spread the message."

"With what money?" Kalan frowned.

"The money Eradore gave me. It should be plenty to convince those greedy minstrels to sing of our plight."

"And how will we eat?"

"Do you want food, or do you want to save our kingdom?"

"I'd like both, and I don't want to be forced to choose."

"Too bad," Gwen said.

They navigated the crisscrossing streets until they found a tavern that had music playing within. Gwen handed Kalan a handful of coins.

"See what you can do," she said.

He shrugged and entered the tavern. Lyra and Gwen waited outside. After a few moments of uncertainty, Kalan returned with a smile.

"That was easy. The man probably would have done it for free."

Gwen doubted that, but she was happy regardless. "Start telling everyone we need their help. When we find places like this," she pointed at the tavern, "or come across bards on the street, we give them some money and keep going."

The three of them spread out across the street and

began stopping passerby. Initially, Gwen found some resistance. People thought she was a beggar who wanted a handout, but when she started talking, they listened with rapt attention. Kalan had been right— people *were* tired of Torian.

Gwen expected their task to take them most of the day, but as they spread through the city, so too did their words. By the time they crossed the bridge into the second section of the city, people were already aware of their message and were spreading it themselves.

"We told people who are interested to meet us outside the city, but we don't have anywhere to host them. We've no tents or bedrolls or anything," Kalan said.

"I thought about that," Gwen replied. "These people live here. They can sleep in their homes until we are ready to march."

"When will that be?" Lyra asked.

"Hopefully at dawn's fight light, but we can't leave until the Prestiges from the Great Library arrive. They are the key to battling Torian's."

"What if they aren't here by then?"

Gwen didn't even want to consider that as an outcome, but it was possible. "Then we go ahead without them and leave them a message to continue to Isentol. Whether we have five people or five hundred doesn't matter now. We just have to get there and get Torian's attention before he focuses his might on Conal and his army."

"Five hundred would get his attention more than five," Kalan said with a chuckle. "Imagine five people showing up outside the castle gates demanding he abdicate the throne. I don't think he'd even notice."

Gwen couldn't help but smile. The sight would indeed be laughable. A commotion nearby caught their attention and Gwen spotted a contingent of soldiers harassing a young boy.

"Vengeance is coming!" the boy shouted as the guards tried to wrangle him under control.

"It looks like they've heard their days are numbered," Kalan said.

Gwen had considered the fact that she or Kalan could get arrested, but she *hadn't* considered that the soldiers might target innocent people. Before she could decide what to do, Kalan rushed to join the fray. He lowered his shoulder and drove it into the back of one soldier, sending him crashing to the ground.

Kalan turned to the next one and grabbed onto his helmet, forcing the soldier's head down onto his knee. The armor clanged as if it had struck a shield and the soldier cried out in pain as Kalan tossed him aside. Gwen blinked several times before breaking out of her reverie. She sprinted to the boy.

"Are you all right?" she asked.

"I am now," he said with a large smile. "Pummel him, sir! Show that pig what for!"

"You should get home," Gwen said. "It's too dangerous for you out here."

The boy looked like he was going to argue, then nodded and ran off. Gwen turned around in time to see Kalan take down another soldier. Within a matter of seconds, he had subdued three of them. The remaining two had drawn their swords, but they were keeping their distance and seemed hesitant to engage Kalan.

"Tell your fellows that if they harass anyone else, the wrath of Her Majesty Queen Gwen will find them!" Kalan shouted.

A bell started ringing a few buildings down and Gwen realized they were near a guard outpost. She cursed under her breath.

"We need to hide somewhere," she said to Kalan. Before she'd finished her sentence, she spotted soldiers bolting out of the building. Someone met with the soldiers and pointed in her direction. Gwen squinted to see who it was. Why would one of the citizens rat them out? As she stared, it almost looked like …

"No," Gwen said. "It can't be."

"What is it?"

"More guards," she replied. "And a powerful enemy. A mage."

"We can take him," Kalan said with a tone of superiority.

"It's a her, and I don't know about that. She's got more runes than most prostitutes body counts."

Kalan gave her an odd look and she shrugged in response. The soldiers started running toward them.

"Here they come!" Gwen turned to Lyra. "Hide!"

"I'm tired of hiding," Lyra replied. "I want blood."

The tone of her voice sent a shiver along Gwen's spine. She nodded. The time for running was over. It was time to fight. Lyra issued a roar as she partially shifted into a dragon. Her body stretched and changed, but only until she looked like a massive lizard. She charged the two soldiers who'd been keeping their distance and whacked one with her tail. The other one she snapped up in her jaws, crunching the man's bones loudly. Gwen blanched and turned to face the approaching soldiers. She held up her right hand and inhaled a deep breath, then summoned the magic of her fire rune.

"Tine," she said, speaking the rune's name.

A wave of flames erupted from her palm and shot forth, engulfing the nearing soldier. He screamed in terror and anguish, his armor melting under the intense heat. He was the first to die. Gwen spoke the rune again, killing another soldier. She watched as more of them came out of the outpost, and she watched them as they died, writhing in the wrath of her fire.

"Watch this!" Kalan shouted.

She kept her focus on the magic but offered a glance in his direction. He was pointing to the sky where a group of birds wheeled overhead. He spoke a word and the birds changed direction, diving down to attack the guards.

"That's nothing!" Gwen shouted back. She cut off the magic and switched hands. *"Tintreach."*

Lightning flashed from her fingertips and forked apart, striking two soldiers simultaneously. They died instantly and the bolts ricocheted, killing two more soldiers. Despite their magical attacks, the soldiers kept coming at them.

"Amateur!" Kalan laughed.

He spun in a circle and held his right hand out, shouting another word. This time, an ethereal ball formed. He threw it at the center of a small group of soldiers. The ball grew as it sped through the air. It landed on the ground, quivered briefly, and then exploded, sending hundreds of spikes airborne.

"That's impressive," Gwen said. "But not as impressive as this!"

She called on the magic of the might rune and waited until a soldier was right on top of her before she punched him in the chest plate as she yelled, *"Láidreacht!"*

The armor caved in under her enhanced blow, crushing the man's chest and sending him reeling. Gwen was just as surprised as Kalan. They continued in the sordid game, pushing each other into more insane ways of taking out their enemies until the street was littered with dead soldiers and none remained. Lyra stalked around like a predator, her head swiveling as she looked for more enemies. The general citizenry had cleared the area already, and as Gwen surveyed their work, she started to feel ill.

She had killed many people, and she had laughed doing it. Bile rose in her throat and she forced it down, gathering her saliva and swallowing it to ease the burning of her tonsils. Their fight wasn't over, though. Bells were ringing all around the city. More guards would be coming, but Gwen wasn't thinking about that. She watched Aimil slowly approach, their gazes fixed on one another.

"I see you've learned some new tricks," Aimil said, casting a glance at the bodies.

"Why are you here?" Gwen asked, clenching her fists. Aimil's betrayal burned in her veins like her fire rune and Gwen wanted nothing more than to obliterate the woman from existence.

"I'm here to kill you," Aimil replied casually. "Torian tires of the rebellion and he's about to stamp the life out of it."

"He can try, but his cruelty lacks our passion. We *will* defeat him."

"Enough talk," Aimil spat, then she swept her arm up and a rush of air struck Gwen, pushing her back a few feet.

Kalan turned her magic against her, using his wind breath rune to turn the direction of the gale back at her. She dove out of the way, rolling aside and coming back up quickly. Her body rippled and suddenly there were five of her, each one identical to the others. Gwen couldn't tell which one was the real Aimil. She spoke the name of the lightning rune, shattering one of the illusions into pieces like broken glass.

The other four scattered and hurled different spells at Gwen and Kalan, putting them on the defensive. A faint blue glow appeared around Kalan and Aimil's attacks bounced off harmlessly. He threw another spiked ball and closed the distance between himself and Gwen, sharing his shield with her. The ball exploded and destroyed two of the four illusions while also sending a wave of spikes into the surrounding buildings. Gwen was glad the area had been evacuated. The devastation the spikes caused would have killed many innocent people.

Aimil knelt and dug her fingers into the dirt between the cobblestones of the street. The ground shook around Gwen and Kalan before a gaping hole opened up, threatening to swallow them. Gwen wrapped her arms around Kalan and summoned the might rune, throwing them backward and away from the hole.

"I think you were right," Kalan said as they got back on their feet. "She's a worthy opponent." He paused. "We might want to run."

"We can't. She'll find us. Aimil won't stop until she's dead. Or we are."

"Then we need to find a way to kill her," Kalan said, stating the obvious.

"I'm open to ideas."

When Kalan didn't offer any, Gwen looked at him. He shrugged. "I can shield us and we can try to get close to her. That's all I've got."

Gwen considered each of her runes. The healing and life rune were obviously no good in this fight. "That might work," Gwen finally said. "If we can get close enough, I can use my dark rune."

"What does it do?"

"It steals life, but I have to be touching her."

"So we have to get *really* close," Kalan said.

"Too close," Gwen replied. "There's no telling what other magic she's got."

"What if we had a diversion?"

"Such as what?"

Kalan tilted his head and Gwen looked in the direction he was hinting at. Lyra was perched atop the roof of a building near Aimil, her reptilian eyes watching the woman intently.

"She must know Lyra's there," Gwen said. "She's been watching the whole time."

"Maybe, but a diversion doesn't have to be a surprise. It just has to draw her attention."

"Can you communicate with Lyra and tell her what we're doing?"

"I don't know if it works with dragons, but I can try." He closed his eyes.

Gwen watched Lyra, but if the dragon could feel Kalan's mind, her demeanor didn't show it.

"She'll pounce on her," Kalan said. "And it was surprisingly easy to touch her mind. Even more than with Korla."

Gwen didn't care about that, but she smiled anyway. Lyra leaped off the building and Aimil immediately turned to face her.

"Hold on!" Gwen shouted and grabbed Kalan's hand. She summoned the runes on her thighs, only a vague idea of what they did as she said, "*Luas.*"

They sped forward so quickly that everything

around them blurred. Gwen barely stopped in time before they passed Aimil completely. Lyra landed beside them, her jaws snapping at Aimil, but the woman easily sidestepped out of Lyra's path. Gwen reached out as her speed slowed and latched onto Aimil's arm, jerking her and Kalan forward roughly before coming to a stop. With vengeance within her reach, Gwen fell into the power of the dark rune.

"Draein saoil."

Aimil screamed in anger and pain as her lifeforce was violently ripped away. Gwen felt the energy streaming into her own body, addictive and powerful. It revitalized her flagging strength and she could feel Aimil weakening. Despite the euphoria, Gwen knew the magic was unholy. It was magic so dark, no one should ever have discovered it. Aimil dropped to her knees and her face looked like it had aged several years within just a few seconds.

It's wrong, her subconscious told her.

Yet it felt so good. Aimil deserved to die. She'd poisoned many elves and some of them had died. This was the fate she deserved, to suffer and die painfully. And yet, there was a fate that could be worse for the woman. An idea struck Gwen and she focused on the stream of life energy flowing out of Aimil. She followed the trail until she found what she was looking for. A glowing sphere of golden light hovered near Aimil's spine. Gwen turned the power of the dark rune on it and with a single thought, she snuffed the light out.

Aimil's *bunús* died, and with it, her access to magic.

CHAPTER 8

CONAL

For two days, Conal's army swarmed north, moving as quickly as possible, yet not so fast as to tire. He spent most of the time either with Lorkan or Storri discussing battle plans and listening to their counsel based upon years of experience. Of especial concern was remaining unnoticed for as long as possible. Scouts had been deployed well to their front and flanks to provided early warning. Likewise, Conal had the two mages pay attention to the skies for messenger birds.

Korla wasn't especially happy to be relegated to birdwatching and decided to check in with Kalan only to have to listen to his boastful exploits of getting to ride a dragon and some adventure in a pub where he threw a table at some of Torian's soldiers. The way he told it, he was having the time of his life.

And here she was, bored, playing second fiddle to some old woman and looking for birds. Conal frustrated her. Why couldn't he see that she was far more valuable than merely birdwatching or checking to see what Gwen was doing. She was a mage, a powerful mage and when the time came, she would show him.

But it was more than that. Ever since he told her to call him Conal and she had politely reminded him that he was a lord and she was a mage, he became distant, almost brusque, especially when that woman showed up claiming to be a mage.

As if reading her thoughts, Madlyn sidled up next to her and spread her lips in a root-stained smile. "Don't worry dearie. Yer secret's safe with me."

"What secret," Korla coldly replied.

"That yer new at this mage business. Just started, have you?"

Korla glared at her. "I was born to be a mage."

Madlyn barked a laugh, shook her head, and dropped back so that Korla rode alone, stewing at the insult.

Riding behind them, Conal saw the exchange, wondering why the old woman was picking on Korla. He was tempted to ride up beside her but didn't want to have to deal with her moods.

Madlyn dropped back far enough to ride alongside Conal. "Relax, young Lord," she grinned. "I know what I'm doing. Up 'til now, all her training's been schoolin'. Never had to kill a man, don't know what it's like to take a man's life, and don't know what it's like to lose her family. She's unsure of herself. Just makin' sure when the time comes, she'll be ready."

"By picking on her?" He looked at Korla whose sour expression hadn't changed.

"It's what she needs," she said with a shrug. "You'll see."

Unconvinced, Conal was about to question her teaching methods when he noticed a rider approaching. The man circled around Conal and reined in his horse to ride beside him.

"Forward scouts have made contact, m'Lord. Per your instructions, two scouts have ridden into the enemy's camp to report to the enemy commander."

"Good work," Conal complimented, his worry increasing. Everything depended on Hafgan believing they were Firyn's army. "Go back to your position."

"Yes, m'Lord."

Before the rider had spurred his mount forward, Conal turned to Voldar. "Tell Storri we're stopping. I want to hear what the enemy commander has to say before we get much closer, but he needs to be prepared in case we have to attack."

As Voldar sped off, Conal issued the same instructions to another courier and sent him ahead to Lorkan. Ten minutes later, both Storri and Lorkan came riding up.

"Once the scouts have returned, we'll know how to position," Conal said.

"It's a dangerous game we play, m'Lord," Lorkan said. "I pray my scouts are not betrayed."

"I know," Conal fretted and for the next hour, nervously waited for the two scouts to return, occasionally looking up the scattered billowy clouds in the early afternoon sky. Every now and then he thought he saw a hawk and would shoot a glance at the two mages whose lack of interest told him not to worry.

Storri and Lorkan had returned to their armies to reposition security in anticipation. It was with great relief when Lorkan returned with the two scouts.

"What news?" Conal asked, his eyes bright with excitement.

"It was a piece of cake, m'Lord," the one scout said. He was a wiry man with russet hair and beard.

"We rode in like we were glad to finally be there. They took us to the commander straight away. She's a tall one, strong and demanding. She started to interrogate us a bit, asking where the rest of us were."

"But we acted the part," the other scout added. She was the same height as the man, sinewy with auburn hair. "I greeted her and said that Commander Firyn sends his respects and asks where she wanted him to position his forces. That seemed to flatter her. My impression was that she wasn't keen on him being there."

"They've got the city under siege," the man explained, "but they're spread thin. They've concentrated most of their forces at the main gates."

"They were halfway finished building a battering ram," the woman said, "when we left, and positioning catapults."

"Could you tell the size of her forces?" Conal asked.

The two scouts exchanged a look before the woman spoke. "From what we could tell, m'Lord, they were less than half what we got."

"Yes," Conal exclaimed.

"Look who I found wandering around," Storri called out riding up, Drustan and a woman of aristocratic bearing riding beside him.

"Drustan," Conal declared. "Where have you been? You've missed all the excitement."

"Good to see you too, my Lord," he replied with a smile.

"Since when have you been so formal?" Conal gently chided.

Drustan shrugged. "You are who you are. M'Lord, this is Meinir, a half-druid like me. I have been absent due to discovering her whereabouts.

When I explained who you are and what you were doing, she insisted on helping."

Conal immediately understood, greatly pleased. "You are most welcome, Meinir."

"Thank you, my Lord," she respectfully answered. Meinir was a comely woman with long raven black hair that cascaded down her shoulders and contrasted sharply with her milk-white skin. She wore the raiment of a huntress: brown leather breeches tucked in darker brown boots, a forest green v-neck, short sleeved top of finely woven cotton, and a thin gold circlet holding her hair back. Two crossbows dangled from the pommel of her saddle.

"So, what's your plan?" Drustan asked.

"Meinir," Madlyn exclaimed riding up. "By the gods, it's wonderful to see you again."

"And you too, Madlyn," she replied with a warm smile. Turning to Conal, she added, "You are indeed fortunate to have a mage with her powers with you."

"We have another," Conal quickly pointed out as Korla eased her mount into the mix.

"So I see," Meinir noncommittally answered, causing Korla to grimace.

"What *is* your plan?" Drustan repeated.

"We infiltrate and attack them from the inside," Conal confidently replied. Seeing the confused looks on the newcomers' faces, he explained, "Their commander thinks we're the forces of her compatriot from down in Blasingdon come here to help her attack Gorwick, which she presently has under siege. Lorkan and his army will move into the enemy camp and pretend to set up bivouac. Meanwhile, Storri's forces will position themselves to attack from the opposite direction."

"Would you like our help?" Meinir asked.

"Absolutely," Conal said before seeing Drustan's tight lips. "That is, if you'd like to. I trust you to best place yourselves where needed."

"Thank you," Drustan nodded, giving Meinir a look of irritation.

"What about us," Madlyn spoke up, "the young'un and me?"

"I'm not a 'young'un'," Korla snapped.

"We don't know if she has mages with her," Conal hastily said, "so I'll need you both to be on the lookout for anything strange. You know best how to deal with that." Looking pointedly at Korla, he said, "Listen to her and do what she says."

"What?" Korla stiffened, her nostrils flaring. "I'll not –"

"Yes you will," Conal growled. "Either that or go back and find that brother of yours with Gwen." Dismissing her from his attention, he turned to the others. "Time to get ready."

While Storri positioned the dwarven army to the east of the city, Lorkan and his soldiers moved up the main road toward Gorwick. Conal and Lorkan placed themselves towards the rear of the army, with the plan of getting as much of his army in position before the deception was discovered. Conal searched for Drustan and Meinir but no one knew where they were.

Much to Conal's surprise and advantage, Hafgan was preoccupied with placing the catapults and berating those constructing the battering ram that she didn't want to be bothered with the new arrivals, expecting Firyn to come to her. It was a battle of personalities as she expected to be the overall commander. Yet when Firyn failed to show up, she sent someone to look for him.

Conal was in conversation with Lorkan when Hafgan's emissary arrived, haughty as his commander. The emissary, a plump staff officer who flaunted his position, rode up and flashed a condescending glance at Conal and Lorkan. "Where's Firyn?" The man arched his back and cast a slow regal glance at the surrounding bivouac.

"He's not here," Conal indifferently replied.

"Well, where is he?" the emissary tersely demanded.

Scratching his head, Conal frowned at Lorkan. "I'm confused. Was it my turn or yours to watch him today?"

Lorkan shook his head. "Y'know, I'm not sure. Tell you what, I'll flip you for it." He reached into his pocket and pulled out a coin. "Heads is my turn, tails is yours."

"Two out of three?" Conal grinned.

"Two out of three it is."

Lorkan had no sooner flipped the coin in the air when the emissary barked, "By the gods, what is wrong with you two? Do you know who I am?"

As Lorkan caught the coin and smacked it on the back of his hand, Conal stared intently at the man, shook his head and turned to Lorkan. "Well?"

Lorkan removed his hand and sighed. "Heads. Advantage yours." He flipped the coin again.

"Did you hear what I said?" the emissary snapped.

Conal raised a hand at him to be quiet though his attention was on the coin on the back of Lorkan's hand. "Hold on."

"Tails," Lorkan triumphantly announced.

Conal swiveled his head to grin at the emissary. "One more tells the tale. Oh the suspense is mounting. The crowd grows quiet."

"I don't believe this," the emissary snarled.

"I said 'the crowd grows quiet,'" Conal chided.

Lorkan flipped the coin once more and happily announced, "Tails. It's your turn."

"Ah well," Conal sighed with disappointment. "As usual, I never win anything." Turning back to the emissary, he knitted his brow at him. "What were you saying?"

"Do you know who I am?" the man snarled.

"Nope." Conal turned to Lorkan and hooked a thumb at the man. "Do you know him?"

Lorkan shrugged. "Never seen him before in my life."

"What are your names?" the emissary angrily commanded.

"You don't know who we are?" Conal asked as though surprised.

"Of course not."

"I guess that makes us even. Listen bub, tell her highness that if she wants to see General Firyn, she needs to come here."

"What?" the emissary exploded. "*General* Firyn? Who does he think he is? Where is he? I will not stand for this insubordination." He went to spur his horse forward when Conal grabbed the reins.

"I wouldn't do that if I were you… friend," Conal threatened.

The emissary's eyes blazed at him, but movement out the corners of his eyes caused him to look up to see a dozen or more soldiers with death in their eyes heading his way. Wheeling is horse around he galloped away, yelling back over his shoulder, "You'll pay for this."

"Well played, m'Lord," Lorkan chuckled.

"Well played yourself," Conal complimented. "Now let's see if we get any reaction."

It wasn't long before the emissary returned with a dozen soldiers who fanned out behind him.

"I demand to see Firyn."

Conal looked at him then the soldiers with him before snorting a laugh. "Really? You come here with twelve soldiers to compel the general to go with you? Are you that stupid? Like I said before, tell her highness that she needs to come here… and take your kids with you." He craned his neck to look up at the early evening sky. "Besides, it's almost dinner time. Tell her to come by after dinner."

"But…but, Firyn has to come, now. She commands him to come."

"She *commands* him?" Conal's face hardened. "Listen junior, you and I are stuck in the middle between two stubborn commanders. You do realize that this will go on all night until one of them sucks it up and goes to see the other. Tell you what. Let's see if we can get them to meet in the middle between the two armies, sort of neutral ground. That way both their vanities can be salved and maybe we can get on with taking the city. Do you agree?"

The emissary pondered a moment before nodding. "What you say makes sense. I'll be back."

Conal watched him ride away, the soldiers with him relieved that that they were not needed.

Lorkan stepped closer to him and lowered his voice. "Storri should be in position by now."

"Good. I want to wait until it's almost dark before we attack."

Ten minutes later, the emissary was back.

"What did she say?"

The man sighed in frustration. "No change. She

wants him to come to her."

"I figured as much," Conal kindly said. "Tell you what. Why not stay for a bit, have something to eat with us and when she wants to know what took you so long, you can say that you were arguing for her. We've got excellent cooks."

The man grinned. "That's the best offer I've had today." He dismounted and stepped closer to Conal and Lorkan. "Name's Kieve, Captain Kieve of Commander Hafgan's staff."

"Welcome Captain. I'm Conal and this is Lorkan, commanders in this army." Turning to a soldier close by, he said, "Take Captain Kieve to the kitchen. Make sure he gets the royal treatment along with our best ale."

"Yes m'Lord."

Kieve stiffened. "M'Lord?"

"It's a sort of running joke," Lorkan hastened to say, giving the soldier an evil look and intoning, "Most people only say it behind his back." He looked back at Kieve. "I'll tell you the tale when we come back to join you."

"Ah," Kieve nodded in understanding, assuming it was some foolish act done in the ignorance of youth. Allowing himself to be led away, he was soon separated from his horse only to discover no one was cooking anything. All too quickly, he was tied and gagged.

"That was close," Conal muttered. Casting another glance at the darkening sky, he was about to announce, "Spread the word," when he saw two enormous shapes filling the sky, followed by an alarm in the enemy camp.

Yet the alarm was late for billows of fire suddenly erupted from the dragons' mouths as they descended and swept across the enemy's encampment.

CHAPTER 9

GWEN

N o!"
Aimil's horrified scream echoed off the wrecked buildings along the street. Gwen could only imagine what she must be feeling. With the *bunús* destroyed, Aimil would never again feel magic coursing through her. She slumped to the ground, tears streaming down her cheeks.

"What did you do?" Kalan asked.

"I took away her power," Gwen replied. "But she's still a threat. We need to keep her close. The last thing we need is her running off to report to Torian."

"What about the guards?"

Gwen looked around them and shrugged. "What about them?"

"Not these ones." Kalan waved a hand at the surrounding city. "Judging by the bell towers, I'm sure we'll be surrounded soon."

Gwen was torn between staying to spread their message of need and leaving the city to wait and see who showed up in support. Lyra shifted back into her elven form and forced Aimil to her feet.

"We should get moving away from here," Gwen decided. "Let's get closer to the noble district. There should be less chaos there."

They marched up the street together, Lyra pushing Aimil and keeping watch over her. Gwen glanced at her rival and saw she was listless, moving along only because Lyra forced her to. For a brief moment, she felt pity for the woman, but then she reminded herself of what Aimil had done in Auleavell and the pity quickly fled.

Gwen turned her attention ahead, where a battle was raging. Commoners were fighting against armed soldiers. The soldiers were outnumbered, but they held the advantage with better weapons and armor.

"We'll go around," Gwen said.

"We have to help them," Kalan argued. "They'll be slaughtered. And we both know we started this."

"Go," Lyra said. "I'll stay here with Aimil."

Gwen hesitated for a moment, then sprinted toward the battle. Kalan ran beside her, a boyish grin plastered on his face. An overturned merchant wagon was in the street, its fresh fruits spewed everywhere. As the press of bodies grew, they stomped on the goods, slicking the cobblestones. One person slipped and fell and was promptly stabbed in the chest by a soldier.

Kalan went for him, tackling the man to the ground and using the power of his steel skin rune to crush the soldier's helm, along with his head. Blood sprayed through the slit in the helmet, splattering Kalan's face. Gwen's stomach churned at the sight, but she ignored her revulsion and grabbed ahold of a soldier, ripping his helmet off and casting him aside like a ragdoll with her might rune. He slammed into the wagon, his face cracking hard on one of the wheels. More soldiers joined the fray, but they were still outnumbered as Kalan tore through their ranks.

He picked up a sword from a dead soldier and became a whirlwind of death. He thrust and spun, blocked and dodged, his footwork a blur of movement. Gwen could see why Kalan wanted to be a warrior—he was born for it. Her attention was diverted as a soldier came around the wagon. He wielded a hefty ax and swung at her, narrowly missing as she backpedaled and summoned her fire rune. A wave of heat and flames struck the soldier and sent him reeling into the cart, which caught fire.

Gwen backed away as the inferno spread, and the battle momentarily lapsed as the heat forced everyone away. Kalan shielded his eyes with his free hand and drove one of the soldiers into the flames. His screams filled the air as his armor heated, melting flesh and hair, the stench fouler than anything Gwen had smelled before.

The remaining soldiers retreated, turning and fleeing into the noble district. The crowd of people shouted a cheer of victory and gave chase. Kalan rushed along with them, and Gwen looked back at Lyra, concerned about their group getting split apart. Lyra waved her on and motioned to the east.

I'll meet you outside the city. Do what must be done.

Her voice penetrated Gwen's mind, jarring and unexpected. Her words were like a headache, pounding with each syllable. Gwen nodded and followed the mob, pushing through until she was beside Kalan. He was covered in blood, gore, and sweat, and was barely recognizable. He added his voice to the cheering as one of the escaping soldiers fell and was trampled to death.

This is madness, Gwen thought. *So much blood and death.*

And yet, she knew it was a necessary evil. Torian would not give any respite, and she was determined to do the same. If her conscious was scarred, so be it. If she had nightmares for the rest of her life, but the people were free from tyranny, so be it. It would all be worth it in the end. It had to be.

The crowd continued to grow as the word spread throughout the city. Farmers came with their pitchforks and scythes, metalworkers wielded hammers, and others had collected weapons from fallen soldiers. The ragtag band of common people slashed and burned their way through the noble district, killing the soldiers and rounding up the nobles. Gwen convinced the people to take them as prisoners, finding some solace knowing that not everyone would be killed.

As the hours passed, more and more of the city fell under Gwen's authority. Soldiers began surrendering or fleeing the city entirely. The few who tried to fight were crushed immediately, their bodies drug through the streets as a warning sign to those who would side with Torian. By the time Gwen's army reached the duke's castle, the city was hers and the duke willingly opened his doors.

Gwen didn't spare him. The people wanted his head, and she gave it to them.

The mages from the Great Library have arrived, Lyra informed her. With the city won, she and Kalan cleaned themselves and washed their clothes in the duke's chambers, then organized the people into two groups, those who would stay in Wespin and those who would march on Havengarde. Gwen appointed leaders among the people and took a count of the men and women that would be marching with her. She was disappointed to find that their numbers were only two thousand but knew it was much better than where they had started.

Kalan chose a handful of people as personal guards for Gwen and they escorted her outside the city to meet with the mages. As Gwen approached, she spotted a mage that stood out from the others. He was tall, towering over everyone else by at least a foot. His head was bald and his arms were covered in runes. The man's most prominent feature was his hooded eyes. They captured her attention and sent a chill down her back. He wore flowing robes that were dyed a vibrant blue and he smiled broadly when he spotted her.

"Quinlee," he greeted, bowing low. "I am Menjing, Your Majesty. It is an honor to join your cause. My mages and I are at your service."

"The honor is mine," Gwen replied. "And please, call me Gwen."

Menjing's smile grew bigger. "The Librarian mentioned you might say that. Very well, Gwen. What is your wish?"

"My wish?" Gwen's brows knitted with her confusion.

"Yes. What do you want us to do?"

"Oh, right. We've secured the city and have an army of two thousand men and women who will march with us to Havengarde. You will help me with drawing the attention of Torian's mages. We will be a diversion and keep him focused on us until Conal and his forces can strike from the west."

"Very good. How will we serve as a diversion? Will we attack the walls to enter the city?"

"That would be the ideal situation," Gwen said. "Though I don't want to assume it will be as easy as it sounds."

"Many of my mages are offensive casters. We will overcome the walls of Havengarde like the waves overcome the ship."

Gwen found his description poetic, but she doubted Torian and his forces would be so easily defeated. "What kind of runes do they have?"

"Our runes range widely," Menjing replied. "We can call fire and lightning, run like the wind, and shatter stone like glass. Those are only a few of our talents."

"Are they battle-tested? It's one thing to say you can kill a man, and another to do it. Trust me, I know firsthand."

"There are a few who have seen battle, but most of their hands have not seen blood. But do not worry," Menjing added, seeing Gwen's frown. "They are capable and want to see Isentol change for the better."

Gwen was worried he might not know his mages as well as he thought, but they were the only spellcasters she had. "We will leave in the morning. You'll find lodging and food in the city, but try not to let them overindulge. A sour stomach and a headache will make the trip worse than it already is."

"As you command," Menjing said, bowing again.

As the darkness of night covered the city in shadows, Gwen met with her army's leaders one more time to go over the many details she had no experience with. Supply lines, materials for their camp, and a weapons shortage were talked about the most. By the time the details had been finalized and Gwen was able to get some rest, she fell asleep immediately.

Morning came and Gwen opened her bleary eyes to see Kalan standing over her. For a moment, she forgot where she was and sat up quickly. A glance around the room reminded her and she breathed slower, trying to calm her racing heart.

"What news?" she asked, yawning and rising out of bed. She had been so tired she'd slept with her boots on.

"Korla says Conal and his forces reached Gorwick."

"That's good, right?"

"Yes," Kalan replied, smiling. "Would you like me to fill you in after you're fully awake?"

Gwen scowled at him. "No. Tell me now."

"They've passed themselves off as one of Torian's companies and have made contact with someone named Hafgan, apparently one of Torian's commanders. Korla seemed distracted, so I didn't get much out of her besides that. And I kept seeing images of an old woman." Kalan shrugged.

"We need to get moving," Gwen said. "It'll take Conal at least two days to reach Havengarde, and we need to be there before him."

"I've already met with the others, and everything is in order. All we need is your word."

"You have it."

When Gwen had heard that their forces only numbered at two thousand, she knew that wasn't enough, but also that it didn't seem like much. As the procession began the march north, Gwen realized that two thousand people was more than she thought. The line of people stretched on and on, making her wonder how they would reach Havengarde with any element of surprise.

They marched all day, stopping just before dusk to set up camp and rest. The next day started slowly as most of the people were sluggish and exhausted. Gwen tried to be patient and had to remind herself several times that these people weren't disciplined soldiers. She wasn't a soldier either, but she also wasn't the same ignorant girl who had left Dawsbury.

After another day of travel, the walls of Havengarde were within view. The fortress jutted up from the ground, an unnatural structure amidst a wild, untamed landscape. Her motley army set up camp safely away from the place, out of range of arrows and, hopefully, magical attacks. Kalan forged ahead to scout the area near the castle and ensure there were no hidden surprises.

Night fell, and Gwen sat in her tent, unable to sleep. There was so much uncertainty, and Kalan couldn't get ahold of Korla, which made her worry that something was wrong. She absently traced the lightning rune on her hand as she stared at the wall of the tent, her mind roaming endlessly.

A sound outside broke her reverie and she looked up as a hooded figure stepped into her tent. She thought it was Menjing, but then she saw the body of one of her guards on the ground outside. Her heart skipped a beat and before she could summon the magic of one of her runes, the figure drew a sword.

"My master Grimmar sends his regards."

CHAPTER 10

CONAL

Get ready," Conal yelled, his voice rising above the tumult in front of the city. Raging fire consumed catapults and battering rams while soldiers staggered and fell, flames engulfing their bodies. A few archers launched feeble attempts to bring down a dragon, but mostly dodged the spewing flames.

Conal turned an excited eye to Bedo who stood next to him, a ram's horn in his hand. "Now, Bedo."

Bedo raised the horn to his lips and blew three loud blasts.

As Lorkan's army surged forward and Storri's dwarves emerged from the forest, Bedo stepped in front of Conal. "General Lorkan told me to remind you that you command, m'Lord."

The runes tingled on Conal and he paced like a caged animal, the urge to join the battle tormenting him, but he forced himself to take deep breaths and remember who he was. Yet one part of his brain argued how could his soldiers respect him if he wasn't in the middle of the fray while the other part argued that he was in charge and responsible for every soldier in his army.

His army… the thought startled him for up to now, they had been Lorkan's soldiers or Storri's dwarves. But combined, they were *his* army. Sure, once he gained control of the kingdom, he would have his own dedicated soldiers and Lorkan and Storri would return to their own kingdoms, but for now, he was in command.

A pulse of vanity flashed through him until he remembered he was responsible for the lives of thousands of soldiers, that thousands of soldiers looked to him to make wise decisions, especially when it came time for battle. The thought sobered him and the raging torment to fight lessened.

"I need to get to a vantage point," he muttered to no one in particular as he shifted a glance around to find a high point somewhere.

"Besides the city walls, m'Lord," Bedo said, "I don't see anything around."

Madlyn walked up, nodding thoughtfully at him. "Can't feel a thing."

"Which means?"

"No mages around."

"That's good," Conal replied, "isn't it?"

"If times was normal, I'd say 'yes.' But times ain't normal. If you was attackin' a city, wouldn't you use mages?"

"Yes, I would. Where's Korla?"

Madlyn rolled her eyes. "She's lookin' fer a secret entrance to the city."

"What? Why?" Conal redirected his attention to the battle, which was no longer much of a battle as the dragons had wiped out over half of Hafgan's army giving Conal's forces a lopsided victory.

Madlyn shrugged.

His mind already dismissing Korla, Conal urged

his horse forward, his bodyguard moving in sync with him along with Madlyn, Bedo and Torgreth. They were met halfway by Lorkan comfortably seated on his horse, leading a defiant and chained Hafgan shuffling behind him.

"You have won another battle, m'Lord," Lorkan announced.

Giving her a brief glance, Conal smiled at him. "Status?"

"Don't have a final status yet, but the severest injury we have so far is a sprained ankle." He shook his head with admiration then held up the chain. "This is their commander, the dreaded Hafgan.

Conal stared down at her. She was a tall, muscular woman who was not unattractive. She wore the battle dress of a commander: padded leather pants, tall boots and a thick leather vest. "Why are you here attacking innocent people?"

When she didn't answer, Lorkan yanked her chain causing her to stumble. "Our commander, Lord Conal, asked you a question."

"Commander?" she sneered. "This young pup knows as much about battle as I do about cooking."

"Yet here you stand," Lorkan grinned, "brutally defeated I might add."

She said nothing, but her scowl remained.

"Why did Torian want you here?" Conal asked. "What was your mission." When she didn't answer, he leaned forward. "Do you who I am?"

"Of course not," she retorted.

"I am Conal," he slowly intoned, "King Kamron's son. You know who he was?"

Hafgan suspiciously eyed him. "Kamron in dead… so are his children."

"Wrong dearie," Madlyn answered for him.

"Kamron had two children. But you know that. That's why you're here. You were supposed to draw him out and kill him." She suddenly turned to Conal. "That's why there're no mages here. Torian knew you'd have some with you and mages here would've alerted you."

"That was your mission?" Conal huffed in feigned disbelief. "To draw me out? To kill me? You? You and your puny army were never any match for my armies."

"Bravely spoken, sitting there high on your horse," she shot back.

"You think you're a match for me?" he taunted. "You really think you can defeat me?"

"I'd carve you like a cold chunk of ham," she sniffed.

Conal slid down from his horse. "Unchain her and give her a sword."

"M'Lord," Lorkan startled. "No."

"Do it," Conal barked.

Lorkan hesitated, yet saw the fire in Conal's eyes. Flipping the chain to one of the bodyguards, he said, "Unchain her. Find her a sword."

Hafgan rubbed her wrists, shaking her head at Conal as she smiled at his stupidity. Now, at least, she had the opportunity to fulfill her mission. Another bodyguard found a sword, tossing it to her before stepping back to form a circle.

Noting the circle of a one-on-one match, others of Lorkan's forces joined in watching, surprised though admiring Conal's bravery. Seeing the battle proven enemy commander, many thought his decision foolish.

Conal reached into his saddlebag and pulled out two sets of iron bars connected by a short length of metal chain.

"What are those," Bedo murmured to Madlyn.

"Don't know. Never seen 'em before."

Lorkan frowned at the strange contraptions. "Do you not want a sword, m'Lord?"

"No," Conal nonchalantly answered. "I'll use these."

Hafgan snorted a derisive laugh. "You will fight me with those? You make it too easy for me."

"We shall see," Conal smiled, silently praying his nunchuk runes didn't fail him. Moving to the center of the circle, he began spinning his nunchuks by his sides.

Gauging the spinning bars, Hafgan sniffed in scorn and took the first step to press the attack only to find the bars spinning at Conal's side were now crisscrossing in front of him like a windmill. Brought up short in her attack, she feinted left then attacked to his right.

With his left hand, Conal flicked a nunchuk at her head, causing her to over-react and lean backwards out of the way. In that instant, Conal attacked as blur of speed, leaping and spinning midair as the other nunchuk whirled in a wide powerful sweep and embedded with a crack on her ribcage, resulting in an audible grunt of pain.

Hafgan reeled backwards, her breathing suddenly exploding pain, and her strength compromised. She lifted her sword too late as the metal bar smashed into her head and the world turned black as she crumpled to the ground.

Conal stood over the prostrate body, staring at the indentation in the woman's skull. She was still alive though unresponsive, blood seeping from her nose and ear. "You really think you could defeat me?" he loudly challenged before pulling up the sleeve and revealing the tattoo on his shoulder. "I'm the Cobra of prophecy. I can't be defeated."

The revelation was electric, and word spread amongst the armies faster than any messenger could ever deliver – the Cobra of Prophecy was their commander.

"What do we do with her, m'Lord?" Lorkan asked, staring at the woman crumpled on the ground.

"We finish the job," Conal coldly answered. "She was sent her to find me and kill me. She was willing to destroy an entire city just to get to me." Dropping the nunchuks on the ground, he grabbed her head by her hair while reaching for the stiletto in his boot. In one quick motion, he sliced her across the throat, wiping his blade across the fabric of her pants to clean it.

He glanced up to see Lorkan's look, a mixture of stoic understanding and disappointment. "What would you have me do? I have nearly killed her with these." He picked up the nunchuks. "I crushed her skull. There is no survival. Oh sure, she might live for a couple of days, weeks, even. I have seen people injured like this, stone masons who failed to pay attention when a stone dislodged and hurtled down to destroy their lives. The lucky ones die immediately. The unlucky ones lingered, the pain worse than dying." He dipped his head to look at her. "I did her a favor."

"I know, m'Lord," Lorkan acknowledged and nodded. "It was necessary."

"What's truly sad is that under different circumstances, she could have been one of my commanders."

"Torian's poison must be cleansed away,"

Madlyn wisely stated. She pointed at the dead woman then narrowed her gaze at Lorkan. "She had a choice… just like you. You chose to fight. She chose to stay. Not everyone's tainted by Torian. Those who chose to yield to him are just as evil as he is."

Storri strode up, looking pleased and disappointed at the same time. "While I'll take a win any day, it wasn't much of an effort." He glanced down at Hafgan. "What happened to her?"

"That's Commander Hafgan," Lorkan said. "She decided to fight Conal."

Storri blinked as his gaze switched between Conal and Hafgan. He noticed the nunchuks in Conal's hands. "You use those?"

"Yes."

"I've seen those used once before. Very dangerous weapons when used by someone who knows what they're doing. You're just full of surprises."

Conal grinned and shrugged. "What's your status?"

"We're all fine," Storri chuckled. "Like I said, easiest battle I've ever been in. The dragons were a nice touch, especially since no one has seen a dragon for hundreds of years. Almost terrified us as much as the enemy. How'd you manage it?"

Conal thought about Drustan and Meinir, deciding they would reveal their dual status when they were ready. "Pure luck. I'll explain later. Let's go see how the city fared."

The city gates were still closed when they approached. In fact, the city was much too quiet. One would expect jubilation, especially anyone witnessing the crushing victory of the army that just rescued the city.

The peephole slide in the smaller door within the left gate door scraped open then closed and the small door pulled open and a plump man stepped out with an ingratiating smile as he pulled the door closed behind him.

"Thank you so much for rescuing this city," he said, as though repeating lines he had memorized for the occasion. "We were in such dire circumstances before your… before your… timely arrival. Yes, you came in the nick of time. Thank you." He started to turn away when Conal stopped him.

"Whoa there, mister. Who are you?"

The man turned back, offering the same ingratiating smile. "I am the burgomaster of the city."

"Are you all OK?"

"Yes. Everything is fine."

"Do you have enough to feed your city?" Conal asked, wondering why the man seemed so anxious to get back inside.

"Yes," the burgomaster repeated. "Everything is fine."

Conal frowned at him then said, "We will need supplies."

The man's eyes widened. "Supplies?"

"Yes," Conal emphasized. "Supplies: flour, water, meats, things like that."

The burgomaster's ingratiating smile vanished as he wrung his hands and started talking to himself. "Supplies. They never said anything about supplies. That wasn't part of the plan. They said it would be easy. He'd show up and she would kill him. Then everything would be fine. Never said anything about supplies."

"This is madness," Storri blurted and stepped towards the door causing the burgomaster to yelp and rush in first, vainly attempting to close the door behind him before Conal kicked it with such force that it sent the man sprawling on the ground.

Conal stepped inside followed by the others. However, once inside, they abruptly stopped. For there in the open space between the city gates and the interior walls were several sets of gallows, a body dangling beneath each rope. One set of gallows contained what looked to be a family: father, mother, and three children all under the age of ten. Looking to his left, more gallows filled with limp bodies lined the street as it curved its way into the city.

"What happened here?" Conal demanded.

The burgomaster's eyes filled with tears. "They killed a tenth of the city then herded the rest east towards Havengarde, my own family among them. We could do nothing to stop them. They said that if anyone said anything about what happened here, they would all die."

"Why?"

"You are the son of Kamron?" The burgomaster gazed at him, his shoulders settling in resignation.

"Yes."

Exhaling a long-suffering sigh, he wiped a tear away. With bitterness in his voice, he clenched his jaw. "Then it no longer matters for my family is condemned. She was supposed to kill you. He promised that once you were dead, everyone would return."

"And you honestly believed that?" Lorkan scoffed. "Wake up man. Your family was doomed before they set foot out of this blighted city." He pointed at Conal. "This man is your only hope. He's more than a king's son." He reached up to touch the sleeve covering Conal's tattoo. "With your permission, m'Lord."

"None needed," Conal replied, pulling up the sleeve to display the snake's head that shimmered with a crimson sheen.

"He's the Cobra who will defeat Torian."

The reaction was what Lorkan had hoped, for the burgomaster dropped to his knees.

"By the gods," the man gushed. "It's true. Save my family, m'Lord."

"I'll do my best," Conal reassured him. Bending down to grasp him by the elbow, he lifted him to standing. "Now tell me what happened."

Twenty minutes later he had heard enough. "So there's no army close by?"

"That's what I overheard, m'Lord. Firyn was supposed to join Hafgan here and wait for you. Once you were eliminated, they were to proceed west. At least that's what I could make out."

"And the families they moved out of Gorwick left several days ago?"

"Yes, m'Lord, headed for Havengarde. They should be closing in on the city by now."

Conal frowned at Lorkan and Storri. "Why would Torian want the distraction of civilians in Havengarde, civilians who don't even live there?"

"Dragons and hostages," Drustan said walking up, Meinir beside him. "By now, Torian is fully aware that dragons do exist and that they are on your side. I imagine he's betting that you won't use them when you attack Havengarde for fear of killing innocent women and children."

"Which would negate the advantage of having dragons," Lorkan observed.

"Exactly."

"Where have you two been?" Conal gazed

knowingly at them.

"Scouting," Meinir answered. "By the way, there's an army to the south headed this way."

CHAPTER 11

GWEN

The figure exploded into motion.

He lifted the sword in an overhead chop, bringing the blade down toward Gwen. She rolled aside at the last second and scrambled to her feet, rushing to the other side of the tent. The assassin came after her, wildly swinging his blade, the sword smashing into everything around him.

Gwen turned to face him and summoned the magic of her speed runes. "*Luas,*" she spoke its name, then charged ahead, slamming into the assassin. They both went flying, crashing into the center poles of the tent. They splintered under the force and the canvas collapsed on top of them.

A cry of alarm echoed through the camp, followed by shouts and the sound of steel ringing upon steel. Gwen crawled under the material, trying to navigate her way to freedom. She heard the material rip, and then something heavy landed on her. It was the assassin. He pummeled her with his fists, striking her over and over. She stifled her groans of pain and blindly tried to grab onto him through the material. It was soft and she couldn't get a strong grip.

"Láidreacht," she gasped, then pushed against him with everything she had.

The weight was gone. She clawed at the canvas and finally pulled it off, emerging to a sight of chaos. Over a dozen tents were burning. Robed figures, more of Grimmar's lackeys, were cutting their way through her army, heading for Lyra. She'd transformed into her dragon form and roared as she stomped the ground in anger. Gwen spotted Kalan. He was gathering a group of people, stopping those who tried to flee and bringing them together.

The assassin who'd attacked her was back. She had no idea how far she'd flung him, but he approached calmly. Clearly, she hadn't injured him. He spun his sword around with skillful comfort and threw his hood back. He was much older than her, and atop his head where hair should have been, the skin was covered with runes.

"You made a grave mistake in coming here," he said.

Gwen didn't bother with a reply. She lifted her left hand and spoke the name of the lightning rune. A lance of blinding white energy left her palm, forking through the air. In the blink of an eye, the assassin twirled his blade and deflected the bolt into the sky. Gwen watched in amazement as the lightning flew high and disappeared.

"Is that the best you've got?" he mocked.

He stalked around her in a circle, continuously spinning his blade, alternating from hand to hand.

"Your master was too frightened to come himself?" Gwen said.

The man laughed. "Hardly! Dealing with someone as pathetic as you would be overkill, so why would Grimmar trouble himself?"

Gwen launched another lightning bolt at him as a distraction, then used her speed runes to close the distance between them. Her might rune invigorated her and she punched him hard in the chest. She felt his bones crack under the blow, but she didn't stop. As the assassin fell backward to the ground, Gwen followed through with a wave of fire. His robes were incinerated instantly, trails of smoke wafting up from his charred remains.

Gwen stood there heaving in deep breaths. She was getting better at cohesively using the runes, but it drained her strength considerably. A look around the camp revealed that more tents were burning now. Kalan's small group had doubled in size, and they were working to put out the fires. Lyra roared again, but the tone was different. It sounded pained. Gwen scanned the darkness and spotted the dragon.

She was surrounded.

A host of robed figures were encircled around her, but there were other people there, too. They were oddly clothed with glowing runes on their arms, and one of them jabbed a spear at Lyra. Gwen expected it to shatter as it struck her scales, but instead, the tip of the weapon pierced her chest. Gwen cursed and ran for her. Kalan called out to her, but she ignored him. As she neared Lyra, she saw a pile of dead bodies on the ground. One was holding a sword and she snatched it up, then drove it into the nearest mage. It was a woman. She crumbled to the ground with a bloody gurgle.

The others turned to face her and drew their swords. Gwen jerked the blade free of the dead mage and held it up before her, having no idea how to wield it. Blood dripped down the blade and onto her hands. She'd rushed to aid Lyra, but now she was second-guessing her decision. She was outnumbered, one mage against a dozen or more.

"There!"

Gwen looked over her shoulder to see Kalan. He pointed and his group of fighters swarmed toward the enemy. The mages turned their attention away from her and she rushed toward the people attacking Lyra. She targeted the one with the spear first, swinging her sword at him in an awkward motion.

The man brought his spear up to block her strike, and the sword collided with the thick wood, sending powerful vibrations into Gwen's arms. Somehow, the blade hadn't carved through the spear. Gwen's hands trembled violently, and she dropped the sword. What was she doing? She wasn't a warrior. She grabbed onto the spear.

"*Tine!*" she shouted.

The spear caught fire. The man howled as the flames licked at his fingers, and he tossed the spear aside. Gwen grabbed him by the throat and looked him in the eyes.

"*Draein saoil.*"

The man's eyes bulged as his life was sucked away. Gwen drained him quickly and dropped his lifeless husk to the ground. The rune wanted more, *demanded* more. Gwen turned to meet the charge of another man. This one had no weapon, but he came at her anyway, his eyes filled with madness. She used her might rune to snap his neck, ignoring the yearning that the drain life rune pulsed through her.

The ground rumbled ominously beneath Gwen's feet. One of the mages had cast a spell similar to the one Aimil had in Wespin, and the ground heaved upward as it split open, swallowing several of Kalan's men. Gwen struck the mage with a lightning bolt. He was too focused on his own spell to defend himself, and his sizzling corpse sailed through the air before tumbling along the ground and skidding to a stop.

Gwen spun around, looking for the next enemy, but Kalan's men had subdued or killed those that remained. Lyra was on the ground, a pool of blood soaking the dirt around her. Gwen rushed over and knelt beside her head.

"Venia? Can you hear me?"

The dragon's eyes were half-open. Her chest rose and fell as she breathed, but the blood continued to seep from the wound caused by the spear.

"I'm fading," Venia said. "The dragon hunters have poisoned my blood. I feel it burning through me even now."

"Can you heal yourself?" Gwen felt anxiety rising within her. It had been a while since she'd experienced the feeling. Just as when Tobias had died, she felt helpless.

"I tried," Venia murmured.

"You can't die," Gwen said. "We need you. And we're so close. We're here at his gates." Gwen pleaded with her, but Venia's eyes started to lose focus and her wound stopped bleeding.

"No," Gwen whispered sadly, stroking her hand along the scales on Venia's face. The magic was tugging at her, but she tried to ignore it. She knew the dark rune wanted to steal more life, but she refused to answer its call. The magic grew more insistent, to the point that it was starting to give her a headache.

Gwen closed her eyes, intending to focus on the magic long enough to shut it out of her mind. And then she realized it wasn't the dark rune calling to her. It was the life rune she'd received from the elf in

Auleavell. She remembered what the elf had done, restoring the vitality of a vine, and she opened her eyes. Perhaps she wasn't too late. She laid her hands on Venia's face.

"Saol."

Energy flowed forth from Gwen and into Venia. The dragon was like a dark well, and the energy vanished as it reached her. Gwen refused to give up, sending more and more energy into the darkness. She was already drained, and the river flowing out of her was exhausting what she had left.

Gwen could feel her eyes closing. She fought to keep them open, to stay alert, but the darkness was so inviting. She startled, one of her hands slipping off Venia. Several blinks seemed to help at first, and she replaced her hand on Venia's snout. There was no air coming in or out. Instead of feeling panicked, Gwen was… content. As her vision faded, the last thing she saw was a faint light beginning to glow at the bottom of the well.

When Gwen regained consciousness, it was dawn. She was lying on the ground under the open sky, a thin blanket draped over her. Sitting up, she saw Lyra was gone. A few guards were keeping watch, but the rest of the camp was silent. Nearby, Kalan lay sprawled out on his stomach, snoring loudly.

The events of the previous night were a blur in her mind, but she remembered enough to piece together the fact that Grimmar had sent assassins after her and Lyra. Gwen rolled her head around, stretching her neck. She'd slept on a rock, and now her neck was sore. She flung the blanket off and stood up, rubbing the sleep from her eyes.

"Kalan," she called out.

He continued snoring, so she walked over and kicked his foot. His eyes snapped open and his body tensed, but when he saw it was her, he relaxed and offered a tired smile.

"I wondered if you'd ever wake up," he said, rolling over onto his back. He lifted his hand and shielded his face against the morning glare.

"You stayed out here the whole time?" Gwen asked.

"Someone had to keep an eye on you."

"You were asleep."

"I literally just closed my eyes." Kalan stifled a yawn and got up, brushing his clothes off.

"You expect me to believe that? You were snoring like a hog."

"Fine, fine. Maybe my eyes were closed for a little while, but the camp was in good hands. Besides, we both needed the rest. The gods only know what Torian's going to throw at us today."

"What? You didn't like his welcome party?" Gwen rolled her eyes. "They almost killed Venia."

Kalan grew somber. "I know. She left a few hours ago. She said she was hungry enough to eat an entire field of cows."

"I'm just glad she's all right."

"That's thanks to you. You healed her."

Fragmented memories floated above the haze and Gwen nodded slowly. "I remember. Sort of."

"They tried to kill you, but they also tried to scare off our army. It didn't work."

"Nobody fled?"

"Well, I wouldn't say that. There were a handful of deserters."

"I can't fault them," Gwen said. "These people aren't ready for what they will see today."

A runner arrived and bowed low to Gwen, then looked at Kalan. "Sir, this just arrived." He handed over a folded parchment. Kalan opened it and read over the contents.

"Torian is demanding we hand you over," he said, looking up at her. "He'll grant a pardon for everyone who marched here if we do."

Gwen made a noise in her throat. "He's a fool if he thinks it will be that easy." Gwen stared at the castle, eyeing the walls and trying to determine the best plan of attack. "Wake the mages. Tell them to report to me as soon as they've had breakfast."

Kalan looked at the runner. "Do as she says."

"Yes, sir." The runner sprinted away.

"What's the plan?" Kalan asked.

"To bring hell to Torian's doorstep."

CHAPTER 12

CONAL

To Conal's good fortune, the army approaching from the south was two regiments from Clagmoran's home guard, commanded by a thick-necked bulldog of a man named Awstyn who barged in to where Conal and the others stood outside the gates of the city, demanding, "Which one of you is Conal?"

"That would be *Lord* Conal," Lorkan not so politely corrected him.

"Oh… ah… huh, never said anything about that. My apologies, m'Lord," Awstyn said, glancing around to see which one was the Lord.

"Apology accepted," Conal replied with a tired smile.

Expecting to see an older man, Awstyn cocked an eyebrow in surprise. "Ah… Lord Kilmaryn sends his respects, wishing he could send more but the security of the kingdom is equally important."

"I am thankful Lord Kilmaryn was able to spare so many." He curved a hand at Storri and Lorkan. "General Lorkan and General Storri are my primary commanders along with Commander Sorcha. You will command your soldiers as the fourth division of this army. Coordinate as you see fit. We leave in the morning."

"Yes, m'Lord." He smiled with contented excitement.

"War council in twenty minutes. Be there."

"Yes, m'Lord… uh where?"

Conal glanced up at the too close city, the ghosts of the innocent dead seeming to hover at the open gates. Looking back over his shoulder at the charred remains of the battlefield, he smelled the acrid stench of burned bodies wood then turned back to Storri. "How about we meet at your tent."

"As you wish, m'Lord," Storri replied, pleased with the specific attention.

"I'll meet you there then," Conal said. "But first I need to talk to Drustan and Meinir. Madlyn and Korla, I also want you two to stay."

Recognizing the tone of dismissal, the commanders slipped away to coordinate boundaries and liaison officers. Conal turned a sharp eye to Korla.

"Don't ever go off on your own again. What you did was stupid. I told you to stay with Madlyn and that is where you will stay from now on. Understood?"

"I was only trying to help," she said, embarrassed to be chastised in front of the others, especially Madlyn.

"You can help by being where you're supposed to be. Had I needed mage support, no one knew where you were." Conal then turned his attention to the two druids. "I hope you know what you're doing," he fussed at them. "While I appreciated the attack on Hafgan's army, you put yourselves in danger. Was that smart?"

"It was expedient," Meinir answered. "Taking the battle to Hafgan on your own would have taken too much time. Yes, you would have won, but at what cost? You now have your army intact and ready to go."

"Suppose some errant arrow found you like it did Bryok?" he pointedly stated.

"We have greater protection as dragons than humans."

"Wait, what?" Korla startled, her embarrassment forgotten. "You're dragons?"

Madlyn shook her head with maternal patience. "Yes, dearie. They are shapeshifters. You're a mage. You should know about that."

"I do, I mean, I've read about them, but I've never seen one in real life." She stared at them with fascination.

"Let's save it for later," Conal gently scolded before turning back to the two druids. "While I'm not happy about you two in the battle, I can still use your talents, specifically in scouting ahead. You can range farther and faster than any of my scouts."

"We can do that," Drustan acknowledged with a nod.

Conal regarded them a moment longer. "Are there anymore coming?"

"They're on their way," Meinir answered. "Hopefully, they should be here in the next couple of days."

Nodding thoughtfully, Conal said, "Would you mind doing a sweep once more before you turn in for the night?"

"No problem," Drustan replied. "We'll wake you if we need to."

As the two druids drifted away into the night,

Conal turned to the two mages, shifting a pointed finger at them. "I have a feeling that once we get into Isentol proper, you two will be very busy." He narrowed his gaze on Korla. "When was the last time you talked to your brother?"

"Just a little bit ago. Gwen has taken Wespin. She has about 2,000 followers with her, mostly civilians. They're on the move to Havengarde"

"2,000," Conal sputtered. "How is she going to attack Havengarde with 2,000?" He began pacing. "This is madness. She'll be destroyed. We've got to hurry."

"He says she has some more mages from the Library with her."

"I don't know what that means," Conal brooded. "We've got to move."

Madlyn placed a hand on his arm. "It means she has some very powerful magic with her to make up for the lack of a real army. In this instance, their magic will more than offset the weakness of her army."

Unconvinced, Conal shook his head. "That may be all well and good, but we've got to get to Havengarde before Torian can throw all his effort at her. We need to make some noise to draw off as much of his part attention and forces as possible."

He abruptly spun around and headed off to Storri's tent.

"Well that was rude," Korla huffed.

Madlyn glanced up at her with a look of pity. "Now's not the time to sugarcoat things, dearie. You got your underthings all twisted and can't figure out why he's not goo-goo eyes over you. All you have to worry about it yerself." She swept a hand at the vast array of campfires and activity. "He's responsible for all of this. He's a future king. You? Like you said, yer just a mage."

Conal burst into Storri's makeshift tent, a tarp raised up with a couple of poles. "We got to move. Gwen's attacking Havengarde with 2,000 civilians probably armed with pitchforks and brooms."

"What?" Storri exclaimed. "She crazy?"

"I know, but we're gonna have to get going, march through the night. You dwarves, while you can't match strides with a man, you can march farther without rest. You can go days on end. That's one of the many things I admire about dwarves. You're strong."

"That we are, m'Lord," Storri replied, flattered. "A word of advice?"

"Please."

"Let everyone rest for now. Give 'em a couple of hours sleep now and they'll be stronger later. We forced marched to get here. A few hours rest now will save us time later."

Torn between rushing off or listening to the wisdom of a soldier, he opted for wisdom. Besides, he was tired himself. What good would it do to exhaust everyone. A few hours nap would rejuvenate them all.

"I defer to your wisdom, my friend. Cancel the planning meeting tonight. We can do it in the morning while we're traveling."

"Smart move," Storri grinned. "We can move out a couple of hours before dawn. That'll give us plenty of time."

"Spread the word," Conal agreed. Sending several of his bodyguards to deliver the message, he headed back to his own tent. As he strode back to his tent, soldiers seeing him pass by called out greetings and he felt their confidence in him. *Let's pray I don't let them down.*

Bedo had a small pup tent sent up for him with a bedroll unfurled inside.

"Get some sleep, Bedo," he yawned. "We'll be getting up early."

"Yes, m'Lord." Bedo waited for Conal to stretch out on the bedroll before wrapping a thick woolen blanket around his shoulders. Settling onto the ground in front of Conal's tent, he curled an arm under his head and closed his eyes.

Though tired, Conal's mind wouldn't settle and he tossed. He was sure that he had just fallen asleep when he felt a nudge and heard Bedo's voice.

"Time to rise, m'Lord."

Conal sat up and rubbed his eyes. Crawling out of the tent, he heard the rustle of activity as fires were doused, bedrolls tied up, tents dismantled. Yawning, he shivered in the morning briskness, silently wishing for something hot to drink.

Numbly standing there, watching Bedo tear down his tent, he felt someone behind him and turned to see Drustan and Meinir approaching.

"Anything?" Conal asked.

"It's quiet all the way to Cwnbriar," Drustan replied.

"How far is that?"

"About halfway to Havengarde," Meinir answered.

Conal frowned. "Seems too quiet. Shouldn't there be some sort of military presence between here and Havengarde?"

"You forget that you've destroyed two of Torian's armies," Drustan pointed out. "Unless he knows his backdoor is open, he'll assume everything is fine."

Conal's frown remained. "He has to have some sort of communications with his military in the west. How is he doing it?"

"That's something you need to ask your mages," Meinir replied. She shifted a look at Drustan. "Let's find a place to rest."

Drustan nodded then told Conal, "We'll catch up with you. I doubt we'll have a difficult time finding you."

"Be careful," Conal warned, suddenly feeling protective.

"We will," Drustan replied with a warm but tired smile.

Lorkan passed the two druids, giving them a nod of friendship, and came up to Conal. "With your permission, I'd like to send out scouts well in advance of our forces."

"Do what you think best, my friend," Conal said, finally waking up. "By the way, Drustan and Meinir say it's quiet all the way to Cwnbriar."

Lorkan's initial reaction was to ask how they knew. Choosing to keep his own counsel, he said, "That should help us move quicker. I've chosen several scouts who know the area and can walk into towns along the way without drawing suspicion."

"I like it," Conal nodded, immediately understanding. "I want to place the mages farther forward. It's been too easy so far and I don't like it. Something's not right." Conal shook his head in misgiving. "I have this feeling like we're being watched... from afar."

"I can place them with my forward elements, if you wish. That way they'll be far enough forward and still have protection."

Conal mused for a moment. "What's the chance of us gaining more bodies as we march through Isentol? There has to be more people like you, willing to take a stand."

"We'll see as we get closer to Havengarde, m'Lord."

Conal nodded. "I guess we will. Are we ready?"

"Yes, m'Lord."

"Let's move. We'll do a war council wherever you are. Once I track down the mages, I'll send to them to you."

Momentarily left alone, Conal glanced around in the darkness, hearing the muted commands and movements of bodies to places in the order of march. The fact that he was in charge sobered him, and he was mindful of all the wisdom his father… his real father, the one in Urve who had chosen to love him like a real son, had preached at him. In this moment, he wished he had his father by his side, for the man always seemed to have the right answer and he would know what to do and how to do it.

Conal chuckled remembering a dictum his father would often say: *When working toward a solution to a problem, it always helps if you know the answer.* His musings were interrupted when Madlyn walked up with a still half-asleep Korla in tow.

"It's too quiet, my young Lord," Madlyn said. "When I was in Blasingdon, I could feel Torian's presence. Not his exactly, but his wizard's work, if you know what I mean. It was like a thick foggy morning where the mist is so heavy it clings to you. I felt it here for a bit, but now it's gone. It's like his eye is turned elsewhere."

Conal immediately thought of Gwen and locked a gaze on Korla. "Have you heard from your brother?"

"Not since the last message I gave you."

"Be careful, young Lord," Madlyn interrupted, placing a hand on Conal's arm. "Mind messages can be intercepted, especially by them that knows it's happenin'. I'm not sayin' you don't need to know what's goin' on. I'm just sayin' it might be best to leave well enough alone. If he's occupied somewhere else, all the better for you."

"Sound wisdom, Madlyn," he nodded, suddenly worried that all the previous chats the twins had might have been compromised, which might mean that he was being lured into a false sense of confidence. "I want you two up with Lorkan's forces. He'll position you where I want. I need all the advanced warning we can get."

Madlyn smiled in understanding and turned to Korla. "Come along dearie. Let's see what mischief I can keep you out of."

"What are you talking about," Korla grumbled as they walked away.

Despite Conal's misgivings, the combined armies made excellent time, arriving at Cwnbriar in the late afternoon. All the stress of scout reports, overhead searches for messenger birds, and frequent checks with Madlyn revealed nothing out of the ordinary. The several towns they passed through, alarmed at the soldiers, were hesitant about providing either supplies or information.

Conal was angry at first until Storri pointed out, "They don't expect us to win. You can't blame them. They've been living under Torian's thumb for so long that they no longer have hope and they're not about to get their hopes up because some stranger shows up claiming he's going to defeat Torian. Nothing will change until Torian is truly gone."

"You are right," Conal acknowledged with a sigh, "as usual. We rest here. War council at your tent in an hour."

Before Storri I had a chance to reply, Korla came racing up.

"Torian knows were here!"

"What?" Conal exclaimed. "How?"

Korla leveled an 'I-knew-it-all-along' look at him. "Madlyn. She's been working for Torian since the beginning."

CHAPTER 13

GWEN

The mages from the Great Library stood in a line facing Havengarde.

Gwen glanced at them, then turned her attention to the stone walls that protected the castle. She shifted her stance impatiently as she waited for Kalan to contact his sister. Despite her initial aggravations with the man, he had quickly proven his worth and had become her trusted right hand.

She looked over her shoulder. Lyra still hadn't returned. She'd told Kalan she was going to find food, but that had been a few hours ago. The dragon should have been back by now. Gwen was worried something had happened to her and offered a silent prayer on her behalf, hoping that she hadn't been caught by dragon hunters.

"Good news," Kalan said as he approached.

"I hope so," Gwen replied.

"Korla says Conal and half of his forces will be in position outside of a tunnel that leads into the city. They're waiting for us to draw attention to ourselves."

"You mean we haven't already?" Gwen smirked. "Where's the other half of his army?"

"They're heading for the west gate, led by someone named Lorkan."

Gwen vaguely remembered him from the meeting in Haddence. "Good. Torian will be hard-pressed to defend his castle."

"What's wrong?" Kalan asked.

"Nothing."

"You look uneasy. What is it?"

"Lyra still hasn't returned. I'm worried about her."

"She's a dragon," Kalan scoffed. "She can protect herself. You should be worried about us."

His words made Gwen realize she was thinking foolishly. He was right—Lyra was fine. Probably.

"I guess we'll have to attack without her. How many archers do we have?"

"Not enough," Kalan said. "Two dozen, maybe."

"Do you think they can hit anything from here?"

"No." Kalan didn't even hesitate with his answer.

"Then we need to get closer. How far can your shield stretch?"

"I've never tried covering more than two people," he answered. "But I like to push boundaries."

"Try to shield the archers. I'll have Menjing and the others get closer. If the archers can take down some of the soldiers on the wall, we're better off. Once we blast a hole in the wall, it's going to get bloody."

"I'll do my best." Kalan jogged off to collect the archers.

"Menjing!" Gwen shouted. The tall man looked at her as she strode over to him. "We need to get closer to the wall. Is that going to be a problem?"

"That is no problem," Menjing said. "How much closer do you want us?"

Gwen eyed the distance. "A hundred feet or so. That'll put us within the range of their archers, but ours can't reach them from here."

"Do not worry for us. We are ready."

Menjing told the woman next to him, who passed the word down the line. They began walking together, moving ahead as an organized unit. Gwen waited for Kalan and the others, then marched with them.

"You should be at the camp to direct your army," Kalan remarked.

"You shouldn't tell me what to do," Gwen replied. "Besides, I'm not a leader. The people we chose are better equipped than I am."

Kalan opened his mouth to argue, but Gwen gave him a hard stare and he kept quiet. As soon as the mages were within range, a volley of arrows came hurtling at them. One of the mages raised her arms and the arrows flashed brightly, the wooden shafts incinerated. The steel tips showered to the ground, their pattering reminding Gwen of a hailstorm.

The archers grouped behind the mages and Kalan motioned to them. They readied their arrows.

"Our turn," Kalan said. "Fire!"

The return volley was pitiful in comparison, and a third of the arrows didn't make it halfway to the wall. Those that did struck an invisible barrier and simply fell from the sky.

Gwen looked at Kalan and shook her head.

"We can try again," he said.

"Let's alternate. Magic, then arrows." Gwen whistled.

Menjing and the others raised their hands toward the castle. There was a moment of silence, and then a chorus of runes was spoken. The ferocity of the magic made Gwen wince and back up a few steps. Lightning bolts, balls of flame and spikes, glowing orbs of energy, and many other magical bombardments lit up the sky.

Gwen held her breath as the barrage struck the wall. Except, none of the spells landed *against* the wall. Like the arrows, they hit the unseen barrier and fizzled out. Menjing glanced back at her, his uncertainty evident. Gwen nodded at him, and they fired off their spells a second time. Again, the magical attacks were thwarted by the barrier. Gwen rushed ahead to join Menjing.

"What is that thing?" she asked.

"Anti-magic," he answered. "It's the work of a sorcerer, maybe a wizard."

"Anti-magic stops arrows, too?"

"It would seem so. Should we retreat?"

"No. We need the focus on us until Conal is ready. Keep attacking, but not all at once. And reserve your strength. The real battle won't start until we're inside." Gwen turned to leave, then paused. "Can you tell if the person casting the anti-magic is on the wall?"

"Mila might be able to. She has a rune that gives her far-sight."

More arrows filled the sky. The mage who'd stopped the first volley raised her arms and incinerated them again. Menjing summoned the woman he'd mentioned, and she hurried to the front of the line.

"Can you see the one who shields the castle?" Menjing asked her.

Mila looked toward the castle and spoke the name of a rune. Her eyes went completely black. A few seconds later, she blinked lazily and her eyes returned to normal.

"Yes. The magic flows from a Prestige near the middle. He's surrounded by soldiers and two mages."

"We need to get rid of him," Gwen said. "Let me talk with—"

A roar drowned out her words and she whirled around, looking to the sky. Lyra had returned, along with three other dragons. Two were blue and the third was jet black. They flew overhead and continued toward the castle. The blue dragons opened their mouths and blasts of lightning flew forth. Lyra breathed fire, and the black dragon spewed a sizzling wave of acid. A cheer rose from among Gwen's camp.

Magic arced over the walls, followed by a barrage of arrows. The projectiles bounced harmlessly off the dragons, but a few of the spells struck the blue dragons and they screeched in anger. Lyra bellowed loudly and the dragons turned away from the castle and landed at the camp.

Gwen looked at Menjing. "Continue assaulting the walls but remember what I said. Reserve your strength." She ran back to the camp, leaving Kalan with the archers. Lyra was conversing with the other dragons as she approached.

"You're back," Gwen said, looking at the dragon's chest for signs of the wound. Lyra's scales were flawless. Gwen's eyes widened in surprise.

"I went to find food and found allies," Lyra said. She lifted a claw and ran it over her scales where she'd been wounded. "Your magic is powerful. There's no scarring at all."

"I wasn't even sure if it would work," Gwen admitted.

"You have done a great service to me, but also for my kind. I am still able to bear eggs, and once we have the city back, I will help restore our numbers."

Gwen wasn't sure what Lyra meant about having the city back. She was just glad to see the dragon was healed and hadn't been captured.

"Menjing says there's a sorcerer on the walls that's keeping us at bay. We need to make some noise so that Conal can enter the city unnoticed, but we need to find a way to get past that barrier."

Lyra looked toward the castle and hummed lowly. "The barrier cannot be removed unless the sorcerer breaks the spell or dies. I vote death."

"As do I," Gwen replied.

"We can drop a few people on the wall. The rest will be up to them."

"Won't the barrier keep you from getting close enough?"

"The barrier blocks magic, but not living things. As long as you humans don't mind free falling a short distance, you'll be fine."

Gwen smiled, knowing just the person to lead such a risky endeavor. "I'll get a team ready."

She returned to where Kalan was and told him the plan. His face lit up like a young child on Yuletide. "Please let me go," he begged.

"The job is yours," Gwen replied. "Pick a few people to go with you. Once you land, do whatever it takes to get rid of that sorcerer. If you can at least break the spell and make him retreat, that's better than our current predicament."

"I'll do that and more," Kalan said confidently. "Be ready for my signal."

"What's the signal?" Gwen asked.

"You'll know when you see it."

Gwen wasn't sure she liked that answer, but she decided to trust him. She just hoped he didn't let her down or die as Tobias had. Kalan pulled the archers back to the camp since they were useless and handpicked seven people to go with him. Lyra was confident that each dragon could hold two people while flying near the walls. The small team armed themselves and climbed onto the dragons, all but Kalan exuding a strange mix of excitement and fear. He was enjoying himself immensely.

The dragons leaped into the air, their powerful wings pushing them higher and higher. Gwen rejoined Menjing and his group, deciding to add her magic to the diversion. As one mage finished throwing a spell at the wall, the one beside them would go next. It kept a continuous barrage hitting the barrier while also preventing the enemy from shooting any more arrows.

"*Tintreach!*" Gwen shouted, sending a bolt of lightning from her palm.

Shadows passed overhead as Lyra and the other dragons sped toward the walls, diving down sharply at the last moment. Gwen couldn't see much, but she did spot the small forms leaping from the backs of the dragons and landing, thankfully, atop the walls. The mages continued their assault, changing the aim of their attacks toward the lower portion of the wall in case Kalan was successful.

The minutes ticked by and Gwen tried not to worry. Kalan was a capable mage and an exceptional fighter from what she'd seen, but his stone skin rune didn't make him invincible.

"The sorcerer is gone!" Mila shouted.

"Dead?" Gwen asked, but Mila shrugged.

"He's no longer at the wall, but I can't say if he's dead. The barrier should be down now."

"All together!" Menjing rallied.

This time, Gwen summoned the lightning and the fire runes, back-to-back, adding her magic to the chaotic mix of the other mages. Every spell struck the wall. The camp behind them cheered again, and Gwen allowed herself to be optimistic. Now that Kalan and the others had dealt with the sorcerer, where were they? He was smart enough to stay out of the way of their magical attacks, but where would he go? The entire city was crawling with Torian's men. She gritted her teeth and pushed the growing doubt aside, throwing herself into the magic.

They needed to blow a hole in the wall to allow the army through. Despite the combined power of their runes, the walls merely blackened under the assault. They weren't making any progress.

One of the mages pointed and shouted something unintelligible. Gwen looked, seeing nothing at first. Then movement caught her eye. The portcullis over the gate was rising. Gwen's eyes widened. Kalan was opening the gates! Gwen sprinted back to the camp.

"To arms!" she shouted, not sure if that was the correct thing to say. "We march on the city!"

The army was small and untrained, but they drew their weapons and shouted war cries. They were ready, Gwen knew. Ready to deliver vengeance for all the years of tyranny at the hands of Torian and his evil followers.

Gwen grabbed a sword and was about to lead the charge when a sound from behind their camp stopped her in her tracks. Her heart felt like it dropped into her stomach. The ground began to tremble, and another sound overtook the first.

"What is that?" someone yelled.

Another person turned and pointed.

"War horns!"

CHAPTER 14

CONAL

"Madlyn?" Conal cocked an eyebrow in doubt. "I don't believe it. Where is she?"

"Gone," Korla flatly affirmed. "Last anyone saw her she was heading for Havengarde. I bet if you ask the scouts, they'll tell you the same thing."

"Are you sure? She didn't say anything?"

"Yes," Korla snipped. "She said it was time to get back to where she belonged and then started walking up the road to Havengarde, walking at a good pace I might add."

"You didn't try to stop her?" Storri asked.

"I… I couldn't."

"Why not?" he frowned.

"Because she's more powerful than I am, OK? Satisfied?" She crossed her arms and glared at him.

Storri's frown deepened and he turned to Conal, hooking a thumb at Korla. "What's her problem?"

Still processing Madlyn's departure, Conal shook his head. "This doesn't make sense. She destroyed Firyn's army. Why would she do that? Just to make me believe she was on our side?"

"It wouldn't surprise me," Storri ruefully

observed. "Those poor fools. All those years of training, weeks and months spent away from family, only to be used as toys for someone's blind ambition." He turned a hard eye on Conal. "When the time comes, and I pray it comes soon, that Torian comes to you in chains and begs for mercy… remember his crimes. He gave no mercy and deserves none. The same applies to those who willingly chose to serve him. Just like a dead tree cannot grow again, they must be ripped out at the roots."

Conal shifted a glance at them. "This goes no further. I want no one else to know, except Lorkan."

"What?" Korla burst. "The woman's a traitor. She had you hoodwinked."

"He's right," Storri sharply said, pointing finger at her. "Now be quiet, woman. You know nothing of military matters. What good would it do to tell soldiers who are about to fight and possibly die that the mage they trusted was a traitor. Is that how you inspire people to follow you? And speaking of you, what makes you think they won't believe the same thing about you?"

Korla's eyes popped wide. "But I'm not a traitor."

"So you say," Storri coldly replied then swept a hand at the assembled armies of men and dwarves. "Tell that to them."

Korla swallowed and blinked in understanding.

"If anyone asks," Conal said, looking directly at Korla, "Madlyn's gone on a mission per my orders. No elaboration, just that's she gone because I have her doing something for me. You don't know what then change the subject. Understood?"

"Yes," she sighed in frustration.

"That's 'Yes, my Lord," Storri corrected.

Korla glanced away so she wouldn't have to look

in his eyes as she said, "Yes, my Lord."

Storri stroked his beard as he mused aloud. "She knows our strength and our position."

"And about the dragons," Korla added.

"Them too. Our element of surprise is gone."

"Not entirely," Conal responded. "Anyone seen Drustan and Meinir yet?"

"Not yet," Korla answered.

Conal curled a hand at them. "C'mon. Let's go find Lorkan and the others."

After explaining Madlyn's disappearance, Lorkan and Storri increased perimeter security in addition to sending out patrols. Drustan and Meinir arrived while they were issuing orders. Conal explained their situation.

"Madlyn's gone and our presence here is compromised. Gwen's committed to battle in the east. We have to attack to take pressure off her. You two know the area. What's the best avenue of approach to Havengarde?"

"The fastest way is straight up the main road," Meinir replied.

"Not exactly what I had in mind," Conal said.

"If Torian knows you're here," Meinir continued, "what does it matter where you attack from?"

"It would be nice to have at least one surprise," Conal sighed.

"You do," Drustan said with a slight smile. "We brought some friends with us."

Out of the darkness, five figures emerged, three women and two men, all dressed in the garb of huntsmen.

"Lord Conal," Drustan said, beginning the introductions with the women. "This is Derryth, Tesni, Amsyr. These two are Elys and Gawyn." As each was introduced, they gave Conal a respectful bow.

Derryth was a striking svelte woman with crisp facial features and long black hair. Tesni was a buxom brunette a hand span shorter than Derryth. Amsyr was the same height as Tesni, with blond hair tinged with emerald highlights that seemed to shimmer in the night. Elys was tall and muscular with a thick neck and close-cropped hair. Though a head shorter than Elys, Gawyn's broad shoulders and brooding face gave him an imposing presence. Two things were unique to them all: their eyes, coal black with pupils like the occasional flicker of simmering coals, and the numerous runes imprinted on their skin.

"There are seven of us here," Drustan said. "Four more are standing by to employ where needed."

"One more thing that ought to be mentioned," Meinir said, glancing quickly around to see who was in earshot. Motioning Conal and the others to close in, she lowered her voice and said, "Derryth says there is a way into the city and then into the castle." She motioned Derryth to join the group.

"There is an entrance," Derryth repeated. "As far as I know, it hasn't been used for many decades. The last time I was there was before Kamron's grandfather was born."

"How old are you?" Korla blurted, earning her glares from the others. "Sorry."

"How do you know about this entrance?" Storri asked, suspicious.

"Derryth is Princess Derryth," Drustan answered for her. "Her parents ruled in Havengarde before the Hunting. She will rightfully rule again when the time comes."

"How long will it take to get to the entrance and then into the city?" Conal asked, his hopes rising.

"I will lead them," she regally replied. "It should not take long, provided your soldiers are strong. It is through the mountains."

"Sounds like dwarf territory," Storri grinned.

"It is," Derryth said, "for dwarves carved it for us an age ago. The hallways and caves are large so an entire army of dwarves can easily pass through. Though it has been a long time since I walked those hallways, I have never forgotten my home."

"That means splitting our forces," Lorkan warned.

"I know," Conal pensively nodded, "but it also means getting someone into the city and castle without them knowing." He peered intently at Derryth. "How far is it to Havengarde?"

"You can be there well before dawn if you left now."

"How long from here to Havengarde for those not going through the mountains?"

"Six hours."

Conal thought quickly. "We attack at dawn. Storri and his army will go with Princess Derryth through the mountains. Lorkan and the remaining combined forces will continue this avenue of approach." He shifted his attention to Drustan. "I'd like to split your group between the two."

"Agreed. Meinir and I will remain with Lorkan, along with Tesni and Elys. Amsyr and Gawyn will go with Storri."

"What about you, m'Lord?" Lorkan asked, already knowing the answer.

"I'm going with Storri."

Both Lorkan and Storri were about to argue when

Drustan spoke. "An excellent idea. That will get the king's son inside the city before Torian realizes it. I have no doubts that there are enough in the city who are ready rebel."

"What about me?" Korla interrupted.

"You go with Lorkan," Conal said. "He'll need mage help as soon as Torian sees the army."

Though disappointed she wasn't going with Conal, she was also keenly aware that Torian's mages were far more powerful than she was. Even Madlyn was more powerful. Suddenly feeling inadequate, she meekly nodded and tried to blend in with the others.

"If we leave, now," Derryth said, "Storri and his army will have a few hours to rest before the battle."

Conal turned to Lorkan. "You know better what to do than whatever council I could offer. As soon as the sun's rays rim the mountains, attack." He stretched out a hand, grasping Lorkan's hand. "We'll meet up in the city. Hopefully we'll have the gates open by the time you get there. If not… improvise."

"Watch yourself, m'Lord," Lorkan replied with a firm handshake. "Once Torian discovers you're inside the city, he won't stop until he finds you."

"And your sister," Drustan added.

"Torian is just a man," Conal snarled. "He needs to worry that I don't find him first." Turning to Storri, he said, "Don't worry. I'll stay out of your way."

"We serve you, m'Lord," Storri nobly answered, hoping Conal would be true to his word.

"Then we better get going."

While Lorkan gave his soldiers an hour's rest, Derryth led Storri's dwarven army along the road to the northeast, a road that would eventually connect with a main road out of Havengarde that went due north to the human kingdom of Tul Cragbyrn. Amsyr and Gawyn lagged behind towards the end of the dwarven army, scanning the area and occasionally drifting off then reappearing.

Walking beside Derryth, Conal noted she moved with a fluid grace, even at the pace they marched.

"Why are you so intent on helping us?" He said it without thinking. "There are so few dragons left. It's dangerous."

She cast a sharp look at him. "Havengarde was my home long before humans took it over. Will you return it to us, or will we have to fight you too?"

Started at the brusqueness, Conal replied, "Hadn't really thought about it. I've been a little busy of late and to tell the truth, I hadn't even thought about what happens after Torian's gone. But I do know threatening me isn't exactly endearing your cause to me. The way I see it, there are eleven of you left. Humans and others eliminated the rest. Seems to me that your threat of continuing the battle only ensures your complete elimination."

That caused her to stutter-step, but she quickly recovered. They walked in silence for a bit before she spoke, though it seemed an effort to be polite.

"You are right, of course. I was wrong to imply any such violence for it is true that we are at your mercy, hoping that you will do what is right and honorable and restore Havengarde to its rightful owners."

"So a kingdom within a kingdom," Conal observed. "And what else will you demand? How much of Isentol will you claim belongs to you?"

"Now see here," she snapped. "Isentol was ours long before you humans took it over."

"And who did you take it from?" Conal shot back. "Are you saying there was no one here when dragons decided, 'Hey, this looks like a good spot. Why don't we build a city here?'"

"So you admit Havengarde is a dragon city."

"I'm not arguing that dragons had *dwarves* build Havengarde. I won't even ask if they were threatened or volunteered, though it does cause me to wonder what treasures dragons had that they hadn't taken from someone else and used as payment... *if* that's what happened."

Derryth's nostrils flared. "How dare you impugn —"

"Come down off your high horse, Princess," Conal interrupted, "or did you forget that I am a king's son and when I regain my throne, a king. My family has reigned in Havengarde for over a hundred years... a hundred years when no one believed dragons still existed. We can talk claims to the city and the kingdom all we want, but the truth is that I have more resources at my disposal than you do."

Derryth's mouth clenched, and she stared straight ahead.

For the next hour, as the evening's light slipped away to darkness, neither spoke and Conal wondered if he hadn't stepped over the line, that perhaps Derryth was leading them into a trap. But then, logically, she'd still have to have his and Gwen's support to defeat Torian. It was when Derryth abruptly stopped that an idea he had germinating began to blossom. A halfmoon's light gave shape to the forest on both sides of the road.

"We're here," Derryth said, pointing into the forest on their right. "Follow me."

Conal continued to contemplate his idea, so much so that he blindly followed Derryth dodging trees, crossing small streams, and clambering over rock formations as the trail she blazed continued to climb. Another hour later she crested on a wide rock shelf covered in vines.

Hands on her hips she sighed and shook her head. "I can't count the number of times I came out here." She tugged at several vines and pried them apart, Conal and others pulling and prying to give them space to get an army through.

When enough space was created, Derryth plunged into the darkness followed by a flash that lit a torch on the wall.

"How'd you do that?" Conal said, impressed.

"I'm a half-druid, remember," she lightly replied, lifting the torch out of the wall holder and handing it to a nearby soldier. "Torches line the entire hallway. Light only enough to find our way."

Soon, enough torches provided dim light showing the ceiling of the hallway was a good fifty feet above them. Conal immediately wondered how long it took to carve this from the stone of the mountain.

"This tunnel will get us into the city," Derryth explained. "I will get us close to the entrance so that we may rest before the attack."

"Lead the way," Storri grinned. Standing inside the mountain and seeing the work of his ancestors filled him with a comfort only a dwarf would understand.

Conal caught up to Derryth. "I have an idea."

"Yes?"

"I will return Havengarde to you in return for your help."

"You already have my help."

"Not this time," he said. "What I mean is, how much of Isentol was yours?"

"About half of it," Derryth answered, her hopes

beginning to rise.

"Which half?"

"Does it matter? Human towns now occupy all parts of the kingdom."

"True. However, my thought is this; to start off, you reclaim Havengarde. Obviously, you don't have enough dragons to enforce your presence. However, over time, that will remedy. But, until then, you will need help, so we enlist anyone who wants to stay. However, it will dragon law that rules."

"OK?"

"As dragon numbers continue to increase, you expand over a specified area that has been demarcated as the dragon kingdom. In the meantime, since the seat of my kingdom is no longer in Havengarde, it will need to move elsewhere. Likewise, I am losing a good chunk of my kingdom. So… I need to make up for that loss."

"How?" She looked at him and cocked and eyebrow.

"Tir Manach."

"What about Tir Manach?"

"You will help me take Tir Manach."

"You're going to conquer another kingdom?" Her frown deepened.

"Tir Manach has been under Torian's spell for years. My other family was murdered and Tir Manach did nothing to prevent it or complain about it. The present king is still under Torian's thumb. This will be justifiable reward for betrayal."

Derryth tilted her head to the side as she led them past side corridors, through large, vaulted rooms, and up and down wide sets of stairs before slowly nodding. "I agree to your proposal. Though frankly the affairs of men are of little concern to dragons, as long as we are left alone."

"Good. We can hammer out the details later. For now, where does this come out?"

"It comes out on the southwest side of the city. The city is built against the mountains." She went on to describe the layout of the city. One street ran along the length of the city walls, stopping well before the citadel. There were seven main thoroughfares that fanned out from the citadel all the way to the walls. With the citadel as the focal point, descending concentric rings of streets connected the main thoroughfares.

"The castle is much like the city with wide hallways, doors, archways, stairways, and anything else you would imagine for a dragon to move comfortably in the castle. The castle sits higher above the city and there are many levels within the citadel, arranged in concentric circles with hallways connecting each circle, just like the city streets. The throne room is in the center, a grand affair with a raised dais where the dragon king used to hold court. It is the throne room your father and your grandfathers used. I do not know how Torian has it arranged, but it will be hard to catch him unawares because he will see you before you can get close."

Not for the last time, Conal wished his highwayman days had brought him here. It would have made things a lot easier now. "Wonder how Lorkan's doing."

"When we begin our attack, I will have Gawyn find out where Lorkan is."

"Thank you."

To Conal's surprise, Torgreth came running up. "Storri asks how much farther?"

"We are almost there," Derryth answered, leading

up a flight of wide stairs that thirty humans could have walked up, side-by-side.

True to her words, she stopped on a broad platform before a set of grand double doors almost as high as the cavernous ceiling and not quite as wide as the set of stairs.

"The city lies on the other side of these doors. We can rest now."

A few moments later, Storri came up and gave the doors a doubtful look, especially at the door handles well above the reach of any dwarf or human. "Who's going to open the doors?"

"Don't worry," she soothed. "I'll make sure the doors open when needed."

Conal glanced around as the dwarves settled in groups and quietly chatted or stretched out where they were. "How do we know what time it is?"

Storri shot him a smug look. "A dwarf always knows what time it is, especially inside the mountains. We made good time. We got another hour and a half before we launch our attack. I've got a regiment ready to open the gates for Lorkan."

Amsyr and Gawyn came up and drew Derryth aside to chat quietly.

"Amsyr says that Lorkan's army arrives unnoticed."

"How does she know that?" Conal sputtered.

"There is more than one secret way into the city," Derryth cryptically replied. "The attention is all to the east where your sister and her mages have engaged the magic of Torian's magical forces."

"Let's pray his attention stays there," Conal muttered.

For the next hour and a half, Conal tried to relax, but his pent-up nerves wouldn't let him, and he was actually relieved when Storri said, "It's time."

Amsyr, Gawyn, and Derryth joined to stand before the doors.

"Give us room," Derryth commanded, "lots of room."

Conal, Storri and the dwarves scooted back off the platform to fill the stairs up to the edge. Conal saw the reddish glow of the runes on their forearms begin to shimmer, brighter and brighter until the forearm was a swath of color. And then the transformations occurred as the human forms bumped and bulged and twisted as three dragons expanded to their original forms.

Derryth was a large coal black dragon with cobalt blue eyes and wings the color of shimmering onyx. Amsyr evolved to just a little smaller than Derryth, an emerald green dragon with eyes the color of liquid gold. Stout Gawyn was the surprise for he was almost twice the size of the other two, all muscle and power, his scales the color of dazzling amethyst and eyes that blazed bright orange.

A hush of wonder rippled through those who watched the metamorphoses.

Derryth stood on her hind legs and reached for the door handle then turned to Conal and Storri. "Ready? Then let's do it."

With a yank, the doors silently swung wide.

CHAPTER 15

GWEN

Turn around!" Gwen shouted. "We're being attacked from the rear!"

She rushed through the camp to the other end, hoping the approaching army didn't outnumber hers. How would they pose a distraction now? Gwen tightened her grip on the hilt of her sword and stared at the impending mass. Something wasn't right. The army was too uniform, too… perfect. A mounted rider broke away from the group and thundered ahead, coming straight toward Gwen's position.

She lifted her hand, prepared to blast the rider from his saddle with lightning. The rider drew closer and closer. Gwen held back her spell until she was sure she wouldn't miss. And then she saw it. The finely crafted armor and the unique helm. That was elvish armor!

Gwen lowered her hand and sprinted forward. The rider wheeled the horse around in a circle, coming to a stop as Gwen reached him.

"Kirith!" Gwen shouted, a smile spreading across her lips.

"I'm not too late, then?" Kirith asked as he slid off his mount. He removed his helm and tucked it under his arm.

"Just in time actually. We're about to march into Havengarde. Kalan managed to get the gates open."

"Excellent news." Kirith looked past her to the gathered men and women and raised a slender brow. "This is your army?"

"It's small," Gwen admitted. "But it was all we could muster."

"That's not a problem, I just don't think they are outfitted for an assault. I'll have my forces take the lead." He looked back at Gwen. "If that's all right with you?"

"That's fine with me. We need to hurry, though. Conal is about to enter through the western side of the city."

Kirith retrieved a horn from his saddle and put it to his lips, then blew three short notes. His army split down the middle, each side going around the camp, and they converged back as one force on the other end of the camp.

"Let us go and take Havengade back," Kirith said. He climbed back onto his horse and offered Gwen his hand. She grabbed onto him and he pulled as she jumped, landing in the saddle behind him. He snapped the reins and the horse sped toward the castle.

"Attack!" Gwen shouted as they rode through the camp. "Fall in line behind the elves!"

Kirith's army was mounted and therefore faster, and Gwen's forces ran along behind them. The two of them rode past the line of mages and took the lead in front of the elven army, continuing to the open gate. As they crossed the threshold, Gwen spotted Kalan and two others. They were covered in blood and running toward the gate.

"There's too many!" Kalan shouted breathlessly.

Gwen pushed herself out of the saddle as Kirith slowed, landing awkwardly on her feet. She hurried over to Kalan.

"What about the gate? Are the others guarding the lowering mechanism?"

"No," Kalan heaved in a deep breath. "The others are dead, slaughtered after we lifted the portcullis. I used my key rune to lock the door behind us, so that should keep them busy trying to get inside to room, but not for long."

"Reinforcements have arrived," Gwen said, pointing behind her toward the mounted elves.

Kalan looked, and the fear that he had seemed to melt away. He turned around and Gwen saw a line of soldiers coming toward them, all holding long shields in front of them, forming a wall of steel.

"You couldn't take them out on your own?" Gwen asked, cracking a grin.

"If it was only them that I had to worry about, then I would have already dealt with them."

The sound of marching steps echoed off the buildings that lined the street, signaling more soldiers were coming. The street was wide enough for two dragons the size of Lyra to walk side by side, and Gwen realized that everything in the city was built bigger than necessary.

Kirith's mounted soldiers clopped onto the cobblestone street and begin lining up beside one another, stretching across the entire width of the thoroughfare. Gwen and Kalan moved out of the way, stepping into one of the buildings. It was a small shop, and the place was empty. Tools and other items were left strewn about, and Gwen guessed whoever had been there had left in a hurry to escape the attack.

More mounted riders filed in behind their fellows until the line was six rows deep, then they began moving further into the city. Gwen glanced out at the gates and saw there were plenty more elves, but they were dismounting and entering the city on foot.

"We need to get to the castle," Gwen said, turning to Kalan. "I'm sure Torian is holed up there, letting his soldiers do the dirty work."

"This place is crawling with them," Kalan replied. "I don't think we'll be able to reach the castle without having to fight our way there."

Gwen figured that would be the case, but she'd been hoping to have some luck otherwise. The sound of battle outside replaced the echo of marching hooves and feet. Cries of both agony and victory mingled with the clash of steel.

"The real fighting has begun," Kalan said grimly.

The elven soldiers on foot began passing by, rushing into the fray further down. Gwen watched as their numbers continued to pour down the street, surprised that Kirith had gathered so many men so quickly. She spotted Menjing among the crowd and stepped out of the building.

"Menjing! Over here!"

The mage glanced around and spotted her, then pushed his way across the street. His mages followed after him and they converged inside the building.

"We need to reach the castle, but Torian's men are everywhere. Can you help us clear the way?" Gwen asked.

"Yes, we can escort you there. What of the sorcerer from the wall?"

"He got away," Kalan said. "We killed his mage bodyguards, though."

"He's probably gone to the castle," Gwen said.

"I'm sure Grimmar will be waiting there for us."

"Torian will likely have his best soldiers and Prestiges there," Kalan added. "We're going to have one hell of a time getting inside."

Gwen considered Kalan's words and wondered what kind of Prestige Grimmar was. If he was a wizard, they would certainly be outmatched despite their numbers. She looked around the room. Each person looked back at her expectantly, waiting for her orders. She didn't want this responsibility, but there was no one else to take the mantle. They had come too far to worry about death now.

"Does anyone know the layout of the city?" Gwen asked. Silence met her question. "Very well. We'll just have to figure out the best route as we go."

"If we follow the wall around to the castle, that should mitigate how many soldiers we encounter," Kalan said. "Now that the gate is open, there's no need for the soldiers to man the walls. They've probably all been withdrawn into the city."

"Anybody opposed to that?" Gwen asked. Again, there was only silence. "Let's go."

Gwen and Kalan took the lead, turning back toward the gate until they reached the wall, then they ran along the wall's perimeter. Gwen continuously glanced left, right, up—wanting no surprises and taking no chances. Overhead, the dragons circled over the city. Gwen wondered why they weren't down in the streets helping fight. There was certainly enough room for their bulk to land. Gwen looked over her shoulder. Menjing and his mages were keeping pace. The buildings to their left provided cover from the side streets, and Gwen didn't see any soldiers on the wall. It seemed Kalan's assumption had been correct.

The castle was still a fair distance away. Gwen slowed to a brisk walk and tried to catch her breath, then asked Kalan, "Has Conal entered the city yet?"

There was a pause, then Kalan nodded. "Yes. Korla says they're inside the city. Conal's also headed for the castle."

"Is Korla as strong as you with her runes?"

"No. She has potential, but she's too fearful."

"Then we'd better hurry. If they reach the castle before us, Grimmar will slaughter them all."

They returned to a jog, but Gwen didn't feel they were moving fast enough. Her impatience was itching under her skin.

"I'm going ahead," Gwen said. "I'll make sure we're not entering a trap."

Before Kalan could argue, Gwen used her speed runes and left him and the others behind in a rush of wind. Her surroundings blurred around her, but as long as she kept her gaze straight ahead, she was able to see where she was going. The closer to the castle she got, the more she felt something heavy weighing on her. She tried to ignore it, but whatever it was would not be disregarded. It assaulted her mind with images, dark scenes of murdered dragons and large glittering eggs that had been destroyed.

Her breaths were coming in short gasps and her head began to ache. The pain pounded against her entire skull, and she saw tiny flecks of light shooting across her vision. She shook her head to clear them, which was a mistake. Her balance was thrown off and she had the sudden feeling that she was going to vomit.

Restore us, a multitude of voices spoke within her mind. *Bring us back to glory.*

"Who are you?" Gwen gasped. She tried to slow

down, but the magic was in full control. The voices in her mind were clouding her ability to cut the magic off.

We are the dead, dragons who were murdered by men in this very place. Restore us, princess. Restore us and make amends.

Murdered dragons? She didn't know what the voices were talking about. Their presence in her mind faded and she had control over her body again. She skidded to a halt. Ahead, the castle towered high into the sky. A group of soldiers guarded the entrance, and other groups were scattered around the courtyard.

She was trying to count their numbers when something caught her attention to her left. She looked just as it slammed into her, knocking her into the wall. Gwen's body exploded with pain and she collapsed to the ground. She looked up to see a tall figure dressed in black robes standing over her. The man smiled, but there was no joy in his expression, only gleeful madness.

A jagged scar ran down the left side of his face, from his forehead down over his eye, ending at his jawline. His hair was dark auburn and cut short. He had no facial hair, and his eyes were green and bloodshot. Gwen had never seen the man before, but she knew who he was.

Grimmar the Mage-breaker.

Grimmar held out his hand and the air rippled briefly before a massive battleax appeared. Gwen realized that she wasn't up against another mage. No, she had the unfortunate privilege of facing off against a wizard. She risked a glance back the way she'd come, but there was no sign of Kalan or the others. She cursed herself a fool, knowing she shouldn't have gone ahead without them.

Gwen slowly pushed herself up and stood. Grimmar made no move to stop her, and she didn't find that comforting at all. Her sword was on the ground at her feet, but she didn't dare make a move for it.

"Pick it up," Grimmar said. His voice was deep, and his accent was so thick it took her a moment to decipher what he'd said.

"Why? So you can cut my head off while I'm not looking?"

Grimmar laughed heartily, then shook his head. "I wouldn't do that, little mage. It wouldn't be fair. And contrary to what you may think about me, I am a fair man."

Gwen snorted. "Right. Is that why your namesake is mage-breaker? You are a Prestige who murders other Prestiges. There is no justifying that."

"Murder is the wrong word," Grimmar said, tilting his ax. He ran a finger over the blade, cutting the flesh. A few drops of blood slid across the blade, and it began to glow with an eerie light. He grinned, a smile full of dark secrets and lies.

"I'm an executioner."

CHAPTER 16

CONAL

In the hour before dawn, three dragons led the dwarven army through the doors into what appeared to be a vast empty room carved out of the mountain. Glow stones lining the center of the ceiling gave dim light to the enormous room. At the far end was another set of doors made of stone.

"Where are we?" Conal asked, expecting to be immediately in the streets and heading to the west gate.

"We are halfway between the west gate and the citadel," Derryth replied, purposely slowing her pace so the dwarves could keep up.

"What is this place?"

"It is a secret place, a refuge when Havengarde was still Dragon-home. We knew even then that man would not let us live in peace." Derryth stopped and glanced around the empty space. "I remember coming here when Havengarde was falling. There were seventy-five of us then. We escaped the way we came in. Now there are eleven." She turned a harsh stare on him. "I have compromised our future because I trust you."

"We've already talked about this, remember?"

Conal shot back then relaxed. "Besides, I like living near the coast."

Derryth frowned and resumed leading the way. Pausing at the doors, she said, "These doors have not been opened in over one hundred and fifty years." Reaching up, she pressed a stone in the wall. "May this room never be used again." Twisting her head to look back at Storri, she said, "Go to the right when you exit here. This is the outer wall. Follow it all the way to the west gate."

The stone doors silently swung open and the morning air swept into the room. The dragons burst through, unfurled their wings and leaped into the air. The dwarf army spilled out behind them, flowing onto the wide streets and fanning out, some heading towards the gate, others ascending the stairs to take control of the ramparts.

Conal stood to the side, momentarily getting his bearings. The doors behind him were cleverly concealed as part of the city walls that blended into the steep sides of the mountain. Tall buildings across the street blocked any view of the city and he suddenly felt clueless as to where anything was. Deciding to get a better view, he followed those clambering up the stairs then suddenly realized the sky was brighter than it should be at this time in the morning. But the brightness seemed to pulse like someone shooting off fireworks

He also found it odd that it was far too quiet here. That lasted until he was halfway up the flight of stone steps when horns blared, and the clamor of gongs filled the air along with shouts of warning. Racing up the rest of the steps, he paused only a moment to see three dragons spewing fire onto the streets below.

Kicking in his speed rune, Conal raced along the

ramparts leaving his dwarven compatriots far behind, bowling over unsuspecting guards whose attention diverted to the dwarves swarming in the streets below.

Halfway to the gatehouse, Conal saw a mage hurling down fist sized fireballs that exploded and spread on the dwarves below. Unaware of Conal's rapid approach, he lifted an arm to toss another fireball when pain exploded as Conal sliced through his arm at the shoulder, the limb flopping onto the stone paving. Blood spurted out as the mage wheeled around and fell to the street below, only to be trampled by the dwarves heading for the gate.

Pressing on another fifty paces, Conal suddenly stopped, confronted by a mage standing in the middle of the rampart, waiting for him. Without a word, the mage flicked a lightning bolt at him.

Conal easily dodged the bolt and closed the gap, raising his sword to strike. Yet the mage was equally fast and Conal swung into empty air, only to find the mage behind him. Spinning around, Conal jerked his head just in time as a fireball flew by him. At the same instant, he flung his sword at the mage whose shocked face morphed to impending doom as the sword's point penetrated through his ribs and pierced his heart.

Wasting no time, Conal yanked the sword free from the crumbled body and resumed his race to the west gate. Thankfully no more mages appeared, and, leaving a path of destruction, he reached the gatehouse well ahead of the dwarves below. Bounding down the stone steps attached to the walls, he hustled around to open the gate, surprised by the dozen soldiers standing watchful guard.

"Yield," he commanded, brandishing his sword.

"The city is about to fall."

The sergeant of the guard, a well-built muscular man, pointed at him and smirked, waving his hands in pretend fright. "One against twelve. We're so scared." His mocking jeer abruptly vanished when the streets behind Conal suddenly filled with charging dwarves.

"Yield," Conal encouraged. "You don't have to die."

"Death before dishonor," the sergeant cried out and leaped for Conal as the swarm dwarves crashed upon them.

In mere seconds, the sergeant and the other soldiers were cut to pieces, not one soldier yielding. Frowning at the willingness to die in the face of overwhelming odds, Conal wondered why such men would choose to do so. Did Torian command that much respect?

"We need help, m'Lord," a dwarf called out, snapping Conal out of his reverie.

The support bars holding the crossbeams were just high enough to prevent dwarves from pushing the crossbeams out. Conal strode through the mass and, using his strength rune, effortlessly lifted the two crossbeams out of the way.

The dwarves watched in shocked silence for each crossbeam required at least two men to lift.

"C'mon," Conal ordered, oblivious to their stares. "Let's get these doors open."

Pulling the doors open, Conal grabbed a torch from the wall sconce and waved it side to side, immediately pleased to see Lorkan's army surging forward, Lorkan in front.

"We saw the dragons," Lorkan exclaimed, running up, " and knew you had gotten in."

Storri appeared by Conal's side with a smile for Lorkan. "Good to see you, my friend."

"And you too, my friend," Lorkan answered with a grin. "Ready?"

"Ready and willing."

"Then let's deliver a kingdom."

"Where's Korla?" Conal asked.

"She's coming," Lorkan chuckled as Korla worked her way through the soldiers.

"Drustan and Meinir?" Conal asked.

"Haven't seen them, along with the others. Don't worry, they'll show up in time."

Korla arrived with Awstyn right behind her.

Directing his attention to Awstyn, Conal pointed to the east. "Awstyn will connect with Gwen's force. Storri's and Lorkan's armies will sweep this half of the city. I'm headed to the citadel with Korla."

"Me?" she squeaked.

"Yes," Conal said, "in case I need your magic."

"We're wasting time," Storri growled.

"Right," Conal nodded. "Let's move out."

Dawn's light rimmed the mountains. Expecting to see dragon's overhead, Conal frowned at the absence of the massive beasts, wondering where they disappeared to. Dismissing them from his thoughts, he headed to the closest main thoroughfare, Korla racing to keep up. Lorkan's and Storri's army moved in sync, fanning out and pushing up through three of the main roads to the citadel.

Conal felt like he was in a tunnel with no roof. Though the street was broad, the buildings that lined both sides rose four and five stories high. The original dragon doors had much smaller doors cut into them, adapting to the size of humans. He wondered why humans would want to live in a city better suited to dragons.

At first, resistance was light with Torian's soldiers retreating in the face of the larger enemy. But with the citadel in sight, resistance stiffened, and archers rained down arrows from upper story windows, causing the armies to slow down for house to house fighting.

Conal's armies pressed forward, the enemy choosing to fight and die than surrender. Conal's speed, endurance, and strength caused him to slice through the enemy, the gaps behind him filled with dwarves wielding broad axes, widening the swath of hacked bodies and the dying. Korla did her best to contribute, flinging small fireballs or lightning bolts. Though effective, her insecurity with her own powers caused her to second guess her abilities.

By the time they reached the wide piazza where the seven streets joined just before the steps to the citadel, the fighting intensified with more of Torian's soldiers pouring out of the multi-storied edifice to join their comrades. Yet the combined strength of Conal's armies overpowered the defenders and they slowly fell back in a retrograde defense, taking the battle inside the citadel.

Once inside, Conal hacked his way through the melee, dragging Korla behind him, up flights of stairs and down hallways.

"You know where you're going?" Korla panted, running to keep up with Conal.

"No," he replied, his sword at the ready as he led her down another hallway that abruptly intersected with a series of adjoining hallways.

"O my God," Korla blurted as Madlyn stepped into the hallway.

"Hello dearie," she grinned. "'bout time you got

here."

Conal swung his blade to meet her.

"No need for that," Madlyn said, shaking her head then flicking her hand to the right and sending a fireball the size of a large watermelon down the hall to her right.

Conal and Korla turned their heads in unison to watch the fireball explode upon a dozen of Torian's soldiers.

"Whose side are you on?" Conal demanded.

"Yours, of course." She frowned at him, the answer obvious.

"You expect us to believe that," Korla sneered, "when you ran off to your master here?"

Madlyn rolled her eyes. "First, I have no master." She flicked a fireball down the hallway to her left. Instead of exploding, it spread like a sheet across the hall, blocking the hallway. "Second, of course I've been working for Torian. How else ya think I could discover his plans?"

"You're telling me you're a double agent?" Conal cocked an eyebrow in doubt.

"Ain't it obvious?" she replied, frowning at them then shaking her head in exasperation. "Think. What happened in Blasingdon? Do ya really think Torian would allow that to happen?" She gave Conal a hard stare. "You were supposed to be dead long before now. Ain't dead, are ya?"

"Then why did you leave?" Korla challenged.

"Figured you'd get here," she replied, tapping a finger to her nose. "Also figured you'd get lost unless ya had someone to guide ya."

"You know where Torian is?" Conal's eyes blinked wide as he lowered the tip of his sword.

"Of course, dearie," she grinned and winked.

"Follow me." She curled a hand at him.

"I don't trust you," Korla snapped. "You're too smooth, too slick. You have an answer for everything."

Madlyn leveled a gaze at her. "It's easy to have the answers when ya knows the questions."

"You see?" Korla complained, turning to Conal. "That's exactly what I'm talking about."

Madlyn narrowed her gaze at Conal. "Yer wastin' time, dearie. Ya want this kingdom or not?"

Conal's lips pursed for an indecisive moment. "Lead on."

Madlyn turned and headed down a wide hallway. "This way."

"You're going to trust her?" Korla blurted, catching up to them.

"Might as well," he cavalierly replied, though his suspicious eyes scanned the hallway.

Madlyn set a quick pace, flinging lightning darts of fireballs as they progressed. Conal noted that the numbers of enemy soldiers increased at each junction. At one intersection, well-lit with ornate sideboards against the walls, Conal battled five soldiers while Madlyn and Korla dispatched twenty more. The next intersection proved even more troubling as fifty soldiers poured into the gap. Yet, with Conal's rune-might and Madlyn's and Korla's mage strength, they managed to overwhelm the enemy.

But cuts on all three of them caused Conal to warn, "We can't take much more of this."

"Posh," Madlyn replied, casting a disdainful glance at the cut on her arm. "Mere scratches." She paused and focused her concentration on her cuts, which closed and healed. She grinned at Conal, about to offer healing, when her jaw slacked open. "Your cuts… they're gone."

"Yeah," he shrugged. "I'm a quick healer."

"Not *that* quick," Madlyn marveled. "Has it always been so?"

"Yes."

They looked in unison at Korla who was struggling to perform self-healing, her frustration evident.

"You're tryin' too hard, dearie. Relax. Let your energy flow into yourself."

Korla tried relaxing but to no avail. "I still can't do it," she whined.

Madlyn gave her a quick once-over. "Yer not that hurt. I'll teach ya how to do it when we finish here. C'mon."

Arriving at the next intersection, Conal was surprised that no one was there.

"We're almost there," Madlyn reassured him.

Focusing ahead, Conal saw that the hallway ended, and he picked up the pace.

"Slow down, dearie. We'll get there in time."

Conal slid a glance at the mage, puzzled at her casual demeanor.

They stopped at the edge of the hall, peering into the vast piazza where the seven hallways met. Except for the numerous sideboards, tapestries, wall sconces, display tables, statues and other artwork, it was empty. Madlyn pointed across the expanse to the set of towering doors tall enough for a dragon to pass through.

"He's in there."

Conal stepped into the piazza, expecting to see soldiers suddenly swarming out from the other hallways, but nothing happened. Looking over his shoulder at Madlyn, he smiled. Lowering his voice, he asked, "Who else is in there?"

Madlyn shrugged. "Don't know. Usual he has Grimmar with him. But there'd be other mages hangin' about here."

"Guess I'll find out." He turned and strode across the floor.

"Aren't you going to help?" Korla fussed at Madlyn.

"Can't do no more," she replied. "You and me need to protect out here."

"But suppose he has mages in there?" Korla argued.

"He might," she agreed then ticked her head at him. "But if he's the one of prophecy, it don't matter."

Korla's frantic stare followed Conal as he approached the smaller set of doors cut into the thick wood of the grand set of doors. Her voice a whisper, she muttered, "Suppose he's not the promised one."

"Then you and me better find a place to hide."

Conal stood before the doors and inhaled a deep breath. Reaching for the handle, he twisted it and pulled the door open and stepped inside the throne room, a vast cavern of impossible height and scintillating walls. At the far end and in the middle of an otherwise empty room, a throne perched on a platform with seven steps leading up to the single throne. A sturdy muscular man with a full dark beard sat on the throne, a drawn sword across his lap. He looked up when Conal entered.

The man's voice carried across the room as though he were standing right next to Conal.

"So you're the brat who's come to take my throne. I should have killed you when I had the chance."

CHAPTER 17

GWEN

Grimmar lifted the ax above his head and his body began to glow with the same light as his weapon. Heat and power radiated from him, so powerful that Gwen had to use her might rune just to stay on her feet. Even then, it was almost too much. When he spoke, the words rolled over her like a thunderclap.

Gwen covered her ears against the sound, tears streaking down her cheeks. He took a step toward her and the ground trembled with his power. The buildings shook around them, and Gwen knew that she would not survive against him. In a blur of movement, she dropped down and retrieved her blade, then tried to stab Grimmar in the stomach as she came back up.

There was a clang of metal as Grimmar's ax blocked her sword. He rotated his wrist, locking her blade between the ax head and the handle, then jerked back. Gwen's sword was ripped from her grasp and it went sailing away, clattering to the ground somewhere behind Grimmar. Before she could react, Grimmar backhanded her. She flew backward, striking the wall again with a crunch, then bounced off to the ground.

She didn't know for sure, but she thought some of her ribs were broken. Gwen whispered the word, "*Leighis.*" The magic began healing her, but it was a slow process. Gwen lurched to her feet, pushing the pain into the back of her mind. She matched Grimmar's intense stare.

I'm going to die, she thought.

And then she rushed him, lifting her left hand. She got close enough to touch his chest before letting off a blast of lightning. Grimmar grunted as he was thrown backward from the concussive force. Thin trails of smoke rose from his robes, but otherwise, he seemed unfazed.

"You've got nerve, I'll give you that. Most of the mages I killed cowered and begged for their life."

"I don't beg," Gwen snapped.

"We'll see."

Grimmar stomped his right foot down. The cobblestones of the street heaved upward, forcing Gwen's balance off. She staggered and tried to keep from rolling her ankle, quickly diving aside. She tumbled a few times, then got back up. Grimmar was there in the blink of an eye, his glowing ax coming straight at her head.

Gwen used her speed rune and stepped out of the way just in time, the air from his swing brushing the side of her face. She dropped to one knee and used her other leg to spin herself around. Using the might rune, she drove her fist into the back of Grimmar's leg, just behind his knee. To her surprise, it worked. The blow forced his leg to bend and he fell forward onto the ground. She stood and leaped into the air, intending to land on him and use her drain life rune.

She crashed to the ground, the air knocked from

her lungs. Grimmar was already gone. She rolled onto her back and saw him standing over her, the ax poised inches away from her neck.

"This has been fun, but I've got a rebellion to crush," he said. The madness in his eyes had intensified, and Gwen pondered for the briefest moment whether or not he was possessed by some foul spirit.

The ax rose and fell, and Gwen snapped her eyes shut, not wanting to see her death coming. Something heavy landed on her and there was a clang. Gwen opened her eyes to see Kalan's face right above hers, his excited grin plastered across his lips.

"If you wanted me on top of you, all you had to do is ask," he said with a chuckle.

And then he was pulled off of her as Grimmar grabbed him by the back of his shirt, flinging Kalan across the courtyard. Gwen didn't worry about him. His stone skin rune could take the beating. Gwen rolled out of Grimmar's range and got up, her ribcage burning with fire. Menjing and the others were there, too. They quickly encircled Grimmar, closing off any escape.

"You're outnumbered," Menjing said. "Give up or die."

Grimmar turned a slow circle, looking at each mage. And then he laughed.

"Fools! This battle is already won." Grimmar tossed his ax aside, but instead of falling to the ground, it spun end-over-end through the air and cut down three of the mages. Their forms crumpled; puddles of blood rapidly growing around them. The ax landed in one of the puddles and the glowing intensified.

Gwen stared in horror. With barely any effort,

he'd slain three people. He was a monster, and he was unstoppable.

No one in unstoppable, Lyra's voice echoed in her mind. *Even dragons can be killed.*

And apparently, they could read minds without permission. Gwen looked at the ax as it began to shake, then it flew through the air of its own accord, striking down another two mages. Those who remained used their runes to erect barriers around themselves. Gwen wished she'd taken a rune like that, and as if in answer, Kalan appeared at her side and used his barrier rune to protect them both.

Grimmar held his hand out and the ax returned, then he gripped the hilt and it vanished.

"Enough games," he growled. Grimmar lifted his arms into the air and clenched his hands into fists. The ground rumbled and the sky began to darken with unnatural black clouds. A myriad of lightning bolts dropped from the heavens, striking everyone and everything within the circle of mages. Cries of anguish and surprise rang out as the blasts cracked and shattered some of the barriers, killing those within.

Dust and smoke blotted out everything. Gwen coughed and covered her face with her arm, peering vainly into the swirling chaos. A dark shape came toward her, swift and silent. Grimmar's face appeared in front of the barrier and Gwen screamed involuntarily, scrambling back. He cackled in response, every laugh laced with his insanity.

Kalan's shield was still intact, but Grimmar tapped it with his finger and it flickered and died. Kalan stepped in front of him, blocking Gwen. He started to summon his spiked ball of energy, but Grimmar grabbed him by the throat and lifted him off the ground. Kalan clawed at Grimmar's hand, his feet kicking wildly in the air as he was strangled.

Gwen used her might rune and quickly placed one hand on Grimmar's wrist, and the other on his elbow. She pulled back on his wrist and pushed his elbow in the opposite direction. The was an audible crack as Grimmar's bones broke. Gwen felt bile rising into her throat and swallowed, forcing it back down. Grimmar's grasp on Kalan's neck was released, and he staggered to the side, gasping.

Grimmar hadn't flinched. He pulled his broken arm close to his body and lifted his other arm toward Gwen. His palm glimmered briefly, and then a blast of cold air sent Gwen reeling. She shivered uncontrollably and her teeth chattered. She felt as if she'd suddenly been thrown into winter. Her lips barely moved for her to call on her fire rune, and the word came out as nothing more than a whisper.

Flames roared from her right hand, striking the ground around her feet. The heat warmed her and pushed the cold away, enabling her to direct the flames at Grimmar. He came at her anyway, the flames casting themselves aside from his presence. Gwen cut the magic off and hit him with another lightning bolt as he reached her, his hand going for her throat. The blast knocked him back a few steps, but he recovered quickly and came right back at her. Grimmar snatched her up by the neck as he had with Kalan.

She gasped as her vision exploded with lights. Grimmar squeezed hard, but Gwen managed to wheeze the name of her might rune. A wave of strength flooded her body, strengthening her enough to keep him from crushing her windpipe. She kicked at him vainly, the blows accomplishing nothing.

Behind Grimmar, the smoke had cleared to reveal the massacre. Many of the mages were dead, their bodies nothing more than smoldering lumps of charred flesh. Darkness was creeping around the edges of Gwen's vision, but she forced herself to look at the destruction, to burn the sight into her memory. The gruesomeness fueled her somehow, giving strength to the dark rune. Gwen clutched Grimmar's hand.

"*Draein saoil,*" she whispered.

Grimmar's eyes widened.

The madness was still there, but Gwen spotted something else. Fear. He tried to release her, but the dark rune would not be refused. It kept him rooted in place, siphoning the life and vitality from him. The energy filled Gwen, renewing her. The healing rune flared within her mind, and her ribs healed instantly. Grimmar's strength was fading, and he dropped to his knees. Gwen pulled his hand away from her throat, but she didn't let him go. She would not show him mercy as she had with Aimil.

Grimmar tried to speak, but all the came out of his mouth was garbled noise. Blood flecked his lips as he gagged, and more trailed from his nostrils. His eyes shrank into his head and his skin became loose. He aged rapidly before her eyes, but she didn't feel revulsion this time.

She felt pleasure.

"You will never again cause torment," she hissed, watching as the look in his eyes became pleading. Gwen clenched her jaw and forced the rest of the energy from his body. The life in his eyes faded, and only then did she let go of him.

She stood over his lifeless form for a long while in silence. She expected to feel guilt or shame for taking his life with the dark rune. Instead, she felt nothing at all. Her emotions were completely absent, her heart hollow and empty. There was movement beside her, and she slowly became aware of Kalan's voice. She looked at him blankly.

"We're not finished yet," he said.

Gwen looked past him and saw a group of robed figures coming toward them, and they didn't look like allies. She nodded at Kalan and pushed past him. She took a few steps and stopped, waiting calmly.

"What are you doing?" Kalan asked. "Get inside my shield!"

She ignored him. Torian's followers would never stop. Whether they were under the influence of magic or some distorted sense of loyalty, she didn't know, nor did she care. All she knew was that death was never satisfied. And neither was the dark rune. It was pulsing across every inch of her body, begging to release the energy it had consumed. Gwen didn't think, she just reacted, letting the rune guide her.

The nearest mage was torn to pieces by a swarm of shadows. Another was sucked into a dark hole that had no end. Gwen tore through their ranks methodically and sadistically. She forced a man to pick up a sword and impale himself. Somewhere in the back of her mind, she knew she was no longer in control of anything. The dark rune dictated her moves, her thoughts. She touched a woman and gave her a disease that ate her alive as Gwen watched.

If she was to become a monster, then this was how she wanted it. A tool of justice, dealing out death to those who deserved it. The remaining mage fell to the last of the dark rune's energy, her skin flayed from her body while she was alive. As the power of the rune faded, Gwen slowly started to feel like herself again.

She surveyed the carnage wordlessly. Had she really killed Grimmar and his mages by herself? She turned around and saw Kalan. He was staring at her as if she were a creature he'd never seen before.

"Where's Conal?" she asked, looking to the castle. "Is he inside the castle?"

Kalan didn't answer. He just continued to stare at her. Gwen walked toward him. She thought he was going to run away from her, but he stayed where he was. She reached him and wrapped her arms around him, then broke into tears.

Kalan hesitantly hugged her back.

CHAPTER 18

CONAL

Sword in hand, Torian slowly rose from the throne. "That you made it this far speaks persistence." He snorted a derisive laugh. "Though do you really think your presence here is because you're some great warrior?"

"Does it matter?" Conal shot back, taking measure of the man. "I'm here."

Torian descended the stairs in slow casual steps. Expecting to see him in royal garb, Conal frowned in surprise to see him dressed for combat, but then figured it was logical since Havengarde was under attack. And then he remembered this man was his father's brother. Was there a resemblance?

"You're here because I wanted to see you for myself." Torian's voice was firm and strong. "Come closer and let me see you."

Conal strode half the distance to Torian, studying him as he approached. The dark beard and hair were flecked with grey. He wore a thin circlet of gold with an emerald in the shape of an eagle in the center. For all Torian's bravura, Conal noticed the occasional shimmer of chainmail beneath the sleeveless tunic of thick leather. Conal smirked to himself. The man was taking no chances. Still, the muscular arms said he had not been idle these past twenty plus years.

"Well, *Uncle*," Conal said. "Here I am." It was then he noticed that Torian's arms were covered in runes.

"Come closer."

"Why don't you come here?"

"As you wish."

Torian touched his speed rune and in an instant was upon Conal who stepped aside just as Torian's down stroke swung at him. On instinct, Conal raised the sword above his head and felt the heavy clang of Torian's second stroke. He bent down and swirled, his sword outstretched hoping to catch Torian's legs, but all he felt was empty air. Instinct had him leap and roll as Torian's sword banged against the floor.

Torian came at him with a flurry of thrusts and jabs, forcing him backwards. Yet with each parry, Conal noticed the force of Torian's strikes seemed to lessen.

Abruptly, Torian stopped his attack and gave Conal a haughty stare. "You fight well. I'm impressed." In a surprise move, he turned his back on Conal and walked back towards the center of the room then turned to face him.

He shook his head at his nephew and sneered, "You don't have the heart to command. I gave you opportunity to attack me from behind and you simply let me walk away."

"Only cowards attack from behind," Conal retorted.

"Cowardice has nothing to do with it. It's called 'opportunity.' You take advantage whenever it appears. That's what kings do."

"No, that's what *you* do. A true king doesn't have

to rule by fear and intimidation. A true king is loved by his subjects. No one loves you."

Torian's arrogant smile vanished. "Bold words from a whelp with no experience."

"Experience has nothing to do with it. Truth is truth. It's a fool who won't accept truth."

Torian's nostrils flared and he composed himself. "Did you come here to bore me to death?"

"No," Conal firmly replied. "I came here for restitution. Death is merely the end state."

"Then you have greatly erred, for it is you who will die."

"I guess we'll see, won't we?"

"You've forgotten one very important point," Torian mocked.

"Oh?"

Pointing to his crown, he said, "You see the stone of the eagle. I'm sure you've been told the prophecy."

"I have."

"The eagle will bear the vipers in its claws. You know that I am the eagle. You and your pathetic sister are vipers, though that is stretching the imagination a bit. But, the result is that you two lose."

Conal sniffed in derision. "You've conveniently left out the most important part. From the west a cobra will rise and strike down the eagle." Conal jerked up his sleeve, revealing the Cobra brand on his shoulder, the brand now a dazzling tattoo of shimmering greens and gold.

Torian stiffened, exclaiming, "Impossible."

Energized, Conal closed the gap between them, attacking a surprised Torian who found himself pressed backwards before parrying and delivering counter blows.

The two opponents traded strikes and jabs,

circling around the throne room floor as the battle progressed.

"I'm surprised you haven't called in reinforcements," Conal taunted as they exchanged blows. "Or would that be admitting your weakness?"

"Weakness," Torian roared, arcing down a powerful hit that Conal easily blocked. "I should have killed you when I had the chance."

"You said that before," Conal mocked. "But then I suppose that's what you're good at, killing babies and women."

With an angry growl, Torian increased his attack, his frustration growing that Conal simply blocked or deflected each strike yet didn't attack himself, as though he was toying with him. At the same time, he felt his strength giving way and silently cursed Grimmar for convincing him he didn't need the strength rune, that he was strong enough and besides, he had others to do his bidding.

But what about all the other runes he had marked on his body? An image flashed of the excruciating pain he endured accepting the speed rune. Truth was, he had nearly died. Only Grimmar's ministrations saved him.

But these other runes? Grimmar convinced him he didn't need fighting runes, that he was powerful enough as he was. What he needed was mystical and magic runes, runes about insight and knowledge. None of the magic runes had worked. In that instant, facing his nemesis, the epiphany burst, and he realized that all the runes he had on his body were nothing more than sugar pills meant to placate him. He had seen what happened to others who demanded rune marks only to horribly suffer and die, for they were not mage-marked.

But surely he was mage-marked. He had to be. He was the king.

Doubt creeped in and Torian knew he needed time to regroup, to come up with a plan to destroy his brother's kids. Where was Grimmar? He was supposed to be here. What was taking him so long?

Sensing indecision, Conal pressed a furious attack, his strength rune dominating the weakening Torian. Suddenly, Torian delivered a series of strikes that momentarily caught Conal on the defense. He was about to step back when Torian spun around and fled towards the rear of the room behind the throne podium.

Surprised at the retreat, Conal reached into his pocket and retrieved a throwing star. He had never used one before, but now seemed like a good time. Praying that the rune-mark worked, he flung it at Torian just as he opened a secret door in the wall. Torian let out a startled grunt of pain as the star tore into his thigh, causing him to stumble and drop to his knees.

By the time Conal had raced across the room, Torian had managed to stand and stagger through the opening. Conal stuck a foot in the doorway to prevent its closing. Yanking it open, he stepped onto a broad landing with five sets of spiral stairs, three ascending and two descending. Torian was nowhere in sight.

Thankful for the embedded glow stones, Conal rapidly scanned the landing, thinking that, with Torian wounded, it would be easier to descend than climb. Glancing down at the floor, he hoped for a telltale sign of blood, but there was none. It wasn't until he checked the second descending staircase that he saw the throwing star on the ground and the bloodied handprint on the railing.

Descending the stairs brought him to long hallway lit with glow stones. Torian was halfway down, hand on the wall for support, dragging his left leg. Blood continued seeping from the deep gash in the back of his thigh. Conal was on him in an instant, bypassing him then spinning around to confront him.

"We haven't finished."

Torian looked up at him, a mixture of anger and fear in his eyes. Inhaling a deep breath, he leveled a paternal stare at Conal. "You just don't understand. Your father was tearing apart everything our family had spent hundreds of years building. You think I wanted his death. He just wouldn't listen. I had to do something."

"Murder my entire family?" Conal retorted.

"That wasn't my fault. Some individuals I called friends thought they were doing me a favor. I found out too late. Surely you believe me."

Doubt slipped into Conal's determination as Torian's voice had a calming effect.

"What about my family in Urve?"

"I knew nothing about that," Torian said, his voice soothing and melodious. "As soon as I found out, I had the perpetrators executed."

"Really?" Conal lowered his sword.

"Yes. I know you believe me. Now come. Help me get to a physician."

Conal took a step forward when a voice rang out. "Liar."

Torian turned as Conal looked past his shoulder to see Madlyn storming up the hallway, Korla on her heels.

"Liar," Madlyn again exclaimed. She stared at Conal. "Can't you see he's using his voice to sway you?" She snapped her head to glare at Torian.

"You're just like Havyrd Smooth-tongue – all mouth and no brains."

"Shut up, woman," Torian seethed. "Why are you here? You're supposed to be helping Grimmar."

"Grimmar doesn't need my help," she replied then pointed a finger at Conal. "Besides, he needs to hear the truth from you, the man who killed his family."

Torian flipped his sword up to stab her only to have it deflected by Conal's blade. Torian twisted his head to look at him, pitiful eyes pleading for understanding. "I'm your uncle, your own flesh and blood."

Conal felt a surge of guilt and stepped back.

"Stop it," Madlyn scolded. "He's using an emotions voice-rune."

"Don't listen to her," Torian continued, his leg throbbing. "She's a traitor. You can't trust her. Listen to me. You need to help me. You shouldn't have hurt me like you did."

"I'm… I'm sorry." Frowning, Conal gazed down at his sword as though he couldn't understand how it came to be in his hands. His first inclination was to toss it on the floor, but that didn't seem right.

"Does it hurt?" Madlyn interrupted, smacking Torian's wound.

"The gods damn you, woman," Torian roared, cringing in pain as he awkwardly stepped away.

In that instant, Torian's voice spell broke and Conal woke to his surroundings.

At the same time, Korla stepped around Madlyn and placed a hand on Torian's shoulder. "Here. Let me help. *Glórach an Bás.*"

Expecting the pain to subside and the wound to heal, Torian waited but a few moments before excoriating her. "That didn't do anything, you stupid woman."

"Ah well," Korla shrugged. "Sometimes it works and sometimes it doesn't."

Torian felt the point of Conal's sword at his side. Turning his head to face him, he used his most persuasive voice. "These two are thorns in our sides. You need to get me to a physician. Then we need to talk about co-ruling. You'd like that, wouldn't you?"

Conal barked a laugh. "Co-ruling? Are you serious? You're not ruling anything anymore."

Torian's eyes blinked wide and he refocused his voice. "But you *want* to rule with me. I'm your uncle. You'd never want to harm me."

"What gave you that idea?" Conal challenged. "I've come to end this, remember?"

Madlyn shifted a glance at Korla, dipping her head in respect.

"You two need to step away," Conal told the two mages before turning his full attention on Torian. "Like I said, it's time to end this."

Dumbfounded, Torian stared at them before tossing his sword on the floor. Glaring defiantly at Conal, he said, "I won't fight you. You'll have to kill an unarmed man."

"Just like you killed my unarmed family in Urve," Conal retorted, swinging his blade.

Torian dodged the attack, grabbing his sword in the process, before limping back several steps then turning to force his legs to carry him down the hallway.

Conal let him go until Torian was almost at the far door at the end. Withdrawing another throwing star, he whipped it down the hall with such intensity that it completely sliced through the chainmail and imbedded itself in Torian's back, propelling him forward to crash onto the floor.

"Stay here," Conal ordered the two mages. An instant later, he stood over the prostrate body of his uncle who was struggling to push himself to his knees. Conal patiently waited until Torian sat on his haunches, blood gushing out of the wound in his back.

"Any last words?" Conal coldly asked.

"Go to hell," he snarled, spitting blood.

"Not very original," Conal taunted, "but they'll do. Remember this?" He pulled back the sleeve to show the Cobra brand. "It will be the last thing you remember." In a powerful stroke, he sliced though Torian's neck.

Torian's head momentarily wavered before rolling forward and down to the floor. His body sat back then slowly flopped to the side.

Though watching Conal stare down at his uncle, Madlyn spoke to Korla. "That was very clever of you, dearie."

"Thank you," Korla smiled. "It was all I could think of at the moment."

"Where'd you learn the spell to counter a voice rune?"

"It was one of the things I was taught. Never thought I'd ever use it."

Madlyn turned to her and placed a gentle hand on her arm. "You're gonna be a great mage, dearie."

Korla studied the older mage. "Were you really working for us all along?"

"How else ya think he and all the others knew what was going on here?" She turned back to gaze at Conal. "He's gonna need our help. He'll have to undo all of Torian's wickedness. That'll take time. And of course, there's the dragons to consider."

581

CHAPTER 19

GWEN

Torian is dead. Korla saw Conal strike the killing blow."

Gwen pulled back from Kalan and wiped her tears. "Then it *is* over," she said. "We did it. We've taken back the throne."

"There are still many things to do, but the worst has passed," Kalan replied.

"Come on, let's go find Conal."

They walked across the piazza where seven streets conjoined and headed up the stairs into the castle. Bodies littered the area, and Gwen was forced to tread carefully to keep from slipping in the blood that soaked the cobblestones.

The inside of the castle was just as bad, if not worse. The bodies of both groups littered the halls. Gwen navigated through the carnage and reached the throne room as Conal and two women stepped out from behind the throne.

"Korla!" Kalan exclaimed.

Gwen looked at the woman who rushed forward and embraced Kalan. Although they were twins, Gwen had come to know they were more different than alike. The other woman stayed at Conal's side.

There was something odd about her, but Gwen dismissed the thought and looked at Conal. He seemed different somehow, but she wasn't sure what it was.

"You killed him," Gwen said, a statement more than a question.

"Yes," Conal replied.

Gwen nodded, remaining silent for a moment. "Was it difficult?"

"A little," he admitted. "These bone runes gave me an advantage, though."

"I meant… emotionally. Knowing that he was your—our—uncle, did that change anything?"

Conal was quiet a moment. "Not really. It's not like there was any sort of bond. And then all I had to do was remind myself that he killed my family… our family."

Gwen listened to his words, but her mind kept replaying the slaughter she'd committed. Grimmar's mages were evil, she knew, but it didn't change the fact that what she'd done had been overkill. There was something wrong with her, and she knew the dark rune was responsible. She needed to find a way to get rid of it.

Conal stopped talking and looked behind her, and she turned to see Venia and several other dragons had entered the throne room. There were a few she didn't recognize. One of them stepped forward and turned its gaze on Conal.

"We summon you to fulfill your oath." The dragon's deep voice echoed off the walls. Gwen didn't understand what that meant, and she turned back to look at her brother.

"What oath? What are they talking about? Are you in trouble?"

Gwen glanced over her shoulder at the dragons. They didn't look menacing, but there was something about their demeanors that told Gwen there could potentially be an issue. The dark rune thrummed in her veins, urging her to do insidious things.

"There's something I need to tell you. This is Derryth. Princess Derryth. She's the leader of the dragons that are left. I'm not sure how much you know about Isentol, but it was originally the home of dragons, and it's the only place where they can breed. I've agreed to hand the kingdom over to them, and we will head west to take over Tir Manach."

Gwen felt a wave of anger wash over her at the fact that Conal had agreed to give the kingdom to the dragons after all their hard work and sacrifice, but she quickly calmed herself. She didn't want to lead a kingdom, and with Torian dead, that left Conal as the only option. It made sense that he would make that decision without her, but she still felt a slight sting to her pride.

"And what of our people here? Will they be forced from their homes?"

"No," Conal reassured her. "The dragons will need our help, food, and things like that. We'll also need people who will stand up for them… here."

As things were being decided, Gwen wondered what her purpose was. If Conal was going to lead, then what would she do? Perhaps she could attempt to find a way to rid herself of the dark rune? Without anyone needing her to lead them, she would be free to do as she pleased. The idea was tempting.

"I was hoping that you might consider staying here with some of your mages," Venia said.

"Staying here with you?" Gwen asked.

"Me and my kind," Venia clarified. "We will

need help and protection."

"Protection? From what? You are the most powerful creatures I've ever seen. What could possibly hurt you?"

"It surprises me how quickly humans forget," Venia said. "Do you not remember how I was almost killed? As long as my kind exists, there will always be those who seek to hunt us down."

Gwen shook her head, realizing her words probably made her sound foolish. She thought back to the previous night when the dragon hunters had mortally injured Venia with a magical weapon. Venia was right—dragons could be killed like any other species. Yet, was it her responsibility to offer that protection?

"I will consider it," Gwen said hesitantly. "There's something that I need to do before I can trust myself around others."

"The dark rune," Venia said.

"How did you know?" Gwen asked. And then she felt it. The subtle probing of her mind. "Stop doing that," Gwen said.

"You need to learn to close your mind from outside presences. If you stay here and help us, there are many things we can teach you. And maybe we can find a way to help you with the dark rune."

"Yes," Derryth chimed in. "We will help each other in beneficial ways. I will consider that the first step on the journey to building trust with humans again."

"Taking Havengarde back wasn't enough to prove that?" Gwen asked, snorting. "And where were you at? Once we entered the city, I didn't see you helping clear the way to the castle. I didn't see you fighting. You were flying safely high overhead.

Many of my people lost their lives to bring Torian down. And it turns out they bled for *you,* so I think that's worth more than a few steps."

"Calm down," Kalan said gently. "She could have phrased that better but imagine having everyone you know hunted down and killed."

"I know exactly what that's like," Gwen snapped.

"Perhaps we should talk about this elsewhere," Conal said to Derryth.

Gwen didn't care what they did. She stormed out of the throne room, fuming as she passed through the halls. By the time she exited the castle and breathed in some fresh air, she was barely holding back her tears. What was happening to her? She slumped onto the stairs and laid her head on her knees.

"It's the dark rune," Venia said from beside her. "It's infecting you from the inside."

"How do I stop it?" Gwen asked, lifting her head. The dragon had taken her elven form.

"I don't know. At least, not yet. But if we work together, I'm sure we will find a way. Dark magic is volatile, and those who use it have short lives. You've done well to control it so far, but you will need more self-control, especially if there isn't a way to rid yourself of it."

Gwen didn't want to consider that she might be forced to live with the rune for the rest of her life, but that was a possibility. She also had a decision to make. Should she live among dragons, or with her own kind? And then there was Conal. She'd lost so much time with her brother, but he was also a stranger to her. Should she go to Tir Manach with him? Could she?

"Your thoughts and emotions are at war with one another," Venia said.

"They always seem to be," Gwen muttered.

"Stay here with us," Venia said. "Take some time to rest and learn who you are."

"Rest? What is that?" Gwen laughed. "I don't think I would even know how to rest at this point." She heaved a sigh and looked out at the courtyard. "But it would be nice to do so. To have the choice."

"You do have the choice," Venia replied. "And the decision is up to you."

For the first time in a long while, Gwen felt as if that were true, as if she weren't being forced into some destiny that she had no control over. It felt … freeing. She stood up and looked at Venia.

"I'll do it," she said. "I'll stay."

CHAPTER 20

CONAL

In the mid-morning daylight, Conal stood on the crest of the road where the forest ended and empty farm fields surrounding the city of Blasingdon began. The armies of Storri and Lorkan spread behind him. Above him, vultures circled the skies, waiting opportunity to descend to continue their feast on the dead.

It felt odd to be here. Well… maybe 'odd' wasn't the right word. Gwen, his sister – he'd have to get used to saying that – had remained in Havengarde, at home with the dragons and mages. Was he disappointed? Part of him had expected her to be here with him, conquering Tir Manach, then ruling as king and queen. Another part said she had her own destiny to follow.

The parting had been more than amiable, though still awkward… sort of like being forced to give a hug to an aunt you've never seen before. Yet there was a connection, a bond that they both knew and felt… and a desire to know each other better, to form the real bond of a brother and sister.

Gwen had wanted him to stick around a little longer, but he knew if he didn't strike now, opportunity would slip through his fingers. Besides, once he had conquered Tir Manach, he could come back to Havengarde anytime he wanted. There'd be time to discover who his sister really was. For now, he had another kingdom to claim.

Storri came up to stand beside him. "Doesn't look like anyone's come back."

"Would you?"

"Probably not."

They stood in silence a moment, watching the macabre display. Conal glanced at the scouts in the distance as they emerged from the forest.

"I appreciate Rorkyn lending me your help."

"I do too," the dwarf grinned. "Haven't had this much fun in a long time."

Lorkan strode up to join them. "It seems strange to come back here," he said, "at the head of an army set to conquer my own kingdom."

"*Your* kingdom?" Storri teased.

"You know what I mean."

"Change is upon us," Conal mused with a thoughtful nod. "The dragons have returned. Time for new beginnings." He twisted his head to gaze Lorkan. "You still OK with this?"

"Why shouldn't he be?" Storri interjected. "He's going to be the kingdom's army commander."

Lorkan shot him a look of irritation. "That's not why I'm doing it."

Storri shook his head and chuckled. "You two need to lighten up. Torian's evil didn't die with him. There is still work to be done. My only disappointment is that Galadyr isn't here."

"And Voldar and Torgreth," Conal added.

"Rorkyn's support only goes so far," Storri observed with a wry grin. "Besides, those two are carvers not fighters."

"Still," Conal said, stepping forward, "I'm more than thankful that you two are here. Let's see what the scouts have to tell us."

The lead scout, a short wiry man, came bustling up, dropping to his knee before Conal.

"Don't do that," Conal frowned, reaching down to touch him on the shoulder. "Just give me your report."

"Besides," Storri pointed out, "we're at war and kneeling before the king lets the enemy spies know who he is."

The man's eyes bolted wide at the obvious mistake, and he gushed, "I'm so sorry, m'Lord."

"I know," Conal replied with a kind smile. "But from now on, let's just all stand and pretend like we're friends. What do you have?"

The man composed himself. "There's nothing at least two to three miles around. Seems too quiet, m'Lord. I don't like it."

"Why?"

"There should be some sort of activity, even if it was just scavengers in the city."

Conal nodded in agreement. "I know. Go ahead and push on out to Pencord."

"Yes, m'Lord." He started to bow then caught himself, unsure what to do.

"Just go," Lorkan said.

"Yes, Commander."

As the man ran off, Conal turned to a runner nearby. "Find Madlyn and bring her here."

"Yes, my Lord."

"We can't sit here all day," Storri groused.

"I know," Conal mused. "Just a couple more minutes."

He thought about his aged mage and the young Korla who decided to remain in Havengarde to gain more knowledge and power. Was he disappointed she chose to stay? Truthfully, not really. Yes, she was exceedingly attractive, but she was too… what was the word? High maintenance. Campaigning and battle were not her strong points.

Yet he was destined to be a king and a king needed a queen. Would Korla be a suitable candidate? Or should he look to align himself with another kingdom by marrying a princess? He slid a glance at Storri. *Uh… maybe I should go north to the elven kingdom or east to what remains of Isentol.*

When Madlyn arrived, Conal directed her attention to the empty city.

"Not surprised," she answered. "Place is cursed. Don't see anyone living there unless they can chase away the ghosts."

"What ghosts?" Storri asked, eyes wide.

"Not them kind, dearie," she said with a smile then tapped her chest. "The ones in here. Them that lost the ones they loved won't come back." She again looked at the city. "It'll be some time before this is a city again."

Conal's attention diverted to a scout on horseback racing towards them.

"A large group on horseback approaches, my Lord," he called out as he came up.

"How large?" Lorkan interrupted.

"Couldn't tell exactly, Commander, but probably no more than a hundred."

At that moment, the newcomers emerged on the main road to Pencord. Conal grinned as they came closer.

"Seren."

"Morning, Boss," she grinned, reining in her steed and dismounting.

"Good morning, Seren. Good to see you."

She took a measure of his greeting. "You're not mad at us for not going along with you to Havengarde?"

"No." He smiled kindly at her. "Your skills are not in combat. Besides, I have other things in mind for you. Which way did you come from?"

"Came from Rexfyrd through Pencord. Thought you might could use a little intel."

"Now we're talking," Storri nodded. "What's happening?"

Seren looked quizzically at him then back to Conal.

"It's OK," Conal chuckled, shooting a bemused glance at Storri, oblivious to the breach of etiquette.

"You've a clear road through Pencord. Word's already spread that a new king arrives. A lot of folks are unhappy with Caldyr's rule and ready to join you."

"What about Rexfyrd?"

"Caldyr still controls Rexfyrd. Folks are afraid to speak out against him. He has at least a thousand soldiers in the city, with more coming from Malvyn and Pharyl."

"Pharyl?" Conal curled a lip.

"Yes, Boss." She smiled a knowing grin. "He's sent a cohort under the command of Captain Cadfyn."

"Cadfyn?" Conal smirked.

"Yeah. All told, I'd figure Caldyr's total between two thousand and twenty-five hundred."

"We still outnumber him more than two to one," Storri calculated.

"And with more joining us," Lorkan added, "we

will vastly outnumber him."

"Let's move out then," Conal ordered then looked at Seren. "Ride next to me."

As the armies moved forward, Seren's small force moved in behind Conal and their leader.

"You know you can't continue as highwaymen anymore," Conal said, though scanning the positioning of his soldiers.

"We sort of figured that," she smiled. "You said you had other things in mind, Boss?"

"Yes." He turned to gazed directly at her. "I want you to be the eyes and ears within my kingdom."

"Like spies?"

"Exactly," he nodded, "with you as my spy chief."

Seren grinned, pleased. "Sounds like fun, Boss. You know you can depend on me."

"I know," he said, returning the smile. "Maldwic spoke highly of you and from what I've seen, I can trust you and you know what you're doing. Oh… one more thing."

"Yes, Boss?"

"Only you and your group may call me 'Boss.' Thus, I will know any messenger who calls me that is from you."

Seren's grin spread wider. "Thank you, Boss. This'll be fun."

Conal laughed. "I hope so."

Just as Seren had reported, the road through Pencord was uneventful except for the addition of growing numbers of citizens who wanted to join Conal's army. Conal rejected most of them on the basis that they had livelihoods to pursue and he didn't know how long the campaign would last. Besides, he didn't want to be responsible for feeding them. Still, by the time they encamped outside the walls of Rexfyrd, Conal's army had added five hundred more battle-worthy men and women.

To no one's surprise, the gates to the city were firmly shut.

Two days later, one gate door yawned open and two men and a woman slipped out. Carrying a white flag on a guidon pole, they guided their mounts to the middle of the gap separating Conal's army and the city. Alerted at the request for parley, Conal, Storri, and Lorkan rode out to meet them.

"King Caldyr demands you disband your army and leave this place," the man in the center coldly stated. He was shorter than the other two, with close cropped hair and beard, and the manner of one used to being obeyed.

"And who are you?" Storri offhandedly asked.

The man sat up straight in the saddle and sneered at the dwarf. "I am General Fynbear, the commander of His Majesty's army."

Storri cast an amused glance at Lorkan and stage-whispered, "Not anymore."

Bristling, Fynbear glared at them. "King Caldyr demands to know by what right you invade his kingdom. This is a peaceful realm wishing only to be left alone."

"He should have thought about that when he threw in his lot with Torian," Lorkan replied.

Fynbear narrowed his gaze at Lorkan. "I know you. You were once a loyal and true man."

"I still am," Lorkan retorted, "though not to that traitor Caldyr. I suggest you think hard about your next move. Caldyr is finished. This kingdom has a new king."

"Him?" Fynbear scoffed, ticking his head at Conal. "He is to be your king?"

"Yes," Lorkan calmly answered. "Just as he defeated Torian, he will defeat Caldyr."

"Then you –" Fynbear abruptly stopped as giant shadows flitted across the ground at the same time that cries of fear bellowed from the walls. Looking up, he cowered as two dragons circled above them then swooped down to land next to them, frightening the horses.

"Good day, m'Lord Conal," said a dragon the color of dazzling amethyst and eyes that blazed bright orange.

"Always a pleasure to see you Gawyn," Conal replied, "and you too Elys."

Elys was a dragon of equal size to Gawyn with a shimmering hue of topaz and eyes of glowing amber.

"Greetings, my Lord," Elys said, dipping his massive head.

"You two arrived just in time. I was about to explain to these individuals that it would be in their best interest to surrender the city and prevent needless death."

Gawyn turned a scaled head to the emissaries. "Tell your master that he has until the sun sets to surrender the city or we will burn it down."

Fynbear wheeled around and raced back to the gates, the other two in hot pursuit.

"How'd you know?" Conal asked as they watched the three riders slip back through the gates.

"Just a hunch," Elys said. "Thought you could use a little muscle."

"Think I'll take a little flight to remind them," Gawyn said then launched into the sky to circle ominously over the city, occasionally buzzing the guard towers.

"He's such a kid," Elys chuckled. "Think I'll join him."

Less than half-an-hour later, the dragon's threat had spread throughout the city. Not long after the news of impending conflagration had coursed it way, the gates opened wide and a prison wagon emerged, driven by a single wagoner. Crowds on foot followed behind. They stopped a short distance away. The wagoner descended and approached. As he approached, Conal knew immediately he was no ordinary merchant for he carried himself with a confident regal bearing.

"I am Prince Brody. Behind me in the wagon sits Caldyr. Do with him as you deem fit. Though I am related to him, I am not like him."

"I have heard of you," Conal said, remembering the attempts on Pharyl's life. "You have no love for your brother-in-law Pharyl."

Brody curled a lip. "He was Calder's man, Torian's man. Fortunately, I finally gained a measure of success. The city is yours to command." He bowed and stepped to the side.

"If you are not like him," Conal challenged, "why are you here?"

"I came in one last effort to make him change his mind. Instead, I was tossed in prison. Only your arrival and threat to destroy the city made my freedom possible."

Conal pondered the response. It would be easy enough to verify. "And your son, Blayne? Is he here with you?"

Brody's lips pursed. "He is dead, my Lord, a casualty of Pharyl's treachery."

"I am sorry," Conal commiserated. Dismounting,

he walked up to the wagon and stared at the man inside the cage whose look of fury told him he was unrepentant.

"Confine him to the dungeon," he commanded.

"As you wish, Your Majesty," Brody said, again bowing. He flicked a hand at a man close by who leaped aboard and wheeled the wagon around. "Let me introduce you to some of the leadership of the city."

He escorted Conal along with Storri and Lorkan to a group of men and women who had positioned themselves in a line. They stopped at the first person, a middle-aged woman with darting eyes and permanent smile.

"This is Lady Ailis, the burgomaster of Rexfyrd."

"Your Majesty." Ailis curtsied.

"Lady Ailis," Conal replied with a forced smile then glanced down the row, already wondering if ruling a kingdom was what he really wanted to do. He noticed a man five people down in line whose look of disapproval seemed to land on Storri. Skipping those in between, he marched down to stand in front of him.

The man was dressed as a wealthy merchant with expensive ermine and silk fitted on a portly frame. His black hair was perfectly cut and greased back.

"I couldn't help but notice your look of concern," Conal said with a smile.

The man bent forward. "It's the dwarves, Your Majesty," he said in a hushed voice. "Nothing good ever comes from dwarves."

Conal's smile vanished and his hand shot out, gripping the man by the throat and effortlessly lifting him off the ground, much to the stunned shock of the other city representatives.

"You don't like dwarves?" he growled. "The feeling is mutual. They don't like idiots."

Still holding the man aloft, he glared at the rest of them while the man's face turned redder. "Effective immediately, dwarves are to be given privileged status. If I hear of anyone disrespecting or mistreating any dwarf in my kingdom, there will be hell to pay. Understand?"

Everyone quickly nodded.

Conal felt a gentle hand on his arm.

"You may want to let him go, Dearie. Don't want to scare the neighbors."

Smiling despite himself, he lowered the man to the ground. As the man gasped for air, Conal addressed the group.

"This is Madlyn. She is the kingdom's mage. You will obey her just as you would me. To my left is Lorkan, now General Lorkan, the commander of my army. The other fine individual is General Storri, my friend and brother. Any questions?" When none came, he curtly nodded then addressed Brody. "You may escort me to my residence. And while you're doing that, I want every one of Torian's followers rounded up. I'll deal with them on a case-by-case basis."

"Yes, Your Majesty." He motioned for Conal to follow.

"C'mon you three," Conal said to Storri, Lorkan, and Madlyn. "Let's see how the other half lives.

Conal settled on the throne and wondered if he was going to like being a king… or was it going to be all headache. People were going to go out of their way to please him, their fawning motivation being something in return. He would have to tread carefully… no changes in the beginning until he understood what was going on and how things worked.

Gazing around the throne room, he smiled at Storri and Lorkan chatting away like close friends do. Madlyn had disappeared to inspect her new home as well as call a council of mages to purge them of any residual Torian allies. The rest of the room was filled with the city's leadership, chatting amiably, all the while casting not so surreptitious glances at Conal.

Peering over the crowd, he recognized two men who stood off to the side. With a grin, he motioned them to come.

Gawyn and Elys weaved their way through the crowd and stopped at the bottom step. Conal stood and raised his hands, immediately silencing the crowd.

"You all know that the myth that dragons do not exist is not true. You have seen that for yourselves. Henceforth, anyone harming or seeking to harm a dragon will be punished by death."

The crowd audibly sucked in a breath.

"Make no mistake," Conal warned. "Dragon hunters are hereby banished from this kingdom upon pain of death. Any dragon hunter found within the borders of this kingdom by the time the morrow's sun sets has forfeited his or her life. No exceptions."

He sat back down and the thick silence gave way to quiet chatter which grew as the people relaxed.

"Tell Derryth this is a start. And thank her for letting you two help. You know you always have a place here."

"Thank you, my Lord," Gawyn said and bowed.

"Blessings on this kingdom," Elys said, "and may all your rulings be equally as wise."

With another bow, the two excused themselves to find a spot to shape change and head home to Havengarde.

Brody approached and said, "Caldyr's confidants are in the goal. Do you wish to question them now or at another time?"

"Now sounds good," Conal said, standing.

Brody led the way through the crowd, down hallways and stairways, Bedo by Conal's side.

"I was wondering where you were," Conal teased.

"I…I'm sorry, my Lord," Bedo stammered. "They wouldn't let me through. Said you already had servants. Thank the gods General Lorkan saw me."

"I do already have servants," Conal said, "which is why I need you here. You are now in charge of them all."

Bedo stumbled a step. "My Lord?"

"You are in charge of my servants. Do you not want the job?"

"Of course I do," he blurted, eyes brimming with a mixture of excitement and thanks.

"Good. We'll get things settled once I finish here."

"Yes, m'Lord."

Brody stopped at the gaoler's door and knocked. A burly bald-headed man opened it.

"His Majesty wishes to assign the prisoners," Brody announced.

"Yes, Your Majesty," the man answered with a reverent bow.

"Are we still branding people these days?" Conal questioned.

"Yes, Your Majesty."

Conal slowly nodded, hating the arbitrary exile of people to a life they did not choose nor want, yet balancing that the fact that some people needed such punishment. Hoping to find some who were repentant, he said, "Fine. As we proceed, I will tell you what brand to use or if they are to be set free. Can you write?"

The gaoler hung his head and mumbled, "No, m'Lord."

"That's fine. Lord Brody will assist us, but I bet you've a good memory."

The man brightened. "The best, Your Majesty."

"Good. Let's get started."

Conal followed the gaoler down the stone corridor to the main containment cell where more than twenty of Caldyr's loyal followers were chained to the walls. Conal paused to gaze in through the peep hole. "Who's in here?"

"Caldyr's chamberlain, the army commander –"

"I met him already," Conal smiled. "What's your recommendation? Are there any in here who you would consider trustworthy?"

Brody thought a moment. "Honestly, Your Majesty… no."

"Good enough for me. Let's get started. Oh, by the way, we have a new category of brand."

"Your Majesty?"

"My guess is that there are few here who are worthy of the normal brands like vipers or… a rose."

Brody snorted a laugh. "Hardly, Your Majesty."

"From now on, we will now have a worker brand, a mark in the shape of a sheaf of wheat."

"As you wish, Your Majesty."

Conal was about to tell Brody to ease up on the 'Your Majesty" crap but decided to wait until he could learn more about the man.

The gaoler opened the door and commanded,

"Listen up. His Majesty is entering."

Conal entered and the first man he encountered was the chamberlain, a pudgy toad of a man who bounced up.

"You Majesty," he fawned with a bow before receiving a cuff on the head from the gaoler.

"Shut yer yap. If His Majesty wants you to speak, he'll ask for it."

Conal briefly studied the man before saying "Wheat."

The chamberlain frowned, puzzled.

"Sit down," the gaoler growled.

Conal continued down the line, announcing "Wheat" with each individual, until he came to a well-dressed middle-aged man who stared back up at him with the eyes of recognition and hope.

"You," Conal pointed. "What's your name?"

"What?" the man sputtered in anger. "You know my name, damn you."

Whereupon the gaoler landed a heavy kick to the man's ribs. "That's the king yer talkin' to."

"He's no more a king than I am," the man sneered, clutching his side. "I should know."

"Then you should know to respect your betters," Brody interjected. "What is your wish, Your Majesty?"

Conal folded his arms, pretending to study the man. "Rose. Then immediately sell him to the farmers to work the fields and tend the cows and goats."

Spinning around, Conal headed to the door, the gaoler and Brody in step.

"What was his name?" Conal asked the gaoler.

"That one calls himself Lord Pharyl, Your Majesty."

Conal smirked and nodded. Being a king did have its benefits.

THE END

ABOUT THE AUTHORS

Richard Fierce

Hey there!

I write fantasy and space opera, and you can find all my books in many different eBook stores. You can check out my website for more information about my books, my next projects, and events I'll be attending where you can meet me and even get signed books.

WEBSITE

www.richardfierce.com

pdmac

pdmac spent a career in the US Army before transitioning to education as a university Academic Dean. He transitioned again and now writes fulltime. He has a MA in Creative Writing and a Ph.D. in Theology. He is a member of the Blue Ridge Writers Guild, the Steampunk Writers and Artists Guild, and the Georgia Writers Association. A diverse author, writer, and editor, he has also edited a Literature anthology, served as managing editor of an archaeology magazine, ghost-written an autobiography, and has had poems, short stories, articles, and editorials published in various literary journals, magazines and newspapers. His most recent short stories appear in the *Short Story America* anthologies III and IV, *Poets in Hell*, *The Mulberry Fork Review*, and the Fantasy Anthology *Chronicles of Mirstone*. He has also sung back-up for Broadway plays, provided voice for radio plays, and acted and directed theater stage productions. In his off time, he and his wife race mountain bikes, kayak, and occasionally backpack sections of the Appalachian Trail. Additionally, he and his wife love to travel, their favorite place so far being Crete, Greece.